John Josteins is a lawyer of British and Spanish citizenship. He was born on 1 February 1965 in Equatorial Guinea, where his father from Mallorca, Spain was an Air Force officer. At that time, it was still a Spanish territory in the Gulf of Guinea in Africa before it became independent on 12 October 1968.

He earned two degrees in Law and Political Science from the University of Complutense in Madrid and speaks Spanish, English and French (as well as Fang, a dialect from his mother's side spoken in Central Africa by the Bantou sub-ethnic group). He is very proud of the mixed European and African heritage that he carries with him in mind, body and soul, and that makes him feel like a citizen of the world, free of borders. As a living example of fraternity between the two continents, it has given him a unique perspective of the world and of life.

He moved to London many years ago where he has lived and worked ever since, eventually becoming a British citizen. He is very fond of the United Kingdom, and in particular London, to him, one of the most beautiful, dynamic and multicultural cities on Earth. He feels at home there in the city that has welcomed him with open arms. It has captivated his soul and imagination such that he feels a special bond with the city, like a friendship with unconditional trust. If a city could have a conscience and be aware of the world around it, the way it has shaped people for centuries, London would be very proud indeed to know the achievements and successes it has made over the centuries that will continue to attract and inspire many generations to come, as it has inspired the author to write this book.

John Josteins

THE MYSTERIOUS ROBBERY OF BIG BEN

AUSTIN MACAULEY PUBLISHERS™

LONDON * CAMBRIDGE * NEW YORK * SHARJAH

A CIP catalogue record for this title is available from the British Library.

ISBN 9781528902502 (Paperback)
ISBN 9781528902519 (Hardback)
ISBN 9781528957281 (ePub e-book)

www.austinmacauley.com

First Published (2020)
Austin Macauley Publishers Ltd
25 Canada Square
Canary Wharf
London
E14 5LQ

London, one of the most famous cities on Earth, is about to suffer the strangest, most mysterious theft ever seen in its existence of one of its most emblematic landmarks. It would be a dramatic event that would leave the United Kingdom and the entire world in shock, without any explanation for how this bold theft could have occurred.

CONTENTS

Chapter One
The Village of Black Cloud

The story begins on a mysterious planet called Oxon, far away from planet Earth. The plot was planned by a middle-aged woman named Moxum who had special powers. She lived with her sister, Eris, and their nephew, Winn Blitzzer. She was around fifty years old with dark grey hair, dyed to hide her true red colour. She had a pretty face with small green eyes and brown skin, a full figure and average height. She usually wore a long white dress with a red short jacket over it and a black ribbon tied at her waist. On her feet she wore light, brown shoes with no heel. Her younger sister Eris was a medium-sized woman in her late forties with short brown hair and deep blue eyes, slim face and high cheekbones. She wore a long brown dress with a blue short jacket and light, black shoes without heels. Their nephew Winn Blitzzer was seventeen years old, of average height, slim with big blue eyes and curly long blond hair. He was very handsome and intelligent and had an easy smile.

They lived in a village called Black Cloud. It was not a normal village, rather a very mysterious, dark place in the middle of the forest located beneath a mountain valley full of green open space. It was neat and clean with a picturesque view of a mysteriously silent waterfall. Each house was separated from its neighbours by a large garden with short trees as a boundary. Ms Moxum's house was the only one that was hidden inside the branches of a huge tree from which the chimney emitted smoke day and night. The forest around the mysterious village of Black Cloud used to be well protected by invisible guardians, as well as heavy spider webs forming an impenetrable boundary around the village. Now only the spider webs remained.

The village had around twenty-five wooden houses, and a school and a temple, but only three of the houses were occupied; the rest stood empty. The front doors were still hanging open on many of the empty houses, as if their owners had left in a rush. The few people left in the village would occasionally see candles lit inside some of these empty houses. Other times nothing but darkness could be seen inside. These mysterious occurrences only made the atmosphere in the village gloomier and bleaker than it already was.

The house where Winn Blitzzer and his aunts lived was two-storeys high. The main wooden doors had a half arch at the top with round windows looking out onto a small garden. The house was large enough for three of them; Winn Blitzzer lived in the upstairs, while his aunts lived downstairs. He had no idea that his Aunts Moxum and Eris were keeping a big secret from him.

In the kitchen hung a big cauldron suspended over a fire from the ceiling with chains. Winn Blitzzer had no idea that this cauldron was no ordinary one. It was a magic cauldron, and his Aunt Moxum could use with her mysterious powers to watch their planet Oxon in it without leaving her home. Its magic powers could show her everything happening in every galaxy, if she wanted it to.

Winn Blitzzer never questioned why the cauldron was over a fire day and night, or why they kept watch over it so intently. He simply thought its purpose was to keep the house warm against the cold of the forest. In fact, the fire was never extinguished because then it would lose its power for good. Because of this neither Moxum nor Eris had slept deeply for years, and never left their house empty to avoid leaving the cauldron unattended. Inside that special cauldron, were hidden many special magical objects which looked like small toys but that could become full sized when needed. These magical objects were safely kept at the bottom of the special pot. Simply by maintaining the hot water on top made it secure enough that not one would ever try to put their hand inside. Ms Moxum called the special cauldron Potsat, which was short for Pot Satellite Radar.

In the other houses at the far end of the village lived two women with their children. They were Lady Dallas and her daughter Yalta and Lady Esra and her son Tovic. After her husband's sudden disappearance over a decade ago, she was very protective of her daughter Yalta, who was 15 years old, slim with long blond hair, small green eyes and a long neck. Tovic was Winn Blitzzer's best friend. His father had also suddenly disappeared over ten years ago. When they first met, it was the first time Winn Blitzzer had ever seen someone his age. From then on he had a friend to play with, go fishing or hunting with, or just to talk to.

Lady Dallas and Lady Esra were the only neighbours who talked to each other, often to share their sadness about their husbands' disappearances. They knew Ms Moxum to be a very bad woman who possessed special powers that she inherited from her ancestors. Although she was supposed to do good with these powers, she used them for bad purposes against those she did not like. In fact, she was to blame for all the evil things that had occurred in the mysterious village of Black Cloud. Lady Dallas and Lady Esra knew very well that Ms Moxum was the one who caused their misery, but they also knew they could not do anything about it. So the two women looked after each other and their children so as to not suffer the same fate as their husbands, family members and friends.

Tovic's mother, Lady Esra, was aware of the friendship her son and Winn Blitzzer had. She knew Winn Blitzzer's destiny and the secret power of the Potsat his Aunt Moxum had. Ms Moxum was aware of her nephew's friendship with Tovic too. She did not know how much his mother had told him about her and she feared that Tovic might tell her nephew more than she wanted him to know. In fact, all the adults knew about the history of Winn Blitzzer's family, only he himself did not. No one dared to reveal anything about his family to him, or who he was, for fear of his aunt.

The only person in the gloomy village who greeted everyone was the teacher, a very friendly woman named Mrs Loly who lived alone.

Although there were no other kids in the village besides Winn Blitzzer, Tovic and Yalta, they could remember a time when there used to be other children, when they were little in the nursery.

One day at school, Winn Blitzzer said to their teacher, "Mrs Loly, I would like to ask you a serious question."

"Excellent, Winn Blitzzer!" said Mrs Loly, cheerful and smiling as always. "I like students who ask questions. Go ahead, I will do my best to answer."

Winn Blitzzer hesitated, still not certain she would not like the question he was about to ask her.

Mrs Loly said to him, "Well, speak up. Don't be shy. We all know each other well here."

Winn Blitzzer said, "Well Mrs Loly, why is the school empty? I remember there used to be so many children here at the nursery. It's like all of them just vanished overnight. What happened to them?"

Mrs Loly's face changed suddenly as if she had received bad news. Winn Blitzzer's question caught her by surprise. There was silence in the classroom; Tovic and Yalta looked from the teacher to Winn Blitzzer, but kept quiet. They already knew a bit of this story from their mothers.

Mrs Loly said, "Dear Winn Blitzzer, I have nothing to say to you on this. I'm afraid your question is beyond my area of teaching. Soon this level of education I teach will be complete. Indeed by the end of this summer I hope you can continue your higher education elsewhere, if you are able. But I will make an effort to explain to you the little of what I know about the question you are asking me, when this course ends for good."

Unfortunately Mrs Loly did not know that as she was speaking, Ms Moxum was just outside the classroom and had heard everything she was saying to the children.

"Thank you, Mrs Loly," said Winn Blitzzer.

Mrs Loly then said to the class, "I won't take any more such questions. I don't want any problems with anyone in this village."

When the lesson ended, Winn Blitzzer walked home and for some reason continued feeling a sense of guilt for having asked his teacher this question. More weeks passed, and Winn Blitzzer, Tovic and Yalta began to look forward to the coming summer holidays, to spending every day playing around in the forest or going fishing.

But on the last day of school something mysterious happened, which would change the lives of the three students forever.

Mrs Loly finished handing out their certificates with outstanding results and wished them all the luck and success they deserved.

She then announced, "After you leave, I will not have any more students to teach, and so I have decided to retire. But before you go, I will fulfil the promise I made you a month ago. The truth is I owe you an explanation. Sixteen years ago a crime occurred here, a shameful act. In just a single day, all the people of the village disappeared…"

Before Mrs Loly could finish her words, she began coughing, and grabbing her throat as if she could not breathe.

The youngsters became very frightened. Mrs Loly reached for the thermos of warm tea she always had on her desk and drank some quickly to relieve her coughing. She smiled as she finished drinking. But before their beloved teacher could say anything more, she vanished before their eyes. Only her clothes and the red bracelet she was wearing were left lying on the floor.

All of them ran out of the school back home. They immediately told their mothers what they had seen. After that day, Lady Dallas did not allow her daughter Yalta to go out anymore. Lady Esra did not want her son Tovic to go outside as often either, or to visit Winn Blitzzer. She and Lady Dallas suspected that it was his aunt, Ms Moxum, who caused the mysterious disappearance of Mrs Loly, probably using one of her special recipes and adding it to her tea. This was what she had done in the past to make all the other people in the village disappear.

When Winn Blitzer arrived at home with a sad face. His Aunt Eris asked him, "What happened to you?"

"Mrs Loly suddenly disappeared," said Winn Blitzzer. "Only her clothes were left on the floor. It was so scary."

"What!" exclaimed Aunt Eris. "This is very bad if it is true. I hope you're not telling a joke."

"I wouldn't joke about this Aunt Eris. Our beloved teacher Mrs Loly has disappeared." Aunt Eris was in shock as well. But Aunt Moxum, who was sitting nearby, did not react at all.

Winn Blitzzer noticed this, and tried to ask his Aunt Moxum if she knew what had happened to Mrs Loly.

She replied shortly, "I have no idea what happened to that woman. Do not ask me again."

Winn Blitzzer tried to press her. Aunt Eris put her finger to her mouth, telling him to keep quiet. He spun round and walked away, but in his mind, he kept running over all the unanswered questions in his head.

Why won't Aunt Moxum tell me anything about the disappearance of our teacher? She was a good person. She greeted everyone and taught us well. Why would someone want hurt her?

As Winn Blitzzer got older, he began to question the mystery surrounding the village of Black Cloud even more.

"Why are we living in the middle of the forest, hidden away and isolated from the city? Why are so many houses empty here? Where are all their owners? There aren't even any pets around. I have never seen a village without dogs and cats."

And the most gnawing question: "Where are my parents?"

Life carried on, on planet Oxon. Nothing changed in the strange village of Black Cloud. Ms Moxum continued watching live images from the Potsat in fire when Winn Blitzzer was not around. One day she discovered that the king, Brelys-1000, was watching a planet called Earth, using the special powerful telescope he had hidden in the royal palace.

Chapter Two
Revelations

Ms Moxum could see he was looking at a city called London, clearly in admiration of what he saw there. King Brelys-1000 was a medium-sized man with a round face. He had short, curly brown hair flecked with white and a small well-trimmed white moustache. He was quite handsome, with a nice smile and soft, deep voice. Although he was well-mannered, he was also known for being rather temperamental at times, making it clear to others by his mood whether he was having a good or bad day.

King Brelys-1000 first saw the telescope and learned of planet Earth's existence some thirty-five years earlier when he was still a young prince. His father, King Bixiz-2, took him to the secret observatory containing the telescope that allowed him to see the planet Earth for the very first time, even though he knew that doing so was going against an ancient code followed by every monarch before him that stated no future king may be brought up to the secret observatory before his coronation day. He was older in age and concerned, he will not be alive after his son's coronation and must ensure that this knowledge is passed on the next king so that, the information will not be lost and his son will be prepared to protect the secret next.

Prince Brelys was stunned when all of this was first revealed to him.

"I did not know there was an observatory here, why didn't you show this to me before?"

"I couldn't bring you here, because it wasn't yet time to do so. As I have already told you, I have broken the ancient code by revealing all these secrets to you, before you become king. But I could not wait any longer." I needed to tell you this secret before as I worried that maybe I will not be alive once you will be by your own, this is the reason why I have broken the ancient code to make you to discover this place.

His father told him the observatory was built by one of their ancestors to study astronomy and learn more about outer space. They had almost given up the possibility of seeing anything, when they caught sight of the image of a city on planet Earth by chance and from that day onwards they kept the telescope at the exact same angle, so that they would never lose their wonderful discovery. For generations, every king and queen had kept the secret of Earth. To know something beyond the planet of Oxon, knowing that they were not alone in the universe as previously thought, was worth being kept secret.

The young prince said to his father, "I will never get tired of looking at it, it is so beautiful. I like this name, Earth. How do you know the planet is called that?"

"Indeed we are fortunate and very privileged to enjoy this view. And I know the name of this planet thanks to the amazing work done by astronomers and scientists years ago. Come, I would like to show you something."

His father opened a large book lying on the table. It was full of colourful drawings of tall buildings with many windows, green parks covered in well-kept flower gardens and a striking clock tower in the middle, all surrounding a great river crossed by many bridges. Other smaller objects dotted the spaces on the ground and even in the sky, which the prince did not recognise, but were called cars, planes and trains. Drawings of the same place at night showed a skyline silhouetted against the horizon, lit up everywhere by tiny bright lights in every window of the tall buildings, along the streets and in the parks, even the face of the great clock tower shone as brightly as the moon in the sky above it. He was immediately fascinated by it all.

"This is an Earth city," his father explained. "The people living there use those lights to see at night. Even if someone dropped a needle, they could find it and pick it up easily with these artificial lights everywhere."

The young prince was so impressed by this and the colourful paintings of places and objects he never would have imagined existed.

"These drawings are remarkable, Father."

"I am glad you like them. I knew that you would," said his father. "Now even before becoming king you know the greatest secret of our kingdom. Remember, do not reveal it to anyone, except perhaps your future wife. That is up to your discretion."

"But if you knew that these kinds of things existed elsewhere, why didn't you or our ancestors try to build similar objects here? Especially the great clock."

"We don't need a great clock here," his father replied. "You need not dream about, or be envious of, the lifestyle these people have on planet Earth. You can see clearly the differences between both our worlds in the telescope. We are happy with the two perfect times we have been using for centuries, day and night. The sun clock for day, and by night, the sand clock. While we on planet Oxon sleep when it is night, and only a tiny minority were engaging in activity like baker and nigh club for the young people, and when we enjoy holiday and festivity most people of planet Oxon enjoy nightlife, but these people of planet Earth have a different lifestyle to ours and need these mechanical objects to read the time whenever they wanted, because they continue to be very busy and active even when the sun has gone down. So, you see, it would really not fit our customs here. Anyway, our technicians and scientists attempted to replicate it but this proved near impossible, without knowing the kind of material it is made of and how it works as it seems to be controlled by some sort of mechanical force from the inside. We don't even know for a fact if it really looks as it is painted."

"I see, Father," said Prince Brelys.

King Bixiz-2 asked his son, "Which image did you like the most from your first time seeing the planet Earth?"

"Let me think, Father," the young prince said. But there was really only one object that had most captivated the attention of the young Prince: the great clock tower. Finally, he said to his father, "I like the great clock in the tower."

King Bixiz-2 was not surprised. All kings and queens who had come before them were also fascinated by the amazing object.

The young prince asked his father, "Do you know what it is called?"

"If it has a name, I do not know it," answered his father. "But I can tell you the name of the city where the great clock is located: London. Just two short syllables, very easy to remember."

"London, London, London," the young Prince repeated the name. "How do you know this name, Father?"

"Well, thanks to the astronomers and mathematicians who recorded this information in the library of this observatory. In fact, I also know how they discovered the name, and it was mostly by luck. They happened to be looking through the telescope one day when six rows of hundreds of people lined up on one of the bridges and formed the letters LONDON. Another day, they saw a huge crowd of people with big banners with writing on them saying, "Welcome to London". From this they have come to the conclusion that this must be the name of that city. But it took sixty years for the mathematicians and astronomers to decode this writing. This was a great achievement, to understand not only the culture and ways of the people in the London, but also their language."

In the end, his father said to him, "My son, this is my advice to you. If you want to live well and in peace, forget this idea of recreating objects from Earth here. Enjoy this view in the telescope, as our ancestors did before us, but remember it belongs to another civilisation, not to us. Think of it more as a dream, something you can only see but never touch with your own hands."

"Yes, Father. Thank you. I can never thank you enough. I am honoured to be next in line to carry on this secret."

The young prince did his best to accept the explanations his father King Bixiz-2 had given him about life on planet Earth as he had no other information to tell him any differently. He never forgot anything about that day, and his fascination with the city he had observed through the telescope never diminished. Years later, when he became king of the planet Oxon, he went up every day to look at the city called London. The artificial lights fascinated him when watching the city at night under a clear sky. It was difficult for him to believe that with these lights the people there could really see clearly at night. King Brelys-1000's interest in having a similar mechanical clock, and his need to know if everything was the way his father had said began to occupy most thoughts in his mind to the point that it became an obsession.

Soon after his coronation, King Brelys-1000 was married to Queen Zam, and they had one daughter, the sole heir to the throne, known throughout the kingdom as the Princess of Light. "Queen Zam was a pretty, slim woman with long, blonde hair that reached her waist. But she was also very intelligent, and bit more calm and reserved in demeanour than her husband." She spoke with a soft voice. However, she never showed interest in topics such as astronomy, and so he never shared with her the secret of the discovery of London.

The royal family managed their duties everyday with the help of their staff. King Brelys-1000 was assisted by a middle-aged man called Zomy, who had been in his service since he was still a young prince. He took his job very seriously. Zomy was a tall, slim man with long, white hair tied back with a blue ribbon. He was always well-dressed in a brown or grey cassock with shining yellow ornaments on the arms and around the neck. He was a vegetarian, with a thin, bony face and long, slim nose. Although he had a friendly, kind smile that gave the impression of an easy-going nature, he was a very professional man and diplomat, one who was never afraid to ask questions or give his opinion.

Although daily life was not always easy in the royal palace, the family was able to find repose from royal duties by spending time playing music together on the piano, cello or violin, playing cards and on some nights attending the theatre. The queen was a patron of the arts and education, while the Princess of Light was most interested in botanical gardens and the ancient architecture of the capital of the kingdom, Ryam. The king's hobby was, of course, astronomy. Every evening, after dinner, the king would kiss Queen Zam and his daughter goodnight and retire to his private chamber. This particular evening, however was to be very different for the king than the ones before.

Chapter Three
A Dream Like No Other

After arriving in his private apartment with his secretary Zomy, his attendants helped him to put on white pyjamas, over which he put on a long white gown with golden embroidery. On his feet, he wore big, thick red socks that resembled moccasins, so the king could step out of bed whenever he wished. He looked like a wise man, with his outfit and his short, curly brown hair and his fine white moustache.

When the king went to bed he was, like always, secretly thinking of the great clock of London. He fell asleep quickly in his big bed, extravagantly decorated with a golden ornament at the head. And then that night, King Brelys-1000 had a dream that he was in London on planet Earth.

The dream seemed so real to the king that he thought he was actually in London on planet Earth, not asleep at home in his bed. He admired the impressive building before him, the Palace of Westminster. He saw the great clock tower that he had always admired so much, and realised that it had four faces not one, as he had previously thought. He finally saw close-up many other objects that he had been watching from a distance in his secret observatory: buildings, bridges, red double-decker buses and small black cars in their actual size and shape. Ships of every size flowed past on the River Thames. The streets were full of statues, lights, and even the famous red telephone booths. Out of curiosity he entered the large red box to see what it was for. The sound of the unending tone when he held the device to his ear was so alien to him, that he dropped it and fled from the booth.

And then, King Brelys-1000 heard for the first time the ringing out of the bells in the clock. He was amazed to hear that it also made a sound, and a beautiful one, and evermore mystified as to how the clock worked. Despite how amazing the experience of the dream was for him, there was something that bothered the king: the realisation of just how much he still had to learn, a realisation that hit him when he discovered what was on the face of the clock. Evenly spaced around the round edge of the clock were more strange symbols, or signs, that all looked the same to him and that he could not understand. And below the face of the great clock he noticed even more symbols, all gilded: *Domine salvam fac reginam nostram victoriam priman*, Latin for "God protect our Queen Victoria the First". He felt frustrated to finally see the great clock clearly, but still not be able to understand everything he wanted to know.

He was walking around among many people who were also looking at the clock and taking pictures of it. He could see that this clock was something very special to the people as well, and that it was not only he who was so impressed and loved this amazing clock. He went to stand below the tower. When the bells rang again he could feel the vibrations throughout his body. The loud sound of the bells was surprising and extraordinary to him. He was about to go see what more wonders the amazing city had to offer, when he saw four people hanging from the tower with climbing gear, sixty metres up in the air. They were cleaners and technicians dressed in black helmets and trousers, red shirts and black boots, who washed the clock every six years, cleaning the three hundred and twelve pieces of wafer-thin glass panels on each of its faces, and checking its inner mechanism. As the king watched, they abseiled down the sides. He never realised how large this great clock was, until he saw the size of the cleaners looking so tiny hanging on the great clock's faces. More people were taking pictures and speaking in many languages; he could not understand a single word.

The road was busy with cars around the Parliament Square. He was very excited when he saw the red double-decker bus in life size. He could not believe that they could carry so many people. Even driverless cars were passing on the road. Then he saw people crossing at the green traffic light to Parliament Square so he followed them, to go see the statues that were there. After he went to see the building called Westminster Abbey whose gothic-style architecture he liked. While standing along the western façade side of the Abbey, far below, he could see statues on top of a large tympanum entrance alongside a woman carrying a baby. He had no doubt that this was a place of worship.

While standing below the St George Column in front of Westminster Abbey, he saw a red double-decker bus 'Number 24' coming along Victoria Street and stopping at the bus stop nearby. People stood waiting in a queue to take it. He crossed the road, running to join them. He went up on the rear door of the bus to experience public transportation. He sat on the back seat looking toward the rear glass with his long white night dress. Some passengers thought that maybe, he was going to a costume party.

When the bus began to drive, he laughed like a child saying, "It's moving, it's moving!"

He was so happy. As they passed the Whitehall, he saw the royal guards sitting on their horses, well dressed in their uniform at Horse Guards Parade. He got off at Trafalgar Square to see the fountains, the four lion statues and the tall column. He looked around the square and all the beautiful buildings around it. Then he saw a big arch with three gates, the impressive Admiralty Arch inscribed again in Latin on top: *Anno Decimo Edwardi Septima Regis*, and then *Victoriae Regina Cives Gratissimi MDCCCCX*. He did not understand the meaning of it, but realised the letter were similar to those on the great clock.

After looking at the Arch, he went through it following the long stretch of the Mall. He arrived in front of Buckingham Palace and saw the royal guards in their smart uniforms marching through the gates. He was certain some sort of royalty lived there.

He walked through Green Park towards Piccadilly Circus, from there he passed the Ritz Hotel, The Burlington Arcade and many others shops with lovely displays selling all kinds of products that he had never seen before, including a large bear standing outside a teddy bear shop. Finally, he arrived at Piccadilly Circus full of people and cars speeding through it. King Brelys-1000 was very impressed by the neon light signs changing colours and advertising different products on the giant screens. Then his eyes fell on the tallest man figure standing outside of Ripley's Believe It or Not Museum. He walked over to have a closer look. He measured his foot against the tall figure, and laughed at how small it looked. Across from that he saw a figure of a man standing with its legs in a funny way and dressed in the uniform of a British police sergeant. He had both hands on his hips and a helmet on his head. On his face was a big grin, his lips pulling back in a funny way, contorting his entire face and hiding half of it under his helmet. King Brelys-1000 burst into laughter when he saw it, small tears coming from his eyes.

A short distance away, he saw the many bells of the Swiss Court. Just as he arrived, they began to chime and figurines of people and animals started moving along the curved wall. He found it just as impressive as the four-sided great clock. There were many other people standing around watching it and taking pictures. Then he walked through Chinatown looking at all the different people of different races walking around and birds hanging in the windows of restaurants, and taking in the smells of different foods. He ended up in Leicester Square watching the crowds of people walking around, the artists, the dancers playing music and singing, others doing acrobatics. Other artists were painting caricatures of people faces so that they were deformed in funny ways.

He said laughing, "This one even looks like me!"

Then he walked into a small park with fountains and benches in the middle of the Square. He saw a small statue of a man standing there wearing a short, tightly buttoned jacket. His baggy pants were quite oversized and loose and he had big shoes on his feet. A tiny bowler hat sat on his head. He had a small, square moustache and a cane in his hand. The king touched it; it was beautifully made.

Who is this man? he wondered. He had no idea that it was of course the statue of Charlie Chaplin, the famous comedian and actor from the silent movie era.

King Brelys-1000 turned away, and behind him the statue reached out and tapped his shoulder. But when he looked behind him, the statue was back in his place and he could not see anyone else there that could have touched him.

He said to himself, "Something touched me. Where is it?"

He was a little confused, but carried on walking. He felt something touching his back again. He looked back fearfully. This time he saw the man walking in a funny way wearing his big shoes on the wrong feet, and at the same time skilfully twirling the cane in his hands. He pretended to fall on the ground, and then stood back up again with incredible flexibility.

King Brelys-1000 laughed in delight as he had never seen anything like this before in his life.

"I knew something touched my shoulder. What is your name?"

The man did not answer and continued performing. Finally, he made a curtsy and reached out his hand to greet his only spectator. When the king held out his hand, he pulled his away and turned around.

King Brelys-1000 laughed saying, "You're killing me with your amazing performance. You're a really funny guy. I wish I could take you with me to my planet Oxon to make my family and my people happy with your amazing performance skills."

After some more funny dancing, the show ended. The actor became a statue again as it was before.

"Please don't stop!" said the king. "Please keep going, I'll never get tired of watching your performance."

He waited a little while to see if the statue would come alive again, but nothing happened.

He left Leicester Square with a sad face and headed towards St Martin Street and Trafalgar Square, where there were many people and artists displaying their talents. Some figures were floating in the air, others had their bodies painted in different colours and were wearing strange masks. He had no doubt that this London was a very vibrant and dynamic place to live. All the people there looked amused with happy smiling faces. From there he had a great view of the great clock again in the background.

He crossed the road to the South Africa House to see the animal heads that were on the façade of the building. Moments later, he saw a red bus coming to stop and took it. But when the bus passed by the great clock without stopping, he realised that he was on the wrong one. He had to get off opposite St Thomas Hospital, and make his way back towards the great clock tower. He stopped in the middle of Westminster Bridge to see the city from there with a wonderful panoramic view of the many landmarks. The London Eye, the bridges with cars and trains crossing them, the dome of St Paul's Cathedral, ships and boats loaded with tourists and planes flying in the sky, and even an amphibious yellow car nicknamed The Duck floating on the River Thames with people inside. He did not know where to look first. Everywhere he looked, he saw something new and beautiful.

Suddenly, he noticed a building on the left side of the riverbank that looked just like his own palace. How could it be possible to have a similar building here in this city on another planet? The building King Brelys-1000 was admiring was the magnificent Whitehall Court. Suddenly the city darkened and the lights came on. When he saw the streets lights shining, he understood everything his late father had explained to him all those years ago.

He reached the end of the bridge and saw a beautiful bronze statue facing the clock of a woman wearing a small crown on her head accompanied by two girls, perhaps her daughters, on a scythed chariot drawn by two racing horses. This was the statue of Queen Boudicca. He could see that this woman must have been a very important figure in this kingdom if she had the honour to have a statue in this city. King Brelys-1000 tried to read the inscriptions on the front of the plinth: *Boadicea (Boudicca) Queen of the Iceni who died AD 61, after leading her people against the Roman invader.*

Suddenly, the great clock chimed very loudly seven times announcing that it was seven o'clock in London. His eyes went up to the face of the great clock tower. He was very happy to hear the sound of the bells again.

But suddenly he began to feel the effects of the bell's vibration through his whole body from head to toe, as though he were being paralysed by the deep sounds of the bells. The smell of the fumes coming from the cars hit his nostrils. He started coughing.

Unconsciously he started turning over in his bed from all the excitement, calling out in a loud voice, "What joy, what joy! I saw it! How beautiful it is!"

Chapter Four
Waking Up from the Amazing Dream

The king woke suddenly from his dream shouting loudly, "I saw it, I saw it, I saw what it really looked like. How beautiful it is with its four faces!"

Zomy heard the king's voice from the antechamber where he slept. He woke up, but though perhaps he imagined it when the voice he heard stopped. He thought to himself that maybe it was he who had been dreaming. He closed his eyes to sleep again. Then a few moments later he heard the king's voice again saying,

"I saw it, I saw it, what it really looked like, it has four faces, it has four faces…"

Zomy felt a bit concerned after hearing the king saying these words. He said to himself, "I am not dreaming anymore the king is really talking. But with whom?"

He decided to go see what was happening with the king. He was there to serve him. He jumped from his bed rather frightened and went to knock on the king's chamber.

"Your Majesty, Your Majesty. May I enter?"

"Enter," the king replied with a soft, smooth voice. The Secretary Zomy opened the chamber worried about how he would find the king as the words 'four faces' made him concerned and a little bit afraid.

When Zomy entered the king's chamber, he saw the king sitting in his bed. He bowed to him and said quickly,

"Your Majesty, I thought I heard you talking in a quite loud voice. I feared something was happening to you, as I know that you are sleeping alone here. I didn't see anyone passing by the antechamber. You know I practically sleep with one eye open, so you can understand why I came to knock on your door at this time of the night."

The king said to Zomy in a surprisingly calm voice, "I never talk at night when I am asleep, maybe it's you who was talking in your sleep, not me."

The king's response made secretary Zomy feel like he was being made a fool of.

He tried to defend his honour saying, "I speak the truth Your Majesty. I heard you talking in your sleep. At first, I thought that maybe it was me who was dreaming, but when I heard Your Majesty talking quite loudly more than once, I was sure that it wasn't me who was dreaming. I also heard very well the words Your Majesty said... All this made me very concerned and scared to come on knock your door."

The king said to Zomy "You have been in my service a long time, almost thirty-nine years now, did you hear me talking in my sleep any night before?"

"Not at all, Your Majesty," Zomy replied. "But just this time now I heard you talking, believe me Your Majesty I would not make this up. My duty is to tell you the truth, and give you my humble advice. I might have even said that I felt fear arising inside me when I heard Your Majesty saying, 'I saw it, I saw it, I saw very well, it has four faces.' I thought you were dreaming of monsters. I believe you may have had a nightmare. Perhaps I am mistaken. But I simply care for your well-being."

The king knew very well that his secretary Zomy was telling the truth, after he repeated the words "four faces" but he could not admit it. Then the secretary asked the king, "Your Majesty, what did you dream of?"

The king didn't answer him, instead he told Zomy, "Bring me a paper and pencil urgently I want to write and draw what I have just seen and lived in my dreams while I still have these images fresh in my mind."

When secretary Zomy was about to fetch the papers and pencil something unexpected happened. The king in his happy and excited state mixed with a touch of madness from his dream's joy made a mistake, and said out loud the words, "Planet Earth," without realising it. He was so filled with emotion from living out his dream as tough it was reality to him.

A few seconds later, he realised his error. He felt guilty at his carelessness in keeping the secrets of the kingdom. When he noticed that secretary Zomy had paused in the doorway before going out, he asked him, "Are you bringing me what I asked for?"

Secretary Zomy was a little confused and distracted by what he had just heard. He said to the king, "Sorry Your Majesty, I didn't hear you properly. What do you want me to bring?"

The king said again, "I asked you to bring me papers and pencil urgently. I want to draw the images I have in my mind before they could be lost. If only you knew what an amazing, unique experience I had in my dream where I went to the city called London on planet Earth."

Before the king finished saying the word planet Earth again, Zomy screamed out loud and repeated the words "Planet Earth", saying, "Your Majesty, did you say planet Earth?"

Zomy was in shock upon hearing those two words, and forgot all royal protocol. After his outburst, he quickly asked the king's pardon and bowed low before the king.

But hearing those words was too much for secretary Zomy. In his mind, he was repeating the strange words one hundred times over, trembling and expecting anger from the king for his behaviour. To his surprise, the king said to him with calm a voice,

"I understand your reaction, and I pardon you."

Zomy was relieved. "Thank you, Your Majesty," he said and bowed again.

Then the king said quickly to Zomy, "I had a wonderful dream… a melody coming from the planet that I named. Yes, this melody cured the back pain that I have been suffering from for so long. Because of that I need you to bring me a paper and a pencil to write down this melody to have it forever, and to use it as a medicine in case I could suffer back pain again. But I don't know if I will remember every note I heard in my dreams."

The king's strange explanation about his dreams didn't convince secretary Zomy at all, because he couldn't recall ever hearing the king complain about back pain before, and had always been in very good health. Still, he ran to fetch a pencil and papers, so the king could record what he just dreamt. As he ran, he remembered when he was just a young man thirty years ago, the last astronomer on his death bed speaking of a secret planet, saying, "Earth, Earth, Planet Earth! There is life outside planet Oxon," before he died.

At that time Secretary Zomy had not taken it seriously, until today. He thought that the old astronomer was hallucinating when he told him that secret long ago. But the king could never have any idea that Zomy would know anything about it.

A few minutes later, Zomy was back with a pencil and some papers, and handed them to the king. He asked the king's pardon again about his mistake for crying out in loud voice in the king's presence.

"It is nothing," the king assured him.

But Zomy was anxious to make up for his mistake and said to the king, "Your Majesty, I understand now why you woke up talking unconsciously in your dreams, perhaps without realising it. Anyone might have done the same if they were dreaming of being on the strange planet called Earth."

"Do not mention that name again!" the king said to him, "I spoke to you of the nice melody I heard in my dream. I am quite happy to tell you more details of it."

"Thank you, Your Majesty. I won't mention that name again," said Zomy.

The king spoke to secretary Zomy about his dreams. But he only told him half of the truth of the sounds and bells he heard. The strange melody he heard, which he said had cured his back pain and how after waking up he didn't feel any pain again was amazing. He didn't know how to describe the sound of those bells. Maybe a "healing and magical melody."

Listening to the king's explanation of his dream, Zomy thought to himself, *What strange dreams.*

The king continued saying, "I am still hearing the vibrations of those melodies in my mind right now. The feeling that healing melody gives me, even my soul feels relaxed. All the worries that I had the night before have vanished with those healing melodies…"

Zomy said, "Your Majesty, I have listened to your explanation. I am very happy about how you are feeling right now. But I would like to say this to you: Do not take very seriously those miraculous healing melodies, which have healed your back pain. I believe it was just a dream like any other or perhaps an unexplained coincidence.

A good night's sleep can help our body and mind feel relaxed and restored to regain strength and energy after long hours of work, as Your Majesty does every day. Working long hours can cause tiredness and stress as well. So, a good night's sleep can make us feel better like the good rest you just had in your dream."

The king looked at Zomy without answering. Immediately, he started to record his dream vision as he sat in his bed.

The secretary asked the king, "Your Majesty, May I take my leave, so that you will be alone to record your dreams and not be distracted by my presence here?"

"No, no wait here maybe I will need you again to do something for me," the king replied.

Zomy waited, watching as the king was writing on the paper without any idea what the king was drawing or writing. The king used up all the papers without being able to draw anything accurately. He felt so frustrated he threw everything on the floor.

Secretary Zomy was alarmed and went to pick up the papers lying on the floor. Before he could touch them, he heard a sharp voice,

"Leave it, do not touch it."

Zomy took two steps backward. The king did not want him to see what he drew on paper.

Secretary Zomy did not dare to look at the king's face after the way he had just shouted at him.

A few seconds later the king said to him, "Just bring me more papers, before I lose the vision of my dreams. I do not want those visions to fade from my mind."

Zomy raced off to get more papers and came back quickly to hand them to the king.

The king began drawing again on a small table sitting on his bed.

Zomy as a good secretary wanted to calm the king. But he didn't know what to do. He took the courage to tell the king what he thought was right.

"With your permission, Your Majesty, I forgot to tell you something very important. After listening to your explanation about the incredible dream you had I don't think you will be able to record what you saw and lived in your dreams alone."

"Why do you say that?" the king asked, "Do you doubt the explanations of the dreams I had?"

"No at all, Your Majesty. I do not doubt anything of your dreams. I believe in the truth of everything you have told me. But after analysing all the details of your dreams, I have come to the conclusion that you won't be able to draw or write much of that you saw and lived through your dreams."

"Why? Why do you say that?" the king asked angrily.

Zomy said, "I would like to explain to you, Your Majesty. First, I do not underestimate your capacity to drawing such things as the dreams you had. But my doubt is about this particular dream. Because you cannot draw or write melodies easily, they were like the air and wind... They come and go and disappear in the mind. I remember when you were still a young prince, you didn't like to write music or enjoy your music lessons very much, even though I know you can play some instruments. These are my concerns.

Secondly, may I suggest to Your Majesty that you tell the master of music Mr Gilmax of your dreams. He can try to rescue these melodies for you. I am sure that he can help make something approximate to what you heard. Let him write this melody for you to keep it safe, so that if you feel unwell someday, they can simply play these melodies to heal any pain you might have in the future… Although I do not want to see you unwell ever.

Your Majesty, I see you are struggling to write these melodies by yourself. My words are just advice from your humble secretary, who really would like to see you have these healing magical melodies with you."

When he finished saying these words, Zomy saw a flash of anger on the king's face. He clearly didn't like his advice at all.

The king turned angrily toward Zomy and said, "I have the impression that you do not entirely believe the truth of my dream. You have been in my services a long time. I have never told you anything like this before."

"I know that, You Majesty," said Zomy. "I believe every word you have told me. I have no reason to doubt anything of your dreams. After all, you were alone in your dreams, as everyone is. Some people are generous to share their dreams with others as Your Majesty is doing for me now, something I am very grateful indeed to hear."

The king replied, "I have no intention of revealing my secret healing melodies to the master of music, Mr Gilmax. I won't take your advice this time. I will keep the secrets of these melodies only for myself. Do you understand?"

"Yes, I understand, Your Majesty," said Zomy while asking himself, *Why did the king not want to share the melodies from his dream with anyone? If he can't write them, they could be lost forever.*

King Brelys-1000 didn't want to say anything more about his dreams for fear of letting something else slip out of his mouth. He must keep the secret of the existence of planet Earth and the great clock just to himself. In fact, the king was unfairly angry against Zomy. Even though everything Zomy had said was logical according to the story the king himself had told him.

All this happened because the king was afraid to reveal the secret of his dreams in full. He was annoyed at his own mistake in pronouncing the name of planet Earth so carelessly. Now his secretary was aware about the existence of planet Earth. Secretary Zomy was now even less convinced with the king's explanation about his dreams, and having some doubts about this story. But he could not say this out loud or contradict the king.

"I believe in your dreams, Your Majesty," said Zomy. "You are my king. I want to see you in good health, if you allow me to say one last thing to you about this particular dream, and about all dreams in general I will be very happy to not say anything more about it."

"Go ahead, I am listening to you," said the king to him with impatience.

Zomy said, "Your Majesty, all dreams are involuntary visions which come into our minds when we fall asleep, like the melodies you dreamed of, anyone would wish these kinds of dreams to last forever. Unfortunately, when we wake up and realise that it was just a dream and not real life, it can have an effect on us, and cause real disappointment, especially those kinds of dreams that are like living a parallel life somewhere else."

"What does all this mean?" the king asked him.

Zomy said, "Dreams are mysterious. No one knows where they come from. They come unexpectedly. Some dreams are bad, others are good. Some believe they can interpret dreams, and explain their meaning. From my point of view dreams are unexplainable whatever rational interpretations some wise man wants to give them. Dreams are always mysterious, and they will remain so as long as life continues. Please, Your Majesty, I would like to suggest to you to not take the dreams you had very seriously because dreams are simply visions without real meaning.

But I am very happy indeed that Your Majesty has heard this melody with healing power, while asleep. My duty as your secretary is to advise you and tell you the truth using my humble knowledge. I feel very proud to serve you, and be assured that you are well. This is all I wanted to say to you, Your Majesty."

Zomy was relieved to hear the king say to him, "I like your explanation about dreams, and I am convinced by your advice. But remember not to reveal to anyone of anything what we have said here."

Zomy bowed to the king and said, "Any secret I know will never be revealed to anyone. Only if Your Majesty ordered me to do so. Nothing I know will ever be found out."

"That is what I wanted to hear," the king said to him.

Zomy smiled for the first time since he woke up. After a few moments Zomy asked the king, "Majesty, may I go now?"

"Yes, yes, you can go now, it is still night and there are a few hours left to sleep," the king said.

Zomy made a low bow, closed the door and went to his antechamber leaving the king alone in his room.

It was a strange night for the king, and for his secretary. The king tried to draw on the papers the things he had seen in his dream without success. He tried to fall asleep hoping to see the same dream again. Unfortunately, nothing of the sort happened; the dreams someone would like to have again rarely return.

Chapter Five
A New Day with a New Project in Mind

Morning came on planet Oxon. Life in the royal court went on as usual. Although his thoughts were filled with last night's dreams, the king was calm. He hid his emotions as if nothing had happened the night before. After having breakfast with his family, he went to his office. He told Zomy he was not to be disturbed, and he would not hold any audiences that day unless it was something very, very important.

The king passed all day in his office trying to draw the clock tower he saw in his dream the night before. He tried over and over again without success, but when he was about to abandon his attempt to drawing it in frustration, he had a breakthrough. He finally managed to draw the clock tower. He was so happy he didn't think again about the sounds of the bells. All he wanted was to have an idea of the design of the clock tower, and find a way to build something similar in his kingdom.

King Brelys-1000 had an ambitious project in his mind to change the capital of his kingdom, Ryam, to make it a modern place with new buildings, avenues, parks and monuments, so that when his daughter the Princess of Light came to the throne of his kingdom it would have a modern look. Most of all the king wanted to build something that would impress his subjects, something they had never seen before, and that would make them feel proud of him for generations to come. What he had in mind, of course, was the clock tower he had seen from his secret observatory, and then last night in his dreams.

King Brelys-1000 loved his only daughter, heiress to the throne, so much that he gave her the name 'Light' because she was a light shining in his life and heart. Still he had never revealed to her the existence of the secret observatory unlike his father King Bixiz-2 did for him when he was still a young prince. Instead he decided to wait to reveal that secret to her on her coronation night, according to the kingdom's ancient code and practice.

The king sat in his office looking at the drawing he had just managed to complete. The floor was still covered in papers from his many previous attempts. He was comparing his drawing with the drawing of the clock tower he had in his secret observatory library. It was almost exactly the way he saw it in his dreams.

"It looks good," he said and laughed. He was very pleased with it.

Three days later he called his most talented painter Marin Zet and the royal architect Klenes Ozz to the royal palace for a secret meeting. Before telling them why he had summoned them, he told them about his project to make the capital city Ryam modern and beautiful.

Then he held up the two drawings of the clock tower and said to them, "I designed something that I want you to build. But first, I want you to make a professional drawing and a small model of them in secret."

Klenes Ozz and Marin Zet were very impressed after seeing the drawings the king presented to them. They had never seen anything so beautiful. The king intended to make the drawings and the small model of the clock tower public when they were ready. They agreed that the drawings and the small model of the clock tower would be presented to the king in three weeks' time. After they bowed to the king and left the royal palace, each one went to their own studios to begin their work in secret.

During this period, the king continued with his royal duties. No one in the royal palace had any idea about his secret project of the clock tower.

Three weeks later the architect and the painter came to present their work to the king in total secrecy. When they removed the cloths, the king saw the small model of the clock tower and the painting, both very beautifully made. The painting showed every little detail of the clock tower very clearly.

"Oh, they are magnificent!" said the king. "They are even better than I ever expected."

He was so happy he couldn't stop smiling. The architect and the painter were pleased too by the king's reaction to their work. The king bowed to them in recognition and admiration of their amazing work. This gesture was something very unusual; something the king had never done before to a commoner. Marin Zet and Klenes Ozz were amazed by the unexpected gesture from the king. They too bowed three times before the king.

The small model of the clock tower was made with clay and mud, covered with plaster and painted with a sandy brown tint that looked like real bricks; it was very beautiful. The king thanked them for their amazing work and looked forward to when this work would be seen in public. He was certain his subjects would admire him and consider him the most intelligent king in the history of the kingdom of planet Oxon.

Chapter Six
The Presentation of the Dream Project

The next day, the king sent an invitation to all the dignitaries of planet Oxon and all professionals and representatives from every social class within his kingdom to come to the royal palace in two days' time. The king supported the principle of a strong monarchy but with democratic values, such that all people within the kingdom were represented.

On this day, everyone invited arrived at the royal palace not knowing the reason the king summoned them. The royal palace was full of dukes, politicians, business people, military officials, architects, engineers, lawyers, doctors, professors, mechanics, carpenters, builders, masons, and many other professions.

All of them were gathered in the big meeting room covered with a richly decorated glass roof. They called it The Glass Gallery. Everyone in the room was talking and holding discussions in their various topics of expertise.

Suddenly the sound of trumpets was heard, *tring, tring, tring!*

The king appeared and everybody stood up to receive him. He was alone, without the Queen Zam or their daughter the Princess of Light. No one had any idea why the king had summoned them there. He made a gesture to sit down. A few minutes later, the king rose from his seat and addressed them.

"Welcome, all of you. All of you know very well of our major project to transform our capital city and we have nearly finished it. But I have called you here today to announce that I plan to build something very special for the culmination of our project. A clock tower, that is to say, a clock that sits high on a tower."

People were confused after hearing such a proposal from the king; they had never heard anything like this before. They were thinking of the sand clock they used to control the hours, asking among themselves how a large sand clock could be placed on a tower. They could not understand how such a thing could be possible.

"What kind of mechanism can make a larger heavy sand clock to turn up in the tower?" they asked.

Some people thought that maybe the king was planning to build a large water clock or Clepsydra to turn it over once a day. One of the assistant engineers wanting to be clever said to his colleagues in a low voice,

"Maybe there is a new technical design that could make it possible to turn the sand clock once a day, so that when one side of the hourglass is full it will easily turn into the empty side each day, via a long chain hanging within the tower. That would make a big difference on the accuracy of the hours in our capital."

The people around him were listening and nodding in agreement.

When King Brelys-1000 heard all these rumours and whispers spreading through the crowd, he realised that some people were going to have some doubts about his proposal. He raised his hand, and the room fell silent. He said to them,

"I understand your confusion, and maybe some doubts as well, about my proposal to build a tower with a clock on top. This is an idea that I know sounds impossible to achieve, but it can be done. We must challenge our current knowledge of architecture and technology to build something fitting for our great city, and make this ingenious idea a reality. This is a real challenge for all of us, even for myself. As your king I really wish us to have this clock tower; it will be a great gift for all to have an accurate means of telling the time with the sound of bells ringing all over the city.

I heard a lot of murmuring and someone saying that maybe my proposal 'will be a big sand clock that can turn once a day only.' This is not a bad idea too if we could achieve it. But my proposal is to have a tower with a mechanical clock that can work using an engine to keep an accurate time for all. The mechanical clock will have bells and ring each hour and every half hour to let people know the time. There will be many benefits if we build it, even those at a distance will be able to hear it too. It could also function as a point of orientation like a lighthouse on ground to help anyone lost to find his way back home safely."

All the people there were impressed to hear his words. The king continued his speech.

"Yes, I know that it will be difficult to make this idea a reality, but nevertheless, I have full confidence in our architects and all of you here today that if we work together, we can achieve this goal. Now I will show you a painting and a model illustrating this wonderful clock. After you have seen it, I will await your comments and opinions as to whether this project is realistic or not."

Secretary Zomy came forward and removed the cloths that covered the painting and the small model of the clock tower; it was the first time Zomy had seen these objects too.

When the people saw the two magnificent ideas presented to them, they were amazed, as they had never seen anything like it before. All of them admired King Brelys-1000's intelligence and his creative ideas.

Immediately, they broke out into applause saying, "Long live the king and his great intelligence."

Never before had any king of the kingdom of planet Oxon planned something like this. In a few moments, people were surging forward to join a long queue to see the painting and the small model of the clock tower. The queue stretched around the great hall; each person who saw the painting and the small model of the clock tower up close was very excited and emotional at seeing its unique beauty.

Everyone was amazed by the king's creativity, and that he had an idea that no one else had. They all admired his idea for the project. There wasn't a single bad comment about it, which reassured the king that it was possible.

After seeing the painting and the small model of the clock tower, the king asked all the people gathered there,

"What do you think about this project?"

"Very good, Your Majesty," they replied.

Then the king asked them again, "So if we work together on this project, is it achievable or not?"

"Yes, it is achievable, Your Majesty," they shouted and broke into applause again.

The king concluded, "If we do this, it will mark a time of great success for our kingdom and our planet Oxon, and we will be leaving an historic landmark for future generations."

Straightaway the king appointed his best architect to start the work on his project and appointed a special team to bring all their ideas together to ensure its success. But the king made it clear that he himself would make all the key decisions if any changes would need to be made in the plan. Because of course, he was the only one who had access to the secret observatory and really knew how the original clock tower of London looked, especially after seeing it up close in his dreams. When the meeting ended, all guests were offered refreshments to celebrate the historic event for their kingdom.

The people awaited the news of the day when the king would lay down the foundation stone to begin the works on the clock tower. However, presenting a model of a project for the people was easy. But to make it a reality was another matter. No one had considered the challenge of how they would actually build it. Even the king and his best architects didn't know what kinds of materials they needed to build the tower and fabricate the mechanical clock strong enough to resist the torrential rain and strong winds which blew across planet Oxon once a year.

Building a real clock tower was a very different matter. During the presentation of this project everybody forgot to ask these key questions. Why people ignored this fundamental question for the success of this project was a mystery, because without real knowledge it would be very difficult to deliver the king's dream project to his people.

Planet Oxon didn't have the right materials to make high quality cement, or enough steel or iron to build a tall tower. The only material planet Oxon had was plaster, clay, stone and water. They used these to make bricks to build their houses by baking them in big kilns to make them hard. In the same way, they could mix large and small stones with plaster to lay down foundations for buildings. The royal palace was very well built using this material. The architects were masters of this material and way of constructions.

Their beautifully built capital city of the kingdom Ryam had three-storey houses, and buildings lining the roads interspersed with parks and gardens, some with fountains and others with statues of the past kings and queens and important people of the kingdom. All buildings were painted in white with windows and doors in blue, green and yellow with the roofs painted in a red and brown colour giving a cosy look to the city of Ryam. In fact, every building in the city was no more than three storeys high, except the royal palace, which had six floors, and was built on top of a hill to make it look even taller and allow it to be seen from a great distance. The clock tower was the first project of its kind to be built in the city that would eclipse the height of the royal palace as a monument of the kingdom.

With this project, King Brelys-1000 wanted to write his name in gold ink in the history of the kingdom. The clock tower was to be built high on top of a sacred mountain commonly known by many Oxonian citizens as the Blue Mountain, for its beautiful trees with blue leaves, so that anyone could see it from far away and hear its bells ringing out the time. By night the clock tower would have candles lit inside to help guide anyone trying to find their way, even at night. This project was a message as well for those impostors of the Mambul sect and wizards who rebelled against the kings Bixiz-1 and Bixiz-2 many years ago and were expelled to live in the forest for good. The clock tower project would send a strong message to them and their followers that the monarchy was solid as a rock, more than their practices and beliefs.

The king was confident in the invaluable services the clock tower would give them all. But many Oxonian citizens gathered there didn't understand the meaning of the times divided into hours by the future mechanical clock. They understood only two times, day and night, perfectly established by nature. But the king was confident that they would soon adjust to the new way of telling time, and would find it useful in their daily lives.

Chapter Seven
The Work Begins

Two weeks later after the presentation of the project, the king went to the Blue Mountain to lay down the foundation stone of the clock tower. Around him, there were some senior dignitaries as witnesses to the historic event, Milos and Arlo, as well as his chief architect Klenes Ozz. After laying down the first stone the king planted a tree to mark the event.

The next day, the works began on the Blue Mountain.

Many ordinary people in the city didn't know what they were building there. There wasn't an official announcement about this project. They just saw architects, masons, carpenters, bricklayers and labourers transporting construction materials on top of the mountain and going to work there every day.

The work progressed quickly. They had already dug half of the tower's foundation in a deep hole in the ground. The enthusiasm and motivation for this project showed in the faces of the people involved. There were many theoretical ideas offered that sounded promising and looked simple enough to accomplish. Now the time had come to put all those ideas into practice to achieve their goal to actually build the clock tower.

Nothing can be hidden when people want to know something that has drawn their curiosity until they discover the truth of it. At some point the rumours began to spread in the capital and all over planet Oxon that they were building a tower with a big sand clock on top, which will turn once a day and keep an accurate time.

Many of them worked voluntarily out of their love and respect for their king and kingdom. By making bricks, transporting water, chopping wood for the bricks kilns, all were motivated to do the project – architects, workers and volunteers alike. The king sent all volunteers a letter of congratulations, thanking them for taking part in the greatest project in the kingdom.

During the day, the king was attentive to the construction. On the left side of his office was a window with a view of Blue Mountain and from there the king was able to watch the works through his binoculars. He wanted to be near it at all times. He received the chief architect every afternoon to inform him about the progress being made. The king was satisfied after every briefing. He had no doubts that this project was becoming a reality according to his wishes.

King Brelys-1000 was like a child playing with his favourite toy when he sat in his palace and looked through his binoculars at the work being on Blue

Mountain. He was already dreaming of the day when he would see the tower completed, rising tall over the city like the real clock from his secret. He constantly checked through his binoculars to see the works progressing When the foundations of the tower were around five metres tall, he called Queen Zam and their daughter the Princess of Light to come see the works through the binoculars from his office. They shared his happiness about the project.

Day by day, the works were going faster than he could imagine. The architects and all the workers involved in the project were so positive about its progress. King Brelys' face glowed with happiness. A few days later the tower was taking shape with the first steel being driven down at each corner to make the strong foundation.

The king was very happy and he didn't hide his joy. He was dancing with Queen Zam every time they met up in every hall or corner of the royal palace. He became very romantic just like when they were married twenty years ago, even though the king was not normally the type of person to show affection easily in public. After the tower reached the height of around twelve metres, the king celebrated the event with his family by sharing a two hundred and fifty-year-old bottle of champagne from the royal cellars.

The work of the tower still had a long way to go, however, to match the ninety-seven metres of the actual clock tower the king had seen in London on planet Earth. The works continued every day without problem or complaint, or any change in the plans as presented by the king.

One week later, the tower was taller still and the structure of the tower could be seen clearly. Since the architects were used to constructing buildings of this height, the foundation and up to the first and the second floors went up quickly and without any setbacks. The royal palace was the only building with more than four floors, not counting the small tower and miradors sitting above the main building. It was very beautifully built with long, slim columns and was six floors in total. But even from the very start of its construction, the royal palace did not have a fixed plan. Over the centuries, it had been altered to make it more and more magnificent. Furthermore, a very old law of planet Oxon kingdom was still in force, which forbade anyone from building anything higher than the royal palace.

One morning, Klenes Ozz and his aid presented the progress of the works to the king and asked him if he agreed for the work to continue, as the tower would soon be higher than the royal palace. The king gave his approval to continue. The way he saw it, the clock tower wouldn't be housing any people. The architect and his aid bowed to the king and left happily but at the same time little worried about the challenge facing them to build this tall tower. They had never undertaken work this massive before. The architects were struggling, as their knowledge and techniques to build such a tall tower were limited. As the weeks went on, progress began to go slower and slower.

Chapter Eight
Work Is Halted

The king received a letter from Klenes Ozz telling him about the problems they were facing:

Majesty,

Despite all of our combined determination and abilities working to complete this great project, I regret that I must inform you we are facing some challenges never before seen in any construction works previously done. Our pace has slowed down considerably since we started because of this. We will require time to develop new techniques and methods and test them out in practice before being able to proceed with certainty. Building this clock tower has certainly become the greatest challenge in all our kingdom's history. We hope you will understand the precautions we are taking with high consideration.

Klenes Ozz,
Chief Architect

The height of the tower at this stage was now around 12 metres high, the same height as the tallest building in planet Oxon, and at the technical limits of the workmen. This was not an issue of mathematical calculations made by the architects, which were perfectly correct but rather a question of material, or lack thereof. The construction would not be possible as previously thought without strong materials like steel and cement. The king was worried after this unexpected news but believed in his heart that these technical problems could be resolved and overcome sooner or later. He didn't lose hope that he would one day see the clock tower of his dreams.

Every morning, the king looked through his binoculars from his office window to see how the work was going on Blue Mountain. He could see that the work had slowed considerably, and there was not any real progress being made. He began to become impatient and disillusioned. His hope of seeing the tower built was starting to fade in his mind. It was not an easy thing to the king to accept this possible reality. His face was no longer shone with happiness. He didn't know what to do to solve this problem. After all, he was the one who came up with this idea to build a tower with a mechanical clock. The architects and builders were simply executing his ideas. They were not guilty for the slowdown in the project. After a time, the king stopped inviting visitors into his office to look through the binoculars from his window office to see the work being done on Blue Mountain.

The king began to lose hope when the work came to a complete stop, something he never imagined would happen. He instructed Zomy to call all dignitaries to an urgent meeting at the royal palace in two days' time. The king could not hide the disappointment on his face. He stopped dancing with Queen Zam when they meet inside the royal palace. She noticed this change and realised that the king was no longer in good mood. Her romantic and jolly husband had disappeared.

Chapter Nine
The Urgent Meeting

Two day later, the urgent meeting took place in the royal palace. The glass gallery of the meeting room was full of dignitaries from every region. Some dignitaries had been at the first meeting called by the king two month earlier, and for others this was the first time they had come to the palace.

Everyone stood up to receive the king with applause when they heard the trumpet's sound. This time King Brelys-1000 was not alone. He was accompanied by Queen Zam and his daughter the Princess of Light, making the meeting even more significant with their presence. The meeting began with some welcoming words from Zomy, and followed by an announcement that the chief architect, Klenes Ozz, would be informing them of the purpose of this meeting. The king would be saying a few last word at the end.

The model of the small clock tower was still displayed in the glass cabinet alongside the painting. The room was silent. Everyone gathered there could see the king's sad face.

Then Klenes Ozz started his speech by saying, "I speak in the king's name as his voice before you. Please excuse me for not having prepared a written speech for this occasion. However I will speak with sincerity from the bottom of my heart about how I feel about this project.

Your Highnesses the king and Queen and the Princess of Light, distinguished dignitaries of the kingdom and guests, His Majesty has called you here today to give you some bad news. Bad news that is partly due to me being unable to make His Majesty's dream a reality. This is not my sorrow alone, but everyone's here today, and all the people of our kingdom. The dream project to build a tower with a mechanical clock here seems very far away now. Although I still have some hope that we can save this project if all of us bring our intelligence and ingenuity together to achieve it."

Upon hearing this news, everyone gathered there began talking and whispering among themselves until Zomy tapped the floor with his stick for silence.

"Yes, work on the clock tower has stopped," said the chief architect. "We need time to study new techniques to be able to build a taller structure. Also, we need to find stronger materials to sustain the tower against the rain, and strong winds that blow in our planet. For centuries, our capital city has changed little with only a few impressive buildings. We still build the same way our forefathers did centuries ago, without changing the style of construction or architecture.

That is not to say that we do feel proud to preserve the old architecture as part of our national heritage. But we must challenge ourselves to create something new. It seems to me that we are incapable of creating a new style of architecture to leave our mark on the history of our planet Oxon. We shall have to commit to a huge effort to build an impressive and modern piece of architecture in our time if we are going to leave a legacy for future generations.

Dear all, the king's dream project is now stopped completely. Therefore I am asking the collaboration of all of you and the bright people you may know to present your ideas to help realise this great project. Let me be clear, His Majesty wants us to have a clock tower here. Any ideas to build a large sand clock as some suggest will not be accepted. This project was the vision of His Majesty, which I am honoured and proud to be part of as chief architect. This project is not an impossible dream but rather something that could become as real as the small model inside the glass cabinet in front of you. These objects should inspire us to not let this project fail."

This part of the speech of the chief architect caused a great emotional response among the people gathered there, and they immediately stood up and applauded when he had finished. The king was pleased with the speech of his chief architect, which seemed to have captivated people's imagination and reignited their motivation to continue believing in his project and get involved themselves.

An old dignitary named Arlo asked for permission to speak.

"Our chief architect was unable to build a small tower?"

There was a silence. Nobody answered him. It seems as though Arlo doubted the challenge faced by architects, as the chief architect had just explained to them.

Another old dignitary called Milos stood up to answer Arlo saying, "My dear old friend, it seems by your question you are a little lost. Everyone here has understood very well, as His Majesty's chief architect explained, why work on the tower was stopped. We must remain united and committed to this great project."

Milos's words were most appreciated by all while Arlo felt embarrassed by his nonsense question and sat back down.

During that time King Brelys-1000, the Queen Zam and the Princess of Light were listening to everything quietly. Klenes Ozz, his speech finished, bowed to the royal family and sat down. Then the king stood up and said, "I have nothing more to say. My chief architect has explained everything clearly. I only ask for your cooperation with one another, that you look beyond social class or rank for the sake of finishing this project. Anyone who can find a solution to complete my clock tower will receive a great reward and recognition for their achievement in the service of their kingdom and king and will become Knight of Honour."

This last part about a reward promised by King Brelys-1000, was to impress everyone in the meeting and beyond. Those who heard the speech first hand stood and again burst into applause. Secretary Zomy was instructed to publish the king's announcement and send copies throughout the kingdom to motivate everyone to get involved in the unfinished project.

With the trumpet's sound, the meeting was closed and the king left with his family. This was one of the best short speeches ever given by the king. Every word came from the bottom of his heart, and had touched all those gathered there. The people immediately began discussing ways to relaunch the project.

During this time, Zomy was already at the royal printing press having hundreds of copies of the king's announcement made, and organised the special royal eagle post services to take the copies across the kingdom. He handed out copies to the dignitaries too, to take with them. Other copies were sent by royal guards to be pasted on the walls of the squares and streets in the cities and towns, even trees in the forests for all to see and read.

When Oxonians read the announcement, they were in shock. They had never heard anything like this before, neither the construction of a mechanical clock tower, nor the king asking the cooperation of everyone in the kingdom. The news was the talk of every household.

But two months passed after the king's announcement and still no ideas came forward. Work on the tower was halted completely without any telling when it would start up again. Each day passing without any work done, seemed to the king an entire month lost. He was desperate. He didn't know what to do. His last hope had been in his announcement to motivate the people. Nothing new had come forward, as he had been expecting, no matter how hard the Oxonians were working to create a solution. The challenge they were facing was a great one.

During this time, the king still waited expectantly for good news to come forward, whenever that might be. He spent more and more time in the secret observatory than ever, keeping himself occupied by looking at the London through the telescope when the skies were clear, hoping that an idea would strike him or to see if there was something he had missed before. Some days, he couldn't see anything because of the clouds covering the city. And he had not had another dream of being in London on planet Earth since the first. All of these frustrations were becoming an unbearable torture for the king. While gazing through the telescope, his heart felt joy. But when the idea or thoughts of giving up this project came into his mind, to accept the reality that he would never achieve his dream, he would shout,

"Never, never, never! I would never surrender the idea of having a clock tower here in my kingdom, never."

Life continued on planet Oxon. The unfinished clock tower was the only bad news, shared by all the good citizens of his kingdom. Many of them tried their best to search for new ideas and techniques, which could build the tower and the mechanical clock, motivated by the privilege and reward the king had promised.

After six months had passed since the king launched his first public announcement and but nothing had resulted from it, his hopes started to drift away like smoke in the air. There was no one on planet Oxon who could find the way to achieve his project. The king became very irritated at being unable to see his dream become a reality, and worse when he slept, that he did not dream of visiting the clock tower in the London. He began to believe that only that magical sound of the bells could heal the sadness and insomnia he was beginning to suffer now.

Chapter Ten
The Princess of Light's Birthday and the Unexpected Letter

On the last day of the third month of the calendar year fell the 16th anniversary of the birth of the Princess of Light. A party would be held on the first weekend of the fourth calendar month. Her birthday was very important as she would now be considered an adult, and so it was a special event across the kingdom of planet Oxon. King Brelys-1000 had waited many years for his daughter's birth, even though he was young. His father King Bixiz-2 had these same difficulties, and Brelys was only born in his father's old age. So the anniversary of the birth of the Princess of Light was very important for planet Oxon, as the sole heir to the throne.

This event was an occasion to put a smile back on the king's face and make him to forget the problems of his project for a few days about. He decreed three days of festivities and beacons lit across the kingdom in honour of his daughter. All the cities of planet Oxon were well decorated with large posters of the Princess of Light wishing her a very happy birthday. The capital Ryam was beautifully decorated and filled with many Oxonian citizens coming across the kingdom to celebrate her birthday. There was a concert with much dancing and singing, while others participated in the many games arranged for this occasion. The dignitaries of planet Oxon were invited to the royal palace. During the celebration of Princess of Light's birthday no one dared to speak about the work on the clock tower which had stopped completely over six months ago, to avoid causing sadness to the king on a day of celebration.

Inside the glass gallery at the royal palace the royal philharmonic orchestra was playing with a choir directed by the maestro of music, Mr Gilmax, by performing a special song he composed called *One Thousand Years of Light, and a Long Life for the Princess of Light*.

Everyone was enjoying the music, dancing and singing along.

"Long live the Princess of Light! One thousand years of light for you!"

She blew out the candles on her birthday cake and they sang happy birthday to her, followed by a toast of champagne. Everyone enjoyed the cake.

Many fireworks were already installed on top of Blue Mountain alongside the unfinished tower; from there everybody would easily see the fireworks when they are lit later after dark.

While they were still enjoying the party, one of the guards blew his trumpet, signalling someone's arrival by horseback.

"Who is coming so late?" some wondered.

Others thought that maybe the horse was sent by an important person to bring a gift for the Princess of Light on her birthday.

But as the horseman approached the gates of the royal palace, the guards noticed that the rider was a royal guard by the uniform he was wearing, and not a dignitary. They opened the gate and a few seconds later the horse entered at high speed, the rider pulling him up quickly making the horse whinny The guard jumped to the ground. His colleagues greeted him with a military salute.

The rider left the horse to his colleagues, saying to them that he will need his horse soon to return from where he had come. He was in a great hurry, and a bit agitated. He was breathing heavily after his long ride.

He told his colleagues that he had a very important message for the king, which he must hand directly to him. One of the guard, an Officer Tolly, led him through the celebration room, where the guests were still enjoying the party. Officer Tolly approached Zomy, and told him about the arrival of a royal guard by horse, claiming to have with him a very special, important message for the king and that he insisted on handing this important message directly to the king himself. Zomy then approached the king and told him this news.

The king told him to call the guard. A few minutes later, Zomy led the royal guard in for an audience with the king. He gave a military salute to the king and announced himself as Sergeant Tomlin of the 17th royal squadron of the southeast region of the kingdom. He bowed and handed him the mysterious letter he brought for him.

The king took the mysterious letter calmly in his hand opened it and started to read. He read it so quickly that his eyes were moving left to right through every line of it and then widened in shock. Then he read it twice more:

Your Highness, King Brelys-1000 of the kingdom of planet Oxon,

Before explaining the real reason which has encouraged me to write you this letter, as I am aware that it coincides with the birthday of your daughter, the sole heir of the throne, allow me to wish a very happy birthday to Her Royal Highness the Princess of Light.

Your Majesty what with the great respect and admiration I have for our kingdom I was very saddened indeed to learn that work on the clock tower has halted; it seems as though there was no one here who can build it. But perhaps I can make your dream come true by constructing the mechanical clock here first, and later building the tower itself. I only have one condition: that you accept my hand in marriage to your daughter. I do not ask for any other title, or any other reward offered for accomplishing this. I will wait for your answer in the same place this letter was found. I know it may not be easy to accept these kinds of conditions from an unknown sender. I hope you receive my proposal with the sincerity, trust and kindness that has always characterised Your Majesty.

Your humble and, for now, unknown citizen,
W.B.

After taking in the contents of the mysterious letter the king asked Sergeant Tomlin, "Who gave you this letter?"

"I have no idea who wrote this message, Your Majesty. I found this letter hanging on the trunk of a large tree in the forest next to the announcement Your Majesty made six months ago. During the six months, the announcement had been nailed to a giant tree in the middle on the forest, a place in fact where few people would pass. But today, I was on a routine mission and to my surprise, I found this letter unsealed on that very tree."

The king opened his eyes widely as he listened to the sergeant's explanation. He read the message again. He made himself remain calm so as not to attract the attention of those at the party. He ran over the letter's contents in his mind. He did not know whether to believe its claims or not. In the end, he burned the mysterious letter with a candle on the table beside him. A few dignitaries watched suspiciously, as he did so. But no one could imagine what kind of news was in that letter; nor did they give it much importance due to it being a private matter. After burning the letter the king stretched his arms and shook his right foot in agitation.

Then he asked Sergeant Tomlin again, "You are certain you do not have any idea who could have written such a letter?"

"I have no idea who may have written this letter, Your Majesty. I was in shock myself after reading its claims and the unacceptable conditions. It took time to convince myself to bring this letter before you, Your Majesty. But my duty as a royal guard is to serve you and because of that I came here today to bring this letter, so that Your Majesty can make the decision you consider best."

The king warned Sergeant Tomlin, "Do not reveal the contents of this message to anyone. All this must remain a secret. We don't know who sent this letter, or who we are dealing with. All we know right now about the mysterious sender are their unacceptable conditions with this fanciful idea and proposal. It could be a mad person with bad intentions looking for some easy reward. Or maybe he wants to test me with this trick letter to see if I would be so careless with my daughter, the Princess of Light."

"Yes, Your Majesty, I agree with you. I will keep it a secret," Sergeant Tomlin replied. "I won't reveal the contents of this message to anyone."

After their talk, the king called Zomy to write a letter in response, dictating the words to him:

To the unknown sender,

I thank you for your unusual letter. We accept your amazing offer with all the sacrifices we must make to meet the conditions you are asking for. In return, I ask you one condition only. Present yourself in person and we will talk. If you can deliver what you claim, you may be able to win my trust.

Signed,
King Brelys-1000

After writing the letter, Zomy handed it to Sergeant Tomlin so that he could return quickly with it to the middle of the forest. Sergeant Tomlin bowed to the king and stepped back, to give him a military salute.

Zomy accompanied him to the gate where the royal guard was waiting for him with his horse refreshed for the return to where he was based in the southeast region. Sergeant Tomlin thanked his colleagues, and in a single movement, jumped up on his horse. He kicked his horse into a gallop, disappearing from view in the dust left behind. Sergeant Tomlin raced to arrive at the big tree in the middle of the forest before nightfall to leave the letter for the unknown sender.

At the royal palace, the party continued. As darkness fell, the guests heard the sound of trumpets and Zomy announced to the royal family and all the guests that it is was time to see the fireworks. Everyone gathered outside looked across at Blue Mountain to see the fireworks. A few moments later, a single trumpet sounded to indicate the countdown to the fireworks. This was the highlight everybody had been waiting for. The royal guards lit the fireworks, and they shot into the sky bursting into different shapes and colours.

Some fireworks exploded into the shape of flowers that wrote "Happy Birthday" across the sky. To everyone's surprise, the last firework that exploded created an image of the Princess of Light inside a ring with the number "16" for her birthday. When the fireworks finished, the sky got dark. Suddenly, the sky suddenly lit up again and to everyone's astonishment, shooting stars flew across the sky in different colours: green, red, yellow and blue, as if nature came to celebrate the Princess of Light's birthday too. This natural phenomenon left no doubt that the heir to the throne was a very special person.

In the city square people were shouting with joy and crying with emotion at what they had just seen and broke out into applause. A few superstitious people were worried by the stars and thought it was an omen. The sky was filled with smoke from the fireworks and the rolling waves of colour from the trail of the stars' lights. On the terrace in the royal palace everybody enjoyed the fireworks and applauded as well. Joy was on the faces of everyone. A big smile was on the king's face with the surprise arrival of the stars. Queen Zam and the Princess of Light herself were very happy too. After the fireworks, parties continued across the city.

All the dignitaries and their wives brought gifts for the princess. These reflected the typical gifts from each region: art, jewellery, diamond rings and gold with the number "16" engraved on them, rich carpets, games, musical instruments, paintings, furniture. Even the timeless flower that lasts forever and the honey flower to which people attribute many miracles. She thanked everyone for their marvellous gifts and for coming to her birthday celebration.

All evening the Princess of Light enjoyed her birthday celebrations, dancing and talking with the people invited to her party. She had no idea about the arrival of the mysterious letter. The king's face did not reveal any sign of the emotions he felt towards the fact that the mysterious letter offered to make his dream come true, or that he was wondering how to find out who this unknown person was, who claimed they could do what not a single person in the kingdom had been able to so far. This question went round and round the king's mind endlessly during the birthday celebration.

Towards the end of the birthday celebrations, the king called over three elderly dignitaries whom he trusted most due to their age, Arlo, Milas and Zilo. He told them the story of the mysterious letter and the nature of its arrival. He told the three elderly dignitaries his answer to the unknown sender to come forward to present himself before him. But the king did not reveal to them all the contents of the letter, specifically the conditions it laid down. He just wanted to hear their opinions about his response to the unknown sender.

No one had any idea who this unknown person could be. The three old dignitaries agreed with the king's answer.

"The mysterious sender of the letter must present himself before the king," said Arlo and added, "Who could be so intelligent in this kingdom that we do not know of?"

Then Milos said, "It is a good idea that this person must present himself before His Majesty the king, above all to see if he is serious or just a fool, or if this is a bad joke."

As for Zilo, he doubted the seriousness of this mysterious person who could give such promise to the king.

"I think he must be mad to make a joke like this and give His Majesty false hope! I don't think this person really wants us to have a clock tower here. I am in no doubt that he is acting in bad faith, and when he is caught, he must be severely punished. It is intolerable to make such suggestions without any possibility of achieving them, especially when everybody knows very well how halting the project has affected the king. His Majesty's own royal architect declared the reason why they couldn't build the tower higher. This mysterious person only gives false hope."

However, all of these ideas and suggestions of the old dignitaries were just hypotheses. They did not know that there could not be another person on the planet who could be just as wise and intelligent.

Finally Arlo said, "We must let time reveal this mystery to us. No one could have predicted that the king will receive this mysterious letter today on the celebration of his daughter's birthday, the Princess of Light. We must wait and see if the mysterious sender will present himself before the king, as commanded by His Majesty."

Milas said to Arlo, "I share your point of view and optimism as the arrival of the mysterious letter coincides with the day of the Princess of Light's birthday. Maybe this is a positive sign."

The king listened to them, and thanked them for their comments and optimism, and told them that their conversation was to be kept secret.

But they had no idea that the mysterious unknown sender of the letter was a woman named Moxum, one of the great-granddaughters of the leading member of the Mambul sect that was expelled from the cities and towns of the kingdom years earlier by the late King Folzy-5. His son, King Bixiz-1, and his grandson,

King Bixiz-2, followed in the same lines of pressure and hostility against the Mambul sect for their mysterious practices.

People like Ms Moxum and the others in the Mambul sect were the last direct descendants of a group of people that was expelled from the cities of the planet Oxon kingdom some forty years earlier due to their practices and beliefs in mysterious sciences mixed with magic and mysticism. They believed there was life elsewhere in the universe and held the secret of how to get there. The king at the time considered these ideas and beliefs dangerous practices that could corrupt people's minds.

They were accused of being witches, a very serious accusation that carried the death penalty. So to be safe from prosecution for their beliefs and to keep safe the secrets of their mysterious practices, they lived deep in the forest in a secret village called Black Cloud. There they kept a special cauldron on a fire day and night with many strange objects boiling inside. The dense forest was safe and nobody would ever notice what they were doing there. This was the place where Moxum and her sister Eris grew up, and where Ms Moxum learned everything about their ancestors' secret sciences. Many years passed until they were forgotten and no longer considered a danger to the crown.

Ms Moxum was the last guardian of the secret of the mysterious practices of her ancestors. She was not a witch, just the keeper of the knowledge of the mysterious sciences. She had thought for a long time about how to avenge the honour of her ancestors who were persecuted by the kings for their beliefs. Ms Moxum knew of the failure and the frustration the king felt after not being able to build the clock tower. Finally she had a weakness and it was time to put her plan into action. She took advantage of the king's frustration and sent him the letter on his daughter's birthday on behalf of her nephew Winn Blitzzer, by sending the letter signed with her nephew's initials W.B., thus keeping her identity a secret. Her audacious plan was for her nephew Winn Blitzzer to marry the king's only daughter, the Princess of Light, thus securing the Mambul sect's presence within the royal circle of power.

Meanwhile, Winn Blitzzer continued with his daily routine without any idea that his aunt Moxum had sent a letter to the king on his behalf claiming that it could make his dream project become a reality by accepting him as the best suitor for the king's only daughter, The Princess of Light.

Chapter Eleven
The Second Announcement

When two weeks passed since the king replied to the mysterious sender who sent a letter to him and no one presented themself before the king, became impatient and frustrated and thought that maybe someone really was playing a joke on him as Arlo suggested. In the end the king made the decision to make a second public announcement aimed at the mysterious sender of the letter. The king instructed his secretary Zomy to write a second public announcement. It read:

King Brelys-1000 of planet Oxon wishes to announce to all of his subjects that anyone who can solve how to build his clock tower shall be offered the opportunity to become a strong contender in offering their hand in marriage to the Princess of Light, if it would be a marriage of love. If it is not a good match and there is no possibility of love between them, the builder of the clock tower shall then have the option to become an honoured knight of planet Oxon, and the chance to enjoy the rewards promised in the previous announcement.

King Brelys-1000

This was the king's tactic to draw out the mysterious sender of the letter, to make them come forward and show themselves. Furthermore the king wanted to prepare his people in case the mysterious sender came forward someday to fulfil the promise of his letter. The new announcement was placed in every city, town and village across the kingdom, even to the forest. This new announcement from the king attracted the attention of many Oxonian citizens again, reigniting their scrambling against one another to solve the question of the unfinished clock. Every household was building their own small model of the clock tower. This was becoming a hobby everywhere whether old or young, rich or poor, those without any idea how to even make a brick did their best to come up with something. After all, no one could say to anyone that his idea was not good enough, now that work on the clock tower had stopped over six months ago.

Chapter Twelve
Unexpected Discoveries for Winn Blitzzer

A few days after the king's second announcement was made, Winn Blitzzer and Tovic headed to the city of Ryam to sell and buy items they needed for their secret village in the forest. They had no idea of the new announcement launched by King Brelys-1000 a few days earlier.

It was not until after they had sold their wares of honey, lard and dried meat in the market and obtained what they needed for their village that Winn Blitzzer and Tovic noticed people reading a large sign on a nearby wall. After reading it people were standing around talking excitedly, while others ran off to tell their families and friends about the latest announcement of the king.

Curious, Winn Blitzzer and Tovic approached the sign. After reading it, they did not react the same way as the other people around them. They glanced at each other and were rather quiet.

Some people gathered there noted their indifference to the king's announcement. Then they heard a voice down the crowd shouting,

"Let me through, let me through please! I would like to read the king's announcement myself."

It was a dwarf with a long ginger beard and a rather scary face with a blue star tattoo, and big protruding eyes. Two large hoop earrings hung from each ear, and he had two rings and his right hand, one black and one red. He was dressed in a blue shirt with black trousers and brown boots. When Tovic looked down and saw the strange dwarf with a tattoo star on his face, he stepped in surprise, right on the foot of the dwarf.

"Ow!" the dwarf cried out with look of pain on his face. "You just stepped on the old corn on my foot. I don't think I'll be able to walk now, it hurts so much."

"Sorry, I am very sorry!" said Tovic kneeling down to speak to the dwarf. "Please tell me what I can do to make up for stepping on you."

The expression of pain on the dwarf's face was replaced with a smile, as if nothing had happened.

He said, "Hoist me up on your shoulders. I would like to read the latest announcement from the king."

Tovic and Winn Blitzzer looked at each other.

Then Tovic said to the dwarf, "I can lift you. That won't be a problem if you don't weigh much."

The dwarf looked at him and said in a low voice, "Do you mean to suggest that I am overweight?"

"I didn't say that sir," said Tovic, his voice breaking slightly. "I only meant to say I hope you are not very heavy for me."

"I do not as weigh much as you think young man," said the dwarf, "but you are paying for having stepped on my foot right?"

Tovic said nothing and bent down to let the dwarf climbed on his back.

"You are a good lad," the dwarf said to him. He read the sign. "So the news is true. Let me down now, boy."

Tovic put the dwarf down and the dwarf said to him, "By the way, my name is Nomy."

He held out his hand in greeting to Tovic with his hand on his chest, and looked up at him.

"I am Tovic."

"A good name," said the dwarf Nomy. "What do you think of this announcement? I'm not sure what to make of it."

"So who will be the lucky man to marry the Princess of Light?"

"It could be you, Tovic," winked Nomy.

"Me married to the Princess of Light?" exclaimed Tovic. "That's a funny joke. I could never marry the Princess of Light."

"Do not say such things, young man," said the dwarf. "Nothing is impossible in life if you believe in it."

He turned to Winn Blitzzer. "How about you, young man? Your friend Tovic doesn't seem very optimistic. Does this announcement mean anything to you?"

"Not really," Winn Blitzzer replied and added, "at first I thought that the announcement was about a tax reduction for the poor, that news could have been very good for all. I do not have any ambition to marry the Princess of Light."

The dwarf was surprised hearing Winn Blitzzer answer the same as his friend. He noticed that unlike the others excitedly crowded around the sign, the boys looked rather indifferent, if not uneasy. People in their vicinity looked around to see who could be uninterested in news like this. They were not wrong in guessing that they were just a couple of village boys who had come to the market to sell. Why would they have any interest in an announcement from the kings?

As the two made their way back home, Tovic asked Winn Blitzzer, "Why do your aunts never leave the house or go shopping in the city?"

"I don't really know why said," answered Winn Blitzzer. "I never asking my aunts anything like that, but it is true that as far as I can remember they never left the house to go to the city. They are always looking after that cauldron fire, day and night."

Said Tovic, "My mother said that your aunts are very mysterious women, especially your aunt Moxum. Because of her my mum doesn't like me visiting your house often. My mother and your aunt Eris used to go shopping together in the city. But after what happened in our village… their friendship ended pretty much after almost everyone vanished suddenly. I don't really know much about it. But because of that there are no other men left besides us. And the few women left do not trust each other anymore."

Winn Blitzzer asked Tovic, "What exactly do you mean, vanished?"

Tovic looked at Winn Blitzzer without saying anything. He had a strange expression on his face.

Winn Blitzzer said to him, "You are hiding something from me. Tell me, what do you know about my aunts? They have never told me anything about my life. I don't even know where my parents are. I have no idea who I am and why we are living in the middle of this forest in an almost empty village. Tell me what you know!"

"I can't, I can't.!" Tovic burst out suddenly. "I cannot tell you anything." He tried to run away but Winn Blitzzer grabbed his sleeve.

"Don't run away Tovic. If you are truly my friend you will tell me the truth about our village."

"I am your friend. I cannot hide anything from you so fine, if you insist on knowing then come to my house in a few days' time. I will tell you the story my mother told me about our mysterious village, and why we were living there in secret. I am lucky to have my mother, at least. And even though I don't have my father right now at least he is still alive. Yours too, Winn Blitzzer..."

"What did you say?" Winn Blitzzer exclaimed. Did Tovic just say his father was still alive somewhere? It was the first thing he had ever been told about either of his parents.

"It's true. We are not alone there in the village. Your mother and your father can see you and hear the things you say every day. If you pay attention, you can feel these strange movements around you sometimes. That is them."

Winn Blitzzer gaped at him.

"It's true," insisted Tovic.

Finally Winn Blitzzer spoke. "I will come to visit you in two days' time. I want to know more. But why didn't you tell me anything before?"

"I couldn't say anything to you," Tovic replied, "I was afraid for my mother. She is the only family I have now. I don't want your Aunt Moxum having any problems against her. Your Aunt Eris sometimes still meets with my mum and Lady Dallas in secret... your Aunt Moxum should never know about this, otherwise who knows what would happen to them too. Promise you won't let anything slip around her."

Winn Blitzzer was in shock at hearing all of this.

"Okay," he promised.

"There's one last thing I wanted to tell you now," continued Tovic. "The dwarf with the ginger beard we saw today, I think it was no accident he was there."

"What makes you say that?"

"Because I just remembered something very important," Tovic said. "Some months ago I heard my mum, Lady Esra and Lady Dallas talking about a dwarf with a long ginger beard and a star tattooed on his face who escaped from our village before Ms Moxum could get to him. The dwarf knew that your Aunt Moxum was planning something. But at the time nobody believed him."

Winn Blitzzer said, "Tovic, it is hard for me to believe such things without having seen any tangible evidence of it."

"Well, my mum wouldn't lie to me or Lady Dallas," said Tovic defensively. "Their husbands, family and friends are all invisible, and they have suffered a lot because of it. I won't force you to believe me. But don't you remember what happened to our teacher, Mrs Loly?"

"Yes, of course, as if it were yesterday," said Winn Blitzzer. "I will never forget it. But how can we know that she became invisible too? And why would that happen to her, or any of them?"

Tovic said, "Winn Blitzzer, you are blind and naïve. But in a few days you will learn the truth about everything."

Winn Blitzzer felt sad and guilty again about what had happened to Mrs Loly. It was he who had asked her the question, "Why is our village empty?" At that point they had arrived back in their mysterious little village and the conversation came to an end.

"See you in a few days' time," Winn Blitzzer said to Tovic. Then they headed their separate ways.

Chapter Thirteen
The Secret of the Magic Cauldron Named Potsat

Winn Blitzzer arrived at his house and greeted his two aunts, handing them everything he had brought back from the city. He told them all about the announcement from King Brelys-1000 and the excitement it was causing in the city. His aunt already knew everything that was happening in the city through the Potsat screen but she was pretending listen to her nephew's news.

"What did the announcement say?"

Winn Blitzzer told her, "The king promises to reward anyone who can build a clock tower, the Princess of Light's hand in marriage as well as other titles."

To his great surprise, his both aunts began laughing. He looked at them, confused.

His Aunt Moxum said, "No one from planet Oxon, even the king, could build a tower here never, never, ever. Even if King Brelys-1000 gambles his throne no one can build this clock of his."

"Aunt Moxum, you don't go to the city, or even leave this house, you too Aunt Eris. How do you know what you're talking about?"

Ms Moxum told him, "Don't worry my dear nephew, I will reveal to you today a big secret, and show you something very special that I think will make you change your mind."

Aunt Eris said, "We know everything that happens in the city without leaving our mysterious village. Even sometimes we see you selling things in the market in Ryam from here."

"What are you talking about?"

Aunt Moxum said, "I have many things to tell you today. It is time for you to know the truth about many things that I have kept from you for so long."

Then Moxum beckoned him to come closer, saying, "Come, I want to show you something."

Winn Blitzzer approached her where she stood next to the big round black cauldron hanging hung by a big chain from the ceiling over the roaring fire.

She told him, "Now you will discover the secret of how we can see everything that happens far away from here and in other parts of universe without ever leaving this room."

Winn Blitzzer smiled, but without any real idea of what his aunt was doing.

Moxum told him, "Close your eyes and only open them when I tell you to do so."

Winn Blitzzer closed his eyes. His aunt Eris made a gesture in front of his face to check if he could see anything.

When Moxum was sure that the cauldron was hot enough she lifted the lid and the steam poured out. On the underside of the lid was a mirror with three small, metal buttons, green, red and yellow. The small lion head ornament revealed two small antenna inside, which she pulled out. After wiping the steam from the mirror, she pressed the green button on the lid and an image appeared. She turned to Winn Blitzzer and said to him, "It is time now to open your eyes and look straight before you."

When he opened his eyes and saw the lid of the cauldron, and the live image of Ryam and the royal palace shining in the screen lid, he felt strange as though he was dreaming, and even a bit dizzy as he stared wide-eyed at the images moving in front of him. This was not what he had expected at all.

He said, "I feel like I am dreaming…"

"You are not dreaming," said Moxum. "This is the way we see things from a distance without leaving this house."

"I cannot believe that I am seeing Ryam right now in front of me. How is it possible? How do you do that? How does it work?" he asked his aunts.

Aunt Moxum told him, "It's a very long story to explain to you at this moment. I will do so in the near future. Your Aunt Eris and I were waiting for the right time to reveal to you this secret. Do you believe in us now when we tell you that we can see you in the city from this cauldron?"

"Yes I believe in you." Winn Blitzzer nodded vigorously. "All this time, the cauldron had this magical power…"

"We know that you had been with your friend Tovic, the son of Lady Esra, today in the city."

"That is true," Winn Blitzzer replied, stunned.

Aunt Moxum said to him, "Be careful, I don't like this friendship with Tovic. He might tell you lies about this village."

Winn Blitzzer felt a little scared, then he asked his aunts, "This cauldron could pick up the sounds of a conversation from a distance too?"

"Yes, of course," Aunt Moxum replied.

Winn Blitzzer did not ask anything more.

Aunt Moxum left the cauldron briefly to get something in her room. Winn Blitzzer took the advantage of her absence by asking his Aunt Eris the question that worried him the most.

"Aunt Eris, how long do these images stay on the lid, all day?"

"No, depends on what Moxum wants to do. But she does not spend more than three hours a day in front of the Potsat," said Aunt Eris.

When Aunt Moxum heard this, she came hurrying back yelling, "No! That is not true. The cauldron can show me images all day long from planet Oxon or any part of the universe or dark galaxies."

She glared at her sister Eris. "Let me answer any questions our nephew has. Remember, I am the sole keeper of the secrets and the power of the mystical sciences. Don't ever say anything to him anymore without my permission. Do you understand?"

Winn Blitzzer was shocked by the angry tone and the way Aunt Moxum addressed her sister. It seemed to him that Moxum wanted to hide something from him. But Winn Blitzzer was even more amazed by the discovery of this secret, the power of this special cauldron.

He said to his aunt Moxum, "I still cannot believe I am seeing the actual market from the city where I have just been. What kind of cauldron is this?"

Aunt Moxum said, "This cauldron is not just any normal cauldron. It has special satellite and radar hidden inside, beautifully made by our ancestors from whom I have inherited all the knowledge of the mystical and mysterious sciences."

Then she looked him in the eye and said, "Now, do not tell a soul about what I have just shown you."

"I would never reveal this secret to anyone," said Winn Blitzzer.

"Something else I will tell you is that the Potsat is divided into two parts. Hot on top, almost cold down below. The water inside the Potsat is not normal water, but a very special liquid to preserve all the magical objects which are inside safe. But it looks very hot with the steam coming off the top. So, if anyone else were in this house, they would only see the boiling hot water and keep their hand away from it. Still, only I may put my hands inside the Potsat without burning."

Aunt Eris looked Winn Blitzzer in the eyes and nodded her head to confirm that everything his Aunt Moxum had just said was true.

Winn Blitzzer still felt like he was dreaming.

He said, "If I understood correctly then this Potsat doesn't only have the power of capturing images from a distance, it also acts as a sort of safe to keep all the magical objects inside."

"That's right, you have understood very well," Moxum replied, and said, "This Potsat is our salvation, and yours too."

"What kind of salvation are you talking about, Aunt Moxum?" Winn Blitzzer asked.

Aunt Moxum replied, "You will see one day."

"Why couldn't I see the live images in this Potsat before?" Winn Blitzzer asked his aunts.

Moxum said, "You couldn't see anything in the Potsat before because the time to reveal all these secrets to you hadn't arrived yet."

Winn Blitzzer was a bit confused by what Aunt Moxum just said. He thought, *If only I could consult with Aunt Eris in private to clarify everything.*

After brief silence Winn Blitzzer said, "It does sounds incredible and a bit hard to believe that such a thing could be possible in a single pot."

"That's why it is a very special Potsat," Aunt Eris replied to him.

"Hush!" Moxum said to her sister Eris. "Don't talk without my permission."

Aunt Eris looked down. Winn Blitzzer thought of what his friend Tovic told him, that his mother, Lady Esra, and Lady Dallas next door often criticised

61

her bad manners and arrogant attitude. It seemed to Winn Blitzzer that his Aunt Moxum may be hiding her true self from him. But he couldn't figure out why.

To change the subject slightly Winn Blitzzer asked, "How tasty would food cooked inside the Potsat be?"

"Very tasty indeed," Aunt Moxum replied, and she began laughing. Aunt Eris laughed too.

"Well," said Winn Blitzzer, "today we must celebrate all these amazing things I have learned. I wish to see both of you talking and laughing like sisters, even with the other villagers. We should be united and not divided!"

"I do not talk to them," said Aunt Moxum. "They are bad people. They envy me because of my inheritance of our ancestors' knowledge."

Winn Blitzzer asked her, "Why didn't you tell me about our ancestors before? I am sure that they are very intelligent and wise people whom anyone could feel proud to be related to if they could have created something special like this Potsat."

"Yes," nodded Aunt Moxum, "they were very intelligent people indeed, with knowledge of the sciences and other beliefs. But I won't tell you much about them right now, another time. I understand very well how you feel, all these new discoveries and unanswered questions going round in your head. But you cannot understand everything in just one day. With time you will understand, and learn more about the power of the Potsat."

"Thank you Aunt Moxum. What can I do for you to tell me more?"

"Nothing yet! Do not rush it. I am still explaining to you the reason why today was the special day I have chosen to reveal these secrets to you. Now Winn Blitzzer. The king's announcement today was the reason I was waiting to tell you everything. It is no coincidence this is all happening on the same day.

The fact is, the clock tower King Brelys-1000 is trying to build on planet Oxon will never be possible. It would never become a reality. No one could ever fulfil his dreams here. His best architects are struggling to build it. King Brelys-1000 thinks he can have everything he wants in life, but not this time."

Winn Blitzzer still did not understand. "I don't see any connection of this story with my life."

"I know," said Aunt Moxum. "But I can assure you that you are the only person who could make King Brelys-1000's dream become a reality."

"Me?" Winn Blitzzer said trembling, his voice shaking.

"Yes, you Winn Blitzzer. You are the only person who could make the king's dream come true."

Winn Blitzzer was astonished. "It cannot be me. I am not an architect to build the king's clock tower. How could I do that?"

"Yes, you can," said Aunt Moxum to him. "If you take my words seriously, and believe in yourself, the Princess of Light could be your fiancée in the near future. Nothing is impossible with the power of the Potsat."

"This is impossible to achieve," Winn Blitzzer said, "I am not a prince to marry the Princess of Light. And how I can achieve something all people of planet Oxon cannot?"

Said Aunt Moxum, "The Potsat was created to accomplish a very special mission far more important than all the money and wealth of planet Oxon combined. Just agree that it could be possible if you believe in yourself and listen to me."

Winn Blitzzer did not contradict her again.

Aunt Moxum said, "In two days' time you will need to go back to the city."

"To do what? I have just come from there today."

Aunt Moxum said, "You are not going back there to sell or buy anything. You will go straight to the royal palace to ask for an audience to see King Brelys-1000 by presenting yourself before him as Winn Blitzzer, the one who can make his dream come true."

Winn Blitzzer asked, "Me, be received for an audience with the king?"

"Yes! You will be received by the king tomorrow," Aunt Moxum replied. "I'll explain why. When construction on his tower could continue no further and he sent out the first announcement asking the kingdom for assistance, I sent him a private letter in your name, telling him that you could help him complete the tower. I will show you a copy so you can read it. I offered him my help in exchange for his daughter's hand, the Princess of Light and sole heir to the throne.

And so, the king made the second announcement to all Oxonian citizens that anyone who could finish his clock would have the opportunity to become the Princess of Light's suitor and possibly ask for her hand in marriage. The king's reaction was a trap I have been waiting for so long for him to fall into. This was the reason I would like you to go to the royal palace tomorrow, and ask for an audience to meet the king. The time is now."

"So you sent a letter to King Brelys-1000 in my name without telling me? Do you really think this was doing things in my interest, without even telling me about them before?"

"Yes! This was the only way," said Moxum. "If I had revealed to you this secret before, things could not have worked out according to plan. I had to do it this way."

"I do not doubt your good intentions in all this, but I still feel your proposal is nonsense. I don't see how the king could receive me in his royal palace."

"Don't worry about that. Look, here is the letter that the king sent in reply." She handed the letter to Winn Blitzzer who took it and read it.

After reading the king's letter, Winn Blitzzer smiled. Aunt Eris looked on in silence.

Aunt Moxum asked him, "Do you believe me now?"

"Yes, I believe you, Aunt Moxum. I don't doubt anything you have said. But put yourself in my shoes. Who wouldn't be in shock after all this?"

Aunt Moxum said, "I understand that. But I want you to be confident. You will go meet the king. Look in the screen of the Potsat again."

When Winn Blitzzer looked, he saw the royal palace and the Princess of Light walking in the garden around a fountain. He covered his mouth with both hands.

"She is very beautiful," he said.

Aunt Moxum said to him, "With this as proof, maybe you can start to believe that anything is possible with the power of the Potsat."

Then she motioned for him to sit down beside the cauldron and they went over the plan and everything he would need to know for his audience with the king the next day.

That night, when Winn Blitzzer went to bed, he lay tossing and turning in his bed, unable to stop thinking about everything Aunt Moxum had told him and showed to him. And the fact that in two days his friend Tovic would be waiting to tell him everything his aunt did not want him to know about the village of Black Cloud, and wondering how he was going keep her from listening to everything they said.

Chapter Fourteen
The First Visit to the Royal Palace and the Encounter with the Guards

Winn Blitzzer woke up early in the morning to the birds singing to celebrate a new day in the forest. He felt as though he had just fallen asleep. He was more aware than he had been before of the warmth spread inside the entire house from the mysterious Potsat.

His aunts had a breakfast of hot porridge prepared for him to warm his body before his first meeting with the king. They did their best to reassure him by reminding him that he would not be alone along the way; they would be watching him through the Potsat.

When he had finished eating, Aunt Moxum took a cup of the strange liquid from the Potsat and told Winn Blitzzer to drink it. "It will be good for your confidence and eloquence, and convince the king to believe in the sincerity of your proposal when you meet him."

When Winn Blitzzer saw the steam rising up from the hot mug, fear showed on his face. "Is it too hot to drink?" he said.

"Don't be afraid, it is not as hot as it looks," Moxum said to him.

Winn Blitzzer took the mug and smelled it. The liquid was odourless and when he tasted it, he found it equally flavourless. He took another sip. To his surprise it now tasted of honey and roses. Instantly a light began to shine out of his mouth from his throat and he began to feel strange. He looked down at his hands and saw a small yellow ball of light circling his body at high speed, up and down and around. He ran to look in the mirror. When he saw himself he could not believe his eyes.

Standing before him was a handsome young man. He looked up at his aunts with a big smile on his face and said, "I feel confident now, more than before. Now I look like someone who would seek an audience with the king."

"Perfect... Everything will be fine," said Aunt Moxum to him and handed him a small bottle with a thick, heavy liquid inside. It resembled mercury but with different colours, shining like a small rainbow. Winn Blitzzer was amazed. He had never seen anything like it before.

"What is this, Aunt Moxum?" he asked.

"Keep it in your pocket as a special gift," said Aunt Moxum. "With one drop of this special liquid anywhere you spill it, you will be able to transform whatever it touches into anything you desire. Just remember, it is not a toy."

"Thank you, Aunt Moxum," said Winn Blitzzer, and put that small bottle in his pocket. As he was leaving Aunt Eris gave him a big hug and said to him, "Remember, do not look back until you arrive at the royal palace."

"I won't," Winn Blitzzer promised and started walking.

And then he was alone below the tree in the middle of the forest. There was light breeze that morning, blowing the leaves and some dry branches fall from the trees to the ground. He felt a bit scared by the noises he kept hearing behind him; it was not easy to not look back. Suddenly, a white bird flew by. He did not know it, but the dove was sent by his Aunt Moxum to accompany him to the city and to help him should he need it.

After a short walk he heard the waterfall of the river Memz nearby. He realised the city of Ryam was near. He was surprised at how quickly he reached it. He crossed the river, walking on top of a big tree laid down across it like a natural bridge and a few moments later, he was in Ryam.

The sky was clear, a sign of a pleasant sunny day ahead. He could see the royal flag, one half dark blue, the other white with a yellow crown in the middle, and a small yellow sun and moon with stars at the top and bottom ends. It was waving over the royal palace from a distance on top of the hill. His heart leapt in his throat. Then Winn Blitzzer saw the white dove again, flying towards the royal palace, and followed it forward.

Winn Blitzzer was becoming paranoid, after having seen the images on the Potsat. He was nervous crossing paths with people in the street, fearing he was being watched all the time now. For second he thought he saw the dwarf Nomy. He tried to remind himself that he was supposed to be acting with confidence and hurried onward.

Finally, he turned in the direction of the royal palace. Gardens full of flowers in every colour, well-trimmed bushes and shrubs, and fountains with statues lined the street he walked down. He had never gone this way before. He slowly approached the gate of the royal palace. It was even bigger, more beautiful in person, and more intimidating. His heart was pounding inside more and he began to feel more nervous. He had never dreamed he would one day meet the king in person.

He tried to remember the advice Aunt Moxum had given him to remain confident and sure in himself. He looked down at himself. No one would have any idea he was just a boy from a village in the middle of the woods. He suddenly found himself thinking of the image of the Princess of Light on the Potsat the night before. This made him feel calm. He noticed the white dove again flying over his head. He was sure now that it was not a coincidence at all. It was following him.

He noticed that on the right side of the gate there was a small glass tower from which the royal guards could watch people come and go from a distance. He was sure they had already seen him. But they were not paying him any mind, having assumed he was one of the staff. The little attention the guards paid him as he was approaching the royal palace gave him more confidence and he straightened his back and walked right up to the gate as though he were meant to be there.

As he approached the royal palace, the massive gate loomed over him. It was elaborately decorated, with two big golden lion statues at the top on either side. Below stood two young royal guards, in red coats and black trousers and shoes. He felt a bit intimidated. But there was no turning back now. The two young guards at the gate were called Erko and Kohla. While Erko was tall, slim, with short blond hair and a kind face with big green eyes, Kohla was medium-height, with black curly hair and blues eyes.

"Good morning, officers!" Winn Blitzzer saluted the guards.

"Good morning!" they replied.

Then the guard Erko asked him, "Are you here for work?"

"No, I came for some other business," Winn Blitzzer replied.

Erko was surprised by his answer and asked him, "What kind of business brought you here so early?"

Winn Blitzzer said, "I came here today to ask for an audience to see His Majesty King Brelys-1000." He nervously brushed back his hair.

The guards looked at each other and began laughing at him.

The guard Kohla said to him, "Show me your documents. No one enters the palace without being checked."

"I do not have any documents with me," Winn Blitzzer replied. The guards began laughing again.

Kohla told Winn Blitzzer, "Without them we cannot grant you an audience to see the king."

Erko asked, "Did you seriously think you could just walk up to visit His Majesty the king?"

The guards were looking at Winn Blitzzer coldly. But to their surprise he answered them,

"Yes, I do. I came here early today to find a way to see His Majesty the king. Please take me to him."

The guards began laughing again. and then looked at him as though he were a mad. Winn Blitzzer started getting frustrated that they were not taking his request seriously.

He insisted. "Take me for an audience please, I have something very important to tell the king."

The guard Erko gestured at Winn Blitzzer. "Dressed like that, you want to meet the king? You must be mad. We cannot grant an audience with the king to someone like you. It would be better for you to go back where you came from."

"I am not mad, I have my reasons for coming here today. You cannot judge people by their appearance alone. My message is for the king and the king alone and something that I can assure you he wants to hear. And if he were to somehow find out that you prevented me from delivering that message…"

The two guards continued to look at him suspiciously but now with a bit of hesitation as well.

Erko said to him, "If you don't tell us what this message is, we will not grant you an audience. Do you understand?"

Winn Blitzzer said to the guards, "I cannot reveal my message to anyone else except the king himself. It's confidential."

The two guards looked at each other. They didn't know whether to take him seriously or not. They had never encountered this kind of a request before, from a young man who was still practically a boy no less.

While all of this was happening, the dove was hiding in the branches of a tree listening to everything that was said between Winn Blitzzer and the guards.

Then another guard arrived, a senior officer called Lahto. He was tall and muscular, with brown hair. He had a long, vertical scar across his face, from an injury he sustained in the war against the imposters of the Mambul sect years ago. But his most striking features were his eyes, which were two different colours, one brown, one green. Between that and the rather severe-looking moustache he always wore, his officers referred to him as 'Neddles' behind his back. He was very serious; in fact no one could ever recall seeing him smile.

Winn Blitzzer saw the guards Erko and Kohla talking to their superior a short distance away. He hoped maybe this officer could help him. When Winn Blitzzer saw him coming to the gate, he again respectfully saluted, hoping this officer would be more helpful. But he was about to find out he was mistaken.

Officer Lahto stopped and stood right in front of Winn Blitzzer with only the high front gate between them. Winn Blitzzer noticed his eyes were two different colours, and then the long scar crossing his scowling face. He took a step back.

With a deep intimidating voice Officer Lahto asked without preamble, "Someone here conspiring against His Majesty, the king?"

"N-no, sir, nobody is conspiring against His Majesty. I just need to tell the king a message," Winn Blitzzer replied.

Officer Lahto made a sign with his head to the guards who came and grabbed Winn Blitzzer to take him away from the royal palace, saying to him, "Go back where you come from."

Winn Blitzzer was desperate. "I must see the king, I must see the king. I cannot miss this opportunity. Don't push me, stop pushing me, like some common criminal, I am a humble citizen who loves his kingdom. Would a criminal ask for an audience to see the king?"

The guards ignored this and continued pulling him away, and in the struggle, Winn Blitzzer completely forgot the small bottle of special liquid he had in his pocket.

The white dove, who had been watching this scene from above, suddenly flew from its perch in the branches, making its way up toward the castle. It fluttered to a stop upon the sill of the king's office window on the third floor where it dove began loudly cooing, attracting the attention of the king himself who was at that time sitting at his desk pouring over the plans for his tower as he had been doing every day since construction on the tower and come to a halt. He came to the window to shoo the bird away. The sight of his two royal guards pulling a young man away caught his attention. He urgently rang a small bell to summon Zomy. The king sent him straightaway to the gate to find out what was going on and why the guards were pushing an Oxonian citizen away from his palace.

Zomy went quickly to the gate; when the guards saw him coming, they stopped what they were doing and stood at attention. He asked the guards what they were doing.

"His Majesty the king himself saw what was happening from his office window and has sent me to find out what is going on. He does not want to see this kind of behaviour outside of his palace gate."

Officer Lahto said to secretary Zomy, "I am responsible for ordering the guards to remove this individual from the palace gate. They were obeying my orders. I take full responsibility. However, when asked to leave peacefully, this man refused. He left us no other choice."

Zomy asked the guards,

"What does this young man want that he refuses to leave peacefully?"

Officer Lahto answered again. "This mad man, so poorly dressed, is demanding an audience with the king without prior notice."

"Do not judge a book by its cover sir." Zomy said to Officer Lahto.

Winn Blitzzer tried to hide the grin on his face. Then Zomy asked the guards,

"This young man told you that he wanted to see His Majesty?"

"Yes, Mr Secretary," the guards replied.

"And he did not say why?"

"No. He refused to give us the reason, saying he must deliver his message to the king himself."

Zomy went through the gate to get a closer look at Winn Blitzzer. "It certainly takes courage, to do something like that."

Officer Lahto made a face but remained silent.

Zomy asked the strange visitor, "What is your name and where did you come from, young man?"

"My name is Winn Blitzzer. I come from a small village far away from here."

"What an unusual name," said secretary Zomy.

Officer Lahto's face was showing signs of the growing annoyance behind it. His cheeks flushed around the scar, while the scar became even whiter.

"This still doesn't answer why he demanded to enter the royal palace to meet the king."

"I didn't come here today looking for trouble. I have great respect for His Majesty King Brelys-1000. I have come here today to deliver a message in person about a very important matter," Winn Blitzzer replied. "I have always been a loyal subject to the king and I know I don't deserve the treatment I received here today. It was no coincidence that His Majesty himself saw what was happening and sent you here. I would have missed the opportunity to tell His Majesty the great news I have, which brought me here today. It was meant to be."

The already red colour on Officer Lahto's face deepened a few more shades. The guards Erko and Kohla looked each other with amazement.

Secretary Zomy said to Winn Blitzzer, "I understand your resentment towards what just happened here. Rest assured, His Majesty will take all the necessary measures. Now what is the purpose of your visit?"

Winn Blitzzer said, "With all due respect sir, I cannot reveal that secret to anyone except the king."

"I am the most trusted collaborator of the king," said Zomy. "For this reason he sent me here. Tell me the reason for coming here, and then I can let you to enter the palace and meet with the king."

Winn Blitzzer said to Zomy, "I do not wish to undermine your position, but as I have said, I cannot reveal this secret to anyone else. If I cannot meet the king, then I would rather go back without telling anyone. But if His Majesty the king would know the message, I am sure he would not be pleased to know I was kept from bringing it to him."

Zomy had no idea that the visit of Winn Blitzzer could have anything to do with the mysterious letter that was sent to the king six months ago.

After hearing this, Officer Lahto said to Zomy. "Do you see? He doesn't want to cooperate. He is arrogant. Can you see now why I had told the guards to take him away from the royal palace?"

Zomy turned to the guards. "I am going to consult with His Majesty on this matter. Keep an eye on this strange young man."

Zomy headed back to the castle. Once he was out of earshot, guards began to laugh again. Winn Blitzzer kept calm. He was still feeling the positive effect of the special liquid from the Potsat that he had taken that morning. He was sure now that when he met with the king, he would believe everything he had to say.

Zomy was not gone long. When he returned, he told the guards, "Open the gate and let in this strange visitor, Winn Blitzzer. The king has agreed to receive him."

The guards were caught completely by surprise. The stood staring for a second before realising they had been given an order and then slowly walked to open the gate.

"Quickly," said Zomy. "The king would like to see him right away."

The guards were silence. They opened the gate to let Winn Blitzzer in. They could not believe that this strange visitor was actually being allowed in, without any prior petitioning, and by the king himself.

Chapter Fifteen
The First Meeting with King Brelys-1000

Secretary Zomy walked with Winn Blitzzer into the royal palace. Just yesterday he never would have dreamed this possible, that he would be standing in the great hall of the king's royal palace. Everywhere inch was covered in lavish decoration, displaying the life of luxury that the royal family lived in, of which he could only dream of from his little village deep in the forest. Zomy led him to a bench and left him seated there while he went to the king's office.

When he returned, he said, "His Majesty the king will receive you now. Come with me."

They walked together down a long hall corridor. Paintings of the kings and queens and princes and princesses of Planet Oxon hung on the walls. Winn Blitzzer's heart was beating fast in his chest.

He said to secretary Zomy, "This feels like a dream."

"Well it is very real. There is no turning back now, the king is expecting you."

Then they arrived outside the hall where the king normally held his audiences. They both entered and bowed before the king.

"Your Majesty," said Zomy, "May I present to you our strange visitor, Winn Blitzzer."

The king was sitting on a big chair with a high back on which was engraved the royal crest. The table beside him, with four seated lions for legs, was covered in papers, quills and ink and an ornamental jug decorated in flowers.

The king noticed that the strange visitor was feeling intimidated by his presence. This was normal; it was the first time ever meeting a king. To make him feel more relaxed, the king said to him, "I saw from my window what was happening with the guards. I wouldn't have noticed if it weren't for a white dove that came to perch on my window and coo incessantly."

Winn Blitzzer smiled.

Then the king asked him his name and where he was coming from, well aware, after the briefing with Zomy, that the boy's name was Winn Blitzzer, and therefore that his initials were W.B.

"Your Majesty, my name is Winn Blitzzer. I come from the tiny village called Green Hill far away from here."

He was looked down at the carpet unable to meet the king's eyes when he lied about his village's name. But he was afraid to give away the real name of his mysterious village, or anything that would lead to the secret of the Potsat and his aunts' identity.

Then the king asked him, "So what is the reason for your visit?"

Winn Blitzzer said, "Majesty, my visit here today concerns your latest announcement."

"Young man, do you know anything about architecture?"

"No at all, Your Majesty. I am not an architect."

The king was surprised by his strange answer. He looked slightly disappointed but also confused.

"So, if you don't know anything about architecture, why are you here about my clock tower?"

"Majesty, I have a plan which could make your dream come true," Winn Blitzzer replied.

The king rose slowly from where he was sitting. "What is that?"

Winn Blitzzer hesitated. "I cannot reveal this secret in the presence of your secretary; only in private."

The king made a sign to Zomy to leave them, who bowed to the king and left.

Winn Blitzzer said to the king, "Majesty, before I reveal to you this secret, there is something else I must tell you first."

The king said, "I will try my best."

"Thank you, Your Majesty," said Winn Blitzzer. "I first wanted to tell you that I know what is hiding in this royal palace. I hope this will act as proof to Your Majesty that my proposal to complete your project is possible."

"Tell me, what do you know is hiding in my palace?" the king asked.

Winn Blitzzer said, "Your Majesty, I know that in this royal palace there is, there is…"

"I am listening. Tell me what you know."

Winn Blitzzer looked at him. "I know that Your Majesty has a secret observatory in this royal palace that only you have access to. I know that from there you can observe another planet called Earth in secret which is where you copied the idea of the great clock tower you are trying to build here."

The king sat back down in shock.

Then he calmly asked, "And how do you know all these things? Who told you this?"

Winn Blitzzer could not answer that. Instead he said, "Your Majesty, I know what I know. No one inside this royal palace ever told me any of this, and I have never even been here before. But it is because of this I am here today."

"How do you know about the planet Earth?"

"I know many things about planet Earth, maybe more than you do, Your Majesty," Winn Blitzzer replied and added, "I know as well that some days from your secret observatory you can't see the images of planet Earth because of clouds covering the view of the city where that clock tower is located."

The king asked him, "Have you been to planet Earth before?"

"Never, Your Majesty. I have never been outside the planet Oxon before. But with the agreement we could reach here today, I could."

The king was beginning to become confused and frustrated with the boy's cryptic answers. It crossed his mind that Winn Blitzzer may be attempting to blackmail him with this information.

He looked at Winn Blitzzer with incredulity. "How could you make build this clock tower when you don't even know anything about architecture?"

"Your Majesty, please believe I tell the truth."

The king looked him right in the eye and said to him, "Young man, tell me the secret now."

"I can confirm that I can provide you an identical clock like the one you have seen in the city on planet Earth. But only if I have your word that you will make me your son-in-law, the reward you offered for doing this."

"How can I when I don't yet know your proposal?"

"Alright. Your Majesty, I can travel to planet Earth and take the great clock from there back to our planet Oxon."

"Did you say you could go to planet Earth?" the king asked, gaping in disbelief. Perhaps the boy was mad.

"Yes, Your Majesty," Winn Blitzzer replied calmly, "I can. If you accept me as your son-in-law. If your answer is yes, then I will bring the clock tower here."

"With what kind of object you could go to planet Earth? If it was true that you could get there?"

"I can get there, Your Majesty," Winn Blitzzer replied. "But I cannot reveal how and with what I can reach planet Earth, otherwise I will not be able to do it. I know I have only my word as my guarantee and the knowledge of what I have just told you as proof."

"I could accept you as my son-in-law if what you are saying is true. But everything you are saying is beyond my knowledge. Your stories are fanciful, and it is very hard to believe them so easily."

Winn Blitzzer said, "I understand Your Majesty. I told you it wouldn't be easy to convince you."

The king said to Winn Blitzzer, "Before I can give you my response to your request, tell me, exactly where is the secret observatory located in this royal palace?"

Winn Blitzzer was clearly stumped. He said, "Your Majesty I cannot tell you exactly where the secret observatory is in your royal palace. I only know that it exists. I know this secret is only known to Your Majesty, and all the previous kings and queens of planet Oxon."

"That will do," said the king.

"We have been talking quite a long time already but without anything in concrete. I would like you to explain to me clearly with details. I still don't see or understand your proposal clearly."

Winn Blitzzer said, "You are right, Your Majesty. To start with, I am not an architect, as you already know. But as you do know, here on planet Oxon it is impossible to build a tall tower with a mechanical clock on top."

The king said, "Yes, my chief architect has already informed me of that. But I am still waiting for your explanation."

Winn Blitzzer continued. "Your Majesty, the architect did amazing work by building the tower as high as he did. Now it will be my turn to find the way to add the mechanical clock. Therefore I will go to London on planet Earth to take the great clock you need from there, and bring it to our planet Oxon."

When the king heard Winn Blitzzer mention the name London, he was shocked and asked him, "How do you know the name of that city?"

"I know the name London because I can go there and take the great clock Your Majesty needs from there and bring it here for you," Winn Blitzzer replied.

Hearing Winn Blitzzer insisting that he could bring the great clock straight from London, he asked him, "How do I know you are not a thief? Perhaps you could steal something from me too, if you could take something all the way from another planet."

Winn Blitzzer felt scared by an accusation like this from the king but answered calmly, "I am not a thief, if I was I wouldn't have come before Your Majesty and given myself away. Believe me Your Majesty, I am just a loyal subject with good intentions."

"Well if you aren't a thief, what are you exactly? With this idea of yours you could cause a war between the two planets."

"Everything I do is with the intention that the Princess of Light could be mine one day," insisted Winn Blitzzer. "There won't be a war between the two planets! It will be a great mystery for the people of planet Earth. They don't really know how many planets are hidden in the vast, deep darkness of the galaxies with life on them. They only know about the existence of around a dozen lifeless planets but not about ours."

"Forgive me, Your Majesty. But I am not a thief and would never be. I am neither a wizard nor a magician, nor a wise man. Only a humble boy from a village."

The king sat straight back against his big chair, and folded his arms across his chest. He looked at Winn Blitzzer.

Suddenly the king asked him in loud voice, startling him, "Do you take me for a fool with your fictitious tales? Do you think you can fool me easily as that, and then accept your request to become my son-in-law? There was only one group of people in this kingdom who believed that there is life on other planets, and they could travel there too. And that was those in the Mambul sect."

Winn Blitzzer felt even more scared by these accusations and said quickly, "Your Majesty, I am not a member of any kind of sect."

The king asked him, "If you are not a member of the Mambul sect, then who are you? If you are not an architect how can you make my dream come true? You cannot be the unknown sender of the letter."

Winn Blitzzer was silent. Then he said, "Majesty, you are right. I was not the person who wrote the letter you had received. Someone else sent it without my knowledge."

"Who did that?" the king asked.

"My aunt," Winn Blitzzer replied.

"What is your aunt's name?"

Winn Blitzzer was scared to say his aunt's real name. But in the end, he said, "My aunt's name is Ms Moxum."

"That sounds very much like the name of someone in the Mambul sect," said the king.

"I don't think so, Your Majesty," said Winn Blitzzer. "My aunt, she could never be a member of such a group."

The king stared at him for a moment. "I would like to believe you, but your stories are too much to be true. And I don't recognise the name of this village Green Hill either."

Winn Blitzzer said, "Majesty, of course it exists, it must not be on any map because it's so small."

"Son the more we speak and the more I hear of your story, the more mystery there is surrounding you!" barked the king, his voice having been getting steadily louder and louder during the conversation.

At the sound of the king's raised voice, Zomy hurried back into the room and bowed, said, "Your Majesty, my apologies for entering without permission. Is everything all right?"

"Everything is fine," the king said to Zomy. "As you were."

Secretary Zomy left them again.

The king turned back to Winn Blitzzer. "Would you ever lie to a king?"

"I would never dream of lying to a king, Your Majesty!" said Winn Blitzzer, "I have never been more honest about anything in my life!"

The king said, "What you are suggesting sounds impossible. And you have not presented me any tangible proof that you can achieve this. All I have to believe you is the fact that you somehow know about what not a single other person in this kingdom has any idea exists."

Winn Blitzzer said earnestly, "Majesty, nothing matters more to me than bringing you the clock and earning the hand of the Princess of Light. I give you my word."

At that the king said, "Fine."

He paused. "Our meeting today is now over. I have a lot to think about. We shall meet again in two days' time."

"Thank you very much, Your Majesty for giving me this great honour of a long meeting."

"Remember, tell no one of what we have discussed here."

"I promise."

"I will remember that promise. You are dismissed, Winn Blitzzer." He rang the small bell to summon Zomy.

Winn Blitzzer bowed to the king and then followed Zomy out to the main entrance and the front gate. Winn Blitzzer bowed to the king and went with secretary Zomy.

The king had no way of knowing that Winn Blitzzer really was in fact the great-great-grandson of the persecuted people of the Mambul sect. Although neither did Winn Blitzzer himself.

The guards were surprised when they saw the strange visitor coming back to the gate. They couldn't believe he had actually met with the king, and for so long. Outside the gate, they watched as secretary Zomy and Winn Blitzzer bowed and said goodbye. Winn Blitzzer walked as quickly as possible through the gate; he could feel Officer Lahto and the guards watching closely behind him.

Winn Blitzzer felt like he was floating as he walked back into the city. He still could not believe that he had been received by the king, just as Aunt Moxum had told him. As he went on his way, the white dove flew past, heading in the same direction. When he reached home, Winn Blitzzer went straight to his aunts with a smile on his face to tell them everything. When they saw him, his aunts cried out, "Welcome home, dear nephew!" Winn Blitzzer immediately launched into an explanation of everything that happened.

"Almost everything went perfectly. Except a small incident I had with the guards at the main gate when I tried to go in. Thanks to the king himself I was able to enter. And the white dove that was following me. If it wasn't for him, the king would have never looked out the window."

Aunt Moxum told him, "We are very happy that your first meeting with the king went so well. This is a good start."

Those words reassured Winn Blitzzer.

Far away from the mysterious village of Black Cloud at the gate of the royal palace the guards still could not believe that the mysterious young man they had refused entry to the royal palace was received by the king and spent four hours in a meeting with him. They kept asking each other, "What kind of information does the strange visitor have that would interest the king? What kind of news is so important to grant such a long meeting with him? Where does he come from?" All these unanswered questions were especially intriguing to Officer Lahto.

While all of this was happening, up in the palace King Brelys-1000 was back in his office, deep in thought. He didn't want to get his hopes up just yet. He would have to wait and see at their next meeting. Hopefully Winn Blitzzer would reveal more to him about where this ability to travel to other planets came from.

Chapter Sixteen
The king Reveals His Secret to Secretary Zomy

It was very difficult for the king to keep the talk he had with the strange boy Winn Blitzzer to himself alone. He called in his secretary Zomy to tell him something about the long meeting before Zomy could start making up his own theories.

The king said to Zomy, "Winn Blitzzer told me such stories that would make some people faint to hear them. He seemed to know many mysterious things about our planet Oxon and beyond, and about the royal palace as well... I don't know how he could know such things."

Secretary Zomy, after listening to this vague explanation from the king, had already made his own conclusions in his head.

"Your Majesty, if you will allow me. After listening to your explanation, my conclusion is this: Winn Blitzzer may be nothing more than a schemer or a liar. Don't take what he had told you seriously."

Zomy was surprised when the king replied, "Even if this boy is as you are suggesting, it took courage to come here and tell the king himself, the way he did. Do you not agree?"

"Yes, Your Majesty not just anyone would do that," Zomy relented. But he was still doubtful.

The king of course did have some proof, just not any he could share with even his most trusted advisor.

In the end he simply said, "I don't agree with your suggestion that Winn Blitzzer is scheming against me. He seemed to know many important things about the royal palace."

"How is it possible that Winn Blitzzer could know anything about the royal palace without having been here before?"

The king said to Zomy "Maybe it was you who shared information and spread rumours about the palace, that now half the kingdom knows."

The strong words of accusation made by the king were not in fact true. He knew very well that his secretary was innocent. But the king wanted to be sure that he would never reveal anything he was about to learn.

Zomy of course had no idea of all of this. In shock, he knelt to the ground before the king. "I swear Your Majesty I never revealed any secret I know about the palace to anyone!"

The king suddenly smiled. "Stand up, Zomy. Do not worry, I believe you."

Now the king felt certain that he could tell Zomy everything without any fear that his secret would get out. "I will tell you about the first meeting I had with Winn Blitzzer to see what you think about all this. I could use your advice. He has made me an incredible proposal."

"An incredible proposal?" repeated Zomy.

"Yes," the king replied, "I would like to have a little talk with you about that now. But before I tell you anything, you must swear to me again that you shall never say a word about what we discuss here."

Zomy said, "I swear before Your Majesty King Brelys-1000. I am your most humble servant. I feel great honour and pride to be trusted with this. I am ready and prepared to listen."

"Good," said the king, "Now, do not write any of this down. I don't want any record of this conversation to be kept."

Zomy was surprised but waited patiently for the king to continue.

"This is what the boy Winn Blitzzer told me. He says that it is impossible for us to build the tower and the mechanical clock here, just as the royal architects have already said. But then he suggested another solution. To do it, he needs to…" The king stopped. He stood up and walked around to look out the window, the same one where the white dove had perched.

He started speaking again. "This Winn Blitzzer believes that he can travel from planet Oxon to another planet called Earth. On that planet, there is a city called London. And in that city is a mechanical clock just like the one we are trying to build here. The boy says he will bring it safely here to our planet Oxon. Although he refused to explain how he could go about doing that. He insists this is the only way we could have a mechanical clock here. Naturally, his only condition is the one proposed in the letter, to accept him as a potential suitor for my daughter and possibly as my future son-in-law."

Zomy was standing with his mouth hanging wide open, the words "planet Earth" sounding over and over again in his ears. Those were the same words the king had muttered after waking up from his strange dream.

"Your Majesty, perhaps the boy is a member of the Mambul sect we thought had gone extinct," suggested Zomy. "I don't see where else such an idea could come from. Perhaps it would be better not to let him come back here again."

The king said, "I asked him if he was. He claimed he didn't know what Mambul sect was. I looked at his hand, and I didn't see the red and black rings they used to wear…" Before he could finish, Zomy fainted, falling onto the sofa behind him.

The king hurried over to him, trying to revive him, shaking his shoulders, saying, "Wake up, wake up! Zomy, your king commands you to wake up now!" Zomy did not respond.

The king urgently rang his bell. Two guards arrived quickly, finding the secretary lying fainted on the sofa and the king beside him. They attempted to revive him but got no response. He was out cold. The king told the guards to take him quickly to the infirmary.

The king was in shock after seeing his secretary pass out, and before they could further discuss everything the boy had said. He considered if he should summon a few of his other most trusted dignitaries to receive their advice but decided that the less people who knew right now, the better.

That night the king could not sleep, still reflecting over Winn Blitzzer's proposal, and how to reach an agreement with him. He had to face that he simply could not build the clock himself. Even his best experts could not. Now it seemed he had a golden opportunity to make it happen. It seemed too good to be true, but if it was true, the king did not want to miss what could be his only opportunity. It would seem that the option Winn Blitzzer was offering him was the only one he had. And even if Winn Blitzzer was telling him the truth, it was risky to accept on the chance that the plan might not work or, that it would very possibly end up revealing the secret of the observatory and that they had knowledge of life on other planets. Still, this was as close as he had ever gotten to having that great clock since his late father had shown him London for the first time.

In the end the king fell asleep and woke up the next day feeling slightly more hopeful. He continued with his daily life at the royal palace. He went to the secret observatory to watch the great clock as he had been doing every day for years, never once missing a day. He would give almost anything to have that same dream every night too, but it hadn't happened since. Staring down the telescope as he had so many times before, the king experienced a mix of emotions from joy to fear to worry, and hope, that maybe someday he could be lucky enough to see and touch that great mechanical clock. The king spent all day thinking and looking forward to his next meeting with Winn Blitzzer.

Chapter Seventeen
Preparing for the Second Meeting

King Brelys-1000 woke up early the morning of the next meeting in good humour. Even the Queen Zam could see a change in his mood, although she didn't know what caused it.

After two days in the infirmary, secretary Zomy had fully recovered from the fainting spell he had suffered. He wanted to go back to work that same day and assures the king that he was in good health. He didn't want to miss the second meeting with the strange visitor. On his way to the king's office, he met with the young secretary Zig in the long corridor. He had been working at Zomy's post since he fell ill.

"I'm back at my job today, fully recovered," Zomy said to him cheerily.

Zig did not answer. He was not happy to give up the prestigious position he had enjoyed the past two days.

When Zomy arrived at the king's office, he bowed and said, "Good morning, Your Majesty! I am fully recovered and ready to continue my work."

"Good morning, Zomy," said the king. "I am very happy to see you well. You gave me quite a shock the other day. Listen, if you are fully recovered as you say, that is fine. But I would personally prefer if you took a brief holiday to rest and recover your health before starting your duties. The young acting secretary Zig could continue to fill your vacancy."

Zomy said to the king, "Majesty, I thank you for your concern, but I have fully recovered now."

The king looked hard at Zomy and then said, "Very good! Carry on with your duties then."

"Thank you very much, Your Majesty!" said Zomy bowing before the king. He did not want to lose his position to the young, ambitious acting secretary Zig.

The king told him to prepare a note to leave with the royal guard at the gate to give Winn Blitzzer permission to enter when he arrives, as well as to cancel all other audiences and meetings that day.

When he was about to leave, the king told him, "When I will meet with Winn Blitzzer, you will sit behind the curtains of my chair to write down everything we talk about. Do not leave out a single detail."

"Yes, Your Majesty," replied Zomy.

The king added, "I hope that you won't faint this time. Be sure you will remain quiet at all costs. Winn Blitzzer mustn't know that you were behind the curtains."

"I understand, Your Majesty," said the secretary Zomy.

The royal guard Erko was amazed when heard the instruction from the secretary. He said to Kohla, "I have been in the service at the royal palace for many years, I have never seen anything like this before. What do you suppose this all means?"

"Maybe he's coming here because he has some kind of secret deal with the king. And we shouldn't rule out that he could be a spy."

When the Officer Lahto heard the conversation between the young guards, he came over and said to Erko, "Show me the note secretary Zomy just left."

Erko handed him the note.

Lahto read the notice, "Allow Winn Blitzzer to enter the royal palace immediately upon his arrival. The king is waiting to receive him."

After reading it Lahto said to the guards, "This sounds like a joke."

Another guard called Tolly, who was in charge of the small mirador, heard his colleagues talking down at the main gate. He asked them, "What are you talking about?"

Lahto said to Tolly, "We are talking about the strange visitor who came here the other day to see the king without any prior notice. Now secretary Zomy just left a notice to let him enter the royal palace as soon as he arrives, without checking him over or doing our duty properly."

Tolly said to Lahto, "Our duty is to respect and obey the superior order. The secretary just brought this message as per the king's order. If the king is to receive the mysterious visitor again maybe it is for something important we don't know about."

Officer Lahto didn't like this answer. "You don't know how he was, that mysterious visitor and the big mouth he has. He doesn't respect or fear the royal guards. You won't take his side when you see him."

Tolly said to Lahto, "I don't support or defend this Winn Blitzzer, I don't know him. I just talk in common sense that if His Majesty is receiving him again, that's not our concern."

Neither Officer Lahto nor the other two guards Erko and Kohla liked what Tolly was saying. It seemed to them as though Tolly was defending the mysterious visitor.

Erko said to Tolly, "Officer Lahto is right, you don't know the big mouth the mysterious visitor has."

Tolly said to them, "I didn't expect you to agree with my comments. But I'll tell you one thing. If you have enough courage to be angry with someone, go be angry at His Majesty King Brelys-1000. He is the one who rules and gave the order to let Winn Blitzzer enter the royal palace."

His colleague became offended at this, especially Officer Lahto, and were quiet.

Officer Tolly returned to his post in the mirador and the young guards Erko and Kohla went to their guards post inside the small grey colour sentry boxes on either side of the gate. Officer Lahto spent the entire day not talking to anyone. He was just sat, stroking his moustache and thinking about the strange visitor.

Chapter Eighteen
A Shocking Discovery about the Truth Hidden in Black Cloud Village

The day after meeting with the king, at around 11 o'clock in the morning, Winn Blitzzer went to visit his friend Tovic at his house. While walking along he noticed a paper in his pocket. He pulled it out and read it with growing alarm.

My dear nephew Winn Blitzzer,

I would like you to have the normal life of a teenager like the other youngsters left in this village. Try to stay in contact with Tovic and Yalta. I don't want you to be controlled by your Aunt Moxum's difficult attitude. I am taking this opportunity to reveal to you a secret I have never told you before. I have a son almost the same age as you called Valger, but I don't know where he is, or if he is dead or alive since the disappearance of so many people from our village more than 16 years ago now. I have been suffering in silence with grief and sadness in my heart. But that's not the only thing I wanted to tell you. This letter contains important information about how your Aunt Moxum uses the Potsat, so that you may have some privacy and meet with your friends without worrying that she is watching. The Potsat could run all day if Moxum wanted it to, but she likes to open it four days per week. If you avoid doing things during these days that could be good for you, so that your aunt Moxum will not be able to control you as she wishes, I will let you know the day the Potsat will be on or off, by wearing a red and blue ribbon tied on my hair as a secret code for you to know, which red colour means the Potsat will be on and blue colour off. For today, I can tell you here that it will be off. Enjoy your free time. Please destroy or burn this letter after reading it to avoid both of us getting into serious trouble. We can continue to communicate in this way in the future.

Take care, xxx your Aunt Eris

Winn Blitzzer was shocked after reading this but quickly looked for a way to burn the letter. When he couldn't find one anywhere, he put the letter back in his pocket to destroy it later.

Tovic and his mother Lady Esra received Winn Blitzzer with a very warm welcome when he arrived. They chatted and drank tea with biscuits. Winn

Blitzzer felt relaxed with them. It was not long before Lady Esra left them in the house to go to the nearby orchard and later to get drinking water from the noiseless waterfall. This was the best time to do this, when they could drink water from the waterfall without fear that Moxum would poison it and make them to vanish like she did with the other people in the village years ago. Winn Blitzzer noticed the table was laid with six dishes of well-cooked food as if his friend Tovic and his mother were waiting for the guests to arrive for lunch, despite so few people being in the village.

Winn Blitzzer asked Tovic, "Do you have a party here today?"

"No," Tovic replied. "This lunch is what I wanted to tell you about the other day. It is a very long story to tell you now. I invited you here to have a special lunch with me. Around 12 o'clock, when the sun at its highest in the sky, we will sit down at the table to eat." Winn Blitzzer had no idea what was about to happen. His eyes roved over the waiting feast.

Even Tovic did not entirely know what would happen later when they sat at the table to eat. He knew that his mother Lady Esra was the cook for the invisible people of the village. Some of them came to eat there once a year to taste the real food they missed so much. But he had never seen the invisible people when they came to eat there, and his mother never talked about these matters with him.

Then Winn Blitzzer said to Tovic, "I too have some very important news to tell you. I met with King Brelys-1000 at his royal palace."

"You have met the king?" Tovic exclaimed. "You must be joking."

Winn Blitzzer said, "I am not. I met with King Brelys-1000. I will have a second appointment with the king again tomorrow."

"What does the king look like?" Tovic ask.

"He looks like a normal person in private," Winn Blitzzer replied.

"Why didn't you call me to go with you?" Tovic asked him.

"I didn't have time to call you, because it was my Aunt Moxum who decided to send me back to the city the day after we came back from there. She was planning a date for me and the Princess of Light."

Tovic laughed and teased, "Remember when we were in the city, I told you that you could be the one to win the king's challenge. Even the dwarf called Nomy said the Princess of Light could be yours one. Guess he was right after all."

"I just remembered," Winn Blitzzer exclaimed. "I thought I saw that dwarf for a split second in the city, but then he vanished."

Tovic ask him, "Are you sure you saw the dwarf Nomy?"

"Yes, of course I saw him with his tattoo of a blue star on his face," Winn Blitzzer replied.

Tovic was silent for a moment then said to him, "I am sure now that the dwarf was not there by coincidence. He came to see you up close up to see if you are ready."

Tovic suddenly got off his chair and knelt down before Winn Blitzzer. "You are the chosen one," he said, "who will bring back our parents again."

Winn Blitzzer was confused and said to Tovic, "Don't ever say such things again. I don't have the power to do that."

Tovic looked up at the window and saw the sky was clear and the sun at its height and said, "Let's have our lunch now." Winn Blitzzer took a plate and served food, fish, vegetable and potatoes. "This food smells great."

He sat down at the table and grabbed a fork and knife to start eating, when suddenly his plate began moving left and right on the table. At first he thought it was Tovic playing a prank somehow, but when he tried to pick up the plate it dodged him and flew off the table hovering in the air, the spoon and fork followed as if they wanted to attack his face. Then he felt his chair pull back strongly on its own, the back legs of the chair lifted up, throwing him forward until he nearly fell on the floor.

Tovic was in shock and was astonished as well at seeing what was happening. They looked fearfully at the table. Suddenly they saw all the dishes on top of the tablecloth with the glasses and jugs of water fly off and hang floating in the air. The cloth turned over, but the food and dishes remained hanging above.

Then they heard a deep booming voice say, "Winn Blitzzer, you are not allowed to eat the food left for the invisible people. We have saved both of your lives; if you had eaten this food you would have become invisible like us now. You are our last hope to be rescued from this invisible world where we are kept against our will by the evil Ms Moxum. Until you accomplish this mission to bring us back as normal again, you cannot eat our food. Our hopes lay on your shoulders. When you will accomplish this on behalf of all of us locked up here, we will be very happy and very proud to share a special lunch with you, but until then…"

They watched as the tablecloth with the six dishes floated slowly back down to the table again without a single one falling off or breaking. Then they watched as the cutlery moved up and down from the table, and the food disappeared from the dishes right before their eyes.

Suddenly, outside the house it got dark as if a short eclipse was happening; the sun disappeared in the sky for an entire minute.

Winn Blitzzer and Tovic ran out of the house in desperation and ran to enter the house of Lady Dallas just opposite. They had never been inside her house before. They expected her to be displeased with them entering without knocking, but to their surprising, she received them with a big smile. Standing with her daughter Yalta, she said, "Welcome to our house, Winn Blitzzer and Tovic. It has been a long time. We were hoping to see you here someday. My daughter Yalta, and I, are very happy to have you here as our guests. Today is a very special happy day for us after seeing the signal from the eclipse that appeared in the sky. You mother, Lady Esra, and I know what will happen soon."

Winn Blitzzer was confused, more than Tovic, by this short speech.

"Take a seat both of you, please," she said to them in a friendly voice, "make yourselves at home. We are all suffering in the same way, although we have never had a chance to talk about it."

Winn Blitzzer and Tovic sat down on the old brown sofa and looked each other.

"What would you like something to drink?" Yalta asked them.

"Nothing for me, thanks." Winn Blitzzer replied nervously.

Tovic said, "I would like a cup of tea with honey."

"Good choice," said Lady Dallas and looking at Winn Blitzzer, she said to him, "You cannot refuse to take anything the first time you are a guest in my house. I know very well what had happened to you at Lady Esra's house. I know you are scared and frightened. Drink something, it will make you feel better."

"You are right, Lady Dallas," said Winn Blitzzer, "please forgive me. I am still in shock. I would like a green tea with honey as well, please."

Lady Dallas said to them, "Do not worry, I know what had happened to you there after seeing the sign of a short eclipse in the sky. It is a good sign, believe me. This was the prophecy that we have been waiting for, for so long."

"What prophecy?" Winn Blitzzer asked her.

"A prophecy that says, you will be the one to bring back life and joy back to our village."

"I don't know what you are talking about," Winn Blitzzer said and tried to stand up to leave.

"Wait," Lady Dallas said to him, "don't be afraid. It's the first time you are here. Sit down please, the tea will be ready soon." Winn Blitzzer sat down on the old brown sofa, his friend Tovic sat quietly beside him and gave him a look that said "See, just like I told you."

Then Lady Dallas said to them again, "Please do not be afraid, you are safe here."

Winn Blitzzer and Tovic looked at each other. They wondered why she kept saying that.

They fell into silence, Winn Blitzzer and Tovic on the sofa, Lady Dallas and her daughter Yalta opposite them, with a glass table between them. Suddenly Winn Blitzzer's realised, who was preparing the tea they were waiting for?

At that moment a big red empty Shirt with a silver tray floated slowly through the air. On the tray were two cups of tea and a cigar.

They jumped on the back of the sofa in fear and sat on top of it, watching the big red Shirt floating towards them. The silver tray came to a standstill before them. Neither of them dared to touch the cups of tea sitting on it. Lady Dallas make a gesture to them to take the cups of tea. They sat back slowly on the sofa. The tray stopped and stood in front of Winn Blitzzer first. He stretched out his hand, trembling, and grabbed the cup of tea with hesitation. This encouraged Tovic to grab his cup of tea too, and after he did, the empty red shirt turned and moved a few meters away while the silver tray hovered slowly down on the table close by.

The red shirt was still standing with the cigar, now lit, floating next to it as if someone was smoking it. Lady Dallas and her daughter Yalta sat as though nothing had just happened, while Winn Blitzzer and Tovic trembled in dead fear.

Suddenly they heard a strange voice coming from red shirt.

"Don't be afraid, young men; drink the tea I brought you. This gesture was not mine alone but on behalf of all people now locked like invisible prisoners. We are very happy indeed after seeing the sign of eclipse just now, the time approaches for us to go back to being normal people. Soon, you will know me and my name."

Winn Blitzzer and Tovic looked at each other again and took a sip of tea. When they wanted to leave the cups on the table they couldn't. The teacups were stuck to their hands like a glue. Only once they drank all the tea, were their hands free of the teacups.

While rubbing their hands, Winn Blitzzer said, "The tea was very good thank you."

Lady Dallas said, "We would never offer you something bad in our house. The invisible figure in the shirt has only come here today to deliver you a message. Listen…"

Then they heard the voice of the invisible figure saying, "Winn Blitzzer, you are the chosen one who will save the people of this village." Winn Blitzzer and Tovic looked towards the red shirt where the voice was coming from. Then they saw the cigar go off and tip ashes into the ashtray. The voice spoke again.

"Winn Blitzzer, you must accomplish this mission if you want to see the parents you have never known. You will need to make a decision, to do this or to stick with the plan your aunt has for you concerning the Princess of Light. She betrayed our agreement to bring us back to normal again after we fulfilled our duties in protecting this village. She is a very bad woman with a very bad heart. But the signal from the sky has spoken, and you are the chosen one who will free us from the prison of the invisible world we are in. Do not be afraid, for we shall help you. For now it would be best to go along with your Aunt Moxum's like normal. You shall hear from us soon."

The red shirt flew up and hung itself, empty, on the back of the chair. They had no idea in which direction the invisible figure went.

They were all quiet for a few minutes. Winn Blitzzer was shaking. The cup of tea fell from his hand, but before it touched the floor an invisible hand caught it handed it back to him.

The voice spoke again. "Winn Blitzzer, to prove to you that we know of the many things happening here, let me tell you that we know you have a letter in your pocket from your Aunt Eris. You don't know how you got that letter, but after reading it you did not destroy it as she requested."

Winn Blitzzer was amazed hearing this. He touched his pocket; the letter was still there. He and Tovic had no doubt that the invisible figure could see and hear everything they did.

Suddenly the letter came out of Winn Blitzzer's pocket and flew slowly through the air. He tried to grab it back unsuccessfully saying, "Hey, that's mine!"

The letter flew slowly towards where Lady Dallas was sitting and began to unfold until it was fully open before her eyes and then remained lying statically in the air. She put on her glasses to read it.

"This letter tells the whole truth," said Lady Dallas after read it, "Winn Blitzzer, now you know the truth about this mysterious village. Do you want to keep this letter or shall I burn it?"

"Yes, burn it please," Winn Blitzzer nodded. Lady Dallas held it over a red candle that was burning on a small table in the corner. Then they saw the red shirt moving from the chair and going up and down as though a person were getting dressed. Then it began to float in the air again. The empty tray swung back and forth slightly beside it. Both objects left the living room for good and went towards the kitchen. Then they heard the voice of the invisible figure one last time saying, "Winn Blitzzer, we wish you good luck and success in this secret mission. Goodbye!"

"Goodbye! And thank you very much for coming," Lady Dallas replied to the invisible figure with her soft voice.

"Finally," said Lady Dallas to Winn Blitzzer, "the contents of the letter were not everything, there is still more to tell you about what had happened here more than 16 years ago."

Winn Blitzzer said, "I am sorry Lady Dallas, I cannot hear any more about this. What I had learned here today was enough."

He rose suddenly and walked towards the front door open. But he could not go any farther than that. Something was blocking his way out. He pushed the empty space strongly with his hand as hard as he could, confused and panting slightly.

"Sit down, Winn Blitzzer," said Lady Dallas in an angry voice, "I have a lot of things to tell you today. I cannot let you run away now. It is no coincidence you are here right now."

Winn Blitzzer went back to sit on the sofa next to his friend Tovic.

Then Lady Dallas said, "Listen Winn Blitzzer, there are some things you have to know about yourself first. Your aunt Moxum is the last descendent of the Mambul sect and the guardian of their special sciences. Although the agreement was that she would teach other people in the village how to use and practice those special sciences, she betrayed our trust and kept all the secrets of the Potsat for herself. She is the reason our village is empty.

Our village used to have invisible protectors working in shifts to keep our village safe. So many men used to do that job with pride, until one day Ms Moxum betrayed all of them. She organised a party for the entire village to thank them, to celebrate the peaceful life our village was enjoying because of the amazing work of the invisible guards who had been keeping us protected from the royal army trying to discover our village of Black Cloud.

During the party she served them a special tea that made every man become invisible, so that she could keep the Potsat power to herself. But she didn't stop there. A few months later, she put that special tea in the pipes carrying water to our homes from the noiseless waterfall to punish all those who criticised her for what she did. They became invisible too after drinking the water. Even all the cats and dogs vanished. For that reason, we take water to drink only after noon, While Ms Moxum is busy watching her Potsat.

Winn Blitzzer, your mother Zilda saw her husband, your father, Moxla, vanish before her eyes. Only his clothes were left on the ground. She went crazy and tried to fight her sister Moxum for what she did. But the oldest man of the village, named Corys, stopped them from getting into a fight. Ms Moxum fell to the ground. She didn't like being exposed and shouted at the old man Corys, threatening him, "I will show you who I am!"

When the old man went to his home, that was the last time anyone saw him. We presume that Moxum made him disappear like she did other people before. As for your mother we presume that Moxum did the same thing to her as well. But no one really knows what had really happened between them. A few days later she too vanished and became invisible after drinking the special tea Moxum left at her house in secret. All of this happened when you were just a toddler. Your Aunt Eris was the one who raised you. Even her husband Laxom was sent to become invisible. As for their son Valger, nearly the same age as you, no one knows really whether he is dead or alive."

Winn Blitzzer was in deep shock after hearing all these stories. Now, he knew his parents' names for the first time, Zilda and Moxla.

"This mysterious tea was the same that made our beloved teacher Mrs Loly vanish?"

"Yes, that is correct," Lady Dallas replied.

"I cannot believe that my Aunt Moxum could be so evil…"

There was a moment of hushed silence on the living room.

Then Tovic said, "I understand now why there were not any animals left in our village."

"Yes," said Lady Dallas, "the evil Ms Moxum didn't leave anything a chance to challenge her. She worked maliciously against everyone. The poor animals were victims too and condemned to disappear like their owners."

Then Lady Dallas pulled something out of the pocket of her dress and said to Winn Blitzzer, "I give you a special gift. Take these blue glass lenses. With them you will be able see the invisible people around here. But you won't be able to see them entirely, just a shadow. That would be enough for you to know the fact that there were invisible people around us alive. But be very careful I beg you, your Aunt Moxum can't know any of this." Winn Blitzzer promised.

She asked them if they had any questions.

"Yes," said Winn Blitzzer. "I would like to know about the bronze statue of the dwarf with a small dog in his hand in the village. Who was that man?"

"I cannot tell you this story now," said Lady Dallas. "But I can tell you that your Aunt Ms Moxum turned him into a statue with his small dog, after he worked to expose her evil tricks. He was a very wise and respected man. His son survived the disappearances in the village, but no one ever saw him again."

Winn Blitzzer asked Lady Dallas, "Can you tell me why some of these houses in this village have their front doors open without anybody inside? And why sometimes we can see candle lights shining and moving inside them?"

"Yes," said Lady Dallas, "it is because people are still visiting their houses even though they are invisible."

Then she said, "You may go now, the door is open for you to go home."

Winn Blitzzer thanked Lady Dallas again for everything she had done for him. Tested his hand on the door, and this time it opened.

"You are welcome anytime you like to come to our house," Lady Dallas reminded them as they left.

During this time Moxum was at home, furious that she did not know where Winn Blitzzer. She knew the meaning of the short of eclipse that happened in the sky at noon.

Winn Blitzzer and Tovic walked around the small garden. Even though they wanted to, they were careful not to talk about what they had just learned.

Tovic said to Winn Blitzer, "Winn Blitzzer, I told you that you are the chosen one, the rare signs we saw today in my house and in the sky confirm that."

"I didn't know anything about it. I don't even know now what I can do..."

"Time will tell you what to do and how," said Tovic.

"I hope all of you are right," said Winn Blitzzer.

"All of us are right," said Tovic. Then, "I am going home now. I am sure that my mother has been looking for me, she must be very worried indeed after seeing the eclipse."

"Me too," said Winn Blitzzer. "I am sure that my aunts are waiting for me. Especially Aunt Moxum. She will be angry with me after I spent so much time out without her knowing where. But before we go, would you accompany me tomorrow for my second meeting with the king? You wouldn't have to come with me into the royal palace, just keep me company along the way."

"Sure," said Tovic, "let's meet upstream by the river Memzs near the waterfall."

"Ok, Tovic, thank you!" said Winn Blitzzer.

When Winn Blitzzer arrived home his Aunt Moxum questioned him about where he was for so long.

He said to her, "Do not be angry with me, please. Tovic and I were walking in the woods not far away when suddenly we saw the eclipse. We were scared and hid ourselves under a large tree. We thought that it was a bad sign or an omen."

Moxum said to him, "You must tell me always where you're going. I do not want to see something bad happen to you. Don't forget the task you have to complete."

"From now on I will always tell you where I'm going," promised Winn Blitzzer.

"I hope you didn't forget that tomorrow you will have another audience with King Brelys-1000."

"Yes, of course, I know that Aunt Moxum," said Winn Blitzzer, "I am looking forward it."

Chapter Nineteen
The Second Meeting with the king

Early the next morning, Winn Blitzzer woke up and got ready for his second audience with King Brelys-1000. He noticed his Aunt Eris wearing a red-coloured ribbon in her hair. After breakfast, Aunt Moxum handed him a cup of the special water from the Potsat and again he transformed into an older, more confident-looking young man.

Aunt Moxum has no idea that this time Winn Blitzzer would be accompanied by Tovic into the city. He knew that before noon his aunt Moxum couldn't see them on the Potsat. He planned to go meet the king and come back before Moxum could watch them, to protect his friend Tovic.

Winn Blitzzer left the house after saying goodbye to his aunts as they wished him good luck. He met up with his friend Tovic and they headed to the capital together. Tovic was almost running to keep up with Winn Blitzzer.

"Why we are walking so fast?"

"I want us to be back before noon, so my aunt Moxum doesn't see us," Winn Blitzzer replied. "She does not know that you are accompanying me."

"How could she know that I am accompanying you?" Tovic ask.

Winn Blitzzer looked at Tovic and said to him, "Listen, you know very well that my aunt Moxum is a very dangerous woman with mysterious powers. She has a very special cauldron, a Potsat, and on the lid screen she can see anything she wants from a distance, and even hear what people are saying."

"What?" Tovic exclaimed. "Let's walk faster then, I do not want your Aunt Moxum to see me and turn me invisible too."

"She will start watching the Potsat from midday today. Because of that we need to get back home before noon to avoid Moxum seeing us."

After brief silence Tovic said, "Maybe we should run."

"We do not need to run," said Winn Blitzzer, "we are close."

Soon after they arrived in the capital of Ryam. The city was vibrant as ever. They were many people walking in the streets going about their business. Winn Blitzzer and Tovic headed in the direction of the royal palace.

Tovic said to Winn Blitzzer, "I will wait for you in the square here in the city."

"Okay, I won't take long I hope."

As they were talking, they suddenly noticed the dwarf Nomy in crowd of people who then disappeared from view.

"I just saw the dwarf Nomy," said Tovic. "I am sure of it."

"Yes," said Winn Blitzzer, "Me too."

"Maybe he is here to help you."

"Why me?"

"Because of the prophecy of course. Go now for your appointment with the king. You can't be late."

Then Winn Blitzzer walked towards the hill with the gardens. It was not long before the palace gates with the two lions appeared up ahead. Officer Lahto was the first person to see Winn Blitzzer, coming a short distance away.

"Here he comes."

That morning, another guard named Kobe was just taking his position at the mirador of the gate. When he heard them saying "He is coming, he is coming", he asked his colleagues, "Who is coming? Someone important?"

"No at all, it is just a villager, the same who came here the other day to see His Majesty, without any invitation. He is the one we were talking about," said Lahto.

Erko asked Kobe, "You don't know that story?"

"No, I was off duty last week. But I heard rumours about an incident that had happened here with a strange young visitor."

The Officer Lahto said to Kobe, "Now you will see, he is the one we have been talking about."

To provoke the Officer Lahto, Tolly said, "I begin to like this young mysterious visitor. He has courage and determination to come to see King Brelys-1000 in person. You cannot envy a weak person, only the strong and ambitious like him."

Officer Lahto furiously replied, "Tolly, if your admiration for visitor is so great, you should go live with him in his village, and go hunting and fishing together."

After hearing that comment, Erko and Kohla burst into laughter at this.

Before Tolly could answer him, they saw Winn Blitzzer arriving in front of the royal palace gate, well dressed with his right hand in his pocket, inside of which he held a small bottle.

He was outside the gates, face-to-face with the three guards who were on duty his first visit. He recognised their faces. They didn't like him at all, Lahto, Erko and Kohla. But he noticed a new face among the guards.

"Good morning officers!" he said.

Only the new guard, Tolly, answered, "Good morning, sir!"

Winn Blitzzer was not surprised by the silence of other three guards. The royal guard Tolly opened the gate with a smile saying, "Welcome to the royal palace, sir."

"Thank you, officer," said Winn Blitzzer.

"The secretary will arrive shortly to take you to your important audience with the king."

Winn Blitzzer was surprised by the kind treatment he was receiving from the unknown guard.

Just then the old secretary Zomy arrived.

"Good morning, Winn Blitzzer. We meet again," said Zomy.

"Yes, Mr Secretary, we meet again," Winn Blitzzer replied.

They walked into the royal palace to where the king was waiting.

"Good morning, Your Majesty," said Winn Blitzzer, bowing.

"Good to see you again," said the king.

Zomy made as though to leave but instead went and took a seat in his secret position behind the curtains.

Winn Blitzzer said, "I am very grateful to Your Majesty for honouring me with another private meeting today."

"I really appreciate your punctuality," said the king. "Even though you live far from here, apparently."

As the king was about to speak, the white dove came and perched on a nearby windowsill.

"What a coincidence!" said the king, "This dove came here on your first visit, and now it has come back again for our second meeting too."

"I believe this white dove has been following me, Your Majesty. Maybe it is a good sign, its presence here."

"Perhaps," said the king. "You seem to know many things, Winn Blitzzer, although at first glance you seem nothing more than an innocent young lad. After much thought, I am tempted to accept your proposal, but this is difficult to do without further proof."

"I have something that will help make up your mind, I hope, Your Majesty."

He looked around and saw a glass vase with three flowers on a table. He approached it, and poured a single drop of the special liquid on it.

Suddenly, smoke came out of the vase and the three flowers became three Birds of paradise birds, which began to fly around inside the hall, singing the songs of their species.

When Winn Blitzzer clapped his hands, the three paradise birds came to pose on his arms. Then he set the birds down on top of the glass vase. With another drop of the rainbow liquid, they became again three flowers in a vase.

The king began to laugh, quite unexpectedly and said, "This simple trick does not impress me at all, it was not difficult to do. You will have to do better than that to impress me."

Winn Blitzzer to felt disappointed when he heard these words. He expected the king to congratulate him for the impressive performance. But he tried again.

Winn Blitzzer said to the king, "Majesty, if this trick didn't impress you, I can try another that I am sure will."

"Go ahead do it," said the king.

Winn Blitzzer looked again at the table. He saw a quill with nice feathers inside an inkwell. "With your permission Majesty, may I use this?"

"Yes you may," the king said.

"Thank you, your Majesty," said Winn Blitzzer. He put one drop of the special liquid inside the inkwell pot. The king looked on without saying anything. Again smoke came out from inside the inkwell pot.

When the king looked inside the inkwell pot, to his surprise, the black ink had vanish and became water. Out of nowhere the quill became a small flame with sparks. A few seconds later and the quill and inkwell became as they were before, as though nothing had happened.

King Brelys-1000 admired this trick and although he didn't say anything right away to Winn Blitzzer, it showed on his face.

He said, "This trick looks quite difficult. I would like to know what you have in that tiny bottle that has this power of transformation."

Winn Blitzzer said, "It's quite difficult to explain, Your Majesty."

"Go ahead, I'm listen," said the king.

Winn Blitzzer hurried to invent a fantastic story to tell the king to hide the truth about the special water from the Potsat he had in the tiny bottle.

"Your Majesty, the story of how I got this liquid is miraculous on its own. It has a sad beginning but a happy ending. Some years ago, I was in the forest and I rescued a small abandoned baby bird. I it home with me and that same day a strange bird I have never heard before came to sing near my house in the trees. My aunt told me that the bird who was singing had never been seen by anyone before. Because of this it is called the invisible bird.

After two days the bird still continued singing without stopping. I thought maybe the small bird I had rescued two days early in the forest was her baby, so the next day I brought the small bird out of the house and put it in small nest. Not long after, its mother came to take it. She didn't fear my presence. The bird cried with joy at being with her baby again.

Suddenly, that bird began to speak. I nearly fell over in shock, and tried to run away. But the bird said to me, 'Do not be afraid young man, we are friends from now on. You are very kind for having kept my baby bird safe. And you are the first person to see me truly as I look, while everybody else assumes that I am invisible. So, I will reward you with something very special, for having brought joy and happiness back in my life. Bring a small bottle, I am going to give you a gift. With this gift, you will be able to make many things and achieve the impossible in your life. By with just one small drop of my tears, you may transform any object into anything you wish.' So, I brought the tiny bottle. The bird said to me, 'When I cry, out of joy not sadness, collect my tears in this tiny bottle.' And so when the bird began crying, I did.

That same day I tried the tears with a wish I had always had since childhood. There was a big tree near my house that I feared could collapse on the roof. I put one small drop of the tears on that big trees, and few seconds later, an incredible thing happened before my eyes. The big tree transformed, its trunk straightened and it became a much smaller, younger tree. It was like a dream. That is the story of how I had got this liquid."

"Fascinating," said the king, "that sounds like a story from fantasy. If I hadn't witnessed the ability of this liquid myself, I wouldn't have believed such stories could be possible."

Then he changed the subject. "The offer I made in my last announcement still stands. Anyone who can finish the clock tower will receive every reward offered including having the opportunity to marry the Princess of Light."

Winn Blitzzer said, "Majesty, my offer has not change either. I swore before Your Majesty that I would risk my life to travel to planet Earth and bring the mechanical clock here."

"Yes," said the king, "however this sounds like nothing more than a fanciful dream. I don't want to hear only words, I want to see action."

Winn Blitzzer said, "Majesty, if these words mean that you accept me as your future son-in-law, then I will proceed to put my plan into action."

On hearing Winn Blitzzer's words, the king could practically already see the clock tower on the mountain outside his window.

But all he said was, "Of course, I accept you temporarily as a potential suitor for my daughter. And I will give my full acceptance to you when you will bring the great clock here. Let this stand as proof that I take your proposal seriously."

"Thank you, Your Majesty. I will do everything I can to bring the great clock here on planet Oxon. I promised to Your Majesty that you will have the great clock here and see it with your own eyes. But in saying this, I would like to ask Your Majesty a favour."

"What is that?" the king asked.

Winn Blitzzer said, "Majesty, I would like you to grant me the honour of meeting the Princess of Light once before I go. Just feeling her hand in mine would give me enough courage to succeed in this mission." He wished to see in person if she was really as beautiful in real life as he saw her in the Potsat.

"Alas, your request is impossible to grant at this time," said the king.

"Why, Your Majesty?" asked Winn Blitzzer.

The king said, "Well to be honest young man, you don't quite look the part yet, shall we say. You are poorly dressed, not at all within the dress code required for Court, and this is not the kind of impression you should want to give a lady, let alone a princess. You are still a potential suitor, but not official one yet."

"I am not concerned about my clothes, Your Majesty. You have received me twice now as I am. Poorly dressed or not I would like to see and meet the Princess of Light. That is all I ask. Besides, I can transform myself as you witnessed like the objects on your desk."

"Well in that case perhaps I can grant your request," said the king.

"Thank you, Your Majesty," said Winn Blitzzer smiling.

Zomy appeared, sneaking quietly from behind the curtain and walking around to the side entrance of the hall. He bowed to the king.

The king said to him, "Call in the Princess of Light."

As he waited for his daughter, he turned to the window and looked in the direction of the Blue Mountain where the clock tower's foundations stood. The white dove was still there perched on the sill; when the king attempted to touch it, it flew away.

Winn Blitzzer took the opportunity to put one drop of liquid on his head. The strange power of that liquid began to make Winn Blitzzer spin so fast he couldn't see. A few seconds later, and he stood transformed in blue and yellow full-dress uniform, trousers with red stripes going down the sides and shiny black boots. He looked quite handsome and elegant.

The king turned, saw him, rubbed his eyes, and looked at him again. Winn Blitzzer looked like an entirely different person.

They heard the sound of footsteps approaching in the corridor. Then the Princess of Light arrived with Zomy. She saw a young man, well dressed, in full dress uniform. Zomy was surprised too, at the change in Winn Blitzzer, but not as to how it had occurred after seeing the tricks he had performed. He left them and went around to his secret place behind the curtains.

The king, after greeting his daughter, said to Winn Blitzzer, "I present to you my daughter the Princess of Light, sole heir to the throne of the planet Oxon."

Winn Blitzzer bowed to the Princess of Light. "My name is Winn Blitzzer. It is a great honour Your Highness, Princess of Light."

He went to kiss her hand but then stopped at the look on the king's face.

The Princess of Light asked her father, "Majesty, where has this elegant gentleman come in his full-dress uniform?"

The king hesitated, unprepared for this question.

He simply answered, her touching her chin, "This gentleman that I have just presented to you, although not an architect, is one of the people who has come to propose how to finish the clock tower. He has been asking to meet you in person."

They exchanged pleasantries and then spoke for a while about the botanical gardens she adored so much. The Princess of Light's visit began to last longer than Winn Blitzzer expected. When he looked down, he could see his new shining uniform had begun to disappear starting at his shoes. The uniform began disappearing at the back, until only the front remained. Winn Blitzer knew that his secret would be exposed if the Prince of Light did not leave soon. The king noticed he suddenly seemed to be wearing his old shoes. He quickly took his daughter by the hand and said, "Thank you my dear! You may go now. I would like to continue talking with our visitor in private."

Winn Blitzzer was relieved. The Princess of Light kissed her father and said to Winn Blitzzer, "It was nice to meet you. Goodbye!"

"The pleasure is mine!" Winn Blitzzer replied to the Princess of Light.

She left, slightly confused why her father would like her to meet this man in full dress uniform when he was there on business to discuss the clock. She had no idea about the offer her father had made.

Meanwhile, Winn Blitzzer had completely retransformed into his old clothes and self.

"Why did you not continue wearing the uniform?" the king asked him. "I am sure that if the Princess of Light comes back here now, she may never recognise you, but your secret was nearly exposed."

"If it please Your Majesty, the transformation was as long as it needed to be to meet the princess."

"Well," said the king, "as you say. Quite mysterious you are young man."

Winn Blitzzer said, "If Your Majesty prefers, the next time I come to the royal palace I will try to dress similarly as I have done today."

Chapter Twenty
A Gift of Dreams

Then Winn Blitzzer said to the king, "Today, I would like to offer a gift to Your Majesty, for the great honour of presenting me to your daughter the Princess of Light."

The king raised his eyebrows. "What do you have to offer to me? What do you, a commoner, have to gift a king?"

"I can reward Your Majesty with something you could never buy with all the wealth you have," said Winn Blitzzer.

The king was intrigued by this. "What kind of gift are you talking about?"

Winn Blitzzer said, "Majesty, I will offer you something intangible, something you cannot hold in your hand, but will leave you with memories."

The king was confused by what Winn Blitzzer was saying. "What kind of gift is this?"

Winn Blitzzer said, "I would like to offer Your Majesty the gift of a dream."

"The gift of a dream?" the king repeated.

"Yes, Your Majesty, I would like to offer a gift of a dream. I can confirm that tonight Your Majesty will have a very amazing dream, the gift of an actual dream with sounds and images of something that will make you very happy indeed. But I don't want to reveal to you what exactly. It will be an amazing and unforgettable experience. Such a gift is not for everyone, only for a person such as Your Majesty."

"How is this possible?" asked the king. "Do you take me for a fool? I do not believe in such things. Let us talk about what has brought you here today, before I change my mind about you."

"Believe me, Your Majesty, I could never lie to you or promise you something I couldn't fulfil," Winn Blitzzer said. "Nobody else can offer such a gift to Your Majesty. Only I, Winn Blitzzer, can do such a thing. The only thing I will tell you is that this dream is something Your Majesty has anxiously waited for every night."

After hearing Winn Blitzzer, the king raised his thick eyebrows and asked in a low voice, "What dreams are you talking about? My only true dream at the moment is to finish the clock tower."

"Your Majesty, tonight you will have a dream about the mechanical clock in London on planet Earth, and you will listen to the sound of bells of that great clock, which you called magical melodies."

After hearing this, the king was in shock. How could he know about this?

"How do you know I had a dream with that great clock before? How do you know I wanted to dream of it again and hear the sound of its bells?"

Winn Blitzzer pleasing his head and said, "We think we are alone and no one sees us, but in fact there are invisible eyes that do not speak but watch in silence. They just watch our conduct in silence, but they can transmit to someone with intuitive powers to be able to read, and reveal the secret that people hide to show them that nothing could be hidden forever."

After listening to Winn Blitzzer's unbelievable and strange speech King Brelys-1000 did not know what to say except, "Well if I don't get your gift of the dream tonight, then I won't believe in your promises of retrieving the clock from planet Earth anymore."

"My promises will be kept just as I promised, Your Majesty," Winn Blitzzer replied. "All of my promises will be carries out in good time."

The king said, "I hope so, in order for me to continue to believe in all this. I think that is enough for today. But you will return tomorrow after I will apparently have this dream you have promised."

"Perhaps I could come next week, Your Majesty," said Winn Blitzzer "It is a long way to travel."

"No, no, you must come here tomorrow," said the king, "That is an order. I won't wait until next week. I want to be certain that you are a truthful man before I even start talking to the Queen about making you a potential suitor. I will not play with the life and reputation of my daughter."

"You have my word, Your Majesty." Then he bowed to the king.

As he was about to leave, he turned back and said to the king, "Your Majesty, I beg your pardon. I have just remembered something very important."

"Go ahead, I am listening," the king said.

"Your Majesty, allow me to reveal to you the name of the great clock in the Earth city, London."

The king opened his eyes widely "Do you know its name?" he asked Winn Blitzzer.

"Yes, your Majesty, I do."

King Brelys-1000 remembered many years ago when he had asked his father if he knew the name of the great clock. But his father did not know. He did not imagine that a clock could even have a proper name. This explanation from his father was not incorrect, because there wasn't any record on planet Oxon to prove otherwise. Now he was about to learn it, something he never would have dreamed would be discovered in his lifetime.

There was a brief silence, then said Winn Blitzzer, "Your Majesty, I will now reveal to you the original name of the great mechanical clock in London. On planet Earth, they call it Big Ben, a very nice, friendly name."

"Please repeat that name to me again slowly, slowly," said the king. "I want to learn it well."

"Of course, Your Majesty," said Winn Blitzzer, "it is my great pleasure." Then he said it again, "Big Ben, Big Ben." Slowly this time, so that the king could hear it well.

Big Ben, Big Ben. The beautiful and strange name was as sweet as chocolate on his tongue. Big Ben, Big Ben. The echoes of that short beautiful name were music to the king's ears.

The king began to do a funny little dance alone with joy. At the same time, he kept trying to repeat the name of the great clock; his tongue was still failing to pronounce it quite correctly. He did not even notice Winn Blitzzer slip out of the room.

Each time he tried to say it, the words came out as, "Big bog, Big Bang, Big bag, Big bong, Big beans, Big bow." He moved his tongue around inside his mouth, making sounds like someone who is warming up his voice to sing. At the same time his face was making expressions like that of a laughing clown. After much repeating, he managed to train his tongue and pronounce Big Ben's name properly. He was very happy indeed after pronounce it right.

"Big Ben, Big Ben, Big Ben."

The discovery of Big Ben's name was an invaluable gift to him. It was priceless. But what exactly did it mean? Suddenly the king realised that Winn Blitzzer had gone. He was alone in the room.

It was then that the king began to question, *How does Winn Blitzzer know so many things about the royal palace? How does he know the name of the clock, Big Ben, something my top astronomers and mathematicians could not figure out? Even without any proof or confirmation he seems certain. How does Winn Blitzzer know so much about planet Earth at all? Has he been there before?*

The king had cancelled all other audiences that day after the long meeting he had with Winn Blitzzer. After it was over the king felt he had discovered another world after the stories Winn Blitzzer told him, and he was distracted for the rest of the day. As he sat going over the moving images in his head, he was completely unaware that there were three dignitaries waiting to be received by him. Even though the guards told them about the cancellation of all audiences that day, they still insisted on seeing the king.

After waiting many hours without being received, they began to ask each other questions, "Who was such an important person that the king gave him such a long audience and cancelled all others?" The royal guards there stayed quiet, but they knew who had been with the king.

Then they saw Zomy escorting Winn Blitzzer out. The Officer Lahto, who was there on guard, was amazed after seeing them come out after two hours with the king. He found it difficult to remain quiet. He said to the three dignitaries, "Here comes the mysterious individual because of whom all audiences today were cancelled." The dignitaries saw the young man passing with Zomy, and could not believe when they saw it was just a poor village boy.

The guard Tolly was standing near Winn Blitzzer who went to greet him and ask his name. "I am Tolly," he said.

"I will remember your name," said Winn Blitzzer. "Thank you for treating me so kindly this morning."

"Don't worry," said Tolly, "I'll make sure nothing like what happened the first time happens again."

"Thank you, sir," said Winn Blitzzer shaking Officer Tolly's hand with big smile on his face. Officer Lahto and other guards Kohla and Erko looked as if they could not believe what they were seeing. Zomy then saw Winn Blitzzer to the front gates, and with a bow, left him to head back to the palace.

Winn Blitzzer walked fast to meet his friend Tovic who was waiting for him in the square. Once they met up, they made their way back home.

On the way Winn Blitzzer told Tovic the many things that had happened at his meeting with the king, especially meeting the Princess of Light.

Tovic asked "Did you really meet her?"

"Yes," Winn Blitzzer replied.

Tovic asked him, "Is she beautiful?"

"Yes, she was very beautiful and very kind," said Winn Blitzzer.

They were walking fast to get back to their village before noon. Soon, they heard the sounds of the waterfall in the forest; they realised they were already far from the city. Then, Winn Blitzzer said to Tovic, "We must walk with a short distance between us, you in front and I behind you, to prevent my aunt from seeing us through the Potsat."

Tovic agreed.

They walked a short distance apart, but continued talking.

Tovic said to Winn Blitzzer, "What will you do now? Follow your Aunt Moxum's plan to try to marry the Princess of Light, or try to free our parents from the prison of the invisible world?"

Winn Blitzzer said frankly, "I don't know what to do yet, I have to think more about all this."

"But is it a good idea to try to marry a woman without being sure that she is in love with you, just because someone else enforces it? Yes, the princess is very beautiful. Anyone could fall in love with her. But to my understanding the Princess of Light may choose of her own free will too, and believe that by mentioning the princess in the announcement the king only wants to motivate people to build his clock tower." Then Tovic said, "Remember Lady Dallas told you when we went to her house that our hope is in your hands. You'll have to choose the best for you and for others. In the end truth and justice must prevail against injustice and darkness."

"Let time tell," said Winn Blitzzer.

Back at the royal palace, Officer Lahto informed Zomy of the three dignitaries who were waiting to be received by the king.

"Despite having informed them of the cancellation of all audiences today, they insist that they see the king. They have been waiting for hours."

"Thank you, officer, for informing of me," Zomy said, "I will see what I can do."

During all this time, the king was still dancing alone at his office like a kid at Christmas, repeating Big Ben's over and over.

"Oh what a beautiful name! I'll never get tired of repeating it. I would like to pass this name on to one of my grandchildren to remember the day I discovered the name of the clock tower."

Zomy stopped in his tracks when he entered the king's office and saw him dancing alone, slowly repeating, "Big Ben, Big Ben, Big Ben." Zomy felt very concerned indeed, imagining that the king was going mad He had never seen the king doing anything like that before.

When the king saw Zomy, he smiled and continued his little dance. The secretary Zomy bowed to him, the signal that he had something important to tell him. But the king ignored him and instead asked, "Secretary Zomy, do you know the meaning of the words Big Ben?"

"No Your Majesty, I have no idea what that name of Big Ben could mean."

"Oh how could I forget to ask Winn Blitzzer while he was still here."

"Your Majesty I am sure that Winn Blitzzer does know the meaning of the name, if he could know a name all the way from another planet and will tell you when he comes again tomorrow. I will be sure to record everything."

"Indeed you are probably right," the king said. "But be careful not to utter those words in front of anyone else. It is my desire that all of this remains a secret. It would not be good for this information to get out. Even to my family. At least not until we can verify the truth of it all."

Zomy said, "All should stay a secret. Your Majesty, I would beg of you on this happy day to make an exceptional gesture and receive the three dignitaries who have been waiting many hours to be received by Your Majesty. Despite having been informed of the cancellation of all audiences today, they have insisted on meeting you."

The king rubbed his chin and said to Zomy, "I can make an exception today to receive those dignitaries. Go bring them in, I want to hear why they insist so much in seeing me. But I better not hear any bad news on this happy day."

"Very good, Your Majesty," said Zomy, bowing. He went back to the three dignitaries and said to them, "His Majesty will receive all of you now, at the same time. This is the best I could."

However the only purpose of dignitaries' visit was to again propose to the king to try to build the tower with timber and wood, something the king already knew to be impossible and immediately refused, ending the meeting right then and there.

When Zomy came back into the king's office after they had left, he was a bit worried as he had been the one to suggest the king receive them. Fortunately for Zomy, the king was not angry with him. He just said, "These people came to waste my time with absurd nonsense proposals. It was not your fault, I am sure they believed they were here for something very important."

Zomy was relieved.

Then the king said to him, "Your duties for the day are not over yet. I would like to put up a new announcement. After that boy revealed to me the name of the great clock, I have decided I would like to see how far Winn Blitzzer can go by accepting his proposal. Write this down."

Zomy took out a pen and paper.

The king dictated, "I, king Brelys-1000, king of the planet Oxon, inform my loyal subjects that the previous offer presented to you seven months ago is now expired. Not a single person came forward to present an idea for how to finish the clock tower. The conditions and rewards related to the Princess of Light in that announcement are now void and null. Signed King Brelys-1000."

He had decided to hang his hopes on the boy Winn Blitzzer. Zomy presented the king with the announcement, he read it, and signed it with the red royal stamp. Within a few hours, the first copies of the announcement were hung up across the capital.

Far away from the royal palace and the capital Ryam, in the middle of the forest in the village of Black Cloud, Moxum worked away, making analyses and doing different tests using her knowledge of the secret mystical sciences in preparation for sending her nephew to planet Earth. Her eyes were concentrated on the Potsat. In fact, she had seen the image of King Brelys-1000 dancing for joy in his palace and repeating Big Ben's name over and over. She saw the image of Winn Blitzzer walking in the forest as well, on his way home after the second meeting with the king.

Moxum was convinced that the secret mission she was planning would be a success. But to be sure of that success, she planned to send a group of birds first to test and evaluate the risk of the mission before she sent her nephew there. Winn Blitzzer was his only nephew she had and only person who had been chosen by his ancestors to restore their honour before the king.

For Moxum to take such a risk was worth it, if it meant being able to honour and avenge her ancestors who were persecuted by the kings of planet Oxon for their beliefs. The current king, Brelys-1000, was not as concerned with these issues of the past as his father King Bixiz II was. Still he carried on the responsibility and the burden of what happened in the past because of his ancestors. Besides, this was the only way her nephew could be near the circle of aristocracy and power in the kingdom. She had always planned that one day he would marry the Princess of Light, fulfilling her dream of restoring honour to her ancestors. Winn Blitzzer's unique mission to planet Earth could make him a hero in the kingdom of planet Oxon. Then he would be the undisputed potential suitor of the Princess of Light.

Moxum and her sister Eris did have some disagreement about the purpose of the secret mission to send Winn Blitzzer to planet Earth. Moxum wanted their nephew Winn Blitzzer to marry the Princess of Light, while her sister Eris wanted her to use Winn Blitzzer's secret mission to form a peace agreement in the interest of the people of the Mambul sect with King Brelys-1000. She believed he should not be hated for the actions committed by his father.

Aunt Eris came to sit and watch her sister as she went about her work. "The king will be very happy with the gift of the name Big Ben. I am sure that the king will accept this proposal gladly. Once this plan is successful, I really hope that you will bring back all the people who have been trapped in invisibility.

I beg you, my sister, to bring them back to the real life to share with us the peace agreement I proposed to you. Everyone will thank you and praise you for doing this. I am sorry if you do not want to hear all this but we are sisters I have to tell you the truth, even though sometimes you may not want to hear it."

She stopped when Moxum turned to glare at her.

"Don't try to teach me about my affairs. I know what I am doing and what I will do with all those people in due course. I am aware that everything I am doing on behalf of our nephew could turn against me in the future. But I will carry out my plans for him. As you know I have never sent anyone outside of our planet Oxon before. I am quite confident in my ability to do this, but as it is rather risky, I would ask you to please let me work in peace!"

Although this was true, that Moxum had never sent someone to another planet with her powers, she had full confidence in the power of Potsat and the knowledge of the mystical sciences and magic she had inherited from her ancestors.

Meanwhile, in the middle of the forest where Winn Blitzzer and Tovic were headed home, the dwarf Nomy hid waiting along the path up ahead of them. He had concealed himself between some low tree branches on the bank of the river Memz. Winn Blitzzer and Tovic stopped at the river to get their feet wet and wash their faces in the cool water. Suddenly, Tovic yelled and leapt back. He had seen the reflection of the dwarf Nomy in the water making faces at him with his hands in his ears.

"What's going on?" asked Winn Blitzzer. Tovic did not answer in his hurry to get away. Winn Blitzzer followed after him saying "Stop, stop! Tovic what is it?"

A few moments later, they stopped running. Tovic was breathing heavily.

"What is going on with you?" Winn Blitzzer asked him.

"Sorry, Winn Blitzzer," said Tovic, "But I saw the reflection of the dwarf Nomy in the water, making a faces at me."

"No, that cannot be true!" Winn Blitzzer exclaimed. "How did the dwarf Nomy got here? He appeared to us early today in the city too."

Then Winn Blitzzer asked Tovic, "Are you sure that it was the dwarf Nomy?"

"Yes, it was him," Tovic replied, "I could see the blue star tattooed on his face. He must have been hiding among the branches of the trees."

"I don't think the dwarf will follow us to our village," Winn Blitzzer reassured him.

"Let's just go home, we aren't far away."

They started walking again. Winn Blitzzer patted Tovic on the back to calm him down. Soon they were laughing again and what had happened at the river was forgotten.

Just before noon, Tovic said to Winn Blitzzer, "I have a very special gift for you, take it."

"What is it?" Winn Blitzzer asked him.

"A whistle."

"A whistle?"

"Yes, a whistle. A very special whistle I took it from my mum's bag. She has four of them. With this whistle she calls to the invisible people to come to eat in our house once a year."

"Tovic, I cannot take such gift, I am afraid I won't use it properly."

"I did not explain well," said Tovic. "This whistle is just to call the pets. It has a higher pitch. In case you would like to see them with the special blue-coloured lenses the Lady Dallas gave you."

"In that case, I will accept it," Winn Blitzzer said. He took the whistle and looked at it, It was sculpted in the shape of a lion's head. "I would like to try and test how it sounds."

"Do not use it now, please," exclaimed Tovic, "do that hidden somewhere in the branches of a tree without anyone seeing you. Do not do it in your home either."

"Okay," Winn Blitzzer said, "but what does it sound like?"

Tovic said, "This whistle sounds like a light wind."

Winn Blitzzer put the whistle in his pocket.

Then few moments later Winn Blitzzer said to Tovic, "Let's stop under the shadow of this giant tree, I would like to show you something very special too. But before that, first let me tell you something that I forgot to tell you before. I will be back to the city tomorrow to meet the king again."

"Why?" Tovic asked him.

"His Majesty called me there tomorrow to check if I am truthful or not. I promised him something and if that promise is fulfilled then he will trust me."

"What have you promised to His Majesty?"

"I promised him the gift of a dream," Winn Blitzzer replied.

"The gift of a dream!" Tovic exclaimed. "I have never heard anything like this before. How is it possible to make such a gift for someone?"

"Yes," said Winn Blitzzer, "such a gift is possible, thanks to a special liquid that I have in my pocket from my Aunt Moxum. With it, I can do many incredible things. I know that it is very hard for you to believe when you haven't seen. But if you would like I could show you how it works. After all, we are friends and you have given me a very special whistle today.

So first you must think of something you would like to see here in the forest. And then I will show you what this liquid does."

"I don't know," said Tovic. "You decide."

"Well, look what I will do now," said Winn Blitzzer and he took the small bottle with the shining liquid from his pocket and opened it, and put a drop below a giant tree near its roots. A few seconds later, the tree began to lower its height as if folding down until it was only as tall as they were, its shadow disappearing and letting the sun through behind it.

The tree continued to shrink until it was as small as a Bonsai. Tovic was shocked after seeing this. He nearly ran away again.

"Don't be afraid," said Winn Blitzzer to Tovic, "this was just a small demonstration for you to see how effective this special liquid is."

Tovic ran his fingers through his hair. "Well, I have no doubt that the king will have the gift of dreams you promised to him, after seeing this."

"Yes, well as you can see this is why I must return to the palace tomorrow," Winn Blitzzer said.

"I won't be able to go with you this time. I need to help my mum with the gardening."

"I understand," said Winn Blitzzer.

"What do we do now with this tree?"

"Shall we leave it as it is now, tiny forever?"

"No, no, no, that is not a good idea," said Tovic. "If we leave this tree in its tiny size here it will get trampled."

"I will put the tree back as it was before then." Winn Blitzzer dropped one single drop of the special liquid. They both stood and silently watched as the small tree stretching its branches and growing, creaking and groaning sounds coming from inside the trunk as if growing so fast took a great effort, and then it became a giant tree as before. It's shadow fell over them again.

"It's time to go home," said Winn Blitzzer.

After they began walking again, Tovic said to Winn Blitzzer, "Your special liquid will make the king very happy, indeed. I have no doubt about it, after seeing what happened with the giant tree."

"I hope so," said Winn Blitzzer. "It also changed me into different clothes, a nice blue uniform, before I met the Princess of Light. I hope this amazing liquid will be more useful to us in the future."

"I have no doubt about it," said Tovic.

The sun was high in the sky now, telling them that it was noon. They walked separately, a short distance apart, to prevent Moxum from seeing them together on the Potsat. But it was too late. She had already seen them walking together in the forest. She said to her sister Eris, "Why did Winn Blitzzer not tell me that he is going to the city with his friend Tovic? Why did he try to hide from me that he will be with Lady Esra's son?"

Her sister Eris said in his defence, "I think that sometimes Winn Blitzzer doesn't like to walk alone in the forest. He needs his friend Tovic to accompany him occasionally."

As the boys walked, they started to smell the smoke coming from the chimney of Ms Moxum's house. They knew they were close. They arrived at their houses and agreed to meet again in two days. Tovic wished Winn Blitzzer good luck at his next meeting with the king.

Finally, Winn Blitzzer arrived in front of his house and went inside.

"Good afternoon, I am back."

"Hello nephew, don't you look happy."

"Yes! The meeting with His Majesty King Brelys-1000 was a success. This time he was very understanding of my proposal. I asked him to present me his daughter the Princess of Light, and he did. He wants me to come again tomorrow after he has had the dream. If all goes well, I think he could really accept me as his son-in-law." His Aunt Moxum jumped with joy.

Then he began to explain to his aunts how he transformed his clothes and then stopped.

"I am telling you this story and forgetting that you can see everything in the Potsat anyway. I am still used to thinking of it as a normal cauldron."

Moxum said to him, "That is alright. For me it is very important that you remember everything and all the rules I tell you. As long as you do this, we will be successful. I am feeling confident after your performance before the king today. You did everything I told you to do. But I would like you to be honest with me."

"What is it, Aunt Moxum?" Winn Blitzzer asked.

"Why didn't you tell me that you are going to the city with your friend Tovic? I saw you both walking in the Potsat. Remember you can never hide from me. I can see you wherever you are."

Winn Blitzzer felt ashamed and began apologising. "I called Tovic to come with me to the city because sometimes I fear walking alone in the forest. He waited for me in the gardens of the city, he was afraid to go to the royal palace. Next time I won't hide anything. I will tell you everything if something like this does happen again."

"I hope so," Aunt Moxum said to him. Aunt Eris wasn't happy about the excessive control her sister Moxum was trying to impose on their nephew, but said nothing.

Moxum said to Winn Blitzzer, "Come here and look into the Potsat. You will see something that will surprise you about the gift of a dream you promised to the king." Winn Blitzzer came close to look into the Potsat and saw King Brelys-1000 still dancing with joy and repeating Big Ben name endlessly. "You see? Our plan is working."

It started to fall dark in the village. Winn Blitzzer mind was occupied with thoughts of the meeting he had had with the king and the meeting they would have tomorrow. Outside he could hear the owls hooting and crickets chirping. Music from the forest he had heard every night of his life.

His two aunts were working all day at preparing and testing different formulas for the success of the test mission they were planning. If the birds arrived safely on planet Earth, Moxum would be sure that Winn Blitzzer could arrive there safely as well. Winn Blitzzer was still unaware of everything behind his aunt Moxum's obsessive actions and plan for him to marry the Princess of Light.

The Potsat was boiling over a fire that had reached 1,200 degrees. Inside the house was like a sauna with a scent of sweet honey, herbs, perfume, and something sour, all coming from the heavy liquid in the pot. The steam from the Potsat helped keep Moxum looking so young for her age. Winn Blitzzer came over to the Potsat and looked inside. The mixture looked like a bright, liquid rainbow with something shining like a light from the bottom. It was mesmerising to look at.

Aunt Moxum said to him, "All this work is to test your secret mission at planet Earth. Trust my knowledge in the mystical sciences. You must be confident for the success of this mission. Everything has gone well so far because you followed all my advice. The same could be when I send you to the planet Earth. Now I think is best for you go to bed, it is getting late. Eris and I will stay here to continue with this work. Tomorrow we will have a very busy day indeed. We are sending twenty-six birds to Earth." Winn Blitzzer said good night to his aunts and went to bed upstairs.

Far away from Black Cloud in the royal palace King Brelys-1000, was already asleep. His secretary Zomy was asleep in antechamber. In the middle of the night he began hearing the king talking and laughing in his sleeping saying, "I saw it, I saw it! It has four faces! What a lovely sound the bells make, it is like magical."

At first Zomy told himself, "I won't disrupt the king's magnificent dreams this time. It is better to let him enjoy it until the end."

But when the secretary Zomy heard the king laughing again and talking loudly as if he was with someone, Zomy felt worried and decide to go knock on the king's door. "Your Majesty, Your Majesty, it is your secretary Zomy."

The king did not answer him. Zomy waited outside a little longer but the king did not speak again. He pushed open the door slowly and entered the king's chamber, walking slowly and carefully to not wake him. He saw the king fast asleep in his big bed. Zomy was about the leave, when the king suddenly coughed. Zomy froze.

Then he began tossing back and forth in his bed saying, "What a magnificent sound, what beautiful faces!"

He was laughing ecstatically. Zomy had never heard him laugh that way before. He slowly crept back to the antechamber.

The next day when the king awoke he sat straight up and said in low voice, "Winn Blitzzer kept his word. I had the dream he promised me."

Chapter Twenty-One
A Brief Meeting with the King

Winn Blitzzer woke up early and after a quick breakfast of porridge and honey, he said goodbye to his aunts and left for the city. Again as he walked it was as though his feet were not even touching the ground. He reached the city in no time at all. He was no longer surprised by these strange occurrences; he was not even surprised when he caught sight of the dwarf Nomy in a crowd of people again as he walked through the capital.

The guards were surprised to see him when he came up to the gates. Without a word they opened them for him. Moments later, Zomy came for him. When Winn Blitzzer saw him coming, he went to meet him in the middle of the garden near a beautiful water fountain sending three-metre plumes of water in the air.

"Good morning, Mr Secretary," said Winn Blitzzer.

"Good morning, Winn Blitzzer, good to see you again," said Zomy, "you are very punctual as always."

"Yes, it is not good to be late for the king," said Winn Blitzzer.

The king was waiting for him with a big smile on his face. He looked pleased to see him. He said, "Last night, I had the dreams you promised me. I had the great pleasure of hearing the loud sound of Big Ben's bells. I thank you for this, for I have never been happier."

"There is no need to thank me, Your Majesty."

Then the king said to Winn Blitzzer, "Now I really do believe that you can fulfil the promise you made to me. You have my word, although without witness, that I will officially consider you a suitor of the Princess of Light."

"I do not need another witness," said Winn Blitzzer. "I am pleased to hear this."

"Very good words, Winn Blitzzer, I can do business with you," the king said. "The final thing I will ask is to see tangible proof of Big Ben in my hands."

"Your Majesty, the next time we will meet will be in a few weeks' time. And at that time, you would hold in your hands objects from the London of planet Earth."

"Good," said the king, "but I do not want to wait for weeks."

"If it please Your Majesty, I will see what I can do." He bowed and made to take his leave.

"I wish you good luck, and success in your mission," said the king to him.

Winn Blitzzer bowed again and left. Zomy accompanied him to the front gate, and there they parted ways. He greeted Officer Tolly on his way past, as officer Latho and the young guards Erko and Kohla watched. As he made his way back home, the white dove kept appearing, soaring high over his head.

Winn Blitzzer hurried home to tell his aunts how happy he was with the meeting with the king.

"His Majesty got his gift of dreams, and gave me his word that he'd accept me as his as a suitor of his daughter, but if I fulfil the promise of delivering Big Ben to him, then he will accept me officially as a suitor of the Princess of Light." Winn Blitzzer thought his aunts would be very happy with this news, especially his aunt Moxum. He was wrong.

Aunt Moxum asked Winn Blitzzer angrily, "Where is the paper signed by King Brelys-1000 accepting you as a suitor for the time being? He gave you only his word as proof? Those are empty promises. What guarantee do you have when you deliver him the great clock that he will keep his word?"

Winn Blitzzer said, "Aunt Moxum, I understand your concern, but I believe the words of the king. He has treated me fairly and besides he made another announcement that he is no longer calling for his subjects to bring forward solutions for the clock tower."

After a brief silence, Aunt Eris said, "Let's give the benefit of the doubt to the king."

"Shut up," Moxum said to her sister Eris, "I told you not to talk about this without my permission."

Winn Blitzzer did not like the way Aunt Moxum talked to her sister Eris, but he couldn't say anything. He feared her too. Shortly after their conversation, he went to bed.

Chapter Twenty-Two
Rules to Be Kept for the Success of the Secret Mission

When Winn Blitzzer woke up early that morning, he was surprised to see his Aunts still at work. The house was hot inside as usual, from the steam rising from the Potsat.

"Good morning, aunts!"

"Good morning, nephew," they answered.

Aunt Eris said, "You're up early. Did you sleep well?"

"Yes, Aunt Eris I slept very well, thank you," Winn Blitzzer, "I can see by your eyes that you are tired. It seems like you didn't sleep at all last night."

"We sleep every night with one eye open to watch the Potsat," Aunt Moxum said. "We are used to it."

Eris said, "Especially you, Moxum, you sleep even less than I do."

Then Moxum put down the large wooden spoon with which she was turning the heavy multi-coloured liquid inside the Potsat to explain to Winn Blitzzer about the rules for the mission. He must keep and obey all of them for the success of the plan.

"Winn Blitzzer, the first thing you will need to do for your protection is to cross secretly near the planets that are hostile against our planet Oxon without being seen by the guardians of the sky there. Especially near the planets of Orion Minor, Orion Larger, Aixias, Neskher and Zexpher. Without this secret crossing, invisible to this hostile zone, you won't be able to travel safely and return here. But with the power of the Potsat you will cross this zone unseen and undetected by the guardians of the sky.

The first rule of the mission is not to look back under any circumstance during your travels. The second rule is, do not to touch the ground of planet Earth with your feet after arriving in London. The third rule is, do not take back any other objects to planet Oxon as a souvenir, a part of the great clock. Otherwise the mission could fail and you could be stuck there without any possibility of getting back to planet Oxon."

Winn Blitzzer a bit worried after hearing that last rule.

His aunt continued. "The fourth rule of the secret mission is to spread Magic Sleeping Powder across London so that everyone there will be left under a dreamless sleep while you take Big Ben away. The work will be done first by the special birds I will send to Earth before sending you there to accomplish that job. Not a single person in London will see you. That will keep the disappearance of the most famous clock in their world even more mysterious. Only you with the special birds will be awake in the London. For just thirty minutes and thirty seconds you will be king of a sleeping city thanks to the powerful effects of the magic sleeping powder. Later, I will show you what you will travel in to get to London. It is called the Free-XL. It is created especially for this mission."

Winn Blitzzer listened carefully to his Aunt Moxum's explanation of the rules for the plan; in his mind he could see himself flying through galaxies, and in London carrying out the secret mission. He was looking forward to seeing what this 'Free-XL' was like. He had never heard of it before. Everything sounded so new and mysterious to him.

Then he said to his Aunt Moxum, "I will follow every rule you told me. It does sound exciting, but also a bit afraid to go there alone."

Aunt Moxum looked at him and asked him "Do you have anyone in your mind who could travel with you?"

"Yes, my friend Tovic," said Winn Blitzzer.

"Never! Never, never," said aunt Moxum angrily. "That is not an option."

Aunt Eris and Winn Blitzzer looked each other after hearing this but said nothing.

"Let's move on," Aunt Moxum said. "You will be making this trip alone."

So Winn Blitzzer asked, "Is there any other advice you can give me or rules I ought to know?"

"Yes!" Moxum replied. "There is still something very important to tell you. Once you reach planet Earth, there are satellites in orbit around it. This technology is like the eyes of the planet. But do not be concerned. You will turn on a ray of special yellow light, which will launch the magic sleeping powder automatically from the nose of Free-XL and will neutralise all of the satellites in the sky. After that, none of the satellites around Earth will be able to record any images during the time of your mission. So the theft of Big Ben will remain a mystery there.

But that is not to undermine the intellect or underestimating the capacity and inventiveness of the humans of planet Earth. They too use advanced technology we don't have here. Our sciences are very different according to our different existences and needs."

For many years, Moxum had been observing many cities of planet Earth in the Potsat but there still existed many devices and different types of technology that she did not understand. Because of this she warned Winn Blitzzer to not touch the ground of planet Earth once there.

Lastly she told him, "I will let you have my magic golden wand. With that you can make incredible things happen. You will even be able to handle the great clock with one hand as if it were a single sheet of paper, practically weightless. But you must not forget a single rule."

Winn Blitzzer felt a bit worried with all this rules. But he said, "Don't worry, Aunt Moxum. I will follow all the rules you have told me. I won't take any risks. After having scattered the sleeping magic powder across London, I will complete my secret trip successfully."

To ease the last bit of doubt he had in his mind, Winn Blitzzer asked, "Aunt Moxum, will I really be able to lift an entire clock with just a wand?"

Moxum said to him, "You will see when you pick up the great clock how easy it will be. You seem to have forgotten the most important rule I told you before: to never doubt what you can achieve. All power begins in the mind. The magic golden wand will do amazing things your eyes have never seen before. You need to believe without seeing. I will give you other instruments as well and further instructions on how to remove the great clock from the main clock tower and bring it here safely.

Tonight, I will test some of these things to see their effectiveness. I will start with the test of the magic sleeping powder, and tomorrow with the test of sending the special birds to the London on planet Earth, and finally I will show you the Free-XL, in which you will travel for your secret mission. Now let's put into practise the first test so that you will see and understand how it will work."

She opened the lid of the Potsat and pressed the yellow button. On it, a small bowl with holes like colander came up to the surface with a small glass bottle containing green powder. She took that small glass bottle in her hand and said, "This is the magic sleeping powder. Tomorrow morning you will see how this powerful magic sleeping powder works."

It was getting dark around the mysterious village of Black Cloud. Moxum said, "Now is the time for the test. Let's start."

She shook that small glass bottle vigorously with her hands, then threw it up, and caught it before it touch the ground, laughing as she did. Moving her big eyes all around, she said, "This magic sleeping powder will make anyone tracking the satellite fall into a deep sleep. And all the people of London won't know what world they are in."

She put that small purple glass bottle of the sleeping magic powder inside small net bag, which she hung outside the front door of the house. Aunt Eris gave the warning signal to the few neighbours around them first by blasting a short horn resembling a snail shell, and said, "May I have your attention please! Tonight we are testing the effectiveness of the magic sleeping powder. We request all of you to seal your doors and windows well and to not come out until tomorrow morning when you will hear this sound of snail shell again. Thank you for your cooperation."

Tovic was scared when he heard this announcement. His mother Lady Esra told him not be afraid. Lady Dallas opposite their house did the same with her daughter Yalta. Ms Moxum opened the small purple glass on top of the magic sleeping power, then shut and locked her front door quickly to avoid the magic sleeping powder to enter their house. That night was completely silent.

Early the next morning when Moxum and her sister looked out the window, they could see animals lying everywhere, fast asleep from the powerful effect of the magic sleeping powder. Aunt Eris went to wake Winn Blitzzer upstairs. She knocked on his door, "Dear nephew, wake up and come outside, we want to show you something."

Winn Blitzzer jumped out of bed and ran downstairs. When his Aunt Eris opened the door, he saw all the different animals asleep in front of their garden and beyond. He was astonished after seeing so many animals sleeping in daylight. His Aunt Moxum said to him, "Here you have tangible and indisputable proof of the powerful effects of the magic sleeping powder. The people of London will be just like this."

Winn Blitzzer went out into the courtyard, lightly touching some of the animals. "How amazing, they are still alive!"

"Of course they are alive, they are just in a deep sleep," Moxum replied.

Walking around, he discovered species of animals that he had never seen before, a type of horse with three sharp horns on its head, other horses with two heads and long black beards, buffalos with horns in the form of stars with five struts, as well as a large antelope with circular horns on his head.

At the end, Aunt Moxum said to Winn Blitzzer, "Now your aunt Eris will make all these animals wake up and go back into the forest."

Eris took the short horn and blew it. The animals woke up, dazed and ran disordered back into the forest before Winn Blitzzer's astonished eyes. They could hear the plants loudly rustling about as the animals leapt through it. And then there was silence. Only the birds were singing. The neighbours woke up at the sound of the horn trumpeting, but preferred to stay locked inside their homes, to avoid catching any remains of the sleeping powder. Aunt Moxum said, "I think all of this speaks for itself."

Winn Blitzzer was confident now in seeing that he would succeed. Then he thought of something else, "Aunt Moxum, where are the birds you said you'll send first?"

"There is no hurry," Aunt Moxum said to him. "Later I will send the birds there. There is something I need to do first."

Chapter Twenty-Three
The Transformation of the Mysterious Birds

Ms Moxum went back over to the Potsat, took the big wooden spoon and started to turn the hot multi-coloured water in the Potsat. The steam that came out from the top was just as colourful as the colourful rainbow inside. She grabbed a small black bag that was hanging from the ceiling nearby. Inside were the special birds she had mentioned the night before. They did not resemble birds at all but were still as tiny as little mosquitoes. She opened the small bag and took out one of those tiny dark specks. Winn Blitzzer looked at her hand and asked her, "What is this, Aunt Moxum?"

"They are birds," Ms Moxum replied calmly.

"Birds?" Winn Blitzzer exclaimed. He repeated with his voice trembling, "These small black things like mosquitoes are birds?"

"Yes! They are real birds indeed," said Aunt Moxum calmly. "They will soon be transformed in the Potsat, and become very large, beautiful birds indeed. You won't recognise them."

Winn Blitzzer found it very hard to believe that these tiny dark insect-like creatures could become real birds. But anything was possible with the mysterious power of the Potsat, as he had discovered.

Then Aunt Eris said, "Dear nephew, these special birds Moxum has in her hand have a very special anatomy composed of two hearts and six lungs, which will make them fly easily across the galaxy without difficulty breathing."

"That is correct explanation," said Aunt Moxum. "I will send them soon to planet Earth. Don't underestimate these special birds by how you see them now."

"I believe everything both of you are telling me," Winn Blitzzer said.

Then Moxum dropped the small black specks into the hot water of the Potsat. Then she began stirring it with the larger wooden spoon, reciting an incantation in whispers. Suddenly, she began laughing out loud. "Now is the time to check if it worked!"

Suddenly, Winn Blitzzer saw a number of small birds with white feathers floating up in the multi-coloured waters of the Potsat. They smelled rather good. "I just saw one floating in the Potsat! How tasty would it be if we ate it?"

"No! Don't ever say a thing like that," Aunt Moxum exclaimed angrily. "Don't touch any birds in the Potsat. They are not to be eaten. They are to test the success of your mission to planet Earth. There are twenty-six birds in total in the Potsat and twenty-six better return."

Aunt Eris smiled covering her mouth with her hand at Winn Blitzzer's innocent and funny questions.

Winn Blitzzer said, "It was a joke. I was just joking."

"That was a bad joke," Aunt Moxum replied in an angry voice and then said, "You should never forget that we and the birds are friends, we do not eat them as other people do. Do not forget it is thanks to the action of the white dove that you were received by the king on your first visit."

Winn Blitzzer said, "I know that, Aunt Moxum, I value what the white dove did for me that day. I am very proud to be friends of the birds. But I don't really understand. What do cooked or uncooked tiny birds have to do with my mission?"

"Be careful about what you are saying," said Aunt Moxum. "The birds in the Potsat aren't cooked or dead, they are well alive and strong. Nothing is impossible with the powers of the Potsat as you saw already. All the birds are very much alive. But be patient and let me finish explaining to you the role these special birds will play in this testing of the secret mission. It is in your interest."

"In my interest?" Winn Blitzzer asked her.

"Yes! In your interest that these special birds will work," said Aunt Moxum. "I will send these birds to London first to test if everything will be safe and go successfully before sending you there. Furthermore they will prepare things there to allow you to take the great clock away easily."

Winn Blitzzer looked at the small birds floating in the Potsat, thinking about what his Aunt Moxum had just told him. All of this seemed like a joke to him. Winn Blitzzer asked his aunt Moxum, "What could these birds with their small fragile beaks prepare for me?"

"Well luckily we will be able to watch them flying in the Potsat. You will see for yourself what these birds can do. We will see if they cross the area of the hostile planets, unseen on their way to planet Earth. They should then be able to cross by the Earth satellites undetected. Then will come your turn to follow them and meet them at the final destination in London."

"Why send these birds and not something else?"

"Because there was nothing better to send than these birds to test the success and safety of this mission. The birds will be our explorers after leaving our planet Oxon, until they arrive at Earth. Anyway the birds are very obedient to the powers of the Potsat. Because of their wings they can fly easily from one place to another without any difficulty. Secondly, they able to cross undetected even in zones of conflict, as no one would be alarmed by a flock of birds."

Winn Blitzzer was very happy indeed after his Aunt Moxum said this. He jumped with joy. He grabbed hold of the wooden bar that ran just under the ceiling from one wall of the room to the other and began to swing on it. He jumped down smiling with joy, like an astronaut who has been selected from many candidates to go to space. But here he was the only candidate.

"I begin to understand now how this secret mission will go. Just one more question. What will these birds do when they arrive in London? You had said it will be in my interest."

"Yes, the birds will wait for you in London and you will all go back together," Aunt Moxum replied. "The success of their mission is linked to yours too. Their discrete work will allow you to take the great clock away quickly without much effort once you arrive. Otherwise you could get pneumonia from the cold weather they have there. We are not accustomed to this kind of weather on our planet. This is the reason it is better to send the birds first. Not one single human being would suspect these birds flying around the tower could have a special secret mission or even come from so far away. Only the other birds in the London would notice our birds aren't from there by their smell. Fortunately, the real birds of planet Earth cannot speak to humans. I think that answers your question."

"Yes, Aunt Moxum. Thank you!" Winn Blitzzer replied.

Chapter Twenty-Four
The Test Mission

Around seven in the morning, Ms Moxum began the preparations to convert the small birds into large ones. Winn Blitzzer was looking at the small birds floating unconsciously in the hot special water inside the Potsat, wondering how they could come out alive.

His aunts had begun reciting an incantation in low voices. Then Aunt Moxum raised her hand up and down on top of the Potsat making bizarre gestures with her hands, as if she was wrapping something invisible in the air. Then she threw a small glass ball inside the Potsat. Suddenly, multi-coloured bubbles began gurgling in the Potsat. Winn Blitzzer was looking at his Aunt Moxum as though he had never seen her before.

Then she raised her hands again. Suddenly a small torch appeared in the air. She took that torch and smiled. She tested the torch fire on her hand but did not burn. The fire seemed as if it was penetrating her hand, but inside her hand the flame of fire was blue and on top of her hand the fire was shades of yellow, orange and red. All this was just an illusion. Then she stuck that small torch inside the water of the Potsat. The fire did not go but continued to glow inside.

A large black bubble went up over the entire surface of the multi-coloured liquid like a lid covering the Potsat. When she took the torch out of the Potsat, the fire did not go out. Then she threw the small torch up in the air and the small torch vanished as soon as it had appeared.

Aunt Moxum blew air from her mouth into the Potsat as though giving oxygen to the small special birds inside to breath. The big bubble covering the Potsat did not break. Immediately, the birds began moving around inside the Potsat. Some birds started putting their small beaks above the surface. They looked like fish in a bowl.

Then Moxum took the big wooden spoon and broke the big bubble covering the Potsat. She stirred the water to make all birds at the bottom come up to the surface. They looked more like little chicks, small white birds, still without feathers, were swirling inside the Potsat, others with their small yellow beaks began to make peeping sounds. When Ms Moxum heard the sounds of the birds, she began to laugh. "How amazing and beautiful and obedient these birds are taking the magic formula in their mouths. They will pass this test with success."

Then she said to the small birds, "Listen well. Now I will turn all of you into larger birds, golden eagles, and then you will be ready."

The birds were chirping even more loudly, as though they understood what she was saying.

Aunt Eris brought a large silver tray and put it on the table. She and Moxum began taking the birds out of the Potsat one by one and giving them some of a special jade liquid that Moxum possessed. After swallowing it, the small birds were converted into golden eagles with beautiful plumage, and grey, red and yellow beaks. Ms Moxum called the first bird who was transformed Ar. Each bird that followed received its own name. Leb, Beg, Gyn, Iris, Mil, White, Tor, Roy, Fog, Vey, Ay, Hef, Chic, Zol, Joy, Or, Kiwi, Kul, Why, Nur, Dia, Grick, Violet, Pir and Ser.

Eris put another liquid on their beaks, saying, "Your little beaks will become strong like iron so that you will be able to cut into the clock tower of like small electric drills."

Moxum then put a special black ring on each of the birds' necks that would allow them to change from golden eagles into a crows when they would arrive in London so as not to draw attention to themselves.

"No one will notice your presence there. With all these safety measures everything will run seamlessly."

Some of the birds were already flying around the house, testing their wings for the long trip ahead. Other birds were perched on the big wood bar near the ceiling, as if saving their energy.

But everything didn't go as well as Ms Moxum expected. The bird called Ser was a bit slow to take in the magic liquid than the other birds. She had to help him get out of the Potsat. In the end, she chose the bird Ar to be the leader of the secret mission, and put a special ring transmitter on his leg that would capture images from a distance.

Then Ms Moxum said, "It is time now to build a special net through which these birds will pass to become the even larger birds so they may fly through the galaxies successfully."

"Call for assistance to build the special net," Moxum said to her sister Eris. Winn Blitzzer had no idea what his aunts were talking about. He saw his aunt Eris blowing the small whistle making a funny weird sound like it was a broken trumpet three times. It was a code of some sort. Suddenly Winn Blitzzer saw three long pieces of wood arriving near their house in the garden, floating in the air without anyone carrying them. They stopped and fell to the ground in front of them. Then small holes began to open up in the ground, while the dirt was thrown to the side, as though someone were digging.

Winn Blitzzer remembered that he had the blue glass lenses. He ran up to his room to observe from there. He saw six pairs of feet standing on the ground, near where the two trunks of wood began to move up and down into the holes as if somebody was pushing them into the ground. This occurred simultaneously, at a distance of about five metres between the two tree trunks.

Then a ladder appeared with four bent legs. A crossbar of five metres in length, rose up in the air and placed itself above the two wooden post about two metres high. It almost resembled a football goalpost without the net. Winn Blitzzer watched in amazement from his hiding place. After completing their work, he saw the invisible feet move, and something pick up the tools and fold the ladder.

Then Winn Blitzzer heard his Aunt Eris blowing the special whistle again. "Thank you for your service!" she called out to the empty space.

The ladder and tools left, floating through the air and disappearing from view in the woods. Ms Moxum took the white foam left over in the Potsat and collected it in small jar. She took a small paint brush and went outside to the wooden structure began to move the brush with white foam, right and left, up and down, in all directions in the empty spaces in the middle as if she were painting something.

Then she said, "The net is ready to do its job." She laughed. "How beautiful it is."

Winn Blitzzer did not see anything where she was looking. Aunt Eris said to her sister, "Everything looks alright for me."

Winn Blitzzer stared intensely between the two wooden posts but he did not see anything in the middle. Only empty space. He thought that it would be better to wait and see.

Ms Moxum went back inside the house. Winn Blitzzer was curious, wanting to discover what this net was. He went to take a closer look. But he still saw nothing, just empty space between the two wooden posts. Then when he put his hands between the empty space, he felt something like a net caught strongly in his fingers. Then he put one foot forward into the invisible net.

The invisible net was indeed real. He caught the net with his hands, as if he was trying to climb it; it held his weight. But how could the birds pass through the invisible net without being caught or trapped by it?

His attention was suddenly caught by the sight of smoke coming from under the door of their house. He went to investigate thinking something had caught on fire, but it was just Aunt Moxum burning incense. The house was full of sweet-smelling smoke. The birds did not cough or seem otherwise bothered by the smoke of the sweet incense. They were quiet, calm.

Ms Moxum raised her hands up saying in loud voice, "In the name of the incredible mystical sciences, and magical powers I possess, an inheritance from my ancestors, dear birds, I have transformed you from nothing but little black specks into magnificent golden eagles you are now. I am very happy with your transformation.

Today, I shall send you all on a very important mission to the most famous city on planet Earth called London very far away from here. I have full confidence in your accomplishing this mission, with your natural genius and original abilities. You are kings of the sky, building your nests in the trees, and with your master hunting skills. With all these of your amazing attributes you have, I command you to go on this special secret mission to cut the brick and iron of the great clock of London. Finally, you will build a large net to hold the great clock. Your work will allow my nephew Winn Blitzzer to take the great clock and bring it here to our planet Oxon. Do you understand me, dear birds?"

They screeched and cawed and shook their heads and flapped their wings, a sign that they understood. Once more Winn Blitzzer was amazed after seeing what the birds had just done.

He asked his aunt Moxum, "The birds understand what you are telling them?"

Aunt Moxum didn't answer him. She was busy with her magic incantation.

She gestured with her hand to tell him, "Wait, I will explain later."

Ms Moxum wanted to make sure that the transformations of the fake birds who could shape shift between different species during the secret mission would be effective and without error. To test it for the final time, she called the bird Ar to come forward. Then she laid her magic golden wand over him. Suddenly, the golden eagle turned into a crow. She tested it five more times. It was like turning a light on and off. Then she laughed and said, "Everything is prepared, you are ready to fly."

Her sister Eris and her nephew looked at her with respect and fear at the same time. The things she did were amazing and beyond belief.

Ms Moxum then said in loud voice, "Dearest birds, I command you to leave this house on the count of three. Fly outside and around this house and wait for my instructions to cross through the invisible net. This will turn you into a larger-sized golden eagle in order for you to fly safely across the galaxy to planet Earth. Ar will fly in front, two rows fly behind him without losing each other along the way. Do you understand me, dear birds?"

The birds looked at Ms Moxum and nodded their heads, as though they understood every word she had just said.

"One last thing. Follow this advice for the sake of your safety: do not touch the ground of the planet Earth under any circumstances, even if provoked by the local birds, otherwise you could be stuck there for good. Just stayed in air and complete your task."

All the birds nodded again. The Potsat was already on, flashing like radar. Ms Moxum said to the birds, "Attention, the countdown begins now! Three, two, one!"

Immediately, the small golden eagles began flying outside the house in two queues and turning around the trees. Once all the birds were out, Ms Moxum came out with her wand and pointed it in the direction of the invisible net. They flew in two queues at low altitude and after passing through the invisible net, they instantly became even larger golden eagles with great flapping wings.

Then the birds formed a rectangular line with a triangle head to fly in in order like a well-disciplined birds. They flew low over the house as though to say goodbye to their master Ms Moxum.

Ms Moxum said to the birds, "Now you may fly to planet Earth. We wish you all a very safe trip, and good luck on your mission. I am looking forward to seeing you all come back soon and safely."

Moxum, with her sister Eris and their nephew Winn Blitzzer, watched the birds flying in four lines, until they disappeared from sight, behind the clouds. But again, the bird Ser was the only one who did not follow well all the instructions given by Ms Moxum; he was a bit slow and distracted in his movement. Ms Moxum was a bit worried at first. But she didn't take the issue too seriously. Everything else had gone according to plan. The test completed, Ms Moxum returned inside the house to watch from the Potsat.

Winn Blitzzer was in disbelief after seeing the birds passing through the invisible net without getting trapped and following all the instruction his aunt gave them. He went to touch the invisible net again to feel whether it was still there. After putting his hands in the empty space between the two wooden posts, he felt the string and the ropes of the invisible net in his hands again. He was amazed. He could not understand how the birds could have passed inside the invisible net without being caught. There were no holes where they had passed through, the invisible net was intact.

Winn Blitzzer went to look for his friend Tovic to show him the mystery of the incredible invisible net. He knocked on the door of his house. Tovic opened it.

"Hello!" Winn Blitzzer said to him.

"Hi!" Tovic replied. "What a surprise."

Winn Blitzzer said, "I came to get you to come and see something amazing and unusual."

"What is that?" Tovic ask.

When Winn Blitzzer told him about that invisible net. Tovic couldn't believe that such a thing could be possible. Winn Blitzzer said to him, "Only when you will feel the ropes of that invisible net in your hands will you believe me."

They walked quickly to go see it. When they arrived Tovic could only see the two wooden posts with the crossbar on top like goalposts, no net in between. But when Tovic put his hand inside the empty space, he felt the invisible net in his hands. He was amazed and said, "It is true, I can feel it!"

Winn Blitzzer said, "Told you. If you want you can climb it, you won't fall either, believe me I tried and it worked."

Tovic asked, "Is it safe?"

"Yes, of course. It's safe," Winn Blitzzer replied. Then he and Tovic climbed up the invisible net. They hung vertically and swung back and forth it.

They began laughing, but quietly, to avoid Moxum hearing them from inside the house. Tovic said to Winn Blitzzer, "I am not surprised actually. The mysterious power of your aunt is well known by the few people left here. Anything is possible in this mysterious village after what we saw the other day."

"That is true," said Winn Blitzzer. "Today I saw the feet of the invisible people who built this wooden structure with the lenses Lady Dallas gave me."

Then Tovic asked him fearfully, "Are you sure that you saw the feet of the invisibles people here?"

"Yes," said Winn Blitzzer, surprised.

Tovic looked at him and said, "I like our village, but all these things seem so strange and mysterious that I feel quite scared sometimes."

As he spoke, Tovic noticed a lit candle with three small whistles floating in the window of an uninhabited house nearby. It seemed to be calling him to come there. He quickly scrambled down the invisible net and ran away into his house, believing that the invisible people knew now that he stole one of the special whistles from his mother to give to Winn Blitzzer.

When Winn Blitzzer saw Tovic running away, he said to him, "Stop, stop Tovic!" But Tovic did not stop or say anything to him, he just kept running.

Winn Blitzzer called, "What's going on? Why are you running away? I still have something very important to tell you."

But Tovic had already locked himself in his house. Winn Blitzzer ran after him and knocked on his door Tovic. He was confused. Then he spoke alone in front of the door, "Tovic, I thought we were friends. You had said to me that I was the chosen one who could bring our parents back from the invisible world. I have to go far away now and I don't know when I'll be back. I guess I'll just leave the small whistle you gave me outside your door. Wish me luck…"

Winn Blitzzer had no idea that after Tovic ran to his house, he stepped into a mysterious icy cold air, despite it being a warm sunny day, which had left his body almost entirely frozen. He was still standing almost frozen behind the closed door when Winn Blitzzer knocked, but he could not open it or speak. He was even more frightened.

Winn Blitzzer headed home. It was already ten in the morning and the sun was strong overhead. He could see his shadow on the ground. Suddenly, he too was hit by a rush of cold air, nearly freezing his body. He ran in fright as fast as he could towards his house. He made it, but then stopped and tried to pull himself together so his aunts would not notice anything was off. He let himself into the house with a big smile on his face as if nothing had happened.

His aunts were busy watching the birds through the Potsat. So far it was going without incident. The bird Ser was still a bit slow and was flying behind the lines of the other birds. Winn Blitzzer watched with them. The birds passed the first conflict zone without being detected by the guardian of the sky of the planet Orion Minor. The successful crossing of the birds made Aunt Moxum optimistic and certain that the mission would be completed.

She said to Winn Blitzzer, "Do you see how the birds fly with confidence? They followed all my advice and instructions. They don't look back, only forward to their final destination. You must follow their example."

Winn Blitzzer was more and more impressed with how much knowledge of the mystical sciences his Aunt Moxum had. He felt like he was only now discovering who she really was. She was like a different person than the one he had grown up with his entire life.

They kept watching the birds fly. Aunt Moxum said, "Soon these birds will cross near the other planets in the conflict zone. That crossing will be the deciding test of this mission."

As she said this, the blue planet Orion Larger came into view, then Aixias in red and Neskher in yellow, and finally planet Zexpher which was a dark grey. All the birds crossed the conflict zone of these planets without being seen. It was the first time Winn Blitzzer had seen another planets before, thanks to the Potsat. Not so long ago he had not even known they existed.

But as the birds entered into Earth's atmosphere, the Potsat lost them behind the heavy clouds in the sky. Aunt Eris put more wood on the fire and the image returned.

"Soon the birds will arrive at their final destination," she said. The small black rings the birds were wearing began turning around their necks. Ar said to other birds, "I think we are close. The atmosphere feels quite different here."

"Me too, me too. I can feel so much oxygen here," answered the other birds.

Then Ar said, "All of you must be prepared for our transformation into crows. You will weigh much less and your feathers will become black."

As they breathed in more and more oxygen, the large golden eagles transformed to small, black crows.

The bird called Kiwi said, "I feel different and very light compared to how I was as a golden eagle."

Another bird called Fog replied, "That is true, everything is as Ms Moxum has told us."

The chief bird Ar knew that their master Ms Moxum saw their transformation in the Potsat. He asked all birds, "Has everyone transformed?"

"Yes, yes, yes, we are, me too!" they all replied in unison.

Ar said, "I am glad. But I want to be sure that everything is going well before we arrive in London. As all of you know, we are forbidden to look back, or turn around to see what is happening behind us. Therefore I suggest we counted aloud one at a time to make sure we are all here. I shall start. One."

Each bird answered in kind, counting up until they reached the number twenty-five. Then there was silence as they waited to hear twenty-six. It was Ser who had not responded. The other birds felt scared flying forward, fearing to look behind. After two long minutes of waiting that seemed an eternity, they finally heard a voice. "Twenty-six."

Everyone sighed in relief. The mission was ready to continue.

"Our great advantage is that maybe we can transform into this Earth species the crow," Ar said now. "Let us test if we sound like them too."

They all began cawing loudly, creating quite a racket.

"Good!" said Ar. "We sound just like the real Earth crows. But remember, if we touch the ground of Earth we can be stuck there forever as Ms Moxum said. We must stay together and always obey her instructions. Now I would like to test our beaks to see how long and flexible they were. With our beaks we will perform our task for this mission." They began moving their beaks up and down, right and left. Their faces looked funny with the expressions they were making to test their small beaks.

"My beak has become long and flexible," said the bird called Nur, and Hef reported the same.

"Mine too," said Pir and finally all the birds said, "Mine too, my beak is working well."

Suddenly, another bird Vey exclaimed, "Ah! Someone just pecked my tail, I nearly fell out of flight!"

"Me too, me too. Someone pecked me too and tried to push me down!" some of the others called.

The chief bird Ar said, "We are not here to play or make jokes. We are on a serious mission in a foreign planet and strange country to us. Anyone who was playing must stop now. Ms Moxum is watching everything we do in her Potsat. Do you want her to put us back the way we were before?"

Ar's scary comments left all the birds in silence. They continued to fly in sombre silence. Ar tried to cheer them up saying,

"Everything is alright. We will soon arrive at the final destination. Everybody knows what they need to do. We are going to make Ms Moxum proud. I will organise the work in teams to work in shifts. Soon we will begin."

The birds started cheering and loudly cawing again. Still, Ms Moxum was very worried indeed about the slow behaviour of the bird, Ser. But she said nothing. The other twenty-five birds were responding well anyway.

Just as the birds were making their descent, they suddenly heard a deafening sound from somewhere the sky. They had never heard such loud noise before and looked around in fright for its source. They did not know that it was a plane making this sound.

"What is this awful noise?" they asked each other although none of them could answer the question.

Then said the bird Leb said, "I smell something strange. It's making me feel dizzy and nauseous." It was the smell of the fumes from the plane's engines.

"Me too," said the bird Violet. "I feel like I could throw up."

All the birds felt the same. Suddenly they flew into a long white road in the sky. It was the contrails left behind by the exhaust from the plane's engine. To them it looked like a long white sheet of smoke spreading without end across the sky. They were afraid at first having never seen this phenomenon before when flying. The chief bird Ar said to them, "Don't be scared; this is normal on planet Earth. This was only the beginning, there are still more strange things to be discovered here."

Just as he said this, they saw a big white object coming from a distance roaring towards them. It was the airplane. Ar squawked in alarm, "Everyone follow me down! It's going to crash into us!"

All the birds followed Ar, nose-diving downward in fright. They could feel the force of the wind left by the plane as it passed over them, blowing them away. Some of them lost their orientation, rolling this way and that, flapping to recover stability as the plane flew away.

The bird Chic asked in shock, "What is that? It nearly killed us. It seems like a big bird that flies without moving its wings."

Ar replied, "We have seen some sort of steel bird that does not need to flap its wings as birds do."

Then said the bird Tor, "It doesn't seem possible, but we have just seen with our own eyes an iron bird and felt its unbearable noise and strong winds."

"You can see now why we must stick together," Ar told them all. "We don't know what kind of surprises are waiting for us where we are going."

Ms Moxum was shocked by what she had just seen in the Potsat. Winn Blitzzer didn't think they were in any danger. But his aunt decided to take extra measures of precaution and changed the time on her nephew's departure time to prevent him from having the same shocking experience as the birds. Winn Blitzzer would have to travel after midnight to crossing with any planes in the sky above London. This would be the best time to travel safely.

The birds were now flying south in the sky over Northern Europe and the Scandinavian countries, seeing spectacular views of mountains and green forests covered with snow along the way.

Aunt Moxum said to Winn Blitzzer, "You will pass all these areas in the dark. You won't be able to see this magnificent view of the mountains and forest covered with snow."

"That's alright Aunt Moxum, maybe I could see it another time."

Aunt Moxum looked at him in a strangely, wondering when he thought he would be going there again.

At eleven in the morning, after an hour of watching the birds flying on the Postat, they finally saw the birds arriving in the sky over the magnificent city of London. Surprisingly, the sky was blue and clear with the sun quite warm for this time of the year. The birds saw again the long white trail in the sky over the city. They were surprised that it was visible even from below. They flew on in silence and then began to sing in celebration as they reached their final destination. They continued flying over London, upstream of the River Thames and soon reached the historic site of the Tower Bridge, flying in between the two towers. They continued their flight upstream passing over many more bridges into the heart of London. The great clock came into view a short distance away. Ar told his birds, "Here is the object which we have been sent here for! Soon we will get to work."

The birds all cawed loudly in response. After passing the Westminster Bridge they arrived at the Palace of Westminster where they could see the clock tower in real size. The birds came flying closer to inspect it all around, making more cawing noises. While this was happening outside, the keeper of the great clock, Mr Martin Smith, was inside resetting and greasing the cogs and gears for the celebration of the New Year, which would take place the next day at midnight. He glanced up at the loud racket of the birds outside. But their presence there did not cause any suspicion. It was normal to see crows flying around there, and pigeons too. Mr Smith continued his work. He didn't give much attention to the arrival of many crows there around the clock tower. Even to think that they could be fake birds, was far beyond his imagination. Nor would he have ever imagined that this was the last time he was checking and greasing the great clock. It was the same job his family had been doing in the tower for nine generations and he was very proud to be doing it. He was now the head engineer and master keeper of the great clock, and with other six people looked after and reset the two thousand clocks in the Houses of Parliament.

Mr Smith was around fifty-seven years old, and of average height. His easy smile would give him a youthful-looking face, if it weren't for his small white moustache and long white hair tied at the back, making him look like someone who plays in a rock band. His small round glasses, however, gave him a more scientific look. He liked trousers with straps. He had on boots and long black wool coat with a scarf of Scottish wool. As he continued with his work, the birds were landing on the roof of the House of the Parliament, taking a short rest after their long flight. They were already planning their work on the clock tower.

From Oxon, Moxum, Eris and Winn Blitzzer watched the birds on the Potsat. Winn Blitzzer clapped his hands after seeing the crows arrive in London. In his mind he was thinking, "*Soon I will be where the birds are now.*"

After the successful arrival of the crows, nothing felt impossible.

Aunt Moxum told Winn Blitzzer, "Now I will explain to you in more detail the reason why I decided to send the birds first on this secret mission. Soon the birds will start the work I have entrusted them to do. As I have already explained, this will make it easy for you to pick up the great clock when you arrive so that you do not need to stay long. Soon the birds will start to strike and give blows with their small beaks around the clock tower just below the clock, cutting the steel and brickwork which has been holding the clock tower together for centuries.

The chief bird Ar has all the instructions to organise the other birds to perform this task on time. They will carry this out in secret. No one in the London will know that the clock tower has been cut out by mysterious fake crows. Only its enormous tonnes of weight will keep it in its place."

Aunt Moxum finished explaining to Winn Blitzzer the details of the mission the birds would perform on his behalf, which would ensure he picked up and carried off the clock in time. But Winn Blitzzer could not understand how the small fragile beaks of the mysterious birds could do such major work without breaking them.

He asked his aunt, "The small fragile beaks of the fake crows can pierce the brickwork and steel?"

"Yes, of course," Moxum replied as if it was obvious. She added, "Naturally the birds with their small fragile beaks could perfectly cut out the clock. Only the doubt in your mind is keeping your from believing this. But to explain more clearly, I put a special powerful magic in their beaks to make them strong as iron. In this way their beaks will be like little electric drills that will cut through the tower easily."

"What amazing idea, Aunt Moxum! It seems like a fairy tale," Winn Blitzzer exclaimed. "Now I understand."

I am glad you like it," said Aunt Moxum, "I don't want you to have any doubts in your mind. I want you to believe everything that I have told you. I would not lie. The only thing I am asking you to do and remember always for your own good, is to believe in yourself, always."

"I do not doubt anything you have told me, Aunt Moxum," said Winn Blitzzer, "I believe everything you have said. You can understand this is a lot to take in at once. I never even knew you had such amazing knowledge or the special power of the Potsat. All this still seems like a dream."

"I can understand that. After all, all of this is new to you," said Moxum. Then she asked Winn Blitzzer, "Do you want to know anything else before I start the preparations for your journey?"

"Yes, Aunt Moxum," said Winn Blitzzer "Why precisely did you choose the crows for this mission to cut the clock tower and not another species of birds like the great golden Eagle? It is much stronger and more powerful."

"Ah, yes. That is a very good question. I have chosen crows for practical reasons. First, because the crow is a very smart bird with a thick and strong beak. And it is a species you can find easily on planet Earth. There are many in London, even living around the clock. Therefore it was an advantage to transform the golden eagles into crows so that they'd be able to go about their work unnoticed. I have taken every precaution in case something goes wrong so that we leave no trace of this behind. I mean, in case any of the fake crows fails to come back to Planet Oxon for any reason, they could still live three days in the city unnoticed before they would turn into ash. No one would ever suspect they were a fake species of a crow.

Only an actual crow would notice the presence of the fake crows. But they too won't be able to do anything to betray them, since they cannot communicate with humans. The anger and frustration the real crow could feel could lead them to be aggressive against the fake crow. This behaviour could draw people's attention to look towards where one group of birds were attacking another. But the small black rings the fake crows are wearing on their neck will save them in case any person tries to capture them. They would turn into ash then too, and appear back here in the Potsat."

As she said this, the bird Ser could be seen on the Potsat struggling to keep up with the rest of the birds as they flew.

"Have you seen how powerful my knowledge of the mystical sciences is? It is more like a magical power. Even with the winter season there now, I have full confidence that the crows will succeed in the special mission I have entrusted them."

Then she began to laugh out loud again, quite pleased with herself. Winn Blitzzer kept watching the Potsat, seeing the birds resting again on the roof near the clock tower in London.

After the crows had rested, they felt strong enough to begin their secret mission. They flew around the clock tower slowly and looked at it saying, "How are you, beautiful clock?"

Their small eyes sparkled inside from the glass reflection of its four faces. Then the bells rang, announcing that it was half past eleven in the morning in London. The birds flew away in shock at the unexpected sound. Aunt Moxum laughed out and said, "I had forgot to warn them about that."

A few minutes later, the clock fell silent again, and the birds began. Winn Blitzzer's aunts hugged him in happiness. Ms Moxum said, quite out of character, "Let's hold hands and dance to this achievement."

And then they danced, leaping about like Irish dancers around the Potsat. Then they embraced again, feeling much like the scientists at NASA after the success of the Moon landing.

As this was happening, Ar was addressing the other birds, "Dear friends, we are now in London. You have arrived safely. I hope we will complete our work on time. We have sixteen hours to fulfil our duties here. Let us not disappoint Ms Moxum."

"No, no!" the birds shouted, "we will fulfil our duties."

Then Ar said, "My dear friends, to make our work a little bit easier I have decided to divide the labour in shifts. We will be divided into groups of five, one for each face of the great clock, in order to spare all of us getting tired at the same time."

"For the six birds left including myself, we will be the Bird Watch Team, divided in two groups. Our job will be to fly one square mile around Westminster area to chase and ward off the real crows in the area to avoid them coming near the clock tower while we work."

Immediately after these instructions were given, the work began; not a second was wasted. All the birds began working together on each side of the great clock, in lines just below it, poking their strong beaks like little electric drills into the brickwork around the clock tower in a rhythmic beat. Ar was watching them work, and then told three birds, Grick, Pir and Ser, to fly around and chase off any real crows they may see. The three birds nodded and flew off, Ser flapping his wings hard to keep up. Ar himself stayed with the birds on his team, Chic and Vey, to guard the area around the clock tower. Far away on planet Oxon, Moxum was very happy with everything she saw the birds doing. The birds were following well all the instructions she had given them. With much encouragement, the crows continued drilling. Suddenly, they saw five real crows arriving near the clock tower.

In fact these real crows were living in a nest on the roof of the building opposite the clock tower. But they regarded Big Ben as their own territory, even though they didn't have a nest there. It was theirs and they were not willing to share that space with any other birds. One of the crows approached the strange birds who were drilling around the clock tower.

"What are you doing here? This is ours, you cannot stay here without our permission. As you can see, there are traces of our droppings here, which means it belongs to us. Your smell is different from other crows. Who are you, really? Why are you damaging our clock tower?"

They were hoping for answers from the strange birds. But they said nothing, just continued drilling their small beaks around the clock tower. After this arrogant attitude from the strange birds, the five real crows flew around trying to land on top of Big Ben to claim it as their own. Before they could land, Ar, Chic and Vey who were on the roof opposite the clock, started chase the real crows to throw them out of Westminster area. They followed the real crows up and down the River Thames and in the sky zigzagging over the bridge, even flying close to people's heads. The real crows kept saying to the strange crows, "You smell strange. You are fakes and committing something illegal to one of our most emblematic landmarks."

People who saw the birds flying around thought that they were just playing. They had no idea the birds were having trouble among themselves. The real crows continued flying, running away from the fake crows, who were chasing them aggressively.

The team of fake crows managed not to let the real crows delay their timed work. The fake crows saw how the real ones went into hiding inside of a large enclosure with four taller towers for refuge. This place was the Tower of London, where ravens were. The fake crows didn't dare to follow them inside there. They stayed outside flying around the tall wall and tower, waiting for the real crow to come out and chase them again. But the real crows stayed inside the Tower of London quite a long time, more than the fake crows could have anticipated. After a long wait the two fake crows Chic and Vey got a bit worried, thinking that perhaps the real crows were getting help from other birds inside to came to attack them later.

Then Ar said to them, "Do not worry about that. They cannot attack us. They fear us, that's why they went hiding within those walls. Besides, we don't have the luxury of wasting a single second. There is a legend, a myth, that inside those walls lived six ravens, and if they vanish, the monarchy would fall. Because of that, the ravens' master clipped their wings to prevent them from flying away so that they would remain inside the walls and the monarchy and the tower would be safe. Therefore there was very little they could do to help the real crows."

Chic asked the Ar, "How do you know all this? I don't think you have been to planet Earth before."

"I don't need to have been here before to know things from here. I have special radar in my brain, which allows me to learn things very quickly from this magnificent London. I can even tell you the name of the ravens living in the Tower of London now: Hardey, Thor, Odin, Gwyllum, Cetric and Munin. They are intelligent and can live to a very old age. Chick and Vey were very impressed by Ar's knowledge. But their faces were still showing signs of concern about the five real crows who had taken refuge with the ravens inside the wall of the Tower of London. They headed back to the clock tower. While they were talking about their little adventure, they saw the others on the Bird Watch Team arriving from their patrol mission. But there were just two flying, Grick and Pir. The third bird Ser had decided to go flying alone to see the London.

They told Grick and Pir about the minor incident they had with five real crows. Grick and Pir were very impressed to hear and envied their colleagues for having had their first contact with the real crows of planet Earth.

The bird Pir said, "We didn't have any contact yet with the real crows. We hope we too can be lucky to meet with them soon. We cannot come this far and not enjoy a little adventure too."

Ar said, "Don't worry, you will meet them sooner or later. There's still plenty of time. We don't know what kind of surprise they may prepare to attack us. I am sure that there are a lot of species of birds here in this city, not only the real crows."

Ar had not noticed yet that Ser was missing. He had no idea that he was perched on top of the legendary Admiral Horatio's Column in Trafalgar Square.

Shortly after, Ar gave the signal to take a break. After resting, they started working in shifts, five birds every thirty minutes. The first part of the work was done well. They had fourteen hours ahead of them to complete their work of cutting out the clock tower completely, before the arrival of Winn Blitzzer.

Violet said, "I feel pain in my beak from drilling so much and the dust is entering my nose."

"Me too," other crows replied.

Ar said to them, "Keep drilling, we are closer than ever to cutting the clock tower. Ms Moxum will reward us for our great work."

The chief bird Ar sent off the Bird Watch again. Before they left he asked them if everything was going well.

"Yes, almost everything is fine," said Pir. "But we did have a little incident I forgot to tell you about."

"What kind of little incident?" asked Ar.

"The one called Ser, I think he is lost in the city. He did not return with us."

"That cannot be true," said the chief bird Ar, "No one is allowed to be alone or get lost. You should have stayed together at all times to avoid this kind of incident. We should go now to look for Ser immediately before it's too late."

Grick said, "I don't think that Ser is lost. He told me that he wanted to fly across the city again to see it well. I regret now having left him alone. I should have stayed with him."

The bird called Nur who had heard all this, said, "I am not surprised. She was next to me on my left side during the flight. I saw myself she was a bit distracted, and slow in her movements. I wondered why she was behaving like this. In fact when we were transforming from golden eagles into crows, she found it hard to confirm that she had been transformed."

After hearing this, Ar sent out all the birds of the Bird Watch to fly together to find Ser. They flew across the River Thames then flew across the entire city, but did not see him anywhere. They returned a half-hour later empty-handed. After a short break, the Ar went with Chic and Vey to search, leaving Grick and Pir to monitor the area around the clock tower. As Ar flew with the others along the River Thames hoping to see the missing bird appear, he was surprised to see a number of real crows and six ravens having a meeting inside the wall of the Tower of London.

When the real crows saw the fake crows flying past, they said to the six ravens, "Those are the birds we are talking about. They are fake crows, who have camouflaged into our noble species to commit a bad act in London. Maybe they are coming to attack us inside the wall. Dear ravens, we must leave you now to keep you from having any problems with these fake crows. Hide yourselves, and thank you for your hospitality."

Then they flew for their lives across the city, the fake crows chasing behind them. They completely forgot their mission to find Ser. But the real crows knew the city well. The fake crows saw some of them flying towards Trafalgar Square and the others towards the Palace of Westminster.

Pir said to his fellow fake crows, "I think the real crows are going toward the clock tower. We must catch them before they get there."

"You are right, Pir," said Grick. "Let's catch them!"

The fake crows followed behind by making strange sounds not familiar to the real crow. Then suddenly they saw the three real crows changing direction and going to land inside the wall of The Palace of Westminster where there were gardens. Two of the fake Crows followed them, trying to inside as well.

Luckily before they could, Ar who was on the nearby roof shouted to them, "Do not touch the ground! Remember, Ms Moxum forbade us. If you do, you could be stuck here forever."

The two fake Crows flew high again, trembling. They flew onto the roof of the building opposite the House of Parliament. "Thank you Ar, you have saved our lives!"

"Don't mention it. But never forget the rules of any mission," Ar said to them.

Before nightfall, Grick and Pir tried a last attempt to find Ser, who was still missing. They flew across the city without finding him. In the end they returned to the clock tower, sad and worried at not having found their teammate, and gave the news to the other birds. After hearing the sad news, there was a brief moment of silence.

The chief bird Ar noticed the change in mood. To cheer them he said to them, "Don't be sad about the disappearance of Ser. I am confident he will be found. Maybe he is lost and following the real crows who know the city well very faraway and he doesn't know how to come back to find us. We still have many hours left in our city. We will see him again, and go back together to our planet Oxon."

And so the mysterious fake Crows continued with their work. Below them on the ground, the three real crows were making loud noises to call attention to the presence of the mysterious fake crows.

During that time, the master clock keeper Mr Smith was still inside the clock tower finishing the final touches on his work and looking forward to come down shortly.

Outside there were polices officers changing guard. The two new officers starting their night shift, monitoring the area around the Palace of Westminster, were Inspector Mark Bing and Sergeant Peter Bank. They had been friends since the day they met at The Royal Police Academy in Gloucestershire. They had never been on the same shift together since they had met. They were rather different characters, Inspector Bing being quite serious and nervous but very attentive to detail, and Sergeant Bank being quite clever with good sense of humour and a bit of a jokester. It was the coincidence of destiny that made them be on guard duty together that night for the very first time. They were happy to be on duty that night, and catch up together about their lives. And above all happy to have a day off on New Year's Day to celebrate with their families and friends. As they took their places, they never would have guessed the nightmare that was awaiting them. It would be a very bad day in their lives and very unfortunate for their careers as Her Majesty's police.

They had no reason to be aware of anything bad happening to the great clock tower. All the police officers on duty at the Palace of Westminster were not really watching Big Ben. They were watching the House of Parliament and the surrounding are. It was not anywhere in the minds of the two police officers to think that someone, somewhere was plotting something against the most appreciated and esteemed Big Ben. Everybody loved that clock and admired it, some even had a kind of affection towards it. Many believed it was the main reason people came to visit London and the reason why many chose to stay and live there. Big Ben was an icon of the city of London and the indisputable, unappointed ambassador of the city. This was why the police officers would never have imagined that something bad was about to happen to the great clock, especially something as unthinkable as stealing it, considering its size and weight.

It was slowly getting dark in London. The city was decorated in multi-coloured lights in the streets and squares from the Christmas holidays a week earlier. The House of Parliament had its big traditional Christmas tree, also beautifully decorated with lights blinking on and off, near the green area of the New Palace Gate. The faces of the clock tower were already beautifully lit with white and green lights below the tower.

At five o'clock its bells rang five times. Inside the clock tower, the sound was very strong; the people who worked there could feel the vibration of the belfry through their bodies. They used to wear earplugs to protect their ears. Mr Smith finished his work greasing the clock and checking all the mechanisms on it so that it would be accurate during the New Year's celebration. He picked up his work materials and other instruments and put them inside a large green bag before taking the spiral staircase down the tower. He put a pre-decimal 2 pence old coin on top of the pendulum of the great clock to balance the time accurately. He was very happy indeed with his work and enjoyed every second of it, working tirelessly every day with enthusiasm as if it were the first day on the job. He never got bored with clocks or watches. He liked their distinctive mechanical sounds. He used to tell his assistants that clocks have souls. They should be treated with care and great respect for their great services to the world. The people of England had great admiration for this particular remarkable clock. Big Ben was well known around the world for its precision. Mr Smith of course had special affection and respect for it, as if it were a person to care for and repair. Ms Moxum, on the other hand, did not care about the virtues of this magnificent priceless clock. She had only one objective in mind, to do everything she could to send her nephew Winn Blitzzer to steal the great clock, without any concern the impact of its absence would have on the people of London and around the world.

At half past Big Ben rang again, just as Mr Smith was going down the spiral stairs and out of the clock tower. As he was closing the small wooden door, he heard the sound of the crows nearby, seeming to him almost like crying or shrieking. He was heading to the House of Parliament to leave the key in the safe inside when suddenly the three crows appeared in front on him on the ground cawing loudly in alarm. He tried to avoid them by leaping over, but the crows prevented him, blocking his path. Mr Smith had no idea that these three crows had been previously driven away by the fake ones he had seen earlier on top of the tower. He managed to jump over the crows, but they followed him continuing to make a loud racket. Mr Smith had never seen anything like that before with those birds.

"What happened, birds? Why are you following me?" Mr Smith asked talking more to himself in confusion at their strange behaviour. He said to the crows, "I have nothing to give you, I don't know what you want from me. Leave me alone. Go away, stop following me."

The three Crows looked at him and ignored this, still following him as he walked to put back the keys. The two police officers on duty had also seen the strange behaviour of the crows.

Sergeant Bank said to Mr Smith, "Master keeper, maybe the birds want something to eat. They've been making this racket our whole shift. Maybe some breadcrumbs would make them happy or at least shut them up."

Mr Smith smiled and said to the officer, "If it's the food the crows want, that won't be a problem at all. I still have half of sandwich leftover in my bag."

He cut small pieces of bread and threw them to the birds on the ground.

But the crows didn't want to eat the pieces of bread he had just thrown to them. Instead they continued crying out looking up at the clock tower where the fake crows continued cutting the clock tower. Neither the master clock keeper nor the officers on guard had any idea they wanted to tell them something very important was happening up on the clock tower. They could not talk with the birds or understand their behaviour. There was nothing they could do for them.

Mr Smith tried to leave again, and again the three crows stood in his way, blocking his path and moving their wings and little leg on the ground, one even pecking at his shoes with its beak, cawing even more loudly and insistently.

Mr Smith said to Sergeant Bank and Inspector Bing, "I have spent years working here at the Palace of Westminster. I have never seen anything like this before. The behaviour of these Crows is very unusual. I don't know what they want from me or what this behaviour means. Sorry poor little birds, I cannot do anything for you."

At Ms Smith's kind warm words, Sergeant Bank said, "There is nothing else you can do to please these birds. You better get on home after a long day at work."

"Right you are," said Mr Smith. "I wish you both a very Happy New Year, and to your families. May everyone be in good health."

"And to you!" replied the two officers.

Then Mr Smith went inside the House of Parliament to leave the keys of the clock tower in the safe, thinking that was the end of it. But he three crows waited outside.

When Mr Smith came back outside, to his surprise he found the three crows still waiting for him.

He said to himself, "*This is not normal. I thought I wouldn't find these crows here again, but here they are. What do they want from me?*"

He jumped over the crows and walked quickly to leave them behind. But the three crows followed behind him making more strong cawing and squawking noises. When Mr Smith stopped at the crosswalk waiting to go to the Westminster Tube Station to catch the Jubilee line home, he noticed the presence of the crows just behind him. He turned in disbelief and saw the same three crows again. One tried to peck his shoes again, this started to scare him; the crows had sharp beaks and were very aggressive. He was lucky that the thick winter shocks he wore saved him from being stabbed.

When the green light came on, he walked faster across the street. The three crows followed him making even more noise. They were not afraid at all of the other people crossing. Mr Smith was beginning to become concerned. People were looking at him as if he had done something wrong.

He muttered, "This behaviour is so strange. Maybe it's a sign of bad luck. No crows have never followed me like this before. I haven't seeing anything like this before in my whole life."

Mr Smith reached his house full of worry but said nothing to anyone about what had happened to avoid ruining the cheery atmosphere in his house at the holiday ahead. No one in London had any concern in their mind that something strange or mysterious was about to happen in their city or that there would not be a celebration of the New Year around Big Ben as there had been for years. Everyone in London was looking forward to the celebration of the New Year like always.

Chapter Twenty-Five
A Boy Found in the Woods

It was around midday on the planet Oxon when Ms Moxum was celebrating her achievement at the arrival of her crows in London. She noticed that the village was still quiet after the powerful magic sleeping powder made the animals fall asleep the night before. Not even the birds sang as they usually did. One of the neighbours, Lady Esra, went to her garden to pick some vegetables. To her surprise, she found a young boy asleep in the woods. She ran back to the village screaming, "Help, help, I had found a boy asleep in the woods!"

The shocking news caught everyone by surprise. The seven people left in the village came out together at once. It was the first time in years that someone raised their voice in the mysterious village. Everyone followed Lady Esra into the forest. While walking, Ms Moxum was very worried thinking that maybe the invisible watchers she didn't want to bring back might have found a formula to return themselves to normal again without needing her help. Perhaps they had sent a young man to come to test her reaction. And a stranger could not easily reach the village without being bothered by the guards or being seen on the Potsat.

When they arrived in the forest, they saw a young boy, still deep asleep within the roots of a giant tree. None of them recognised him. Finally, Winn Blitzzer got the courage to wake the stranger. He touched his shoulder; the stranger turned without waking. Then Winn Blitzzer touched him again and said, "Wake up, wake up stranger! How did you get here? And where do you come from?"

The young man awoke, frightened at seeing so many unfamiliar faces before him. He pushed himself back deeper into the roots of the tree.

"Do not be afraid," Winn Blitzzer said to him, "we just want to help you and to know who you are. What is your name and where did you come from?"

The young boy stood up cleaning off the leaves stuck on his clothes. Then he said, "I came from the capital, from Ryam. I do not know really how I got here. I just remember a dwarf with a long ginger beard and a blue star tattoo on his face gave me some sweets and told me to take the path in the forest. He said it would take me back to my village and my family. But I don't know what he did to me exactly. I was just walking half asleep without knowing the way to where I was headed. Then I saw many animals and birds asleep almost as if under a magical spell. Then I also fell asleep until you woke me just now.

Thank you for finding me here. But my aunt Lilas with whom I live in the city will be looking for me. I have to get back now."

"Wait," Winn Blitzzer said to him. "We would like to know more about you."

There was no mistaking that the young man looked much like Eris' husband Laxom who was in prison in the invisible world. The strange young man found in the woods had Laxom's round face and green eyes, long blond hair and average height. He must have been around sixteen years old. There was no doubt that he was related to someone from the village.

Then the strange young man said, "By the way, my name is Valger."

"Valger?" Eris asked stepping forward, her eyes wide. Then the ladies Dallas and Esra looked at her saying, "Without any doubt this is your son who disappeared on the day of the mysterious tea party."

Eris ran forward with tears in her eyes to hug her son. Everyone was in tears at the unexpected reunion. Only Ms Moxum did not react, or show any emotion on her face. But incredibly, she said, "Welcome dear nephew Valger. I am very happy to have you here. It is divine providence that has brought you here today for I really needed someone for a very special adventure and you arrived at just the right moment. I couldn't be happier. Come hug your aunt Moxum!"

She opened her arms.

Everyone stared at her with her and then greeted Valger as he came to say hello to all of them. His mother Eris said to him, "I present you to the people of the village. This is your aunt Ms Moxum, your cousin Winn Blitzzer. Lady Esra with her son Tovic. She was the one who found you in the woods." Valger thanked her especially for having found him. He greeted Lady Dallas with her daughter Yalta as well. Then they returned to the village.

Once back, Ms Moxum said, "Today is a very happy day. We have a new member in our village. I will organise a party in honour of my dear nephew Valger. All are invited. I really hope that the miraculous arrival of this young man here can unite us once more as before. We must trust each other again to bring some light and joy into our gloomy village. We expect all of you around 1 o'clock to celebrate his unexpected arrival."

The shock and flood of emotions were almost too much for Eris. She wanted to learn about her son, at the same time worried that Valger would ask her about his father's whereabouts. But Valger and Winn Blitzzer quickly got along well and Valger seemed to adapt to the new village life easily. He was happy to have two boys of his age in the village, Winn Blitzzer and Tovic.

After taking a bath and receiving a change of clothes from his cousin, Valger was served something hot and delicious to eat. His appearance had changed almost completely at the joy and happiness of finding his mother. And after drinking some of the mysterious water of the Potsat, he felt very happy indeed among them, as if they had known each other forever.

Then Valger asked his mother, "Where's my father? Hunting or on trip?"

Aunt Moxum glared.

Eris noticed and snapped at Valger, "Quiet son, do not ask such things here yet. I will explain to you all these things in time. Let's enjoy your arrival here today, and with time you will know this place better."

Valger didn't say anything more. Winn Blitzzer made a gesture to him with his hands as though saying, "be patient."

Half an hour later Ms Moxum rang the bell and called loudly, "The party starts in ten minutes."

The ladies Esra and Dallas came with their children and the cakes and drinks they had prepared. They brought their own cups to drink from. They did not trust Ms Moxum or take any risk using her cups after what she did to their husbands and friends.

When they arrived in front of the small garden of Ms Moxum's house, they saw a table set with eight chairs. When the ladies Esra and Dallas tried to go between the two wooden poles with a crossbar on top to get to the table, Tovic said to them, "Mum, Lady Dallas, don't pass between the two wooden poles, there's an invisible net."

"Invisible net?" Yalta asked him in astonishment.

"Yes, it's an invisible net," Tovic replied. "Look I will try to pass through. But I won't be able to pass through the empty space."

He tried and said, "See, I cannot pass."

Yalta was amazed to see this. "It's very hard to believe that there is something there when all I see is this empty space between the poles."

Their mothers looked at each other and Lady Dallas said, "I am not surprise at all with the strange mysteries of this village."

When Ms Moxum heard them talking outside, she came out to meet them with a big fake smile on her face. But after seeing they had brought their own cups with their cakes and juices, Ms Moxum realised that they did not trust her at all. They would never eat or drink anything she could offer to them. She did not like this. Her anger was clear on her face. The situation of the village was not going to change with the mysterious arrival of the young Valger as she had hoped; the mistrust remained.

Eris came out with her son Valger. She and Winn Blitzzer avoided passing within the invisible net. Valger tried, but felt trapped in the mysterious empty space.

They applauded him saying, "Welcome to the mysterious village of Black cloud."

He smile and passed around the other side and went to sit at the table between Winn Blitzzer and Tovic.

His mother stood up and said, "I thank you all for coming to this impromptu party at the unexpected arrival of my son Valger, who I did not know was alive for many years. I am very happy indeed, happier than I've been in years. I look forward to seeing more surprises like this, with our loved ones who we miss every day. I have recovered some of my happiness at the unexpected and miraculous arrival of my dear son Valger. Please stand up for a toast to him."

After toasting in his honour, Valger stood up and said, "I thank every one of you for having me here. I will consider every one of you my family. But I have noticed something a bit strange here. Why do more people not come this party? I can see that there are more houses in the village, more than the eight people who are here. Do some people not accept me here?"

"Do not say things like that, son," his mother told him. "We will have time to talk about all these things later."

Valger said, "Okay… It is just so much quieter here than in the capital."

"You won't be bored here even though it seems quiet to you," said Esra. "It does have its fun side too as you saw with the invisible net by surprise a moment ago."

"That is true," said Winn Blitzzer "my cousin Valger, you were trapped a while ago in an invisible net, that only birds could pass through without being caught."

Valger was shocked to hear this.

"How such a thing could be possible?" asked Yalta.

Winn Blitzzer said to her, "This invisible net is one of the wonders my Aunt Moxum can do."

When Yalta tried to ask more about the mysterious invisible net, her mother said to her, "Do not ask more questions."

Then Winn Blitzzer said to Lady Dallas, "I am happy to explain to your daughter Yalta anything she'd like to know since it is rare we meet like this."

"Thank you for your kindness, Winn Blitzzer," said Lady Dallas. "But we came to get to know Valger, the new member of this village. We are not interested in other topics."

After a brief moment of silence, Valger asked, "Where are the men of this village? It cannot be just us with so many houses here. The others must be in their orchards or hunting or even fishing now. I do not see any animals around either. It's very strange to be in a village without any pets."

"Please leave that topic for now, we will have time to talk about it later. For now we will just enjoy your presence here with us," Eris said to her son.

Then Lady Esra said to her son Tovic, "Could you and Winn Blitzzer take Valger to show him his new home?"

"Yes, Mum. Good idea," said Tovic.

"I agree," said Winn Blitzzer.

Then they left to show Valger the village. They took him first to show him the honey tree. When they arrived there, Valger saw only a small wooden house built around a large tree trunk surrounded by several hundreds of species of beautiful flowers around. Bees were buzzing about, working away without attacking them.

"It is a very lovely place," said Valger.

"Yes," Winn Blitzzer replied. "But we brought you here to show you the miraculous honey tree where we get the honey we usually sell in the city."

"Honey tree?" exclaimed Valger, "I have never heard something like that before, that cannot be true. You are joking."

"We are not joking, we are serious," said Tovic. Then Winn Blitzzer opened the door of the small wooden house. Inside he opened a layer on the tree where there was a kind of wooden tap. When Winn Blitzzer opened it, thick honey began pouring slowly out. Valger's eyes widened in surprise.

"Try the honey and tell us what do you think of it."

Valger tasted the honey with a small wooden spoon. "It's so nice and sweet. I have never had honey before in my whole life." He was very impressed.

"We were sure you'd like it," said Tovic.

Winn Blitzzer said, "Let's go now. There are other things to show you in our village."

Next they came to the noiseless waterfall where the drinking water came from. Valger was very impressed at the noiseless waterfall. Nearby there was the statue of the dwarf with the small dog in his hands.

"Who is this man?"

"I know a little bit of the story about the man in the statue," said Tovic. "I can share with you that secret, but please do not reveal it to anyone. It seems that this dwarf was one of the wise people of this village with his smart little dog. Then something mysterious happened many years ago and left him like this. The statue you see was not carved by any sculptor. He was turned into a statue alive. But someday he will be a normal person again."

Valger was in shock hearing such story.

Then said Tovic to Valger, "The village of Black Cloud is a nice place even though it seems sinister and depressing sometimes. But it has its charms that you will soon get used to."

As they walked around, Valger noticed that there were some houses with burning candles inside. This was not so strange. What was strange was when they entered inside the small temple and saw five lit candles in different colours floating in the air.

Valger was astonished and asked, "Why are all these strange things happening?"

"It is too long a story to tell you now," Winn Blitzzer replied.

As they were talking, they had no idea that there was something behind them. When they turned to leave the small temple, they found themselves face to face with three empty T-shirts floating before their eyes in the air, one red, one green and one yellow. They seemed to be two adults and a young boy. The unexpected apparition gave him such a fright, Valger fell to the ground on his knees to the ground and almost passed out. Winn Blitzzer and Tovic, carried him by the arms and pulled him across the floor to hide behind some big cabinets nearby.

From the hideout, they watched the three empty T-shirts blow out the five candles and then leave. They crept out of their hiding spot and went to look through the holes in the windows, watching the empty shirts float away and disappear from view.

Valger said agitated, "Let's go back home. I've seen enough already. There are too many mysteries here."

"You are right," said Winn Blitzzer. "But I advise you not to be afraid of the strange things you might still see around here. They will never harm you or anyone."

Before they went their separate ways, Tovic said to Winn Blitzzer, "I would like to apologise to you for what had happened. I did not refuse to open the door when you knocked. I was almost frozen by a very strange icy cold air that covered my entire body after running away from the invisible net. Later, I saw the special whistle you had left outside the door. I felt so bad."

"Don't worry about it," Winn Blitzzer said to him, "I had the same experience. I was almost frozen too, but lucky for me after entering my house, where it's always warmer inside, I recovered very quickly."

"Thank you for understanding," said Tovic to Winn Blitzzer, handing him the small whistle back. Winn Blitzzer took it and put it in his pocket.

Then Tovic said, "If I remember well, when you knocked on my door I heard you saying that you wanted to tell me something about a special trip you were going on. Is that true?"

"Yes, is true," Winn Blitzzer replied and said, "but if you will excuse me I cannot talk about it now. Aunt Moxum has forbidden me to speak about it. She is still working on it."

"I understand that," said Tovic. "Maybe your cousin Valger could accompany you, so you won't have to go alone."

"Maybe," Winn Blitzzer replied

"To go where?" Valger asked.

"You will know in time," Winn Blitzzer said to him. "It is Aunt Moxum who will decide everything. I cannot say anything more about it."

Then they said goodbye to Tovic and headed home. The little party in Valger's honour was already finished when they arrived. They did not know that Moxum and Eris had been talking about the planned trip.

Moxum said to her sister Eris, "The arrival of your son Valger here today was a blessing. Winn Blitzzer will have someone to travel with to London on planet Earth rather than going there alone."

"It is not good idea to send Valger on such a trip, not because it was too risky or because he is my son. I love my nephew Winn Blitzzer as well. But Valger has just arrived here, he is still new to us. He and Winn Blitzzer barely know each other yet, and certainly not enough to travel together on this secret mission that has been prepared for Winn Blitzzer alone. Plus, we do not know if Valger can endure high altitude or if he would suffer dizziness or if he would like to fly or not."

"Do not worry about that, I will talk with my nephew Valger. But I do know that young boys love flying high like the birds. I am sure that he will accept my proposal when he sees the transformation of the Free-XL taking shape."

"Well, we'll see," said Eris.

Just then Winn Blitzzer and Valger arrived.

Aunt Moxum asked Valger, "Are you enjoying your new life here?"

"Yes, of course. I have finally met my mother, and my new cousin and the other people of the village. I didn't know I could have a nice family like this. But I did see quite a few strange things in this village here already. It is definitely not as boring as I thought before."

"Good! I am glad you like it," said Aunt Moxum. "What do you like most?"

"I like everything," Valger replied. "I do not feel strange here, my soul belongs here. So far I have discovered an invisible net, trees of honey, T-shirts floating in the air, and the noiseless waterfall. I confess that I love these mysteries."

Eris was surprised to hear her son Valger saying all these things.

"You sound like a very brave young man," Moxum said. "I would like to offer you a trip of a lifetime as a gift. What do you think?"

"I don't know," Valger replied. "To where?"

"Far away from here," Aunt Moxum replied.

"Ah!" exclaimed Valger. "I see, the trip Winn Blitzzer mentioned. What will you offer me if I agree to go on this trip with him?"

"Oh!" said Aunt Moxum, "Well I don't really know what I can offer you. Let me think about it. I will give you my answer later, but if you have any wishes please tell me."

"Yes, I have a wish," Valger replied, "I would like to see my father. I never meet him as you might know. This is my wish, to meet him."

"Well, well, well!" said Aunt Moxum, "I will see what I can do, but you have to travel first and later we will see what I can do."

Eris looked fearfully at her son and Moxum glared at Eris. Valger noticed this. He asked, "The trip will be safe?"

"Yes, of course," she replied, "your unexpected arrival here in the village is a blessing for my experiment of whether the magic sleeping powder is effective. After finding you deep asleep in the woods, thanks to the powerful effects of the magic sleeping powder, I have no doubt that it will leave all Londoners deep in asleep too."

Valger was confused by this statement but only said, "If I accept your offer to travel with my cousin Winn Blitzzer, you will fulfil my request as promised?"

"I told you that we shall see," Aunt Moxum replied.

Valger did not feel encouraged by her answer. "In that case I cannot take such a risk, travelling to unknown worlds without a real answer. I know that you can do it easily, if you are sending us to another planet as you say. It should not be difficult for you. Anyway, what would we travel in? I do not see anything here that would make me believe we even can."

"Do not rush, you will see it later," said Aunt Moxum.

"Well I don't think it wise for me to travel with all this risk involved and the uncertainty I feel. Besides I have just arrived in this village. To make such a big decision is not easy for me. I'm sorry Aunt Moxum, I will not travel to the unknown world. Winn Blitzzer can travel alone. I wish him good luck."

"Fine!" said Moxum. "If this is your decision, I will respect it. But I am sure that you will change your mind when you see the object Winn Blitzzer will travel in, all transformed and ready to fly."

Chapter Twenty-Six
The Transformation of the Free-XL

Aunt Moxum grabbed a large magnetic spoon hanging on a chain tied from the ceiling and put it inside the Potsat. Out came a beautiful, well-decorated small blue box. She put it on the table. She opened it with a special key on the nail of her left index finger. A big bubble came out of the top as if to protect what was inside. She took out ten small white objects that looked like toys. Somehow they were all dry as if they had not just come out of the Potsat. Out of curiosity, Winn Blitzzer tried to touch one of them.

Aunt Moxum yelled, "Do not touch it! I'm still working. If you touch it now, it will not work!"

"Sorry, Aunt Moxum," said Winn Blitzzer, "I didn't know that you kept toys inside the Potsat as well."

"These objects are not toys, these are very special objects which will be transformed to a bigger size to transport you to planet Earth."

Aunt Eris, Valger and Winn Blitzzer looked at each other doubtfully.

"Are you joking, Aunt Moxum?" Winn Blitzzer asked her.

"I am not joking," said Aunt Moxum. "These small objects you see on the table are your vehicles to travel in."

"What?" exclaimed Winn Blitzzer, dumbfounded, "These tiny pieces of glass and plastic are my transportation? How could I fit inside? All these small objects could fit in my pockets, Aunt Moxum. I thought you were going to put special magic wings on my back, so that I'd be able fly like a bird and hopefully return here safely."

"I was right to refuse to go on this trip," said Valger. "I've never heard so much nonsense in my life."

"Shut up both of you!" Aunt Moxum said loudly. "Let me finish explaining. You seem to not appreciate the amazing things that you saw happen in the Potsat. Winn Blitzzer, what you are suggesting is the stupidest thing I have ever heard you say. How can I put wings on your back to send you to another planet? You do not have the same anatomy as those birds. Let's suppose that I could put wings on your back as you suggest, how would you be able to bring the great clock here? The great clock with its bells inside weighing tonnes."

Winn Blitzzer did not have an answer for Aunt Moxum's questions. He felt embarrassed. Valger was looking at him mockingly.

Then Aunt Moxum said to Winn Blitzzer, "You must believe in yourself completely to achieve this successfully."

Winn Blitzzer listened quietly; he didn't say anything else.

Then Aunt Moxum took all the small objects on the table and put them inside a red cloth and said to Winn Blitzzer, "Follow me out in the garden. I am going to transform these objects there before your eyes. If I do it here they won't fit inside this house."

In front of the house, Aunt Moxum put the red cloth with the tiny objects on the ground. Then she waved her short magic golden wand and blew air over them. Like a magic trick, the small objects began to move one by one as though some invisible hands were reassembling them together part by part. Slowly, the tiny objects took the shape of an egg with four legs and began to inflate like a balloon. When it was done, standing before them was a big and sleek white machine with glass on the front door, two noiseless turbine engines in the back and two short wings with a span of just one metre on each side up. The nose had a single powerful light. Eris with her son Valger and nephew watched the transformation in disbelief.

"This object is called the Free-XL," Aunt Moxum told them. "It was invented by our genius ancestors. With this object you can travel unnoticed from here to planet Earth and return safely without being seen by any guardians in the galaxy or any humans on planet Earth."

"Thank you, Aunt Moxum," said Winn Blitzzer, "it's amazing. I am no longer afraid of this trip. How beautiful this Free-XL is. I still cannot wrap my mind around the fact that the tiny objects I saw a moment ago are now this great, beautiful machine. All this still seems like a dream to me.

I'm sorry Aunt Moxum, I shouldn't have doubted your knowledge before. All these things are still new and strange to me, although after seeing all the wonderful and unthinkable things the Potsat has done, I should be used to it by now."

"I understand that," said Aunt Moxum to Winn Blitzzer, "But why don't you just believe everything I tell you. As I have already said, seeing is not always believing."

"You are right Aunt Moxum," said Winn Blitzzer, "I should have accepted everything you are telling me and what I witnessed in the Potsat. From now on I won't doubt anything you say."

"I hope so," said Aunt Moxum.

Winn Blitzzer went to touch the Free-XL.

"Go inside to test it and learn how to drive it," said Aunt Moxum. "It is yours."

As Winn Blitzzer was about to open the door to go inside the Free-XL, Valger said, "I change my mind, Aunt Moxum. I would like to be part of this trip too."

"You are very welcome to, my dear nephew Valger," said Aunt Moxum, "I already told you that you will change your mind after seeing the Free-XL. Go inside the vehicle too and test it."

Winn Blitzzer and Valger sat in the soft white seats inside the Free-XL, looking at the cockpit and the radar with three buttons green, red and yellow, and the yoke to drive it. Aunt Moxum explained to them how easy it was to fly, the green button to take off and land, yellow to control the speed, and red to stay stopped in the air. The yoke was of course to control the altitude. But in reality Aunt Moxum herself would control the flight route from the Potsat for their safety. Then they tested the engine. The turbine began turning noiselessly; only by the red light on the cabin could they see that it was running. Winn Blitzzer and Valger looked very excited.

Valger asked Aunt Moxum, "Are we leaving now?"

"Not now, at one o'clock in the morning," said Aunt Moxum, "You need to get some sleep first and then we will come and wake you to come to get dressed. Now do not ask me anymore useless questions."

As they were climbing out of the Free-XL, the trees in the forest suddenly began swaying without any strong winds, as if they were dancing and shaking themselves. The noise of the trees was so strong that they could be heard miles away. Winn Blitzzer and Valger tried to run towards the house.

Eris said to them in a whisper, "Do not be afraid, it is a good sign. It is the invisibles guards, making the trees move as a sign of joy for their approval of your secret trip to London. Their return to normal people depends on your success."

After hearing that, Valger asked, "So is my father an invisible watcher? Is that why I couldn't see him here today?"

"We will have time to talk about all these things on your return," his mother told him.

The trees stopped moving in the forest, when suddenly they saw another strange surprise. Although it was daylight, still around five o'clock, a large star flashed in the sky, changing colours from blue to red to white. People across the planet Oxon were afraid at the sight of it and locked themselves in their houses, until the strange phenomenon disappeared, as many Oxonians considered this an omen. But for ladies Esra and Dallas, this sign was good news; they knew that according to the prophecy, it meant their husbands would return soon after Winn Blitzzer's secret mission. But their children Tovic and Yalta were as scared as the other Oxonians at the flashing star in the sky. Their mothers reassured them.

Back inside the house Aunt Moxum said to Winn Blitzzer and Valger, "It is time now for you to go to bed, a long trip is ahead of you. But first, before you go to bed, you need to shower with the waters of the Potsat to sleep fast and deep."

Winn Blitzzer and Valger did this and went to sleep on the twin beds upstairs. For Valger it had been a very special day, discovering his family and so many incredible things after just arriving at the mysterious village of Black Cloud. While they were sleeping, Moxum and her sister Eris continued working, mixing and testing formulas inside the Potsat for the success of their secret trip to London.

Chapter Twenty-Seven
One Day Away from the New Year

Life continued normally in London on the second to last day of the year. People were very happy and there was a joyful and festive mood in the air throughout the city. They were just one day away from celebrating the New Year. That night the inhabitants of the London would go to sleep looking forward to the festivities of the next day without bad thoughts or worries on their minds that anything so strange and mysterious could happen to their magnificent beautiful city.

For centuries Big Ben was the central celebrity on stage every last night of the year, with millions of people gathered in London to celebrate the arrival of the New Year. People would gather on the many bridges along the River Thames and along the riverbanks to see the fireworks after hearing the bells of Big Ben welcoming the New Year. But the epicentre of the celebration was in front of the Palace of Westminster. The House of Parliament alongside the clock tower also had a magnificent view from which to watch the hands of the great clock and hear Big Ben's bells as it turned midnight.

The crowd of people over the Westminster Bridge stretched until St Thomas Hospital on the other side of the River Thames. It was massive with Londoners mixed with thousands of tourists who came from all around the world to celebrate the New Year in London. A fee had even been imposed to stand in that area to reduce the crowds. But it had little effect. People were still coming in the thousands to be near Big Ben during the celebrations, no matter the weather.

Scotland Yard would close the entire area off to allow people to walk around freely and avoid accidents. The crowds of people covered all of the Westminster area up to Trafalgar Square, even reaching Piccadilly Circus, making it almost impossible to approach the tower that night. People would get there extremely early to claim a spot with a good view. Some more adventurous ones would camp out inside sleeping bags in street. Others were happy to stay at Trafalgar Square; from there they could see the great clock in the background and hear the great bells of Big Ben just a short distance away. Other people were happy to celebrate the event just by hearing the sound of bells from a distance, followed by the fireworks and music.

Not a single Londoner walking in street going about their business, nor any tourists who was taking pictures, videos and selfies with Big Ben that day before the last day of the year, imagined in those moments that the crows they were seeing around the four faces of the clock were anything more than normal, innocent birds. They were in fact fake crows in disguise, from a mysterious planet far away with a mysterious secret mission. The birds they saw during the day seemed to like biting something around the clock tower. In fact they had almost already cut out the clock with their magical beaks. The tourists had no idea that the pictures, videos and selfies they were taking would be the latest images ever taken of the most famous clock.

The birds, with their privilege of flight, were the only animals who could easily get to the top of the clock tower whenever they wished. Many birds did so every day. The birds and the wind were the only silent friends of the great clock visited it every day reaching its height in the sky since it began ticking in 1859. The birds were scared away every time Big Ben's bells would ring, always when they least expected. Each time they would fly off in a rush leaving the great clock behind them, only to come back when the noise of the bells ceased. But then only to panic again when the bells struck fifteen minutes later. This playful game was like an endless dance every day for the birds. For centuries the birds tried to resist panicking at the sounds of the clock bells. But they never could. Every time they were sent into a panic at the sound, as if it was their first time hearing it.

By contrast the silent agreement between the great clock with the wind was simple. The winds wiped away condensation from the four glass faces of the clock with its smooth cool breezes. It cleaned away the bad odours of pollution from the cars, motorcycles, airplanes, ships, and industrial smoke. Nobody would ever know the silent agreement between the clock and the wind. If there was a change in the air and the winds that day, no one in London had noticed.

Still, the great clock was officially cleaned once every six years from the abseiling cleaners who climbed on it for weeks, working sixty metres up in the air to clean its wafer-thin glass panels. The glass panels over the clock were becoming terribly thin and fragile, because the dials were originally lit by gas. Birds could even fly into them and break them. So the window cleaners had to be extremely careful. The clock dials in the iron frame were massive, measuring twenty-three feet in diameter. One face of the clock was cleaned each day from Monday to Thursday. Usually the cleaning would also give the technicians a chance to carry out any essential maintenance. Some of the glass pieces could be removed for an inspection of the hands. Whenever Big Ben's bells were out of action, Great Tom from St Paul's Cathedral did the honours, ringing its bells every hour for the people of London.

Big Ben had looked down upon London with its four faces day and night for centuries, reflected over the same water of the River Thames, the only mirror in which the clock tower could see itself in its various forms, day and night, in every season. There was no one in the world who did not know the name Big Ben. No celebrity could ever rival Big Ben in fame, whether movie stars, musicians, writers, politician, artists, doctors or scientists, its legacy worldwide was extraordinary and unbeatable.

The number of images of Big Ben were countless. There wasn't a computer that could calculate the amount of pictures taken of the clock every day since its inauguration. From paintings and photos to the massive production of post cards, from films to television, not to mention the billions of gadgets and souvenirs in Big Ben's image, paper weights, jars, mugs, shirts, hats, pens, rugs, diaries, calendars, key chains, clocks and all kinds of memorabilia, the great clock has been forever immortalised.

Thousands of tourists were coming to London every day to visit Big Ben with the same attraction and excitement others had for centuries, silently welcomed by the clock, who seemed to greet each person who visited. Many believed Big Ben belonged to them and perhaps saw it as an old friend.

Many countries tried to emulate Big Ben's success by building their own clock towers in its Neo-gothic Revival style. But the great clock still holds the title of the World's Largest Four-Faced Chiming Clock. And even though it is no longer the biggest clock, nor has any longer the biggest bells, it is still the most famous. All these factors made Big Ben a worldwide icon.

Back in the mysterious village of Black Cloud on planet Oxon, Moxum continued to be unconcerned about the impact on the people of London the disappearance of the clock would have. The Elizabeth Tower without its great clock above would be reduced almost in half with an empty space in the skyline and a distortion in the beauty of the historical architecture around the Palace of Westminster. But Moxum was thinking only about carrying out her plan.

She said to her sister Eris, "I am sure that they will build a new clock like they built this one."

She was prepared, and tested many magical formulas from the mystical sciences to send her nephews Winn Blitzzer and Valger on the secret mission that night. From her Potsat she continued watching her fake birds working hard at cutting and drilling and hitting their small sharp beaks deep inside the tower. She was very happy with their work; they had followed all the instructions and guidelines she had given them.

Around one o'clock in the morning on planet Earth, the birds finished their task with success. While waiting for the arrival of Winn Blitzzer, the only thing that remained to be done was to build the net as Ms Moxum had commanded. A group of birds them went to cut off the ropes on the ships around the Westminster Pier and build a net with the same great skills they use to build their own nests. Ten birds held five lines of ropes with their beaks, while the other ten birds flew with the ropes in their beaks and weaved them inside over and under until net was complete. Then Ar took three other birds with him and went to cut off the flag flying on the top of the Queen Victoria Tower at the House of Parliament and put it inside the net to protect the great clock within. Then they tied it off with a knot and went back to other tasks inside the tower. Below them a ship was floating away along the River Thames, without its ropes to secure it.

At that time, the two officers Peter Bank and Mark Bing inside the Palace of Westminster taking a break in their guardroom, a narrow space near the Parliament entrance where they had a small bunk bed, three chairs and one table with papers and pens. Two thermoses of coffee and tea with cups and teaspoons were also on the table. A red-coloured phone hung on the wall alongside a new calendar with Big Ben's picture on the cover, opened to New Year's Day. They were drinking coffee to stay awake during the night. Sometimes they used to sleep in shifts. For some reason they did not go outside again that night. They stayed inside their small room and both fell asleep.

Chapter Twenty-Eight
Trip to London to Steal Big Ben

Midnight struck in London. It was New Year's Eve on planet Earth, the last day of the year. It was one o'clock in the morning on planet Oxon in Black Cloud. Eris woke her nephew Winn Blitzzer and her son Valger to prepare for their secret trip to London.

They washed their faces and came downstairs. They saw their Aunt Moxum dressed in long black dress with bright little pointed stars on it and a black crown on her head with a three long points on top. In her left hand she held a long stick with a crystal ball on top and a brightly glowing light inside.

"Good morning, Winn Blitzzer and Valger. I hope you have slept well before your trip."

"Good morning Aunt. Yes, we slept well. Valger and I are ready."

"Good!" said Aunt Moxum, "Everything is ready and waiting for you to leave soon."

After taking some special food that would prevent them from becoming tired or afraid on the trip, they noticed some small items like toys on the table: two small pairs of black boots, two small white helmets, two small flight suits in khaki and blue colours and two small pairs of brown gloves.

Aunt Moxum said to them, "Dear nephews, these objects are your flight outfits and equipment."

Winn Blitzzer and Valger looked at each other without saying anything. Then Moxum took her magic golden wand from her dress pocket and said to her sister Eris, "Help me dress the boys, just follow what I do."

She handed her another wand and put her own on the small flight suit. When she lifted the wand, the suit stayed attached as though by a magnet. She put it against Winn Blitzzer's body. The small khaki flight suit became a larger size that fit him exactly with a long zipper from the waist to neck and nice ornamental wings and sleeves on his shoulders like a real officer. He could not believe it was him when he saw himself wearing that flight suit. Eris did the same to her son with the blue one; the boys looked happy. It all seemed like a game to them, with any real danger far from their minds.

They did the same with the small boots, gloves and helmets.

Aunt Moxum said to them, "With these special helmets that have a technology called 3-D Display Systems, you will be able to see many things from a distance and of course have a nice view of London as well."

Winn Blitzzer tried the helmet on his head, seeing everything in 3-D inside their house. He looked quite smart in the flight suit.

Aunt Moxum said, "The first test had been done well, now the second part is coming."

She packed other small toy-like items inside the small box that Winn Blitzzer would carry with him. Among these items were small Pyramid-shaped crystals with a magnet field, two small round glass bracelets and a magical golden wand in the shape of a small broom.

Aunt Moxum said, "I won't transform these small items here because they'll become too big. You will do that in London with the small magic broom I have lent you. Here are the instructions for you to read during the trip."

Winn Blitzzer took the paper and put it in his pocket.

Finally, from inside the special little box Aunt Moxum took three rings with precious blue sapphires. She gave one to Winn Blitzzer and the other one to Valger. She herself was wearing a ring with a brown-coloured stone gem. Then they put the three rings together gently, as though making a toast with wine glasses. A small light appeared inside the rings like blue and brown fire. Winn Blitzzer and Valger were amazed.

Aunt Moxum said to Winn Blitzzer, "With these special rings with mystical fire shining inside, you will be able to handle my magic broom to perform your duties."

"Thank you, Aunt Moxum for trusting me with this," Winn Blitzzer said while rubbing the special ring and looking at the mystical fire alight inside.

Then Aunt Moxum said to Valger, "I am glad for your final decision to take part in this secret mission. I knew you would. For this reason I am making you the pilot of the Free-XL. Please take your wings, captain."

Valger smiled as she placed his wings on his shoulder.

Finally Eris picked up the special box.

"Boys," said Aunt Moxum, "it is time now to accompany you to the Free-XL for your trip."

She lit a torch and placed it in the front yard of the house. Then she took the small bottle of magic sleeping powder. They walked out together, Aunt Moxum ahead, then Winn Blitzzer and Valger, and Eris following them carrying the small box with special items inside. Outside was pitch black. But the big stars with six points that had appeared in the sky that afternoon were still flashing on and off in the sky.

The Free-XL was before them, standing on its four legs. Winn Blitzzer opened the door. Aunt Eris left the box of mystical items inside the Free-XL while Aunt Moxum placed the jar of sleeping powder in the special compartment just below the seat where there was the small hole from which the powder would spill out.

Before they stepped inside the Free-XL, Aunt Moxum handed Winn Blitzzer her magic golden wand in the shape of a small broom, saying, "Dear nephew Winn Blitzzer, I hand you this magic golden wand with all its mystical power, its legacy, an inheritance from our ancestors that it may bring you success on this special and secret mission to the city of London on planet earth, that you will leave and return safely and unseen. So be it."

Winn Blitzzer took the magic broom from Aunt Moxum in both hands. He bowed to his aunts. Then the four of them hugged each other. Aunt Moxum and Eris wished them a good trip and good luck.

"The birds are there waiting for you to take Big Ben away. And we are waiting for your return."

Winn Blitzzer and Valger sat down inside the Free-XL, the lights of the cockpit and radar shining on their faces. Valger tested the yoke with his hands.

Aunt Moxum asked Winn Blitzzer, "Do you feel alright?"

"Yes, Aunt Moxum," replied Winn Blitzzer.

"You don't look very happy," said Aunt Eris kindly. "Is something wrong?"

Winn Blitzzer looked at his aunts without answering. Then he said, "Yes something saddens me a little."

"What is it?" Aunt Moxum asked him. "You cannot travel to the planet Earth if you are not feeling confident."

Winn Blitzzer said, "Do not worry my dear aunts, I am fine. I can travel. I am happy to do it. The only thing that is saddening me, and of course my cousin Valger as well, is that you have forbidden us to bring anything else back, apart from the clock, and to not touch the ground. You see, we will go so far away to a new planet and a new world without bringing a single thing for ourselves or friends, or at least feeling the ground of London beneath out feet."

Moxum and Eris looked each other.

Aunt Moxum said, "I forbade you and Valger to touch the ground of the planet Earth because your mission could fail. But to make you happy, I shall allow you to bring a few small objects back with you, nothing heavy. But you must send Ar to go and take them for you. But I don't want you to take any objects for free without paying for them."

She took something from her hair and handed it to Winn Blitzzer. "I give you this blue diamond of the galaxy to send with Ar to leave in the shop as a payment for your chosen items. The magic broom has a pen inside with which you will write an apology note to the owner of the shop for shopping there during closed hours."

Winn Blitzzer and Valger smiled and said, "Thank you very much, Aunt Moxum."

Then Aunt Moxum and Eris came to hug them one last time. They closed the door of the Free-XL and turned its engine on. At two o'clock in the morning, the Free-XL took off vertically from the ground and flew higher and higher into the sky in the dark night as everyone on the planet Oxon slept.

The Free-XL flew at top speed noiselessly, quickly leaving the planet Oxon behind and entering another the galaxy in half an hour. Winn Blitzzer and Valger were excited and curious to visit another world. They knew that Aunt Moxum and Eris were watching them in the Potsat screen and controlling their flight route. Everything was going well. Winn Blitzzer and Valger noticed many different stars appearing in the galaxies. There were shooting stars like balls of fire, moving up and down, flashing and flying about. They did not feel scared, on the contrary it was one of the most beautiful sights they had ever seen. They were talking along the way about the knowledge that they were making history, being the first people of Oxon to travel outside their planet and no one would ever know. Their story would be forever hidden from other Oxonians. Soon they began crossing the hostile area of the planets Aixias, Orion Minor, Orion Larger, Neskher and Zexpher without being seen by the guardian of the sky there. That crossing made them more confident for the success ahead. Moxum and Eris at home felt the same.

While Valger was keeping control of the Free-XL, Winn Blitzzer took the opportunity to read the instructions for the mystical items. He was amazed to learn the incredible things those mystical items could do. It was not long before they began seeing artificial lights appearing in the sky. Winn Blitzzer and Valger realised that the planet Earth was close. The lights they saw were satellites from NASA, ESA, Russian and Asian satellites. The Free-XL switched on the powerful light installed on its nose automatically to neutralise all the satellites, rendering them useless. All the people below working to keep track of the satellites fell asleep. They were the first victims of the mission. They could not be allowed to record anything in space at that time. The Free-XL passed every satellite undetected.

The Free-XL began shaking and crashing as though hitting bumps, signalling that the Earth's atmosphere was changing. The two boys began screaming and clutched their seats as the Free-XL quickly lost altitude. A few seconds later it entered inside a very thick white layer of clouds. Winn Blitzzer and Valger felt scared seeing the clouds in the glass window. They could feel the change in atmosphere and temperature in their bodies. Far away at the mysterious village of Black Cloud, Ms Moxum noticed the change in atmosphere too. She knew this was the sign that the Free-XL was approaching the mysterious secret passage over the North Pole into the lower layer of the atmosphere that would lead them south directly towards London.

After the being jolted back and forth inside the Free-XL and passing through the low clouds caused by the winter of the Northern hemisphere, small lights began to appear in their view again; it was Scandinavia. But they did not know this. Winn Blitzzer and Valger smiled with joy, thinking they had finally arrived at their final destination. But the Free-XL didn't slow down; it continued flying south as Ms Moxum had planned, still descending. They knew they could not be far.

Chapter Twenty-Nine
Arrival in London

It was just a few minutes after three o'clock in the morning. Many tiny lights came into view and the Free-XL began to slow down automatically. Winn Blitzzer and Valger smiled. Winn Blitzzer cleaned off the window to see the city better, more and more lights appeared in.

He said to Valger in whisper, "I am sure that this is the great city of London."

But at that high an altitude they could not distinguish the exact point where the clock tower was. The Free-XL continued flying at three miles altitude above the city. Then suddenly it stopped mid-air. The magnet radar had captured the central point of London. It shined a powerful light below onto the left forefoot of the statue of a horse ridden by King Charles I. It was the centre from which all measurements of distances from London were taken. It was marked with a bronze plaque "Number 11860" on the ground. Written on it was the inscription: *City of Westminster. On the site now occupied by the statue of King Charles I was erected the original Queen Eleanor's Cross replica of which stands in front of Charing Cross Station. Mileages from London are measured from the site of the original cross.*

The Free-XL was still hovering in the air. Then it began spinning and turning, in a spiralling motion. Luckily Winn Blitzzer and Valger did not get dizzy. Then the small window opened below and the small green bottle poured out the first dose of the powerful sleeping powder. Slowly, the green powder began to go fall over the city like snow, putting people into a wakeless sleep. The power of electricity was also decreased across the city by its powerful effects to prevent the CCTV from recording anything. Winn Blitzzer and Valger looked down at the green powder falling over London, entering into every house through the windows and doors, chimneys and every small hole so that it would make every living being in the city fall fast asleep. Only Ms Moxum's birds around the clock tower stayed awake, as they were immune to the powder's effects.

More and more strong doses of the powerful powder fell on the Westminster area where the secret mission was about to take place. It was early Saturday morning. Young people were heading home from a night out, all of them falling asleep where they stood or walked, some standing like statues in the middle of the pavement, others asleep sitting at the bus stops. The policemen who were supposed to be on duty also fell asleep standing strangely in front of the Palace of Westminster, even the Queen's guard at Buckingham Palace and the police officer at the gate of number 10 Downing Street and MoD, all of them were victims of the powerful effect of the powder. It covered every single nook and cranny of London like an invisible blanket of cobwebs, sealed off and tightly shut to keep the powerful effect strong so that it would not wear off too soon. When Winn Blitzzer and Valger saw the streetlights reducing their intensity, they were sure that the magic sleeping powder was working very well indeed.

After the Free-XL stopped spinning in the sky above London, it went lower as though pulled like a magnet, the vehicle being guided south-east until they arrived in the area of the Prime Meridian at the Royal Observatory in Greenwich. The Free-XL turned twice above the dome of the observatory, commissioned in 1675 by King Charles II. On the right side, they saw the impressive skyline of Canary Warf and the royal gardens below them. There wasn't a sign of life at that time in Greenwich. Winn Blitzzer took off the special helmet to see the image of the city with his own eyes.

"I'll keep mine on," said Valger.

The Free-XL flew at low speed over the Queen's house and continued to the former Greenwich Hospital. From there, the Free-XL lowered about five metres above the River Thames to fly upstream towards the centre of London. On the left below they could see the famous Cutty Sark ship and two small Domes in red dark on both side of the River Thames. This was the Greenwich foot tunnel crosses beneath the River Thames from Cutty Sark Gardens to Island Gardens. They followed the course of the River Thames further towards central London, seeing beautiful landscapes of houses and apartments and other impressive buildings on both sides of the riverbank. They passed the O2 Arena, the former Millennium Dome, with its unusual roof structure that looked to them like a giant cobweb roof.

To their left and right each new view was different and strange to them. They didn't know where to look first to see all the amazing things in this strange world. Their eyes did not get tired of seeing it all. Their second biggest impression of London came when they arrived in front of the famous Tower Bridge, with the Shard, the skyscraper with pyramid-shaped glass a few metres away on the left. Everything went so fast. Their minds were full of thoughts after seeing so many amazing things in so short a time on their way to meet with the birds.

Winn Blitzzer was very, very impressed and said to Valger, "What a wonderful bridge and tall buildings. Everything in this city is amazing, and we haven't even seen the great clock tower of Big Ben yet. I am sure that there are more surprises still ahead. If King Brelys-1000 could borrow my eyes to see the wonderful things I see right here and now he would be the happiest man in the universe, as I am now. Who knows, maybe it would have driven him mad."

Valger flew the Free-XL slowly between the two towers of the Tower Bridge. Just as they looked at the road below on the bridge, they saw the face of a human for the very first time. One man and two women were standing on top of the bridge, sleeping under by the effects of the powder. They saw two cars stopped nearby as well, another small ship and the biggest ship there called the HMS Belfast. Not one single soul was awake across the city. Everything was at a standstill. There was not any doubt that the magic sleeping powder worked. Winn Blitzzer and Valger felt like the kings of London.

After the Free-XL crossed the Tower Bridge, it passed over other famous bridges along the River Thames. Among them were London Bridge, Cannon Street Railways Bridge, Southwark Bridge, Millennium Bridge, Blackfriars Railway Bridge and Blackfriars Bridge. From there the Free-XL flew high again towards St Paul's Cathedral and turned twice around the dome, continuing past the Bank of England and other impressive buildings and skyscrapers towards Oxford Street. It flew low, just eight metres above the road, to see London better without any fear of anything seeing them.

Then the Free-XL stopped in mid-air again at the crossroads of Oxford Street as if deciding which way to go. It took the direction towards Regent Street to Piccadilly Circus. Winn Blitzzer and Valger enjoyed the curious displays of stores with decorated windows filled with clothes and dolls dressed in the winter fashion. The streets were well decorated with Christmas lights and trees still, although none were shining now.

When the Free-XL arrived at Piccadilly Circus, they saw giant screens on the buildings. All of these things seemed to them like big toys. The giant screens stretched to three hundred and fifty square feet until the corner of the street. On the left side was a nice building with lovely entrance called the London Pavilion on Coventry Street. The Free-XL moved to the right side and approached a fountain made in bronze opposite buildings with names like Criterion Theatre, Criterion Restaurant and Trocadero Centre. Winn Blitzzer saw the fountain of Eros's statue nearby with a small winged man on top, standing on one foot with a bow in his hand. Even though he was a man he had a young boy's face.

Winn Blitzzer said, "I don't think this bow is for violence but instead to distribute love and friendship. I love this statue. I wish it was alive."

Valger said to him, "How do you know that this bow was to create love? Maybe that bow could destroy our Free-XL by being so close. Let's move away from here."

"Don't say that. This statue looks friendly and harmless to me."

"I do not trust anything here. We are in a strange land and must be careful Winn Blitzzer. You seem to forget that we are not from here. It's a good thing you cannot open the window of the Free-XL to touch this statue. What if you touched it and something happened to us or perhaps it came alive? We came here on a mission, not to fall in love with this city. We are almost criminals by coming here to steal the great clock when it belongs to the people of this city."

Winn Blitzzer said to Valger, "I am just curious, don't be so pessimistic."

Then Winn Blitzzer noticed young people sitting below the steps of the Eros fountain, like another statue. Some of them were holding hands. Others were kissing. Others had one foot forward as they had fallen asleep while walking. But everything was still.

He said to Valger, "Look down. All of these young people sitting asleep, they are the victims of the powder."

This ensured them again, that they were alone awake in that city.

Free-XL left the Eros Fountain, flying very slowly just around the corner before taking the road to Hyde Market. Winn Blitzer saw another water fountain below with four horses, their legs up as though they were about to jump out of the fountain and run away. These were the Horses of Helios. They were beautiful and made of bronze.

"Look at these beautiful bronze statue horses."

"Sorry I cannot look everywhere while driving the Free-XL at the same time. I need to be very careful we don't fall to the ground here. But I appreciate that this London is more beautiful than even the capital city of our kingdom."

The Free-XL continued flying slowly over Hyde Market with splendid buildings on both sides, the Theatre Royal and Her Majesty's Theatre. The cinema complex and the New Zealand House were on the right side of the Pall Mall East with the statue of King George III and on the left was Waterloo place. Then as they flew towards Trafalgar Square Canada House on the right side and the National Gallery on the left.

The Free-XL was hovering in air in the middle of the square between the National Gallery and Trafalgar Square. And then Winn Blitzzer saw Big Ben. It was shining a short distance in background.

"Look, there it is."

"Yes, it is so beautiful," Valger replied. "Look on my left there, a large tree with many tiny lights."

Right below it were two fountains with mermaid and dolphin statues. When they were in Trafalgar Square, Winn Blitzzer and Valger had no idea that one of the birds sent by their aunt, Ser, was on top of Admiral Nelson's statue on the Column. They left Trafalgar Square behind passing near the statue of King Charles I again and going towards Whitehall to take the great clock. Winn Blitzzer's heart was full of joy. They passed many more statues, one of Prince George, Duke of Cambridge, one of Spencer Cavendish, 8th Duke of Devonshire and the statue of Earl Haig. Then the monument of the Women of World War II and nearby the Cenotaph, the war memorial of World War I. On the left was a large building, the Ministry of Defence, with statues of Viscount Slim, Viscount Alanbrooke and Viscount Monty of Alamein standing with pride and dignity. Winn Blitzzer imagined these men must have been very important people in this country, if they enjoyed the high honour of having statues being erected there.

Finally, the Free-XL arrived at Parliament Square. Below were many more statues of important statesmen and notable individuals. In front there was the great clock tower with four faces looking out. Winn Blitzzer and Valger felt a bit intimidated, knowing the actions they were about to commit.

When the birds saw the Free-XL arrive, they knew straightaway that it was Winn Blitzzer. All of them came to circle the Free-XL, wishing him a very warm welcome to London and cawing as though saying to him, "We have done our duties; it is your turn now."

The birds were surprised to see a strange face they did not know. Valger tried to greet the birds from the window of the Free-XL by smiling to them, but the birds ignored him. He looked disgruntled.

The Free-XL stopped, hovering in the air near the top of the clock tower.

Winn Blitzzer said to Valger, "Our time here is just thirty minutes and thirty seconds so we must do everything fast. I hope you will manoeuvre the Free-XL well. My life and fate is in your hands. If I fall down I won't be able to return to our planet with you. I may even die if I fall from this height, or if I am lucky I will surely break every bone in my body."

"Do not worry Winn Blitzzer, everything will be alright, trust me," said Valger holding the yoke of the Free-XL in his hands.

Winn Blitzzer took the magic golden wand his Aunt Moxum had lent to him reassembled all the mystical objects he would need. He looked in his special mystical ring Aunt Moxum had given him. The blue fire was still alight inside. He looked around seeing the many beautiful buildings and the river below. Then he opened the door of the Free-XL, which extended into a kind of small bridge with a small chains and ropes on both sides for protection. Suddenly a cool breeze and with the smell of London blew past, wrapping around his body as though hugging him. He coughed bit. The birds were already lined up along the sides of the small bridge of the Free-XL cawing and shrieking like they were cheering him on.

Valger drove the Free-XL to the top of the clock tower where there was an object like a golden cross. Winn Blitzzer took the small blue box with all the mysterious items inside and walked out of Free-XL and across the bridge slowly. From a short distance away he saw a big wheel, London Eye, standing still at that moment. And below the Westminster Bridge, to the left the Hungerford Bridge with ships tied at Westminster Pier below, and at the far end of the Westminster Bridge St Thomas Hospital. The silence in the city was immense. The only sounds he could hear were the birds and the breeze. The water of the River Thames continued to flow quietly, the magic powder had not ceased it.

Then his secret mission began. Winn Blitzzer placed the crystal pyramid with the magnet atop the golden cross. The small crystal pyramid held well. Then he held the magic golden wand over the small crystal pyramid. Suddenly the small crystal pyramid began melting as if it were a heavy glass liquid, covering the clock tower inside from top bottom. It was like a big Boa snake swallowing an animal whole. Winn Blitzzer and Valger could not believe their eyes. The small crystal pyramid they underestimated at first sight, was doing its job very well.

Winn Blitzzer said, "Aunt Moxum was right. What a magnificent idea to keep this amazing great clock well wrapped inside this amazing crystal."

The liquid crystal was almost swallowing Big Ben entirely inside, only a small space was still left open underneath. Winn Blitzzer swept the magic golden wand over the great clock. The top part of the tower moved slowly upward, around half a metre high, separating from the main clock tower.

He lifted the magic golden wand and then suddenly he was holding the clock with one hand as though it were weightless. If he had not experienced it himself he would not have believed it. At the same time, the mysterious crystal pyramid created an illusion, reducing the real size of the clock inside the glass. It now resembled a figurine of the tower inside a large snow globe.

Valger was amazed seeing his cousin holding Big Ben with one hand. His hands shook a bit on the yoke and the Free-XL started to lean slightly. Winn Blitzzer lost his balance, his right foot slipped from the bridge, and he nearly fell to the ground, managing to grab one of the ropes. He screamed at the sight of the ground below him and shouted to Valger "What you are doing, nearly I fall down to the ground!"

"I'm so sorry!" said Valger balancing the Free-XL into a straight position.

Winn Blitzzer still managed to keep Big Ben in his hand during all of this. The Free-XL raised a few meters higher, leaving the remains of the clock tower with a gaping hole below.

Then ten birds entered inside the half tower to cut off the mechanism and the chains that linked and held the great clock together while more birds tied the rope in a knot over the button of the electrical transformer to cut off the power and prevent Winn Blitzzer from suffering any electric shocks or causing a fire. Everything was done quickly and safely. Winn Blitzzer raised the magic broom, separating Big Ben from the main tower for good.

This was the first time the clock tower with Big Ben was separated since their construction centuries ago. If the people who had built this great clock, Edmund Beckett Denison MP and Sir Benjamin Bell, could have seen Big Ben floating in the air held weightlessly in a single hand, they would not have believed what they had seen before their eyes. After all the labour required by so many people to lift Big Ben with sixteen horses and put it up in the tower, this could have been the story of all time if anyone had seen it.

While Winn Blitzzer was still holding the clock with a single hand hanging like a magnet from the magic golden wand. The birds approached him with the net. When he saw it with a large Union Jack flag inside, it gave him an idea to bring a flag with him as a gift for the king.

Ar said to Winn Blitzzer, "We have built this large net to pack the great clock inside to take it home."

"I appreciate your idea," Winn Blitzzer said to the birds, "but we won't need this large net. We will carry the great clock another way."

The birds were surprised to hear this. They were expecting thanks for having built the net with great skill.

Winn Blitzzer laid the clock inside the large net to allow the crystal liquid to swallow and seal off the great clock underneath. The twenty-five birds were holding Big Ben in the net with their small beaks, flapping their wings furiously to keep the great clock from falling into the River Thames below. When the liquid crystal began melting again slowly covering the clock underneath, Winn Blitzzer had some doubts and whispered, "*I don't think this crystal pyramid will be able to swallow this big clock entirely.*"

Suddenly, the liquid crystal stopped melting. The liquid crystal was not enough to swallow the great clock entirely; a small hole was left open in the bottom. But at that moment Winn Blitzzer did not give much importance to it.

Valger approached slowly with the Free-XL. From below, two long arms twisted out of the Free-XL, like the claws of a crab. They took Big Ben, wrapped inside the crystal, and took it right inside the Free-XL for safekeeping. The large net was left empty with the flag still inside.

Winn Blitzzer said to the birds, "Take the large net away. We do not need it anymore. Leave it hanging on the bridge down there. But bring for me the flag to take home."

The birds did all this quickly. He thanked them for their amazing work. Then he took the two small round bracelet crystals and put them on the far end of his aunt's magic golden wand and blew them into the air as if he were smoking. The two crystals blew like smoke into air. Four birds came and took them, pulling at them like rubber. Once they were long enough, they cut them with their beaks, and shaped them into a sort of solid crystal chain. Finally they hung them from the bottom of the Free-XL, having made themselves a place to hang on the Free XL as it left the Earth's atmosphere until they could change back into golden eagles again.

Everything was done. The Free-XL was almost unrecognisable with the long glass nose of the clock tower inside the crystal sticking out. In fact, it was now shaped like a fighter jet with the cabin of the Free-XL on top. Valger moved a short distance with the Free-XL over the Westminster Bridge. When they looked back, they saw the look of the Palace of Westminster had already changed without Big Ben on top. Valger flew back slowly closer towards the half tower again. Winn Blitzzer put a small glass on top of the magic golden wand and blew; the empty space of the tower was covered with a glass roof to protect the spiral stairs of the tower from being damaged. They were about to leave London in a few moments' times. This gesture seemed a small consolation for the impact the mysterious theft of Big Ben would have, but it was the best they could do.

Winn Blitzzer finally smiled. The first part of the secret mission was complete and with great success. Now he wanted to bring something for himself as a souvenir and other small gifts for his friends, even a small gift for King Brelys-1000 too. But he was scared that if he broke the rules he could be stuck for good on planet Earth. He was happy to please himself in another way.

He said to Valger, "Now it's time to look for something for ourselves to bring back home."

Valger said to him, "I don't really know what I would like, but do send the birds to bring for me a packet of sweets or biscuits. That will be enough for me."

"That's all you want after coming so far?" Winn Blitzzer asked Valger with amazement and dismay.

"Yes," said Valger, "only sweet and biscuits. I don't know what kind of things there are in this city to try."

"Well, it's your choice," said Winn Blitzzer looking at the streets around and the shops from inside the Free-XL. He saw something he liked in the window of a shop nearby.

He said to Ar, "Take nineteen birds with you, and go to this shop and take some items for us there which you will find most beautiful in the store there, please. I trust your tastes. Work together in coordination by taking small net into the shop and putting each object inside them and bring them to me as soon as possible. Our time in this city was timed, as you know." Don't forget the sweet package for my cousin Valger.

Then he pointed the magic golden wand at the display of the House of Parliament shop and followed the corner toward the shop on Parliament Street. The glass window of the shop began melting like a heavy thick liquid leaving a large hole in the shop wall.

The birds flew towards inside and began working. Ten birds were carrying the small net in their beaks while other birds were pushing the items from the shelves with their beaks and their back feathers into the small net. They did everything very quickly, and came to deliver them to Winn Blitzzer and Valger. While Winn Blitzzer was surprised by the beautiful objects that the birds chose for him "The small Big Ben towers gilded in gold, snow globes with figures of the landmark of London inside, small flags, pairs of sunglasses, pack of six shirts, teddy bears, pocket watch, luxury pens, typical London toys, postcards, and books." Look my pretty objects Valger I don't know how many there were in total I am very excited I will count them back home. But Valger did not even wait to bring his sweet at home, he opened the packet of biscuits and began eating them.

"Oh! This biscuit is very nice!" he said. "If I knew they were so nice, I could have asked for more."

Winn Blitzzer said to him, "It's too late now."

Ar said to Winn Blitzzer, "Master, everything is done. We can leave now to go back to our planet Oxon."

"Not yet Ar," Winn Blitzzer replied. "There's one last thing."

He took the piece of blue galaxy diamond his Aunt Moxum had given him to pay for the items.

The tip of the magic golden wand he brought with him became a pen and with it he wrote a note on a piece of paper in his own language.

Sir,

I apologise for shopping after closing hours. I badly needed some items inside your shop. I didn't have your currency to pay you so please take this invaluable piece of blue diamond in exchange for my intrusion on your premises. I am very sorry for any distress and offence my actions may cause you. Please, don't tell anybody about this. Thank you for your understanding,

W.B.

He put that note with the blue galaxy diamond inside the small net hanging on Ar's beak and said to him, "Go leave this small net inside the shop counter for the owner to see it tomorrow. It is a gesture of good will."

The bird flew to go leave the message in the shop and came back quickly. Then Winn Blitzzer pointed the magic golden wand again towards the window of the showroom. Immediately the glass display rose up again like water mixed with thick plastic liquid until it was intact again, without any sign of a break in. In all this excitement, none of the birds had time to think about the bird Ser who had disappeared and was still missing.

Winn Blitzzer began to feel that the mission was a success and it was time to go back to Oxon. Their time in London was over and the effect of the magic sleeping powder as well. The birds hung below the Free-XL on the long crystals next to Big Ben wrapped inside the crystal. Winn Blitzzer closed the door of the Free-XL, then Valger flew at a medium altitude downstream the way they came before. The Free-XL started moving slowly fifty metres over the bridges along the River Thames. The weakened lights of the London Eye were turning on and off very slowly. Winn Blitzzer loved the large wheels of ovoid-shaped glass on the London Eye. While passing the bridges along the River Thames, Valger was very happy and little bit distracted by everything they saw there; he knew the buildings along the River Thames he was looking at were his last view of London. He took his hand off the yoke to put his 3-D helmet on before gaining altitude. At that moment, the Free-XL was close to the famous Tower Bridge, passing between its towers. The risky manoeuvre nearly made the Free-XL crash into the upper part of the Tower Bridge, narrowly missing it by ten centimetres.

Winn Blitzzer screamed, "Oh, look out or we will collide with the Tower Bridge!"

He covered his face in his hands to not watch. When the Free-XL passed between the towers safely, Winn Blitzzer opened his eyes in relief.

"We were very lucky," he said to Valger.

After that, Valger did not distract himself anymore. He took the control of the Free-XL very seriously indeed to return home safely.

They arrived at the Royal Observatory of Greenwich again. The Free-XL took them downstream near Woolwich where they saw a massive structure in the middle of the river. This was the River Thames Barrier with ten large steel gates shining with lights, spanning over five hundred metres across the River Thames. They had no idea that these massive gates protected Central London from flooding. Each main gate stood as high as a five-storey building. This wonderful structure at first seemed to Winn Blitzzer to be large turtle shells in the middle of the River.

He said to Valger in whisper, "This is wonderful architecture from another planet, indeed."

Then the Free-XL flew back towards the Prime Meridian of Greenwich like a magnet attracted by some kind of force field. Just after arriving above the Observatory's dome at zero latitude, the Free-XL flew at higher and faster, so fast it matched the speed of sound and then vanished in the clouds. It was 3:28

in the morning, Greenwich time. Only two seconds were left of their secret mission. Winn Blitzzer looked down to see the tiny lights of London slowly blinking on.

He said quietly, "Good bye London, beautiful and unforgettable city. I would like to visit you again someday and touch the ground. Even live there one day. Who knows?"

Valger heard him and said this was impossible, too much to even dream about.

"I could do it, one day. Anything is possible now after this trip and all these discoveries. I didn't know about the existence of London before. I do want to return to London one day. The charm of this magnificent city has captivated my soul. I am very sorry for having taken away their magnificent iconic landmark, called Big Ben. I am sorry London, for what I have done to you. I am an instrument of others. I did not choose any of this. Please forgive me, London."

Valger said to Winn Blitzzer, "Stop saying such nonsense. With this adventure the Princess of Light could be yours."

"That could be or it could not. The Princess of Light is not for sale or for trade. Who knows maybe we could be friends at least, if there is no love between us. You cannot force anyone to love you, otherwise you will never be happy in life. But I do have another plan that I'll tell you later."

"Forget the idea that you could see London again in your lifetime," said Valger. "Look, I have something here to make you feel a little bit closer to London. Try these biscuits, they are very nice. You won't be disappointed since you seem to like everything about London."

Winn Blitzzer looked at Valger and took the biscuit and ate it. It was very good. "They are very nice biscuits, as I was expect anything from London to be."

By the time this conversation between them ended, the Free-XL was headed toward the air space above the Scandinavian countries. The birds below the Free-XL holding the strong chains with their small beaks felt the strong cold winds. While flying Winn Blitzzer remembered the fast manoeuvre Valger had made around the Tower Bridge in London to save the Free-XL from colliding with it. He congratulated Valger for having managed to avoid a disaster by just ten centimetres. His reflexes were incredibly fast.

The Free-XL was flying at high speed towards Iceland. A few moments later, they were near the southeast of the island above the Jökulsárlón lagoon near the glacier of Vatnajökull, when they saw the Northern lights appear in the sky in many amazing colours. They were headed at high speed right toward them as if to come and cover the Free-XL. They became afraid and Valger hurried to pull the yoke back to make the Free-XL gain altitude and avoid the lights. But they noticed that the Northern lights had mess with the flight instruments due to the proximity of the Free-XL to the lights. Valger pulled the lever back even harder to gain more altitude, with the same manoeuvre he had used at the Tower Bridge. The crystal around Big Ben shook with the vibrations of the Free-XL as it rose straight up into the sky.

A small part of the great clock fell down to the ground of a small town on the northern coast called Húsavík, on the shores of the Skjálfandi Bay. It was a metal tube-like part of ninety centimetres with the serial number GC-118-GB. It had come out of the hole in the crystal, from the spot that had been left uncovered and unprotected. The hole that Winn Blitzzer had been worried about. Neither he nor Valger nor even the birds saw this happen.

Bit miraculously that small part landed on top of a large chunk of snow, hard as stone, below the mountain behind the town of Húsavík. Thanks to that hard strong snow, the small piece did not become lost inside the snowy mountain. Instead, it went tumbling down from where it landed towards the centre of the town of Húsavík, coming to a stop in the front of a white wooden church, the most famous landmark of the town built in 1907, Húsavíkurkirkja Lutheran Church.

They continued onward, passing over the small island of Grímsey, twenty-five miles off the north coast of the main island and into the Arctic Circle, heading to the far north end of Greenland. After arriving there, just before the North Pole, was a zone with a mysterious magnetic force. This was the gate or portal that would connect them back to their planet Oxon. When Valger saw the beeping on the radar and felt the yoke being pulled in his hands, he put the Free-XL on full throttle. They flew through the sky towards this gate, white as snow with a light shining from inside.

The gate was opening and closing every six seconds. When closed, it looked white as the clouds surrounding it, as if nothing was there. Valger concentrated, focusing the Free-XL in the right direction to not miss it. As the light shown from inside it again, the Free-XL shot forward into the gate and back in the direction of Oxon. Valger was pulling the yoke back all the way with the nose of the Free-XL practically pointing upward from the speed.

Just a few moments later they were flying through the galaxy with an incredible view of the stars and other celestial bodies. Winn Blitzzer and Valger were very happy indeed and shouted with joy, "Yes! We did it, we did it, we completed our mission!"

They realised how deep in the galaxy they were when they saw the birds retransform again into the golden eagles they were before, breathing with their six lungs and two hearts.

The golden eagles were shouting too, or rather cawing, "What an amazing feeling, becoming a golden eagle again!"

Others were saying, "Yes it is an amazing feeling, we feel so much better and different now, like before!"

Winn Blitzzer's mind was full of so many thoughts. He took off his helmet to look at the wonderful views of the galaxy. He was laughing at the golden eagles flying on either side of the Free-XL as though escorting them. Some of the birds continued to hang by their beaks from the crystal chains below. But Winn Blitzzer's joy was short-lived.

Counting the number of golden eagles flying alongside the Free-XL, he saw ten birds on the left, and ten on the right. There were five birds hanging on the crystal rings below. He realised that one bird was missing. He was certain that aunt Moxum had sent twenty-six. He didn't know what to do, or what happened to the missing bird.

He said to Valger, "We have a problem. One bird is missing."

"What?" Valger asked him "Are you sure? Maybe it is flying far behind."

"I am sure that one bird is missing, but we cannot turn back," said Winn Blitzzer. "Aunt Moxum forbade us to look back. Now we are returning with only twenty-five. Everything went almost perfectly, and now this at the last minute."

Winn Blitzzer good mood was lost at this unexpected incident. He asked himself, "Where is this lost bird? Is it following behind as Valger suggested?"

He didn't have any idea how the mysterious disappearance of the bird could have happened.

Valger could see how concerned he was and said, "Do not worry yet, we will know for sure when we get home."

"Yes, you are right Valger," said Winn Blitzzer and then added, "If I could open the window of the Free-XL, I could ask Ar if he knows anything about it."

Valger looked at him and said, "We are in space without oxygen right now, we cannot do anything to find out what happened to the missing bird, and worse we cannot turn back anyway if we did."

Neither had any idea that Ar knew about the missing bird Ser. But he had forgotten to tell them while they were in London.

After a brief moment of silence Winn Blitzzer said, "I would like to believe that the missing bird is coming behind us as you suggested Valger, maybe it was the same bird Ser who was having problems at the start of this mission, although I can't be one hundred per cent sure."

"Do not worry about it," Valger said to him. "We should be very proud of what we have achieved. Aunt Moxum will tell us later what to do."

You're right. I should forget about this incident for now and not let it take away my happiness. Aunt Moxum won't be happy about the mysterious disappearance of the bird either though. But I am sure she already knows more about it than we do."

Meanwhile in Black Cloud, Ms Moxum and Eris were following their return in the Potsat. Ms Moxum was very happy with the success of the mission. Now she was sure of the effectiveness of her knowledge of the mystical sciences she had inherited from her ancestors. This was the first time she had ever sent anyone to another planet with success. But she was a little concerned and disappointed about the missing bird Ser who was left in London on top of Nelson's Column.

Neither Winn Blitzzer nor Valger had a clue what might have happened to the missing bird. But Moxum and Eris did, thanks to the Potsat where they saw how everything had happened. But Moxum did not want to see this mission as a failure because of one little incident; everything else was going well, nearly to perfection, with the other twenty-five birds. She was confident that Ser, would vanish into ashes in a few days' time, in accordance with the magic she had used on all the birds. But if Ser did not disappear within in three days then this incident would become very concerning indeed. It would not be good for her if the humans discovered the true identity of this fake crow, and that it was not in fact a species of crow from planet Earth. So if the humans were to discover the truth about this fake crow, then the theft of their clock would no longer be as mysterious. The humans could glean an idea of what might have happened to their great clock Big Ben. She thought to herself, *Only time will reveal to me if this secret mission will remain a mystery as planned, and as I would like it to remain forever.*

Chapter Thirty
Return to the Planet Oxon

The Free-XL continued flying though the galaxy towards Oxon. The sight of the solar systems passing in the window was breath taking. The Free-XL crossed unnoticed through the area of the hostile planets again without being seen by the guardian. That gave Winn Blitzzer and Valger some peace of mind. A few moments later they were entering the galactic space of their planet Oxon. They felt safe and secure again. Their thoughts were on landing safely in Black Cloud in the dark. They knew that Moxum and Eris were watching them through the Potsat.

As the Free-XL was approaching the planet, Winn Blitzzer and Valger saw many shooting stars dancing in the sky. Some even seemed to be falling down around the Free-XL as though giving them and the birds a very warm welcome after their round trip in London on planet Earth. But Winn Blitzzer and Valger were a bit scared of them, thinking they could break through the glass, and put their helmets back on their heads. They had never seen so many shooting stars dancing in sky like this. Even though they looked wonderful, there were too many to even appreciate them all.

Winn Blitzzer said to Valger, "Aunt Moxum was right to tell us to wear our special 3-D helmets at all times during the flight. I feel safer wearing it."

After a short flight inside the shooting stars, the Free-XL finally reached the atmosphere of planet Oxon. It was still very dark there, still around four o'clock in the morning. Everybody was asleep. Winn Blitzzer and Valger were very happy indeed and relieved at the success of their mission. No one saw them leave and no one should have seen them coming back. In a few minutes, the Free-XL arrived in Black Cloud and stopped in mid-air as if a powerful magnet was repelling it. They did not know that their house was just below and the powerful magic of the Potsat was holding the Free-XL in the air there, as Aunt Moxum planned. It was very dark below; they could not see right in front of their faces. But Moxum and Eris saw their arrival in the Potsat, and came out to welcome them as heroes.

When Winn Blitzzer and Valger saw a torch moving downward as a signal to land slowly, they knew that it was Moxum and Eris. But the birds flew first towards Ms Moxum and her sister Eris after seeing the lit torch with them and began screeching and flapping around them in greeting or as if to say, "We did it, we completed our mission!"

Ms Moxum told the bird to go back and detach the great clock below the Free-XL to make it easier for Valger to come down. The golden eagles flew back below the Free-XL and began to untie the large crystal with Big Ben wrapped inside like a larger snow globe. Then the Free-XL lowered its four mechanical legs, at the same time lowering the great clock down to the ground and standing it on four short and solid rocks. At that moment, the big six-pointed star that had been blinking on and off in the sky since before their trip exploded like fireworks, lighting up the entire village. Winn Blitzzer and Valger were surprised at how bright it was.

Finally, the Free-XL landed a few metres away from the front yard of the house. Winn Blitzzer opened the door and they came out just like astronauts back from space with their high-tech flight suits. They went to hug Moxum and Eris. They stayed in a long group hug without saying anything, even Aunt Moxum who was not the kindest or most affection person. But this a special moment. The mission her nephews had just accomplished was something very special to be very proud of.

Aunt Moxum said to them "You have done it, you have done it, I am very proud of you. Even the mysterious star in the sky was happy as you can see."

Before they started talking about their trip, Winn Blitzzer handed back all the mystical instruments his Aunt Moxum had lent him.

Moxum said to them, "Both of you have been very brave. I am pleased at how well Valger drove the Free-XL, and as for you Winn Blitzzer, well done at having taken the great clock with my small golden magic wand. You and your cousin are very special team indeed. His miraculous arrival here before this trip was a blessing. Nobody saw either of you leaving or returning to planet Oxon to steal the most famous clock on planet Earth, including King Brelys-1000. The mission shall remain a secret."

Winn Blitzzer said to his aunts, "Valger and I have so much to tell you. I do not even know where to begin."

Aunt Moxum said to him, "I don't have any doubt about that. You will tell us your wonderful stories later, but first you need to rest."

"You're right Aunt Moxum," said Valger, "but I cannot go to bed before telling you and my mother what I saw with my own eyes. I will be glad to tell you now about all the amazing things we saw in London."

"We have no doubt about what you saw," Eris said to her son, "if it looked so incredible from a distance in the Potsat, being there in person must have been an unforgettable experience."

Then Winn Blitzzer said, "I present to you the great clock. It is time for you to see it inside the crystal."

His aunts were amazed at Big Ben's beauty when they saw it.

"Would you like to open the crystal and touch it?" asked Winn Blitzzer.

"No, no! I cannot do that," Aunt Moxum exclaimed with fear in her eyes, almost trembling. Her answer surprised Winn Blitzzer and Valger, and even Eris. They looked at each other confused.

"Why can't you open the crystal? Just to get a better look," Winn Blitzzer said.

"I cannot do that right now," Aunt Moxum replied, "because this clock came from another planet. It might have the smell of pollution on it. I do not want that spreading around our planet. Before I can open it, I need to pour some water from the Potsat on it to kill the pollution and any bacteria that could be growing on it."

"I understand, Aunt Moxum. I didn't think of that."

Then Moxum told Eris to bring her small pitcher of water from the Potsat. Eris went quickly and came back the pitcher and handed it to Moxum.

Moxum poured the water over the crystal saying, "With this special water from the Potsat, I remove the smell of pollution and kill any bacteria or other organisms that might be on it."

A furl of smoke was coming off the crystal. Then suddenly to their surprise (even though nothing should have surprised them at this point), Aunt Moxum flew into the air by some invisible force. In seconds she was high in the air floating over the great clock.

Moxum took her magic wand and held it over Big Ben saying, "I order the crystal pyramid that has swallowed the great clock to remove itself and return to the small size it was before."

Instantly the crystal began moving, stretching and unfolding from below the great clock until the cross on top, sticking again like a magnet to the wand Moxum was holding in her hand and becoming a small crystal pyramid once more. As Moxum floated back down, the great clock started growing to its actual size without the crystal to contain it. When she touched the ground, the small glass pyramid stuck on her wand lit up. She threw it upwards into the air where it remained suspended, casting a light over them like a street lamp. The four of them held hands and went around and around the great clock. Thanks to that light they could see Big Ben clearly in the night.

Aunt Eris said, "This great clock is a so beautiful. I have never seen something like this before in my whole life, or dreamed it could exist."

Winn Blitzzer said to her, "Aunt Eris, my eyes have seen many things in London I cannot explain or even remember all of it. The thirty and a half minutes Valger and I had spent in that city seemed like an eternity. Everywhere I turned there was something more amazing to see."

Moxum looked at Big Ben closely and said, "This great clock is very beautiful and larger than I thought. We all look like dwarfs beside it. I can understand why King Brelys-1000 is so obsessed. I might say that it must have been geniuses that built something so magnificent and beautiful. Can you imagine how King Brelys-1000 will react when he sees and touches this great clock in person? If he was so obsessed with watching it through his secret telescope from a distance, how he will react when he sees this great clock, dancing or crying with joy? I hope he keeps his promise to you anyway."

"Yes, Aunt Moxum, the king will keep his word," Winn Blitzzer replied.

After a moment of silence as they gazed at the clock, Winn Blitzzer to Aunt Moxum, "Without the crystal, the great clock must be over two hundred metres tall and wide. We cannot just leave it outside unprotected where someone could see it. It could get damaged. What should we do?"

"Leave it to me. I'll take care of it," said Aunt Moxum, then she tapped her magic wand on the clock, instantly reducing its size to just one metre high and half a metre wide. Then she told Eris to bring a large waterproof cloth of a dark colour to cover it. She had the golden eagles spread the large cloth over the great clock to avoid the invisible people coming to see it, or trying to touch it. Then they all placed four stones at each side of the great clock to protected it.

Then Aunt Moxum said, "Dear nephews, it is time now to return the special outfits I gave you. They must be returned to miniature sizes like before to keep them safe."

Immediately she put her magic wand over Winn Blitzzer and Valger; the flight helmets they were wearing became as tiny as toys hanging from her wand, followed by their flight suits and boots. Winn Blitzzer and Valger stood there in their old clothes from before their trip. Finally, they handed Aunt Moxum the special rings with the mysterious fire lit inside. Aunt Moxum gathered everything together with her own ring; instantly the fire went out inside of the rings. Eris put everything inside the special blue box so that later her sister Moxum could hide them in the bottom of the Potsat.

When Ms Moxum was about to reduce the Free-XL to small size, Winn Blitzzer said to her, "Wait, wait, wait, Aunt Moxum, please. I need to take out my souvenirs."

He climbed in and grabbed the small box. Mrs Eris was surprised to see her son Valger without anything in his hands. Then aunt Moxum asked Valger,

"You did not bring anything back with you?"

"Nothing special. I had a packet of sweets and biscuits but I ate them all during the flight. They were so good, I couldn't make them last any longer. Even Winn Blitzzer tried some too and he liked it."

Moxum pointed her wand at the Free-XL, and seconds later it was the size of a toy. Winn Blitzzer and Valger were just as impressed as when they saw it transform before their trip.

Finally Winn Blitzzer said to his Aunt Moxum, "Thank you for giving us a way to make Big Ben smaller. I think that it will also be easier for us to carry the great clock in the future, when we deliver it to King Brelys-1000."

"Yes, Winn Blitzzer, but first, the king needs to fulfil his promise. We will not deliver the great clock for free, after so much work and sacrifice."

Ms Moxum told the light floating in the air above them, "Follow us inside."

And strangely enough, it did. Winn Blitzzer and Valger were amazed again. Once inside, Aunt Moxum raised her hand caught the magic wand from the air and with a wave turned out the light. Then she out the glass pyramid inside the blue box her sister Eris was holding, then she did the same with her wand, finally placing the box with everything inside on the bottom of the Potsat.

"Now we can talk about other things," said Aunt Moxum.

Now inside the house, Winn Blitzzer was very excited to open the box to show his aunts the items he had brought back from London, things they had never seen before. Among the objects they were "Four small Big Ben towers gilded in gold, four snow globes with figures of the landmark of London inside, four small flags, two pairs of sunglasses, one pack of six shirts of different sizes and shapes and colours, four teddy bears, one pocket watch, two luxury pens, one with glossy yellow ink, one pack of a typical London car, a red double-decker bus and black taxi, one toy of the airplane Concorde, one packet of twelve 3-D postcards of the most beautiful landmark of London, four books, one small English dictionary and history book of the United Kingdom with all their best inventions and of course two pictures books telling the story of Big Ben" Aunts Moxum and Eris were very impressed after seeing all those beautiful objects. Winn Blitzzer said to them "Our round trip to London has been very successful as you can see these amazing object, the city of London look amazing, it was an unforgettable experience for our lives" After a brief silence Winn Blitzzer took one snow globe and a small gilded Big Ben and handed them to Aunt Moxum saying, "Take it, touch it, feel it something from another world in your hands."

Moxum didn't want to touch the snow globe even though it looked very beautiful. She had a look of fear on her face.

Winn Blitzzer approached her saying, "Take it, Aunt Moxum, please."

But Aunt Moxum took one step backward.

Winn Blitzzer said to her, "Don't be scared of a snow globe, Aunt Moxum, you are a wise and strong women."

But Aunt Moxum ran to the other side of the table.

Winn Blitzzer said to her, "Please Aunt, take it. You are the one who had sent us there, if it wasn't for you, I would have never known of the existence of planet Earth or the amazing city London."

But Aunt Moxum was still hesitant to take the snow globe in her hands. When Winn Blitzzer approached her again, she stepped back screaming, "I cannot touch them without first pouring water from the Potsat on them to clean them, otherwise my powers could be lost forever!"

Winn Blitzzer was shocked.

Then Aunt Moxum ran away and locked herself in her room. Valger, Winn Blitzzer and Mrs Eris laughed together; they had never seen Aunt Moxum scared of anything like this before. The snow globe was quite lovely and defenceless; they couldn't understand why Aunt Moxum was so scared and couldn't touch it.

Aunt Eris said to Winn Blitzzer, "Let me feel this beautiful object from London in my hand. Touching something from another world is a privilege that I never dreamt of."

She took the snow globe in her hand and looked inside, "It is very beautiful," she said.

"Yes, Aunt Eris. What you see inside there is the great landmark of London. I still have three more snow globes in the box and other things too, like some t-shirts, two small flags and a large winter one that will be a gift of goodwill to His Majesty. And of course two books with nice pictures telling the story of Big Ben and history book of the greatest inventions of the kingdom and a dictionary to learn the language of this kingdom. I will give some of these special items to my friends Tovic and Yalta."

"I would like to keep one of these objects too," said Aunt Eris.

Winn Blitzzer said to her, "You can take this snow globe, it's my pleasure."

Ms Moxum shouted from inside her room to her sister, "You are not allowed to take any of those items without my approval."

And then to Winn Blitzzer, "Take all your souvenirs and keep them in your room now. I still have very important business to deal with before dawn. I am glad that Valger at least did not bring anything from Earth to distract."

Valger felt a little relieved after the shame he was feeling at coming home empty-handed.

Winn Blitzzer obeyed Aunt Moxum's request and took his souvenirs to his room. Only then did Aunt Moxum come out of her room.

She went directly to the door and said to the golden eagles, "I congratulate all of you for your wonderful work in London. A great achievement which allowed Winn Blitzzer and Valger to take Big Ben quickly and unnoticed. Bravo! Because of your success, we will continue working together in the future.

As for the bird Ser who decided to stay in London reasons only he knows: if by luck he returns here, he will be punished for life. Never again will he be sent on another secret mission. Now is time for you to be given the reward you deserve for your success. I have decided to keep all of you alive as real birds forever to be of use to me. You shall no longer be returned to lifeless, senseless birds as tiny as mosquitoes locked in a bottle as you were before. Your first task, starting now, will be to guard the clock and keep the invisible people away from it. Soon I will train you to hunt these invisible people."

After hearing this news, the birds flapped their wings gracefully and sang songs of joy at the happiness they felt for the trust Ms Moxum had in them.

"Shut up, shut up!" said Ms Moxum at all the noise the excited birds were making. "I have not yet finished explaining everything to you. Listen before I change my mind."

The birds fell silent immediately, still quietly shaking their wings.

Then Ms Moxum said, "You are still large in size, therefore I command you to fly through the invisible net again to become normal-sized golden eagles."

She pointed her magic wand towards the invisible net. The birds flew in two rows through the invisible net, and came out returned to normal size again. Then they took their places on the branches of nearby trees and on roofs to watch over Big Ben. Now everything was done, the retransformation of the birds was complete and Ms Moxum was very happy indeed. She began laughing uproariously.

"What magnificent knowledge of the mystical sciences I possess! No one will take them from me and I will never bequeath this inheritance to anyone; this knowledge shall die with me. Things shall always stay as they are in this village. There will be no more people here nor will anyone left be allowed to leave or come back here again."

When she heard this, Eris looked at Winn Blitzzer and Valger. She knew that her sister Moxum's words meant her denial and rejection of the invisible people ever coming back to normal again. But she did not make any comments about what was just said. After a brief silence, she prepared a hearty meal for Winn Blitzzer and her son with a special drink that looked like white mercury.

She said to them, "This special meal and drink will make you feel better and help you to recover your sleep. Above all it will make you forget some of what you have seen on your journey."

"No, Aunt Eris I do not want to forget what we saw!" said Winn Blitzzer. "I would like to keep this memory forever in my mind. It is the most unique experience of my whole life. If you could see what we have seen I am sure you would understand. I know that you could see London through the Potsat. But it is not the same as actually being there and experiencing as we did."

"I know that and I understand," said Aunt Eris to Winn Blitzzer, "but now you need to eat the special food I prepared for you both to recover your strength. My dear nephew Winn Blitzzer, do not worry. If that is what you wish, your thoughts and memories of London will stay with you forever. They will never be erased from your mind, ever."

Winn Blitzzer felt very happy for her understanding and thanked her.

Then he and Valger began eating the food she made them.

Winn Blitzzer liked it very much; it was tasty. Valger liked it as well. After eating, Winn Blitzzer drank the special liquid from the mug as though he were drinking a very thick soup. When he had finished it, a small ball of yellow light up lit in his mouth and went down his throat to his stomach. Instantly his body shone from inside, with the small ball of light circulating at high speed up and down his body. Valger dropped his mug in shock.

But Winn Blitzzer was not afraid. He had had a similar experience before. A few moments later the small ball of light disappeared from Winn Blitzzer's body.

He said to his aunts, "I feel great."

"That's a sign it's time for you to rest," said Aunt Eris. Valger took his drink too and the same small ball of yellow light shone from his body.

Then Aunt Moxum said to them, "You will have the best sleep you've ever had in your lives."

Finally, just before dawn, Winn Blitzzer and Valger headed to bed without any idea that they would be fast asleep for three days and nights.

Chapter Thirty-One
The Ordeal of the On-Call Police Officers

In London it was half past four in the morning on the last day of the year. It was still dark outside. No Londoner knew yet what had happened in their city that fateful night. The powerful effect of the magic sleeping powder still had everyone asleep in their beds, or where they stood, almost hypnotised. Soft snow was falling across the city as though cleaning up the powerful effect of the magic sleeping powder. Early that morning, the effects of the powder started to wear off. In some houses people were starting to wake up, moving around and turning over in their beds, feeling rather limp still, while others were recovering more slowly.

The two police officers on duty that night at the Palace of Westminster, Sergeant Bank and Inspector Bing, were still asleep too on their bunk beds in the guard's room. They were unaware that something very serious had happened to the great clock that night. Normally when the officers were on duty they would sleep in shifts. While one napped lightly with one eye open, the other was awake and on duty. They would change shifts every two hours until morning. They had learned tactics in the Royal Police Academy to withstand the long hours of the night, especially in the winter season. When the toll of Big Ben every hour helped them to stay awake too, keep track of the time.

When Sergeant Bank and Inspector Bing fell asleep, they did not realise that they had left the door of the guardroom ajar. The cold air entering their room made Sergeant Bank on the top bunk wake up first. Then he saw the door ajar.

"How forgetful, no wonder it's so cold."

He climbed down and looked outside and saw soft snow falling down. He closed the door. His colleague Inspector Bing was still snoring from the lower bunk. Sergeant Bank did his morning exercises then poured himself a cup of coffee and started writing a report for the guards coming for the morning shift.

He looked at his watch; it was quarter to five in the morning. But he didn't hear the great clock ringing. He said to himself, *Maybe my watch is fast. Or the battery might be low. It's never failed me before. I'll wait for when Big Ben rings to reset it.*

It was an old Breitling watch. He bought on credit with his first salary. It had taken five years to pay it off. He had great affection for it. He rarely took it off. It was a personal gift to himself, a childhood dream he always wanted to fulfil from when he used to look at them in the magazine. He could not believe it was already faulty.

When he finished writing the report, he looked at his watch again. And again he did not hear Big Ben ringing.

He said out loud, "Maybe I'm going deaf. I don't know. I was fine yesterday."

Little did he know that his and Inspector Bing's faces would be known to every British citizen and millions of people around the world. They would soon have to answer more than a million questions from other police officers and journalists that no one would know the answers to. Neither of them had ever given an interview in their lives. They were just normal police officers doing their jobs. But their quiet, anonymous lives were about to change forever that day.

Sergeant Bank looked at his watch again. He still had not heard the bells. Maybe Bing was right the other day and his ears were failing. He covered his ears with hands and then patted his cheeks, worried and restless. There was only way to find out what was happening to his ears and his watch and that was to check the time on the face of the clock tower itself. Sergeant Bank looked outside their guardroom and left as Inspector Bing slept on. He walked down a long corridor in the northwest wing leading to the New Palace Yard near the Elizabeth Tower in the foreground of Parliament Square.

He took his watch off, looking at it so intently that he did not see where he was going. He tripped over a cobblestone and nearly fell face down on the ground. His precious watch slipped from his hands and flew through the air. He watched it desperately and ran to save it before it smashed on the ground. Being in good shape, he managed to save his watch like a goalkeeper diving to catch the ball in his hands. He clutched it tightly in his hands like a treasure or a Fabergé egg, lying on his stomach on the ground. All this because he was looking at his watch and not watching where he was going. He put the watch back on his wrist and wiped of his hands.

He walked around the corner to an exit gate with an arch. He saw the multi-coloured lights of the Christmas tree shining on and off in front of him at the New Palace Yard. It was still dark outside mixed with morning fog and mist and the light snow still falling slowly. Finally he arrived at the New Palace Yard with the small green trees lined around it. Sergeant Bank looked up at the clock tower to check the time on the face of Big Ben.

But then the surprise of his life happened. His eyes looked up at the clock tower and saw nothing. Big Ben was not on top of it, where it had been for centuries. He stood and stared for a few seconds but it felt like an eternity. He shook his head and rubbed his eyes and looked at the clock tower again. Nothing there. He began to feel dizzy as though he was about to suffer a heart attack. He would have yelled aloud in shock if he had not thought at first that his eyes were deceiving him. He considered maybe he was hallucinating or going mad. Or perhaps his vision was failing him now too.

But standing there Sergeant Bank felt a sinking feeling of dread that left him frozen without knowing what to do or how to react. All of this exceeded his imagination and was quite beyond what he expected guard duty would entail. Her Majesty's Royal Police Academy, had not prepared them for this.

He gazed helplessly at the empty space where the clock tower should be. He felt his knees trembling. He knelt down on the stones without feeling the cold and wet at a loss for what to do. A few seconds passed by as he attempted to collect his bearings. This was too much for him alone. He stood up, tried to run forward and then stopped and went backwards, then turned twice around the Silver Jubilee Fountain without realising what he was doing, throwing his arms up in the air in despair.

Then he ran the short distance towards the arched gate, and then stopped and come back again to check if Big Ben was really not there. He walked slowly through the arched gate. Then he stuck his head out slowly to look up at the clock tower again for the last time. Big Ben was no longer there; only empty spaces where the great clock used to be.

He said desperately, "It's true, Big Ben isn't there. No wonder I couldn't hear the bells toll..."

Then he sprinted to go tell Inspector Bing. He was going so fast he ran right by the guardroom. He braked quickly, his shoes sliding, almost putting holes in the heels. He flew into the guardroom. Inspector Bing lay there, fast asleep and softly snoring, not a care in the world.

Sergeant Bank woke the inspector, shaking vigorously saying, "Wake up, wake up, wake up! We have a very serious problem here! I don't know where and how to begin but it's very bad, very bad indeed and while we were here on duty..."

The inspector awoke and sat up quickly, frightened at Sergeant Bank's rambling. "What's going on? What is happening? Why did you wake me like that? What are you talking about?"

Sergeant Bank did not have time to answer Inspector Bing's questions. He was shaking and running in place. Inspector Bing stared at his colleague unfazed. He took the thermoses and served two cups of tea.

"Sit down and drink this tea, and then calmly explain exactly what happened."

Sergeant Bank could neither answer nor drink the cup of tea he was offered. Instead he continued pacing around the small guardroom. Inspector Bing began to be concerned that his colleague sergeant was going mad. He knew very well that Sergeant Bank was normally a quiet man and a bit shy. This was quite out of character for him. Something serious must have happened to him. He tried to get the sergeant's attention by startling him.

He shouted, "Tell what's wrong!"

But Sergeant Bank still did not answer and continued pacing. He tried to speak but found he could not. He was still in shock. Inspector Bing tried to help Sergeant Bank into the chair, but he refused to sit down, instead, pointing his finger down the long corridor from where he had just come. Inspector Bing looked in that direction without seeing anything there.

"What do you want to tell me?"

Sergeant Bank did not answer. Instead he pointed a shaking finger at the new calendar hanging on the wall with Big Ben's picture on the cover.

Inspector Bing looked at it and said, "I don't understand what you mean sergeant. What do you want to say? I cannot understand gestures. Calm down, stop running around, and explain to me what has happened."

But Sergeant Bank continued pacing as though he did not hear.

"Maybe you've had too much to drink."

"No, no, no," Sergeant Bank made a gesture with his hand impatiently.

"What's happened to you then?" Inspector Bing asked him, frustrated.

The sergeant stopped moving. He pointed his finger again at the new calendar with Big Ben's picture on the cover.

Inspector Bing did not understand. He looked to the new calendar hanging on the wall.

"I see a calendar. I don't see anything else there. Explain to me, what exactly do you want to say?"

Sergeant Bank took a deep breath and said, almost crying, "My dear friend, I apologise. The reason for my behaviour is something beyond belief that has taken place in London last night. I hope you will believe me but if not, you will be able to see with your own eyes.

Our precious great clock, Big Ben, has disappeared. Don't ask me how it happened. I have no idea how. Just believe me when I tell you that it is not there. You have seen how I was just now after discovering this. But if you still don't believe me you can go see for yourself. It's no longer there!"

Upon hearing this, Inspector Bing burst out laugh. He was sure the sergeant was joking.

"You think you can fool me so with this kind of joke? With your theatrics and everything. You really thought I'd believe that? I am not so easy to fool, you know. Try another one, that one wasn't very funny."

He took a sip of tea.

He was surprised when Sergeant Bank became angry.

"It's no laughing matter, this is a very serious matter indeed. Do you think I am a liar? I understand that this is unthinkable and very hard to believe if you don't see yourself. I almost fainted with shock, I tell you. You could have found me lying on the cold wet ground at the Elizabeth Tower."

Inspector Bing's face changed when he saw that Sergeant Bank was serious. But he was still unsure.

"How did you find out that Big Ben had disappeared?"

"It's too long a story to tell you now," said Sergeant Bank. "We don't have much time but I'll do my best to describe what happened. I woke up early. I did not realise that I had fallen asleep during my shift, in fact I felt cold because our door was half open. I did my daily morning exercise then I wrote the report. It was as I was drinking a cup of coffee that I noticed I had not heard Big Ben ringing as usual. At first, I thought it was my watch that was off. I even asked myself if I really did have hearing problems. But after a quarter and half an hour passed without hearing the bells, I decided to go see for myself.

When I arrived there and looked up, there was nothing there where the clock is supposed to be. The fogs was heavy so I thought that maybe I couldn't see right. I walked around by the Silver Jubilee Fountain looking down and then tried looking up again. But when I looked up the clock tower really wasn't there. I couldn't believe it myself what I was seeing, thought maybe I was losing it.

Then I realised was fine, the clock had really just disappeared. How could this happen? I'm still I shock. I'll never forget that moment, looking up and seeing nothing."

Inspector Bing said, "I'm going to go check myself. I just want to see if you're really in your right mind first."

Then he asked Sergeant Bank, "What is the oldest and the only original part left of the Palace of Westminster?"

"Alright fine, if you insist on doing this… First on the sixteenth of October in 1834, the great fire destroyed the House of the Parliament. The only and original medieval structures to survive were the Westminster Hall erected in 1097, the oldest building in the Parliamentary state. It has played a central role in over one thousand years of British history. At one point it was the largest hall in Europe."

He did not stop there. "Secondly, the cloisters of St Stephen's, the chapel of St Mary Undercroft and the jewel tower survived the great fire as well, thanks to the heroic efforts of the Superintendent James Braidwood and his team of fire fighters of the London Fire Engine Establishment. I could keep going.

The great painter, William Turner, who witnessed the unfortunate event of the fire of the Palace of Westminster along with many other Londoners, painted that dramatic moment for posterity which we can still see today. It's called *The Burning of the Houses of Lords and the Commons*. The Romantic painter John Constable witnessed the blaze as well and sketched the fire from a hansom cab on Westminster Bridge. What more can I say to prove you that I am fine?"

"Alright, alright!" said Inspector Bing. "I do not doubt that you are sound in mind, and I am very happy for that. But allow me to go check the clock tower alone if what you told me is true and it has had such an effect on you."

"I told you the whole truth, no more, no less," said Sergeant Bank. "Believe me, I could never lie to you, or joke about such matters. We should go together."

"No, thank you!" said the inspector, "I would prefer to go alone."

"Ok, ok! But remember I warned you."

"Thank you, my friend, for your warning and concern," said Inspector Bing. "I think I will be able to handle this on my own."

He downed the rest of his tea, touched his fine moustache and rubbed his hands. Then he walked swiftly from the guardroom towards the garden in the New Palace Yard.

He arrived and looked up. He saw nothing. He rubbed his eyes. He walked around the yard to get around the small green trees blocking his view. Then from the main entrance of Parliament Square, he looked up at the clock tower again. But Big Ben wasn't there anymore as if it had disappeared just like that. Only empty space was left.

Inspector Bing couldn't believe his eyes.

He said out loud, "Bank was right, it's not here. Where could it have gone? Who took it? And where?"

He ran as fast as a speeding bullet back to the guardroom where Sergeant Bank was waiting. Like the sergeant, he too passed right by the door and had to slammed on the brakes with his feet and then backpedal. He entered, agitated and in shock. He went straight to his colleague and apologised to him.

"I am so very sorry, I didn't believe you. It's really true. Someone must have stolen it!"

"We cannot say that without any proof," said Sergeant Bank.

"What kind of proof do you need?" said Inspector Mark Bing, "Big Ben has disappeared suddenly, mysteriously. We were on duty here and heard nothing."

"How could you explain that? I do not want to speculate anything far-fetched," said Sergeant Bank. "Maybe it fell into the River Thames. That could be verified."

"I do not agree with your hypothesis," said Inspector Bing, "a clock tower cannot be separated from the main tower just like that as you say, and disappear without leaving any trace behind. I checked below the tower. I saw no sign of debris there. I wish it could be true so that we could recover it and put it back."

Suddenly he started running in place like Sergeant Bank had been doing before, saying, "What do we do, what do we do now? Big Ben has disappeared, God help us."

He was in an even greater shock than his colleague a few minutes ago.

When Sergeant Bank saw the inspector trembling and running in place, he felt sorry for him.

"Take a seat and drink a cup of tea to calm your nerves. I warned you, didn't I? You didn't take my advice seriously."

But Inspector Bing did not seem to hear him.

"Inspector," said the sergeant, "it is time now for you to stop this, it won't solve anything. We must decide what to do next as quickly as possible. We need to tell Chief Milk right away. Worrying away here we will solve nothing."

He grabbed the inspector's shoulders to make him stop. But he too was trembling again without realising it. Then both were running in one direction. Their shoes came flying off without them realising it.

"It is time now for you to stop," Sergeant Bank said again.

"Do you see yourself?" Inspector Bing asked him.

"Yes, I see myself. I'm not moving around like you," Sergeant Bank replied.

"Ha! If you say you are not moving then something really is wrong with both of us. To be honest with you, I feel that if I stop I might faint."

They asked each other, "What can we do? What can we do?"

"Call the chief superintendent?" suggested Sergeant Bank again.

After a brief silence, they both jumped and threw themselves at the phone to inform Chief Milk about the situation. Their heads collided hard and the pain was so strong they did not know where they were for a few seconds.

After becoming conscious of the strong pain in their heads, they asked to each other, "What happened? What's going on with us?"

Suddenly the inspector fainted. Sergeant Bank reacted quickly and attempted to administer first aid. But he wasn't responding.

"What I can do now?" Sergeant Bank asked desperately, "If something bad happens to Bing, then we have another serious problem on our hands. We are on duty together, we must confront this together."

Then in desperation, Sergeant Bank grabbed a mug of cold water and splashed it on his head. It worked well. Inspector Bing sat up gasping and quickly regained consciousness. His head was wet, his pillow as well.

"Why am I all wet?" he asked, stunned.

"Inspector it was me, I was trying to revive you after you fainted."

"Fainted!" exclaimed the inspector, stunned. "I do not remember that at all. I do remember hitting heads."

"Well, that's enough proof for me that you're recovered. That's why you fainted. I think it's important that we work together to confront this. I couldn't imagine such pressure alone."

"Did you inform the chief superintendent?"

"Not yet," said Sergeant Bank. "It's better we do it together."

"I agree," said the inspector, "but before we inform him, I would like to suggest that we go check the clock tower one last time to be sure. Maybe it's something we ate or drank, if you know what I mean."

"I do, but that isn't the case here. I had made this coffee and tea myself. I had checked twice and saw no tower, no clock, just empty space. For me there is no doubt and we must accept this."

"Okay, fine," said Inspector Bing, "but let's go check the clock tower one last time to be sure before informing the chief superintendent."

Sergeant Bank assented.

They walked back outside. Before looking up, they decided to count to three and check together. They saw nothing. The beautiful Gothic revival clock tower was almost in half without the clock on top. They both felt the urge to scream again, despite expecting it this time. They quickly closed their mouths with each other's hands to avoid making so much noise so early in the morning. Then Sergeant Bank spoke in a low voice.

"The only truth is that Big Ben has disappeared. We are not drugged. We are not imagining things. It is time now for us to accept the reality of this situation."

A tremendous thrill of fear hit them. And then guilty that it was they who had been on duty that fateful night. They felt responsible for this mysterious tragedy.

Inspector Bing found it very hard to accept what his eyes were seeing. His brain did not want to believe it. The empty space left in the tower without the great clock on top was unbearable to look at. Millions of unanswered questions were circulating in their minds.

"We can no longer deny it," Sergeant Bank said shaking his head. "Our beloved Big Ben is no longer here."

Inspector Bing could not taking any more of it; he fell to his knees on cold stone ground, raising his hands to the sky in despair. When the sergeant saw him doing this he said, "It is not yet time to pray, you will have time for that later. Let's go first to inform the chief superintendent."

"I am not praying," said Mark Bing "I feel as though I might cry for the loss of our great Big Ben. I feel guilty for not having protected our great clock well enough as I should."

"You need not cry. You are part of Her Majesty's police. Do not feel guilty of anything yet. We have protected the Palace of Westminster and the clock tower without any problems before. Be strong."

"I want to pay tribute for the loss of our great clock," said Inspector Bing, "I am only human."

He began wailing, "Oh, Big Ben, where are you? Who has taken you away from us? Why, why, why? I am sure all the people of the United Kingdom and around the world will dearly miss you and cry over your loss when they hear. I am so sad, but glad at the same time, to be the first person who cried for your mysterious disappearance."

Sergeant Bank could not stand hearing his colleague mourning like this. He tried for the inspector's sake to be strong. He was afraid too, but he hid his feelings; he did not want to appear weak in front of his colleague, but rather brave. He pushed his fears aside.

"Stop this mourning. You won't achieve anything by doing that. We must not take all the blame and burden of this mystery. We need to inform our boss. I must be honest with you. I too knelt down before without realising it and I made the sign of the cross after finding Big Ben missing. But I did not cry. Instead I was felt a kind of emptiness, a sense of loss and hopelessness within myself. I had to pretend to be strong when I saw you almost crying just now, in fact I was feeling as fearful you. But we must be strong to protect ourselves. We will have a very long and uncertain day ahead of us."

Inspector Bing looked up at him. "I am very glad to hear that you did that. It shows you are not made of stone. It is very hard to come to terms with this. The silence of the bells is so strange and eerie. I feel terrible for not having protected Big Ben well enough."

"You can't think like that," said sergeant Bank. "We did our duty as always, but last night something beyond our understanding happened. My dear friend be strong. We have a lot of uncertain things ahead of us today."

Inspector Bing did not respond. He just stared ahead.

Suddenly he stood up.

"The mystery surrounding of the disappearance of Big Ben must involve thieves. They took our great clock away with them. I am convinced they could even be extra-terrestrials! They must have come from another planet with some other kind of strange technology that made this possible, without anyone seeing it or hearing anything."

Sergeant Bank stared at him incredulously. "Are you sure of this ridiculous hypothesis?"

"Yes, I am sure," replied Inspector Bing and added, "Look, the people who did this took something weighing over thirteen tonnes away so easily, so quickly, and without a sound. We are very lucky to be here today, that they didn't come looking for people, or we would have been the first to go. We'd be gone like Big Ben now."

"What exactly are you saying, Inspector Bing?" Sergeant Bank asked him.

"I mean that maybe London had strange visitors last night who stole our priceless clock with its famous bells. There is no other rational explanation. Maybe I am wrong, but who knows. Look Sergeant Bank, there's something else I noticed. Why was a vibrant city like this so quiet this morning? Even in the early hours of the morning one can always hear the sound of cars. We haven't seen any street cleaners or any buses or people heading to their business and home. London has never been so quiet. It's like we're the only people awake."

"Don't exaggerate," said Sergeant Bank.

"I'm not."

"So what you are suggesting is that a group of aliens are the ones who took Big Ben away?"

"Well, yes," said Inspector Bing, "I don't see another rational explanation. I've read a lot about this stuff. There are other civilisations and worlds entirely unknown to us. I strongly believe that only aliens could have done something like this. Nothing else could have done it."

"Personally, I do not believe in such things," said Sergeant Bank. "Our many satellites in space have never found life anywhere else in the galaxy."

Sergeant Bank was shocked at hearing all this although he was beginning to think Inspector Bing's hypothesis was the only plausible one.

"I'll stick with my hypothesis," said Inspector Bing, "I believe strongly that this mystery was caused by the alien. I don't see how any other force could have taken our beloved Big Ben away so easily without a trace."

Sergeant Bank asked with desperate voice, "What can we do now?"

"Nothing we can do to change the fact," replied Inspector Bing. "Before it is too late, let's go make a call to our chief superintendent."

"Yes, you are right," said Inspector Bing.

As they were talking, Sergeant Bank noticed that the inspector was barefoot.

"Where are your shoes?" he asked.

Inspector Bing looked down at his feet. He was in fact barefoot. He was surprised he had not noticed it before. Then he looked at Sergeant Bank's feet and saw that he too was barefoot.

"My friend, you are barefoot like me. Before looking at my feet you should have a look at your own."

"What? I have my shoes on."

But when he looked down too and saw his bare feet, he exclaimed, "Good lord! Where are my shoes? I was wearing my new pair of shoes a little while ago."

The began to feel cold, now that they had discovered this.

When they arrived back at the guardroom, they saw their shoes on the floor where they had been left after having been kicked off during their panic earlier.

Sergeant Bank looked at his watch; it was now five in the morning.

"It is time to tell the chief superintendent."

"Go ahead," said Inspector Bing.

Chapter Thirty-Two
Informing the Police Chief

Peter Bank phoned the chief superintendent John Milk to inform him of their discovery. The phone rang and rang but no one answered. Inspector Bing suggested they call New Scotland Yard.

"Good idea," said Sergeant Bank, "I hope they can do something about this."

But his hope was short-lived when no one answered there either.

"This is impossible!" said Inspector Bing. "Her Majesty's police headquarters cannot be empty. Something is wrong. This is not a normal situation. Can we try another emergency service?"

"Yes," said Sergeant Bank, "Let me try the London Fire Brigade."

He rang but nobody answered the phone there either.

"How can all the emergency numbers in London be silent? Something is seriously wrong, something is not right," he said uneasily.

Inspector Bing coughed softly and said to the sergeant, "Why not try calling BBC Radio? Then they can inform the world."

"No, no, no! We cannot do that," said Sergeant Bank. "We must inform the chief superintendent first before he hears it from somewhere else. If he doesn't hear this from us first, he'll think we deserted our post. That could lead to a very serious disciplinary action against us."

"I understand," said Inspector Bing, "but we don't lose anything by trying to call BBC Radio to inform them. If we are unsuccessful then we can try New Scotland Yard again. Or the fire brigade again. We have to keep trying until we reach someone."

"I appreciate your advice," said Sergeant Bank, "but I would prefer to contact our boss first again before trying other sources."

"Fine," said Inspector Bing.

While Sergeant Bank was putting in the number to call Chief Milk again, Inspector Bing turned on the radio. To his surprise the radio broadcast was repeating the same programme from three o'clock in the morning. Then he tried the television. All the news was from before three in the morning. The other channels were just static.

Inspector Bing said loudly, "Something's very wrong here, the radio and television don't work, all the news is old."

This was of course due to the effects of the sleeping powder. They were the first people to have woken up that morning while almost everyone was still asleep.

Sergeant Bank was still on the phone. After five attempts, his efforts finally paid off.

"'Ello, 'ello! Who's this?" Chief Milk asked, sounding like he had just woken up.

"Good morning sir, it's Sergeant Bank on duty at the House of Parliament. I am very sorry to wake you so early. I need to inform you of something unthinkable that I know you have never heard in your whole life. I am really hoping this will not disturb you too greatly on the last day of the year. Sir, I do not mean to give orders, but let me advice to you to prepare yourself for this. Are you sitting down?"

"Why the long Gospel?" Chief Milk asked. "Officer, just tell me what's going on that you have waken me so early in the morning."

"Yes, sir. I would not have called if it were not important," said Sergeant Bank. "Sir the thing is, the great clock has disappeared, that is, half the Elizabeth Tower is missing. Big Ben is gone. Sir you have to believe me."

There was silence on the other end of the phone. The chief superintendent did not react as Sergeant Bank and Inspector Bing were hoping. They were surprised by his calm attitude. Still the silence was like an eternity for them.

"No one can steal Big Ben. It's far too heavy and besides the clock and main tower are one unit, inseparable," said calmly the Chief Milk. Then the tone of his voice changed.

"Officer I will have to take disciplinary action against you for this. If there is any premature celebrating going on over there, that is a very serious offense and will not be tolerated in Her Majesty's police force."

Sergeant Bank tried to defend himself.

"Sir, please, my colleague and I are completely sober, we haven't had a drop. What we are saying is true, we just wanted to make sure we reported to you first, before you hear from some other source."

But Chief Milk hung up the phone before Sergeant Bank could finish explaining everything to him.

He tried to call back but Inspector Bing stopped him.

"Keep calm. I am sure that when he finds out we told him the truth he will apologise. Might I suggest to you that we try calling Scotland Yard, the London Fire Brigade and BBC Radio again to cover ourselves before it is too late? Time is against us, we must do something fast."

"You try this time," said Sergeant Bank, handing Inspector Bing the phone.

First Inspector Bing called the headquarters of New Scotland Yard in Victoria Embankment London not far from the House of Parliament. But mysteriously still no one answered his call. He left a message on the answering machine.

"Urgent. Please come immediately to the House of Parliament, we are dealing with a very serious incident never dealt with before. This is Inspector Bing on duty at the Palace of Westminster number R-67089-S. Thank you."

Then Inspector Bing tried his luck again at the headquarters of the London Fire Brigade on Union Street, who thankfully answered his call.

He made a small smile at his colleague Sergeant Bank to confirm they answered. After presenting himself as the inspector on duty at the Palace of Westminster, he explained to them the mysterious incident. They too did not believe his story. The fire fighter on the line told him the same as the chief superintendent, that they must be drunk.

"They didn't believe me," said Inspector Bing after he had hung up. "Our last hope now is BBC radio."

"Call them right away. It's getting close to dawn. I am sure they'll believe us."

Inspector Bing rang the BBC Headquarters. This time they were lucky; a friendly-sounding woman answered.

"Good morning, Alice Mary speaking. How can I help you?"

"Thank you very much Alice for answering this call. My name is Mark Bing, I am an inspector on guard at the Palace of Westminster. I have some very bad news to inform the BBC of which is why I'm calling so early."

"Go ahead. I'm listening," said Alice.

"Well," said Inspector Bing, "before I can tell you, please let me say this. I have been Her Majesty's police force for twenty-five years and many times on duty at the House of Parliament. I had never seen the unthinkable event I have encountered this morning. Please accept what I am about to say as truth, no matter how ridiculous it may sound. So far no one else we have called has. BBC is our last hope."

"Thanks you, Inspector," said Alice, "you are in good hands with the BBC. Officer, please tell me, why did you call the BBC radio so early?"

A brief silence passed then finally Inspector Bing said, "Big Ben has disappeared. Our beloved Big Ben is no longer on top of the Elizabeth Tower where it has been for centuries. We don't know how or why. Please do not laugh, this is a very serious matter indeed."

But Alice was already laughing.

"Inspector, if you really are one, I could die laughing after this. This is one of the best jokes I've heard in my entire career. It's New Year's Eve, not April Fool's. This fantasy story you want to sell to the BBC is a bit early, but I advise you to wait until April and call us back. You might win a prize."

Alice fell on the floor laughing but she still did not hang up the phone. Inspector Bing could hear her laughing and her colleagues asking her, "What happened? Why are you laughing so hard?"

"She doesn't believe our story," whispered Inspector Bing to Sergeant Bank.

Alice was now explaining to her colleague why she was laughing. Everyone else was laughing as well; they thought it was a joke. At the Palace of Westminster, the two police officers were in despair. No one believed their story.

"BBC radio was our last hope," Sergeant Bank said. "But I still believe in them. We have to call them back and insist they take us seriously. Let me try again once more." He called BBC again. This time a man answered.

"Good morning, my name is Andrew Steward. How can I help you?"

"Hello sir, I would be very glad if you could help me. My name is Peter Bank, I'm a sergeant on duty at the House of Parliament. My colleague Mark Bing just called to explain a situation to your colleague Ms Alice Mary, but no one took our story seriously enough to come check that it's true. I repeat to you the same sad news: Big Ben has disappeared. I swear on the Union Jack flag as Her Majesty's police officer, I would not do anything to jeopardise my job. Everything I do is to protect the public and the country. Could anyone there not come see for himself?"

Andrew Steward said to Sergeant Bank, "Your news is very hard to take seriously. The only thing I can do for you at this time is wish you a very happy New Year."

"What happy New Year are you wishing me, sir, when we have a tragedy like this? There won't be any celebration today in London without Big Ben!

Neither our boss nor the fire brigade believed us. We called Scotland Yard and no one picked up the phone there. That in itself is another unexplained mystery. The BBC, the great broadcasting service in the world, is our last hope. Please I do not presume to tell you how to do your job, but I do know that it is your duty is to keep the world informed. Do so now."

"If your boss and the fire brigade do not believe your story, it is because it is impossible to believe. Everyone here thinks it is a joke. As journalists we strive to report the news, yes. But news that is true. This could damage the prestige and reputation our broadcasting service maintains around the world. So my sincere advice to you is to call Scotland Yard."

"It is a true story, believe me," said Sergeant Bank, "As I said, we already called Scotland Yard. Doesn't it seem strange to you that they have not answered? Look Andrew, this issue isn't my problem alone, it is yours too and all the peoples of London and the United Kingdom, even around the world. Only God knows what has happened here. I beg you to be the first journalist to report this to the world. I understand how insane it sounds. If you hang up this phone, you'll regret it later."

"There is nothing we can do for you at this time, officer," the journalist Andrew Steward said calmly and hung up the phone. He turned to his colleagues and they all started laughing again.

Off to the side was a journalist named Michael James, putting up the first bulletin for the morning. He said to Andrew, "You just said it was a joke, what the police are insisting about. How do you know it is a joke?"

Andrew Steward said, "Oh, I just meant it's joke we cannot take seriously."

"And nobody here cares to investigate this apparent joke?"

No one answered him. They were too busy laughing.

At that time in the Palace of Westminster the two police officers were very discouraged and frustrated. They had done everything they could to inform people about the mysterious disappearance of Big Ben.

Inspector Bing asked himself, "What more can we do now? All we can do is wait until dawn and the sad news will reveal itself."

"We should not give up," said Sergeant Bank looking at his watch; it was ten past five in the morning. "I would like to try one last call to BBC Radio again."

He dialled the number. This time another journalist took the call.

"Good morning this is Michael James. How can I help you?"

"This is Peter Bank, sergeant on duty at the House of Parliament. This is our third call to BBC Radio, my colleague just spoke with your two colleagues there Ms Alice Mary and Mr Andrew Steward. Neither wanted to take his story seriously. So I would like to try again. We insist that you believe that Big Ben has disappeared."

"Well third time's the charm," said Michael. "I mean I don't think you would insist this much if it were a joke."

"You are very kind. I would like to confirm to you for the last time that Big Ben, the only one of its kind, has disappeared. It is not something I enjoy informing you. Therefore, please believe us. Your name will be printed and forever immortalised for being the first person who brought this news to the world. I feel like Atlas with the weight of the world on his shoulders."

These last words shook the reporter.

"Officer, I will see what I can do for you but I can't promise anything."

After hanging up the phone, Michael James turned to his colleagues.

"I have been a journalist here for thirty-five years. During that time I have never heard this kind of news before. I don't really know what to do, whether to take it seriously or not."

All his colleagues told him, "It's just a dumb joke, no one can actually steal Big Ben."

"That is true. I believe so too. But I remember my one teacher at university, Professor Smith, used to say to us: never undermine news from any source as insignificant as it may sound. Look more into it. It is your duty to bring the truth to the ears of the people. Now don't take me for a fool. I would like to go check myself whether or no they are telling the truth. Anything I find there I will let you know immediately. I don't want to go down there for nothing, but it is my duty as a journalist to do so."

Chapter Thirty-Three
Verifying the Truth

Michael James left the radio-broadcasting house and went to pick up his car in the garage, an Austin Healey 3000 MK III convertible with two doors, green, 1966 model. While driving from Portland Place towards Oxford Circus and then Regent Street, he noticed that his car was the only one on the road. The city was deserted. He also noticed some white statues holding hands on the pavement, covered in snow that he had never seen before. And then again, at Piccadilly Circus, he noticed nine more statues covered in snow standing just below Ero's fountain. He thought they were just new Christmas decorations.

Meanwhile, the two police officers at the Palace of Westminster were in despair wondering how Londoners will react when they will find out the clock is gone. They could not believe their luck that on that fateful night of all nights, they were on duty.

"We need to stop asking questions we won't get the answer to," said Sergeant Bank. "We'll face this in the morning. Let's not ask nonsense questions and wait and see if anyone else has heard anything."

During this time the reporter Michael James had found the road blocked from Trafalgar Square to Whitehall. He could not see Big Ben from there as usual, he supposed the fog was too thick. He drove his car towards the Mall, seeing Buckingham Palace and the Queen Victoria Fountain at the end of the road. Then he went left road towards Horse Guards Road, passing Churchill War Rooms and Clive Steps, and followed the road, turning left again towards Great George Street. Then he arrived at Parliament Square. He looked upwards at the clock tower and saw nothing there. He slammed on the brakes, making his tyres squeal on the pavement. Inspector Bing and Sergeant Bank heard the noise from inside the iron gate of the New Garden Yard. It was the first sound they had heard outside all morning. They looked out on the street to see where the noise came from. They saw nothing.

But nearby on Great George Street, was a parked police car, with four police officers asleep inside. They woke with a start at the sound of the tyres.

"What was that?" they asked each other. "What's going on?" They couldn't see outside their car covered in snow. They were stunned when they realised, they had all fallen asleep on patrol. The driver looked at the clock. It showed the time as half past three in the morning. But it was five thirty.

Then they saw the dark smoke coming from the tyres of a car down the road. A man got out of the car and ran quickly towards Parliament Square. He looked like he was trying to call someone on his mobile. The police found they could not react as quickly when they made to follow him. They could not understand why they felt so tired.

Michael James had managed call to the BBC and was confirming with his colleagues the unthinkable.

"The apparent joke was not a joke at all, it is true. Big Ben is gone. I am seeing it with my own eyes, the Elizabeth Tower is now empty without the clock atop. Do not release any information yet, I would like to investigate more. I will get back to you as soon I can. Please send a van here immediately."

As he hung up, Michael James was approached by the two officers who had called the BBC, Inspector Bing and Sergeant Bank.

"I am Michael James, the journalist of the BBC radio you talked to on the phone. I came to check what you told me. I owe you an apology on behalf of all my colleagues. We have behaved badly. We should have believed you."

"Thank you for coming," said Sergeant Bank to the reporter. "Unfortunately you are the third person who sees this sad image."

As he spoke Sergeant Bing saw four police officers coming towards them. When they were close to the statue of Sir Winston Churchill, they shouted to them, "Officers, this man must get a ticket for speeding. Why did you not have him remove his vehicle from the middle of the street?"

Inspector Bing and Sergeant Bank quickly explained to the four police officers that the man they were chasing was a reporter from BBC radio who had come to help them to reveal to the world that Big Ben had disappeared. After turning around and seeing what they said was true, one police officer fell to his knees in the shock after seeing the Elizabeth tower without Big Ben above.

Michael was already running fast across Parliament Square to hide behind Nelson Mandela's statue. When he looked back he saw the police talking with Inspector Bing and the Sergeant Bank. He thought that they had forgotten about him. To his surprise, he saw two of them coming towards his hidden place. He ran again towards Little George Street and hid behind the statue of the President Abraham Lincoln. From there he could see them from a short distance away. But the police did not chase him for long. The shocking discovery of the disappearance of Big Ben was more important than pursing a reporter for having left his car on the road. Mobilisation began and back up was called to block all road access around Parliament Square and Westminster Bridge until St Thomas Hospital.

During that time all the central computers and satellites in space started to restart as the effects of the powder wore off, including the radio and television stations. Some clocks started to reset to the right times automatically and many other machines started waking up. People as far as central London were slowly waking up.

The four police officers were taking to Sergeant Bank and Inspector Bing.

"We have the contact number of the Secretary of Defence Mr Henry Gordon Grass. We will call him to see what he thinks should be done next."

The Secretary of Defence actually answered. The police informed what was happening. Secretary of Defence could not believe such a thing could be possible.

"I will be there soon," he told them. His house was in Belgravia, not far from the House of Parliament.

The Secretary of Defence immediately informed the Prime Minister who was in deep shock. He told him to attend a special COBRA meeting at 10 Downing Street at six o'clock that the morning. Then the Prime Minister called Buckingham Palace to inform Her Majesty the Queen about the mysterious disappearance of Big Ben on New Year's Eve.

"Ma'am I am very sorry to wake you at this time in the morning. This call is not good news, I'm afraid. It seems our London has had some strange visitors last night and they have taken our beloved clock with them. Big Ben has disappeared, Your Majesty."

The Queen was calm.

"This is very bad news indeed. Keep me informed and assure people to remain calm. Try your best to find out who would do such a thing and why. Maybe there is still a chance of getting it back."

"Thank you Ma'am, for your words in these uncertain time," the Prime Minister replied.

After he hung up he told his private secretary to contact the other cabinet members and the army staff about the COBRA meeting. His secretary tried to call without success. No one answered the phone, which was very unusual.

The Prime Minister informed the allies of the United Kingdom around the world of the mysterious disappearance of Big Ben in London: Washington, Paris, Berlin, Japan, Italy, Madrid, Belgium, Amsterdam, Sweden, Denmark, Finland, the Kremlin in Moscow, even the Chinese government was informed. Washington immediately sent out its intelligence agency to investigate. If Big Ben had been lost perhaps other national monuments had been too.

The Secretary of Defence arrived at the Palace of Westminster to see for himself the unthinkable. He looked up at the empty clock tower in shock. He exchanged words with the police on call that night, and with the four police officers who had just arrived on scene.

"Officers, it is very hard to come to terms with the fact that our beloved Big Ben has been taken away from us. What kind of force or technology could do this?"

The journalist Michael James was watching them from his place behind the Abraham Lincoln statue, already writing his report to send back to the office. He saw two officers walking with the Secretary of Defence going towards Whitehall Street. He left his hiding place to follow them a short distance away. Then he saw them go to 10 Downing Street.

Michael James crossed the road near the underground and walked slowly on the other side of the pavement, passing in front of the Red Lion Pub until he came to the statue of the legendary army general Monty. He could see the Secretary of Defence talking to two police officers standing on guard behind the gate.

"Good morning, officers, open the gate please. The Secretary of Defence, Mr Henry Gordon Grass, has an urgent meeting with the Prime Minister this morning."

To their surprise the two police officers standing on the other side of the iron gate did not answer them or even make any sign that they had heard them. There just stood like statues with a layer of snow covering them. Only their faces were clean of snow, thanks to the police helmets they were wearing.

One of the police officers put his hand between the iron gate and tried to touch one of the guards standing inside. He got no response. Then the other officer climbed over the iron gate and jumped inside. He stood in front of the guards who did not react. He realised that they were asleep standing up. He patted them on their cheeks to wake them. When he touched their shoulders all the snow on their coats fell to the ground.

Suddenly they woke up and gave a military salute to their colleagues, as if nothing had happened.

"Mr Secretary, what a surprise to see you here so early in the morning," one said.

The Secretary of Defence said to them in a serious tone, "You are not allowed to sleep on duty, especially not at the Prime Minister's residence."

Then he asked them, "What time did you fall asleep?"

"We did not sleep, we never, ever asleep on duty," the police replied.

But the police officer who climbed the iron gate said to them, "You were asleep standing. I had to jump over the gate to wake you."

Michael heard all of this. He realised that maybe the figures he saw on Regent Street and below the Eros fountain in Piccadilly Circus were real people, stuck and trapped in the same mysterious situation as the police here.

Then Michael heard one police officer ask, "You didn't hear any noises around here last night?"

"Not at all; we didn't hear anything out there," the two police officers replied.

Then the Secretary of Defence told them, "Big Ben has disappeared. Someone has stolen it. You were standing here close by and heard nothing? You are Her Majesty's police officers. You must behave as such. Now Big Ben has disappeared. How do you explain that?"

The two police officers looked at each other, smiled and said, "Surely you are joking, Mr Secretary."

"Look towards the clock tower and see it for yourself, if Big Ben is still there." When the two police officers looked to their right and did not see Big Ben they, they started running like mad men towards the Palace of Westminster. They could not believe what they were seeing.

Michael came out from his hiding place to speak with the two police officers in the middle of road. They were surprised to see someone there so early morning. He introduced himself as a BBC reporter. They spoke about the mystery of the disappearance of Big Ben.

Then Michael asked them, "What time is it now?"

They looked at their watches and saw they still said three in the morning. They wondered how that could have happened.

The reporter whispered, "That is the same hour that I saw on clock in the office before I left to come here. I do not think this is a coincidence. It seems likely the mysterious disappearance of Big Ben occurred at this time. I could send my full report now to broadcast this to the world later."

He was searching for a safe place to send his report in secret, when he stopped outside the famous Red Lion pub at 48 Parliament Street. Then he walked around the corner towards the end of Derby Gate nearby. Just there he saw a figures like a statue covered in snow in the middle of the small street, a very unusual place to see a statue. He approached the figure. It looked like a real person, tall and slim, walking with his hands in the pockets of his coat.

Michael was quite certain these figures were not statues. They had to be people trapped asleep like the guards. He decided to wait for the cameras to arrive to reveal this to the world. But he needed to alert Scotland Yard.

Michael sent his full report to his colleagues at the BBC radio studios and requested again the van and equipment to broadcast the live images of the mystery surrounding the disappearance of Big Ben.

It was Alice who received the confirmation of Michael's full report.

"Oh God help us it is true. Big Ben has disappeared! Michael has just confirmed it in his last report. We need to get this news out there. Someone needs to go to the Houses of Parliament with the equipment."

"What? Big Ben has disappeared?" all the reporters in the radio studio sat, stunned. No one could believe it was not a joke was true. Andrew felt a bit guilty for not having believed the two policemen. The director of the programme gave the green light to prepare the full report. But due to the seriousness of the incident, they had to wait for the Director of BBC to give the go ahead after consulting with the authorities and the BBC Trust Board before doing so.

Chapter Thirty-Four
Informing the World about the Disappearance of Big Ben

The radio programme started by playing the unofficial national anthems of England, 'Jerusalem' followed by 'Nimrod' by Edward Elgar. It was very unusual for the BBC radio to start the broadcast this way. People from around the world, where the effects of the sleeping powder had not reached, were not aware anything had happened during the night. At half past six, the BBC informed the world of the news. After the five beeps, journalist Steven Max with his distinct voice went on air.

"This is BBC broadcasting services from London around the world. Good morning! Today is 31st December, the last day of the year. Dear listeners, I would like to start this programme by saying I won't be wishing you a happy New Year tonight at midnight, because today here in London is a very, very sad morning indeed. We have some very sad news to inform you of this morning. Please prepare yourselves. We have never made an announcement of this kind in the almost century since we have been broadcasting."

Those who were listening to the radio that early morning in London and across the United Kingdom and around the world began to get worried after hearing the unusual introduction from the host. They asked themselves, "What's happened? What is happening in London?"

The broadcast continued.

"Dear listeners, at this time I can hardly believe the sad news myself. I hope that all of you who are listening to our broadcast at this hour are ready."

Everyone listening was on tenterhooks, waiting to hear more.

"Dear listeners, I must inform you that the great unofficial ambassador of London, our beloved Big Ben, a symbol of England and a unique, iconic figure recognisable around the world, has been lost. I repeat: Big Ben has disappeared. It is no longer here in London on top of the Elizabeth Tower. The clock tower is now empty and almost in half without the icon of our city on top of it. The details of its disappearance are unknown at this time.

Not only did this great clock offer us a free public service, it was a friend to all, at home and abroad, offering a steady, reliable companionship to anyone who came to the city. Like a star, its face appeared in the same place in the sky every night, offering guidance and drawing admiration from millions of people worldwide. Today in particular, New Year's Eve, the clock would have been the centre of celebration for Londoners and tourists gathered here.

This will be the first time that people in London will spend New Year's without hearing the familiar sound of the bells of Big Ben, The Prince of Timekeepers, as it was called by clockmaker Ian Westworth is no longer with us. I don't really know what more to say about this mysterious loss or theft or disappearance…"

Then Steven Max said, "I will not draw out this sad news any longer. I advise you, faithful listeners, in the spirit of the holiday to spend time with your loved ones, and be safe."

The sad news ended with 'Loyalty Hymn' played in Big Ben's honour.

The news of the disappearance of Big Ben hit listeners worldwide like a bombshell. At hearing the news, people felt chills down their spine and got goose bumps. In the countries further south, where the sun was already high in the sky, there were people running like mad in the streets asking others "Did you hear the news? Big Ben has disappeared in London."

Many people did not believe this and wrote it off as nonsense. But those who heard the sombre radio announcement were insistent that others hear it themselves. Even in Jerusalem, after hearing the news that early morning, a group of Rabin went to pray on the Wailing Wall. But few people in London had heard the mysterious news yet. Most of them were still asleep. The Westminster area was still as quiet as a ghost town. Only ten people were awake there. The eight police officers, the Secretary of Defence and the journalist Michael James. But not for long. People were waking up slowly in their houses, their bodies feeling too tired and heavy still to get out of their beds. The magical cobweb that covered the city like a blanket had almost completely evaporated into the air. But thanks to the radio, people abroad and in other parts of the United Kingdom heard the news first thing that early morning. Some tried to contact their loved ones and friends in London without success. This was also very mysterious; that every single person's phone should be off at the same time.

The BBC van arrived at Parliament Square thirty-five minutes past six ready to broadcast live to the world. Among the reporters were Anthony Silvester, Nygel Boos and Alice Mary the blond-haired woman who had taken the officers' phone call earlier. Alice went immediately to hug her colleague Michael.

"I would like to go to apologise to you and the two police officers for having doubted their story before."

"You will have time later. Today we have work to do, more than ever before in our careers."

Then Michael James told all his colleagues, "The news you denied is true, as you can see for yourself. This is all in the past now; I have more strange news to tell you. I think I have found some people who are standing asleep like statues covered in snow in the Derby Gate nearby."

When the four policemen who had chased Michael earlier saw the BBC van stopped in front of Parliament Square they came to join them. They recognised Michael. He told the police officers that he had seen people around Regent Street and the Eros fountain at Piccadilly Circus frozen like statues.

"How do you know that they were people and not Christmas decorations?" the officers asked him. "What kind of proof do you have to confirm that?"

"I have strong evidence to prove it," Michael replied. "I saw with my own eyes when the police who accompanied the Secretary of Defence to number 10 Downing Street, woke the guards there who were asleep standing. After removing the snow off them they woke. I am serious. If you want to verify it go to the gate of number 10 Downing Street now and ask your colleagues there. They'll tell you what I am talking about."

Just then, an officer called Jack arrived and said to his colleagues, "I am the one who jumped over the gate at 10 Downing Street to wake the police who were on guard there. Both of them were sound asleep standing up."

"I am sure that there might be more people like this," said Michael.

So the police took their car and went to look for any unusual snow-covered statues in the streets of London to remove the snow and see what was underneath. They started on the Regent Street and Piccadilly Circus, where the reporter Michael had mentioned seeing them. They were amazed to find living people after removing the snow that covered their bodies. But none of them could remember what had happened to them.

Chapter Thirty-Five
Chief Milk Receives Confirmation of the Unthinkable News

At twenty minutes to seven, Chief Milk received a phone call from his friend Ronny Clark Smith. They had a bet going with a large bottle of champagne for whoever could wake the other first on the last day of the year. When the phone rang, Chief Milk woke and saw Ronny's number. He said to his wife Melanie Flores as he answered the phone,

"Ronny has won the bet! Good morning Ronny you have just won a bottle of champagne. You're the earlier riser, but it's only because I received a prank call at five in the morning from two of my officers. They interrupted my sleep otherwise I would have been up earlier."

"Hello John, thanks for that, anyway," said Ronny. "I actually didn't call you about our bet though, so you can keep the champagne. I called you precisely about the call you mentioned you received from your officers on duty at the Palace. I think it is a very serious matter indeed. I have just heard some strange news on the radio not long ago. I don't know whether you were aware of this or not. Although it does still sound almost too strange for me to believe fully."

"What's going on, I haven't heard any news yet," said Chief Milk.

Then Ronny said to him, "As strange as it sounds, I think it's real and verified. I mean, the BBC wouldn't share such kind of news on the New Year's Eve if it was false. They have reported that Big Ben has disappeared, believe it or not."

"What did you say, Ronny? Are you serious?" asked John Milk.

"Yes, I am serious," replied Ronny.

"Oh my God! It was true then," said Chief Milk, "Earlier this morning the two police officers on duty at the House of Parliament called me telling me this very thing, but I didn't believe them at all. As a matter of fact, I got rather angry and told them off for waking me to tell such nonsense stories. But they were telling the truth. What do you think about this strange news, Ronny?"

"I really think that this sad news is true unfortunately, although I haven't seen any image of it on the television yet. By the way, my wife told me BBC's 24-hour news is off, that too is very unusual. Lot of mysterious things going on this morning, it's hard to deny they're true."

After hearing this, Chief Milk threw down the phone and jumped out of bed in his blue pyjamas with thick black wool socks and leapt into his slippers before he even realised what he was doing. Just before going out the door he grabbed a fleece dressing gown in cobalt blue and put it on over the pyjamas, tying it around his waist as he went. He had no time to think about changing or taking his car in the cold winter. In fact, he lived at 50 Tothill Street right near the Palace of Westminster. When he looked at the Elizabeth Tower without seeing Big Ben on top, he gasped in shock and ran even faster from his house and crossed Parliament Square to the House of Parliament. There were already six police officers there and a few journalists with their recording equipment ready and waiting for the order to broadcast the live image of the missing Big Ben.

The six polices officers recognised the chief superintendent and saluted him; not all of them had noticed the way he was dressed. But he did not pay any attention to the police officers, just made a small gesture of acknowledgment with his right hand looking very worried indeed. He could not tear his eyes away from the space where the missing clock tower should have been, hardly believing what he was seeing. He was still breathing heavily from running so fast and could barely speak. His eyes were almost rolling into the back of his head as though he might faint. Finally, he managed to gain control of himself, and apologised to the two police officers on duty last night, Inspector Bing and Sergeant Bank.

"I am very sorry for not believing your story before officer. I should have the first time when you had reported this to me early in the morning. I should have come to assist you. Forgive me, I have behaved badly."

"It is nothing to apologise for, Chief Milk," Inspector Bing said to him. "It isn't easy news to believe if you don't see it with your own eyes. It has been very hard for us to believe all this too when we first discovered it. Still is now."

Moments later, the reporter Michael James came with Alice Mary, who also came to apologise to the officers for not believing their story when they called earlier.

"I am very sorry and ashamed of the way I had behaved when you needed someone to believe in you."

"It's nothing to apologise for," said Inspector Bing. "Such news is not easy to believe, you are not alone in that. But now that we are here, we need to work together to find out what happened to Big Ben."

It was then that Inspector Bing and Sergeant Bank and the other reporters noticed the way Chief Milk was dressed, including himself.

By now half of London was awoke, but still lying in bed tired and weak. The COBRA emergency meeting was still being held at 10 Downing Street. Chief Milk took the initiative and attempted to take the control of the situation by requesting from the first four police officers that they accompany him as he knocked on the doors of the neighbours of the Palace of Westminster and the surrounding area to see if they had heard anything strange last night. Even though he lived nearby, he had not heard anything. They decided not to tell anyone why they were waking them so early in morning and to leave that for later.

Before leaving he asked the two police on duty that night, "Have you asked the residents inside the Palace of Westminster if they heard anything about this?"

The two officers looked to each other.

"Chief Milk," said the inspector, "we didn't asked or knock on anyone's door inside the Palace because we wanted to inform you first."

"Very well," said Chief Milk. "Follow me then, officers. We need to start our investigation right here. Let's go knock on the door of the official resident of the Speaker of the House. He lives practically underneath the tower. I am sure that if both of you officers didn't hear anything, maybe the Speaker and his family did. Something so big and so heavy could not be removed almost above their residence without them hearing it or feeling their house shaking."

"You may be right, sir," said Inspector Bing. "But we will be very surprised if they heard something we didn't."

They headed to his residence and knocked on the door.

"Right sir, sorry to wake you. Could you please answer the door?"

But no one answered. They tried again, and were met only with silence.

"How strange that no one answered," said Chief Milk. "Well, we'll come back here later. Let's try some more houses near the Palace of Westminster. We should start with the priests of Westminster Abbey, I am sure he must have heard something. Inspector Bing, Sergeant Bank, stay at your post at the Palace while we continue this investigation."

"Yes, Chief Milk," they replied with a salute.

Chapter Thirty-Six
The Investigation of the Mystery Began

Scotland Yard had begun their investigation. They started at the houses in the area. No one answered the door. Then they went toward Derby Gate but only a few people answered the door there and talked with them. Nobody had heard any strange noises around there last night, not a sound.

But there was one thing in common of the few people they spoke with. They had never slept so deeply before. In the end they went to Westminster Abbey and began to wake the missionaries around there to ask them if they had heard any strange noises, or seen anything odd last night. It was impossible to believe that someone could have taken Big Ben away so easily weighing without making a single sound or waking anyone in the area, even if they were in so deep a sleep. The noise of the bells should have been heard from far away.

The residents of Westminster Abbey woke to the sound of the police banging on their doors so early and thought they came to arrest someone. A young priest came down, peered through the spyhole in the door and saw a police officer standing there. He went to call the Bishop Jack Paxman. The Bishop opened the door smiling to keep the situation calm. He saw the police with another man dressed in blue pyjamas with a fleece dressing gown thick slippers in a shape of a dog's head with long ears almost touching the ground.

The Bishop made no comment about the sight before him, but in his head he wondered what kind of strange dress code they had adopted in the force for winter.

"Good morning, Most Reverend Jack Paxman. We are very sorry for waking you so early morning, and in such manner. I am Her Majesty's Chief Milk in charge of security at the House of the Parliament and surrounding area of Westminster. Although I am still dressed in my pyjamas as you can see, this is in fact a matter of emergency. In fact we have a very serious problem which occurred here last night, if you could help us and answer some questions."

"Yes, of course," the Bishop replied, "we are happy to help."

"Thank you," said Chief Milk. "To start, I would like to be clear that there is no issue with you personally Most Reverend, or any other clergy. Instead, it is a problem that concerns all Londoners and the United Kingdom, even the whole world. We have just come here first because you are the closest neighbours to the Palace of Westminster."

"I see," said the Bishop, "go ahead with your questions and we will do our best to help. That is, after all, what we are here to do."

"Thank you for understanding, your Excellency," said Chief Milk. "As I said, something strange and mysterious happened near the Abbey last night. We would like to know if you heard any strange sounds around here? Including the bells of the clock?"

"We didn't hear anything from Big Ben actually," the Bishop replied and added, "but last night we slept like never before. I am really grateful that you have come to wake us up so early. Without you we were almost late for our morning prayer. As you know today is the last day of the year and we need to prepare many things for the mass on New Year's Eve and the celebrations afterward."

Chief Milk said to the Bishop, "Your Excellency, I don't think there will be any celebrations tonight or tomorrow…"

"Why do you say that, Chief Milk?" the Bishop asked.

"Your Excellency, may we talk in private please? I would like to tell you some disturbing news that I don't want spreading around just yet."

"Of course, we can talk in private," said the Bishop. They went into another room.

"Your Excellency, this is why we came to wake you so early morning. Big Ben disappeared last night."

"Big Ben has disappeared?" the Bishop asked in disbelief. "This cannot be true. How Big Ben could have disappeared? That can never be true."

"With all due respect, I would never come wake you like this so early morning if it wasn't for something very serious."

The Bishop did not answer and ran out into the Abbey Yard to look at the tower. He saw nothing. He cleaned his glasses, put them back again and looked again. Big Ben was not there. The Bishop was in shock, and knelt down to pray right there in the yard. Some other priests came out to join him.

"Your Excellency," they asked worriedly. "What is happening? Where is Big Ben?"

He said to them with worried face, "We must pray." The young priests too were in shock after seeing the empty clock tower without Big Ben above.

After a short prayer, the Bishop commanded the priests to immediately prepare an impromptu mass at the Old Palace Yard opposite Westminster Abbey near the statue of King Richard the Lionheart. Chief Milk came to thank the Bishop for his patience and cooperation. The Bishop said something strange to the chief superintendent before he left.

"I strongly believe that strange creatures visited London last night while we were asleep. I don't have another rational explanation about this great mystery. We will sorely miss the sounds of the bell telling us the time as they have for years. We are at your disposal, whatever we can offer you to help solve this mystery."

"Thank you, Your Excellency, for your kind words. We really needed them at this moment," said Chief Milk. And then he land the other police officers left to continue the search for Big Ben.

Chapter Thirty-Seven
Scotland Yard and the BBC Reporters

The other team from Scotland Yard continued with their own investigation in the Westminster area too, asking people the same question: whether they had seen or heard anything last night. But they still held off from saying why.

A few police officers and two reporters from BBC crossed Westminster Bridge to St Thomas Hospital to ask the staff and patients there if they heard anything last night. When they arrived at St Thomas Hospital everybody was still asleep, even the two security guards at the main entrance still dressed in their uniform of white shirts and blue trousers with black shoes. They rang the doorbell repeatedly to wake them. The security guard eventually woke up and came to open the door.

"Good morning, officers!"

"Hello," they replied.

"Can I help you?"

"We hope so," the police replied. "We would like to see someone in charge."

"Wait a moment," said the young security guard. "I'll go find the night manager."

He returned with him a few minutes later.

"Good morning, officers. My name is Charles. I am the night manager. What can I do for you?"

"Hello sir, sorry to bother you so early," said the police. "We would like access to your hospital to interview some of your staff about a very serious incident that had happened near here last night."

He did not specify what.

Charles said, "Officer, the hospital is still quiet at this time in the morning, many nightshift staff and patients are still asleep. Only a few people were awake during the night, if that would be enough for you. I can grant you the access to the hospital to interview them."

"Yes, that would be enough," said the officers. "Thank you, Charles. This is very important."

They managed to talk with some medical staff and one patient. No one heard anything suspicious there the night before.

The young journalist Alice Mary was in the maternity ward, where women and staff were normally awake looking after their new-borns and feeding them. She found one woman awake and greeted her.

"Good morning, ma'am. Congratulations!"

"Hello, thank you," she replied.

"Boy or girl?" Alice asked her.

"She is a baby girl," the mother replied, "I named her Britannia Mary Johnson."

"A lovely name," Alice said. "What is your name, please?"

"Clara Lexi Horton."

"Hi Mrs Horton, I'm Alice Mary, a journalist. I would like to ask you a few questions if I may. Sorry to bother you so early morning."

"Yes, I can," said Mrs Horton, "go ahead."

"I would like to know if you recall hearing Big Ben chiming last night?" said Alice.

"Yes, I did," said Mrs Horton smiling, "I heard Big Ben's chimes around half past one in the morning when I was feeding my baby. After that we both fell asleep."

"Since you have been in hospital did the sounds of Big Ben prevent you from sleeping well at night?"

"Not at all, its chimes have not bothered me."

"Thank you, Mrs Horton for your time," said Alice. "I wish you a very happy New Year and congratulations again."

"I wish you the same as well," Mrs Horton replied.

Alice left and went to meet with her colleague Anthony Silvester who was with the police officers waiting in the long corridor. They were about to leave when they saw a man with a friendly face sitting on a bench in the corner. He was waiting for his discharge letter to go home to celebrate the New Year with his family.

The Anthony approached him.

"Good morning, sir, sorry to bother you so early morning. We were wondering if we could ask you a few questions. Don't worry, nothing personal. My name is Anthony, Silvester, I am a journalist for BBC Radio."

"Hi, my name is Phillipe Herberg Martin, but you can just call Phil. How can I help you?" he asked.

"That's great, Phil," Anthony said. "Can you recall if Big Ben's chimes prevented you from sleeping last night?"

Phil smiled and said, "For me personally Big Ben's chimes have never been a bother since I was admitted here a week ago. But there are some patients who are unhappy at the sound of bells waking them up at all hours. Frankly, I think some of them are exaggerating. But you cannot please everyone…

For me and many others it has been a privilege hearing Big Ben chiming so close day and night. I can sincerely say its chimes sped up my recovery. Still I am looking forward to going home today. But last night I slept so well like never before in my whole life, but maybe that was just the drugs."

The policemen and the journalists looked at each other after hearing the same testimony about deep sleep as the other people they had questioned before. Then Phil looked at his watch and said, "How curious, I still have not heard Big Ben's chimes today and it is ten to seven in the morning. Maybe I am going deaf or maybe it's all this fog."

Anthony did not answer this. He thanked Phil for his time and kindness and wished him a full recovery and very happy New Year.

"I wish you the same," said Phil.

They left St Thomas Hospital still without any clear idea of what might have happened to Big Ben. The only thing they all seemed to agree upon was the deep sleep that everyone had had. They arrived back at the Palace shortly. When Chief Milk saw them coming he came up and asked, "Did you get any answers?"

"Nothing important so far, sir," they replied.

"I spoke to a new mother at St Thomas Hospital," said Alice. "She claims she heard Big Ben around half past one while feeding her baby, and then after that she fell in a deep asleep."

But no one could explain yet why the few people they had spoken with had all slept so deeply.

The mystery remained unsolved. They waited for the decision of the cabinet at the COBRA meeting, of whether or not to broadcast live images of the clock tower yet or not. Many unanswered questions were still spinning in the minds of the reporters and the police.

Chapter Thirty-Eight
The Londoners Wake Up from their Mysterious Deep Sleep

At just five minutes to seven, bus twelve was sitting at the stop at Elephant and Castle. Suddenly the driver woke up and began driving the bus without any idea that they had been stopped there since three in the morning. No passengers looked at the time or ask any questions, they had their headphones in, listening to music as though nothing had happened.

After leaving Elephant and Castle on Lambeth road, the bus passed below the railway and iron structure of Waterloo Station, near the roundabout at Circle Hotel towards the Westminster Bridge. Just when the bus was about to arrive at the St Thomas Hospital bus stop, he saw the police sign blocking road access. He slammed on the brakes, tyres squealing on the asphalt. All the passengers were thrown from their seats and looked around to see what was happening. The fog was heavy they could not see far. At that moment, the bus driver discovered Big Ben was missing. He sat behind the wheel, staring to be sure that what he had seen was not his eyes playing tricks. But he saw nothing where Big Ben used to be.

The passengers jumped as the bus driver started shouting.

"Good Lord, may God help us!"

He jumped out of the bus, abandoning it to run towards Westminster Bridge and get a closer look. There was panic inside the bus. They quickly left the bus to see what was happening. After looking where the driver had gone, they too caught sight of the impossible change in skyline ahead of them. The Elizabeth Tower was empty with no Big Ben on top. Everyone stood in shock; many began to scream and panic.

A young woman with blue hair and a nose piercing was walking around asking, "Am I dreaming? Am I dreaming? Big Ben could not just disappear, we must be somewhere else."

"This is London, young lady," said another passenger. "We are not dreaming. You can see St Paul's Cathedral and the London Eye and other buildings from here. Big Ben is missing. I can understand why the driver acted the way he did."

Many of the staff at St Thomas Hospital went out to see what all the commotion was about. Some patients looked from their windows. They were surprise to see a group of people running towards Westminster Bridge. Then they too saw that Big Ben had disappeared. A panic rose in the hospital. Some patients tried to go out to the bridge too, but the nurses stopped them. The night manager Charles realised why the police and reporters had been there earlier that morning.

"They knew that Big Ben had disappeared, but they did not say anything to us, maybe to avoid us getting so scared."

Then the friendly patient Phil found out the truth about the missing of Big Ben, and Mrs Horton as well, and then other patients in the hospital were looking out the windows in disbelief, some so affected that they began crying.

More and more people were approaching the bridges towards the Palace of Westminster. The four police officers on duty there could not do anything to stop the passengers from the bus from running towards the bridge. They just stood watching them standing at the end closer to the tower. People had begun trying to contact loved ones on the phone, but their mobiles were not working. Every network was somehow off. This was another mystery to everyone and the panic only deepened.

The reporter Anthony was taking picture of people running to gather at the bridges to see the empty clock tower closer.

"Soon the Westminster Bridge area will be filled with people. The police will have a tough job trying to contain so many people."

"That seems true," one of the officers replied.

Chief Milk said to Sergeant Bank and Inspector Bing, "Be prepared and think as far back as you can to remember anything that could be a clue. You are the first responsible for having been on duty here. You must be ready to tell the world what you may know."

And then cameras and lights and microphones were installed in front of the two officers to record what they would say. They had become unlucky and unwilling celebrities overnight.

The journalists asked them, "Could you tell us if you saw something strange around here last night? And how did you discover this in the first place?"

"We don't have any rational answer to give you, all this is mystery for us too," Inspector Bing replied with a sad face, and then fell silent.

Sergeant Bank added, "I am the one who discovered it was gone in the early morning. I went to check the time after I thought my watch was broken because I wasn't hearing any bells. I wasn't aware of anything bad when I headed there. No one could ever have expected the clock would disappear. But when I arrived there without seeing Big Ben above the clock tower, almost I fainted. Then I ran to tell my colleague here, Inspector Bing. At first he didn't believe me, he thought that maybe I was hallucinating. But when he himself discovered the truth, he almost went mad.

Then we tried to contact the Chief Milk present now to inform him. But he didn't believe us. He has since apologised of course. We understand that no one could have believed something like that without seeing it first. We tried to contact Scotland Yard, but no one answered the phone, which was also strange. We were getting pretty desperate so we tried the fire brigade. They didn't believe us either. So we decided to contact BBC Radio as our last hope. We called them three times. But they didn't believe us either. We had almost lost hope when we saw a man coming and introducing himself as a journalist from BBC Radio, Michael James. He apologised to us as well on the behalf of all his colleagues for not having believed us before.

Then we saw four police officers come running towards us saying, wanting to ticket the journalist for speeding. We told them under the circumstances maybe we could let him off. Frankly, we do not have any other important news that we can tell you at this stage."

Sergeant Bank and Inspector Bing tried in good faith to answer everything as the reporters continued to bombard them with questions. Around this time, the urgent COBRA meeting ended and the Secretary of Defence gave order to Scotland Yard to start the investigations and search of the great clock at a larger scale. They would leave no stone unturned. Soon after, the BBC Director gave the approval to broadcast the first live images of the empty tower to the world.

The first live image broadcasted to the world caused a huge impact and commotion worldwide. The effects of the sleeping powder had now completely evaporated across the city. More and more people woke up across London, unaware of any bad news. Most were focused on the New Year's Eve celebrations coming up. But after hearing the news about the missing Big Ben, thousands of people left their homes to see the Palace of Westminster for themselves. The public transportation and even the streets could not cope with that many people all at once. It was busier than rush hour at that same time in the morning.

At the headquarters of the London Fire Brigade, a group of young fire fighters saw the unthinkable news on the television.

"It is a true story, Big Ben has disappeared!" they shouted.

"We must go now to the House of Parliament," one of them said, "and apologise to the police officers who had called us early this morning for help and see if there is anything we can do."

They raced to one of their trucks, and headed towards the Palace of Westminster from Lambeth Bridge. They could see the empty clock tower without Big Ben on top. All of them were shocked. They could not imagine something like this ever happening to their city. After parking near Parliament Square, they ran to where the journalists were still interviewing the two officers on duty the night before. The chief fire fighter went right up and apologised to them and offered their moral support now.

Chapter Thirty-Nine
The Reporters Seek Answers

"We have tried our best to find help from the State, but unfortunately no one believed our story. Only the journalist Michael James trusted us, and came to see it for himself. We are very grateful to his support," Sergeant Bank was saying to the reporters.

Every television channel based in London was at the House of Parliament looking for more information about this mystery and waiting for the green light to broadcast the interview of the two officers on duty last night. There a lot of lights and cameras focused on the faces of Inspector Bing and Sergeant Bank, and microphones set in front of them.

"Who stole Big Ben?"

"Who took Big Ben away and why?"

"Where will you start looking?"

"How could our beloved clock have disappeared like that and right before New Year's?"

These were the question Sergeant Bank and Inspector Bing could not answer. But they were the only people were expecting to tell them what happened. After all, they were the only people who were on duty that night and this unfortunately meant that they were primarily responsible. They could not wash their hands easily of this and claim that it was a mystery beyond their control. People wanted answers.

After asking many rounds of questions Alice from BBC Radio asked them, "Did you fall asleep last night?"

Yes, I think so," Inspector Bing replied, after a brief silence. "It seems we fell asleep mysteriously last night. We both slept better than we have in years. But we don't really know how that happened. When we are on duty, we normally nap in shifts."

After Inspector Bing's honest answer, the journalists and the police officers looked at each other. It was becoming clear that all of London experienced this deep sleep last night.

Another reporter asked them, "Officers, could you tell us if you remember seeing anything strange yesterday?"

"Yes," answered Sergeant Bank. "I remember seeing something little strange yesterday, but I'm not certain that it's related to this event."

"What did you see yesterday?" the reporters asked him at the same time.

"Yesterday afternoon, Inspector Bing and I saw something rather odd here. Three crows were screaming very loudly and chasing Mr Smith the master keeper of the clock. We thought the birds wanted to eat something. But the birds refused to eat the breadcrumbs we offered and kept attacking Mr Smith's shoes quite aggressively. It shocked all of us, we had never seen crows behave that way before. They even followed him across the road. But we did not take this strange phenomenon seriously at the time, even now I don't think it is relevant to Big Ben disappearing."

Another reporter asked, "Where is the master keeper?"

He must be at home," Inspector Bing replied.

Chief Milk sent two police officers to find the master keeper.

Then Inspector Bing said, "Personally, I think aliens may have visited London last night and stole Big Ben and put us in a deep sleep. I do not see another rational explanation for all this."

"Do you believe in aliens?" asked the reporters.

"Yes, I do," Inspector Bing replied. "I have read many books about them. I don't think we are alone in the universe and there is other life on other planets, even if we haven't found it yet. Big Ben was in the clock tower just last night. Who else could have took something weighing tonnes so easily? Only aliens could have done this."

"This is a very big declaration to make on your part without proof," Anthony said.

The Chief Milk answered now.

"I defend my officers whether or not I agree with their hypothesis. The Bishop of Westminster Abbey suggested something similar to me earlier. We have never dealt with something like this before. It is unthinkable that an object so heavy could have just vanished like that without anyone hearing it.

There will be an enquiry to get to the bottom of this. Especially into what the satellites captured last night. With the mysterious disappearance of Big Ben they seem so far quite useless."

"Aliens or not, you were still the first responsible on guard here last night," a reporter name Julie Claire said to Sergeant Bank and Inspector Bing.

"That's true," said Sergeant Bank, "but we are not guilty of anything or any wrongdoing. It is not fair to try to blame us for this. We are only human, and very unfortunate ones at the moment, for being on duty when this occurred. We are guilty of falling asleep, but do not forget we are not only ones watching the Palace of Westminster or all of London, for that matter. Something else assists us every minute of every day that is more efficiency and does not get tired or need a change of guard. It allows the police to monitor the streets and public spaces and can also be used as a part of wider operations in conjunction with the City of London Corporation. I'm talking of course about CCTV. They could never fail at their jobs. So, if we didn't see anything that had happened mysteriously here last night at least the 500,000 CCTV cameras dotted around Greater London could have recorded something."

There were murmurs among the reporters, some of them saying, "Scotland Yard has got to check all the CCTV cameras. Maybe they recorded something that last night."

Inspector Bing and Sergeant Bank felt relieved and even vindicated at the reporters' and their colleagues' acceptance that this event was out of the ordinary and beyond their control.

As Scotland Yard left to check the CCTV, Chief Milk said to the reporters, "There is still one last mystery to reveal to you which may be troubling. I have been informed that they had found the two guards at 10 Downing Street asleep on duty as well. But standing, covered in snow, until rather forcefully awakened to allow the Secretary of Defence in."

"That's true," said Michael, "I witnessed that myself. I am the one who told the police to go wake the other people I saw around Regent Street and Piccadilly Circus. They were standing like statues too."

"How could this be possible?" his fellow reporters asked him. Many doubted this was true. "How could anyone fall asleep standing without falling to the ground?"

"I just know what I saw," said Michael.

Just then Chief Milk received the report from Scotland Yard on his phone. He stepped away from the cameras to read. Not a single recording made by CCTV had been saved last night. Chief Milk was beginning to get frustrated with the lack of leads. He was relying on CCTV to tell them at least something. He began pacing back and forth on the pavement. His left slipper fell off.

Oh! I just noticed you're still in your pyjamas!" said Alice.

"Who is in his pyjamas?" Chief Milk asked.

"You sir," said Alice.

Chief Milk looked down at himself and saw his blue pyjamas with his cobalt blue dressing gown. He looked at his feet and saw his soft toy Beagle slippers with long floppy ears and black eyes. It had the exact look of that determined little hound with the classic tri-coloured fur, right down to the white-tipped tail. They looked so real they seemed like they were about to bark.

"Excuse me, everyone," said Chief Milk. "I did not noticed that I was still dressed like this. I am very sorry. I will go change into my uniform and be right back."

A police car came and took him home. A few moments later he was back wearing his police chief officer uniform with its rank insignia and division number on the collar.

Chapter Forty
The Unveiling of the Truth about the Statues

The discussion about the statues continued, with the many doubts that it could be real people somehow trapped asleep.

"It is possible, believe me," Michael insisted to other reporters. "I have undeniable proof that I can show you not far from here. I would like to ask the police to accompany us. Please follow me with your cameras."

All the camera crews followed him towards Derby Gate just outside the Red Lion Pub. When they got there, they saw a white statue of a man standing with his hands in the pocket. After staring at it, one officer said,

"There has never been a statue in this place before. We have a record of all the statues in London."

"Officer, could you brush the snow off this man, please," asked Michael. Maybe he can tell us what happened."

"Certainly," said the officer.

All cameras were focused on the officer as he started to clear the snow off of the figure. He was a tall, thin man with short blond hair and blue eyes in a thin, gaunt face. He had on a long grey coat with jeans and boots. But their surprise came after the officer touched its shoulder. The man awoke and smiled at the officer, then noticed the presence of the many cameras focused on him.

He looked around, confused but otherwise unharmed. The officer asked him, "What is your name, sir?"

"My name is Alex Mel."

"Where do you live?"

"I live in Oval not far from here. Why so many questions, is something wrong?"

"No, sir," the officer replied, "We just want to know something if you could tell us about."

"I don't know what you mean, or what you are talking about, even I don't know what I am doing here in first place."

The officers said, "We just came here to help you, that is all. We just found you asleep standing and covered in snow."

"Me? Asleep standing up?" Mr Mel asked with dismay and astonishment.

"Yes, we just rescued you," the officer replied. "Look at the ground, you can see the snow around you that was covering your body. Somehow you are not wet, that itself is another mystery."

Mr Mel touched his hair, which was quite dry and said, "I don't understand anything. I am confused."

"We understand you," the officer said.

Everybody was amazed to see this man alive who had been standing like a statue just a few seconds ago. It was like something out of this world. Some people began to believe Inspector Bing's hypothesis that maybe the aliens really were the cause.

Then Michael approached Mr Mel.

"I am the person who found you here early this morning."

Mr Alex Mel looked to Michael with a blank stare as though he did not hear anything he had just told him. He swayed a little, as if he lacked balance. This was normal after spending hours standing asleep like a statue.

Michael asked Mr Mel, "Could you tell us what happened to you, please?"

"I do not remember anything," Mr Mel replied. "I don't even know what I am doing here. The only thing I can remember is that I was at a party with my friends on the restaurant ship R.S. La Hispaniola on the Victoria Embankment. My friends had already left, and then later I walked home alone. Or so I thought I did until I saw your faces here before me. By the way what time is it?"

"It is nine o'clock in the morning," said Michael.

"What?" Mr Mel exclaimed. "Nine o'clock in the morning? I will be very late for work today. I am telecom engineer and I'm supposed to be on call. Please let me through, I have to go now."

He became fully aware of his situation. He was fully awake and seemed to have regained consciousness. The officers asked him,

"Can't you remember anything that might have happened to you last night, at all? Did you hear anything strange?"

"I do not remember anything, officer," Mr Mel replied. He was very agitated after learning what time it was and the way he had been found. "I am ashamed of what happened to me."

"You shouldn't be embarrassed about what had happened to you at all," said Michael. "This is a mystery for all of us too."

"I still cannot believe that I was found asleep standing like a statue. This must be some sick joke."

"It is not a joke. It is a very serious matter indeed," said Chief Milk. "We have just rescued you. You were asleep, standing like a statue covered with snow."

"Are you sure about that?" Mr Mel asked.

"Yes, we are sure about what we are saying. Look at the snow around you like the officer said."

Mr Mel crouched to the ground to touch the snow and felt it cold on his hands. He shook his head in amazement. Then he got up and thanked the police for rescuing him and thanked especially Michael for having discovered him there.

The police then explained to Mr Mel about Big Ben.

"That cannot be true, you must be joking," he said after hearing the news.

"We are not joking, and neither are all the reporters here. You can yourself, go ahead and look."

Mr Mel went to the main road to check. When he saw that it was really not there he fell to his knees and said,

"The people who did this could easily have taken me away like they did Big Ben. I don't feel safe out here anymore. I might never go out alone again, ever." He turned to the police standing there. "Please, officer, you have to take me home. I don't want to walk alone."

"We would like to help you but we can't," the officer told Mr Mel. "All the bridges of the River Thames are full of people looking for the answers to the disappearance. You can go to your house safely. I assure you, nothing bad will happen to you."

"Yes, thank you, officers," said Mr Mel. He walked towards Westminster Bridge and vanished in the crowd.

Then news came that the Metropolitan Police had freed four people who were standing asleep like statues on the Regent Street and nine other young couples by the Eros fountain in Piccadilly Circus. All the people rescued were grateful to the police. But they could not remember a single thing. A short while later they heard from Scotland Yard that they had just found three more people in the same situation on Tower Bridge.

One of the officers said, "I am sure that this is not the last case of its kind."

Scotland Yard reported on the news that they did not find any recordings of the theft on the CCTV. This was another mystery that the security cameras could have failed all across London. People were impatient and troubled at the lack of explanation. More and more people were arriving around the House of the Parliament to see for themselves the unimaginable image of the Elizabeth Tower without Big Ben on top.

Chapter Forty-One
The Strange Story of the Master Clock Keeper

Then Mr Smith, the master of the great clock, arrived with the police at the House of Parliament. When he saw the Elizabeth Tower empty without Big Ben on top he could not hold back the tears coming to his eyes. Some reporters approached him and said,

"Master clock keeper, you are the last person to touch Big Ben yesterday afternoon. Do you remember anything suspicious or unusual you may have seen around there?"

"Yes, yes, I remember seeing many black birds flying around the clock tower as they do every day. But this time they were many more birds than before," said Mr Smith.

The reporters all shouted more questions at the same time.

"How many birds and what species were they?"

"They were crows, around two dozens of them, maybe more, if memory serves."

"How are you sure that they were more than usual?"

"Yes, I am sure I remember it well. When I came out of the clock tower, I saw three of them standing in front of me, but their behaviour was very unusual. I tried to dodge them by jumping over them, but they blocked my way. The two police officers here, Inspector Bing and Sergeant Bank, witnessed it. They told me to feed the birds. Something I did with great pleasure. But to my surprise, the birds refused to eat the breadcrumbs that I gave them and continued shouting, screaming and yelling at me. They were even trying to peck my shoes, luckily for me I wore thick winter socks, otherwise they could had cut my feet quite badly with their sharp beaks.

This unusual and aggressive behaviour scared me. After leaving the key I walked towards the Westminster Tube Station, but the three crows followed me screaming behind, even crossing the street to follow me. I think people thought I'd done something wrong to them. Some found it funny. For me it wasn't a joke or a laughing matter. Indeed their mysterious behaviour towards me had no rational explanation.

I was relieved to take the tube and leave them behind. I arrived home scared and very worried indeed. I managed to calm down and pull myself together. I couldn't say anything to my family to avoid being called superstitious and to not spoil the party that's about to take place tonight.

Unfortunately it will no longer be possible to celebrate anything after a tragedy like this. Big Ben was like a friend or even family to me, after so many years working to keep it running. I would even speak to it from time to time. I could tell which pieces needed oiling just by the sound. I know that might sound a bit mad to you, but it is no ordinary machine. I have been very fortunate and very privileged to have the honour to work alongside Big Ben. I feel an emptiness inside me without the great clock that I saw just yesterday when I left an old 2 pence on the pendulum as all master clock keepers did before me. That is all I can say at this time."

"Thank you, master clock keeper for your touching account of these events," the reporters said to him.

The emotional tribute of Mr Smith left the people gathered there and listening abroad in silence.

"I've just noticed that something very important is missing here too," said Mr Smith.

"What is it, what's missing?" shouted the reporter, trying to shove their microphones closest. Chief Milk, Sergeant Bank and Inspector Bing paid attention more closely.

"The standard symbol of our great nation, the huge Union Jack flag is missing. It was waving on the Victoria Tower just yesterday. Who took it?"

Everybody looked in that direction and saw that indeed the flag was not there.

"Where is the flag, where is the flag? How could the winter flag as big as half tennis court disappear just like that?" people anxiously asked each other.

Scotland Yard mobilised again to investigate the question of the missing winter flag. They were never so busy since Sir Robert Peel founded them in 1829. The person on duty to raise and lower it assured them that the flag was there yesterday as always. The police searched for the flag everywhere but found nothing.

"Who could have stolen the winter flag from the Victoria tower? The same people who stole Big Ben?"

This was another unexplained mystery. Very few people had access to the Victoria Tower. Then after the master clock keeper spoke again.

"I would like to see inside the clock tower."

Amazingly, no one had thought to look inside yet. They unlocked the door and walked inside, looking around. A surprise awaited them. The tower was not open in the top like they had thought. It was covered with a thick layer of snow as though it had a roof.

The master clock keeper, Chief Milk and the on-duty officers stared in amazement.

"What kind of people could have done a thing like this?" asked Mr Smith. "What was their intention, to protect the staircases?"

None of them had an answer. They went back outside where the reporters were waiting.

"How does it look the Elizabeth Tower?"

"It just looks like an awful, sad empty space without Big Ben," Chief Milk replied.

Then the journalists asked him, "Could you allow us to take pictures inside the tower?"

"No, sorry I cannot allow you to do that, safety precaution. The structure of the clock tower and the staircase is very fragile."

Fortunately, the reporters left it at that. But then overhead a helicopter could be seen flying by taking pictures of the tower. The photographer above was surprised to see in his photographs that the tower was covered with snow.

All the bridges across the River Thames were filled with crowds of people, their eyes on the remains of the Elizabeth Tower.

Chapter Forty-Two
Complaints of Theft and a Strange Net on the Bridge

Scotland Yard received a complaint from the manager of the House of Parliament's Gift Shop. Someone had broken in last night and left a note behind apologising for having shopped during closing hours. The police were astonished that the note even mentioned the lengthy list of items they had taken. Thirty-three in total were missing from the shop, valued at over five thousand pounds. But most surprising was the priceless blue diamond they left behind in compensation. The alarms had not gone off, the manager told them, nor had any door or display been broken. The clock on the wall had stopped at five minutes to three. It had been working fine when the store manager closed the shop yesterday afternoon. The break-in was added to the growing list of mysterious occurrences from the night before. The forensic police arrived at the House of Parliament Shop and began working quickly, searching for evidence and maybe an actual lead. While they worked, the clock on the wall suddenly reset the time by itself.

All major television channels were keeping people informed of all this. Scotland Yard received another strange complaint from the owner of a tourist boat that someone had stolen one hundred metres of rope from his boat. Scotland Yard mobilised again to try to solve this theft as well. They found nothing. But they took samples of the ropes left on the boat to be analysed by forensics.

People watching on the bridges of the River Thames began to lose hope and patience screaming, "We want the truth, we want the truth, where is our Big Ben?"

One hour later people found a large fishing net hanging on Westminster Bridge. The huge net was made with quite large spaces between it. It was clearly not for catching fish. They called the police to come investigate, who arrived quickly. After comparing the samples of the ropes they had taken from the tourist boat they found the ropes matched. They were clearly cut with something sharp. But no one had any answers as to who may have cut off the ropes of the boat and why. How and why had they built a huge net and abandoned it? Many unanswered questions. But at least they were starting to put pieces of evidence together to paint some sort of picture.

When the police officers went to take the huge net away for further analysis, they felt electric shocks on their hands. This was not any normal net.

They quickly let go of it and it fell into the River Thames smoking. They could not figure out how ropes from a boat built into a net could cause an electric shock. As they watched it floating in the water of the River Thames, the water of the River Thames suddenly began churning slowly, bubbles and whirlpools forming and then small waves started to appear until the river began to turn white with foam. And then it froze. From Waterloo Bridge to Lambeth Bridge, it completely froze like one large piece of ice floating on the water.

Voices screamed from in the crowd.

"Maybe Big Ben is hidden under the water!"

"It is could be possible," other voices replied fearfully.

Everyone stood and watched the frozen chunk of the river floating like a small white island while the rest of the water ran normally downstream. All television channels began updating their story to include this new mysterious turn of events. People began to believe perhaps it was the end of the world.

Immediately Chief Milk sent a special underwater search unit to investigate it. Later they were joined by professional divers to look for the great clock under the waters of the River Thames.

Chapter Forty-Three
A Piece of Big Ben is Mysteriously Found in Iceland

During this time, far away from London, another mystery was unfolding in the small town of Húsavík in northern Iceland, more than 1,182 miles away from London. It was still quite dark there in the early morning of winter. A priest named Johannes Jensen woke up early that morning for early mass for the sailors of the small fishing town before they left to go fishing. While walking to the small white wooden church, to his surprise, he found an unusual single metal object outside in the courtyard. It was quite clean and grey in colour with a serial number GC-118- GB.

He picked up the metal object and studied it. After opening the church and leaving it in the basket of lost and found items, the priest walked to the alter, made the sign of the cross and genuflected. After lighting the candles, people began entering the church. They were mostly sailors, young and old, and some old and young ladies dressed in traditional jumpers and winter coats. They greeted the priest with smiling faces.

"Good morning, Father Johannes."

"Hello everyone!"

All of them knew each other well in a town that small. None of them, including the priest, had listened to the news on the radio or watched the television yet that morning.

The priest began his sermon.

"Dear brothers and sisters, as you know today is the 31 of December. We are celebrating the first mass of the last day of this year and tonight we will celebrate as well at the final midnight mass, *Gamlarskvold*. This will be followed by the first mass of the New Year at one minute past midnight, *Nyarsdagur*. We pray for all the best in the new year ahead, for good health and safety of all people of our town, and all of Iceland and throughout the world. A special prayer for our sailors at sea. There were no tragedies this year and we hope the next will be the same with the blessing and the protection of God the creator of heaven and Earth. Amen."

Johannes Jensen was reading the Gospel of Matthew when a man entered the church. He walked past the pews directly to the altar and spoke to the priest in low voice, making urgent gestures with his hands. He seemed frightened and agitated as if something bad had happened. The people in the pews were looking at each other, wondering if something had happened at sea. They waited nervously to find out. Every home had someone in the fishing business in their harbour town.

The man went to take his seat and the priest stood up and said to the congregation,

"Dear brothers and sisters, I have just been informed of some very sad and unusual news from London."

"I have just been told that the great clock of London, known as Big Ben, disappeared last night."

"What? What happened?" the people asked among themselves. "Big Ben has disappeared?"

The good mood and expectations of the celebrations for New Year's Eve at midnight changed to grief. The priest calmed them and reminded them to have faith and hope.

"Let us pray for the sad loss of the most famous clock in the world." Shortly after the service ended and before people left, the priest Johannes Jensen showed them what he had found.

"I would like to show you a piece of metal I found in the courtyard of the church this morning. Perhaps one of you knows what this is. Maybe it is something for the fishing boats. Obviously it's really not my area of expertise."

He took the small object out of the basket.

"Here it is. If no one has any idea what it is or come to claim it leave it in the basket so that the owner can find it here someday."

A man named Anderson Byerk, a naval mechanical engineer, took it in his hands and examined it. He saw it had a serial number GC-118-GB. He had no idea what that could mean.

"Father, this object is not a part of a boat engine, I can assure you that."

Another man said, "Father, this does not belong to a boat."

"Thank you," said the priest, putting the object back into the basket.

Before going their separate ways, they spoke again about the mysterious tragedy that had happened in London.

"When a tragedy like this happens anywhere in the world, we must remember that it could happen anywhere. At this time, the only thing we can do is to pray and be in solidarity with the people of London and the United Kingdom. In the meantime we'll keep following the news for updates."

But when Father Johannes went home he was still very concerned about what happened in London. Then he had the brilliant idea to take a picture of the strange object he had found outside the church and send it to the local newspaper to publish it online so the owner could see it and come collect it from the church. Then he began to pray for the mysterious disappearance of Big Ben.

Thousands of miles away from Húsavík in London nobody had any idea that a piece of their famous clock was sitting in a lost and found box in a church in Iceland.

Chapter Forty-Four
A Man Found Sleeping Under a Blanket of Snow

At this time in London, an underwater search unit and the professional divers were searching for Big Ben under the frozen waters of the River Thames. But the brave divers found nothing. The crowd cheered for them anyway for their courageous efforts. Just after the divers had climbed out of the water, it began to thaw and the massive island of ice disappeared only to be replaced with a large circle of bubbling water and then hundreds of roses in red, white and blue appeared forming a large circle, white in the middle, followed by blue and red roses around the outside. Everyone gasped and shouted as six dolphins appeared leaping around the rings of roses and some of the roses floated together to form six letters reading 'Big Ben' After a few seconds those flowers letters changed again into a large heart with the initials 'BB' Then all the flowers mixed together and separated again to form the Union Jack flag. The six dolphins appeared again, playing and jumping about among those beautiful roses and completely ruining the pattern. The flowers begin spinning in the river, making bubbles and whirlpools and disappearing entirely beneath the waters of the River Thames.

People standing on Westminster Bride were speechless. Another mystery had just happened on the River Thames. They wondered how something like this could have happened. Was it a magic trick or tribute made by someone in honour of Big Ben? Word and video footage spread to those not on the bridge, and many were afraid of what this could mean. No one had seen this sort of behaviour from nature before.

At the Westminster Bridge, chanting was heard from the crowd.

"We want the truth, we want to know the truth about all these mysteries! Are we safe here or not anymore? We want the truth!"

But no one could give them any. Nobody had any rational explanation yet. The only truth they knew was that Big Ben was missing. The reporters had turned back to getting more answers out of Sergeant Bank and Inspector Bing. Suddenly they heard shouts and murmurs from the crowd.

"Help, help, help, please!"

It was coming from the people standing around the plinth of the Queen Boudicca statue. Many were running away in shock and fear. Some of the reporters ran over in time to see a man's hand coming out of the snow on the ground.

They alerted the police nearby. A few officers ran over to find a large tall man with long brown hair and beard, brushing the snow off his coat His hair was still covered with snow, but was not wet. He was wearing a long brown coat with faded jeans and black boots tied tightly as if he did not take them off his feet often. But amazingly, neither he nor his clothes were wet. They were dry as if he had not just been buried under the snow all morning. He stomped his feet to clean the snow off his boot. He seemed as though he might fall down, swaying a bit at the hips. He leaned back against the large, granite plinth of the statue, making strange motions with his hands as though about to bless the people around him, his eyes half open. Finally he clasped his hands to his chest.

The strange man looked out at the crowd and smiled in a funny way, showing the blackened teeth of heavy smoker. He did not say anything.

"Sir? Are you alright?" the police asked him.

"Yes, I'm fine. I believe so," he replied.

"Would you like us to call the paramedics?"

"Yes, if you say so. But nothing is wrong with me. I am fine," he replied.

"Thank you for your cooperation," one of the officers said to him, "it would be best to have you checked by a professional after being asleep out in the cold under the snow."

The strange man looked at them with a blank stare as if he did not hear or understand what the policeman had just told him. The paramedics checked him, taking his pulse and blood pressure. They were amazed after their assessment to find that he was in perfect condition. He did not have hypothermia, a cold or a fever at all. He was as well as if he had slept in his bed at home.

Michael said to Alice, "This is more proof of whatever happened in London last night…"

The crowd watched the strange man in amazement at the man who should have not died or lost consciousness but was walking and talking as though he had not just slept under the snow all night. After being checked by the paramedic the strange character walked the short distance from Westminster Bridge to Parliament Square, cameras and reporters following him and asking him questions all at the same time.

"Do you remember seeing any strange things around here last night? Did you hear any noises?"

"I heard nothing," he replied.

One reporter asked him, "How were you able to endure such low temperatures for so long and stay as dry as you are now?"

"I have nothing to say. I do not remember anything that happened to me. All of this is strange for me as it is for you. I started partying a bit earlier yesterday and I had had quite a bit to drink, more than I should have apparently. The only thing I remember as I was going home was bright lights appearing from nowhere, focused over Big Ben with red, blue and violet colours. After seeing that, I got scared so I hid myself beneath the Queen Boudicca statue. After that I remember nothing, and then I woke up now under the snow surrounded by a crowd of people."

"Could you tell us more about these strange multi-coloured lights you saw?"

"I do not remember anything else," he replied.

There were so many people around him that he could barely walk forward.

"Stop following me," he said loudly. "I have nothing to tell you."

More and more cameras followed him. Finally, he walked towards the Parliament Square and sat down on the white steps near the statue of Gandhi. He seemed a little lost and confused by the cameras and reporters following him like he was a celebrity.

Michael said to Chief Milk, "I would like to talk with this man and ask him a few questions myself. This is similar to that man Mr Mel asleep under the snow, but even more extraordinary."

"Go ahead," said Chief Milk.

"Thanks," said Michael. He approached the man. "Sorry sir, what is your name and where do you live?"

"My name is David Wise, I was born and raised here in London. Nowadays I live in Pimlico Churchill Gardens."

"How do you feel now after being woken up under the snow?"

"Please do not ask me why I fell asleep in the street in the snow. I didn't feel cold and that's all I can remember. I'm not proud of myself. I just started celebrating New Year's Eve a little bit too earlier."

"Don't worry," said Michael, "Everyone here including myself thinks you broke a Guinness World Record for this. You are a strong and special man indeed."

"Thanks but I'm no hero," David replied.

"I'm not trying to flatter you. I've never seen anything like that," said Michael. "There's something you should know. The reason you see so many Maybe you noticed something missing?"

"I don't see anything missing around here," he replied with his eyes still half open.

"Mr David Wise, perhaps you did not notice but Big Ben is missing. Our priceless clock has been taken away from us."

At hearing that, David looked up at the clock tower with his half-open eyes.

"Big Ben is still there as usual. Who could have stolen something so big anyhow? If Big Ben was truly lost, I know the watchmakers who have been repairing it so it's ready to ring tonight to celebrate the New Year and they will bring it back soon."

The people around them were surprise to hear such funny comments. It seemed like this man did not take the disappearance of Big Ben seriously.

The police told the reporters, "You're wasting your time here. Do not believe what this man tells you. We've seen him before, roaming the streets of London. He does like to drink."

David listened to everything the police said about him without saying anything. Some reporters started leaving. Then he raised his left hand to stop them as if had just remembered something very important.

All the reporters looked at him expectantly. But then he put his arm down and said nothing, just stared at the ground. After a brief silence, during which the reporters turned to leave in disappointment, he said, "If I tell you what I know about the whereabouts of Big Ben, what can you offer me in exchange?"

"Whatever you want," all the reporters answered him excitedly.

"Are you sure?"

"Yes, we are sure," the reporters replied.

"Good," said David calmly. "I will tell you what little I know. Please excuse me if I do not remember everything just now. My memory is still a bit foggy."

One reporter asked him, "Do you fancy eating something? You need to get your strength up."

David Wise just looked at the reporters and said in soft low voice, "Eat something? I don't think so."

He moved his mouth but no sound came up. He touched his throat and chin. "I don't feel hungry at all, but I would like something hot to drink to warm me up." It was a reasonable request.

The soft feminine voice of reporter Julie Claire came from the crowd.

"Do you fancy a cup of tea? That would do you good."

David Wise looked at her with half a smile on his face. "Thank you for your kindness, miss. But I'm afraid a cup of tea won't be quite strong enough after a night under the snow."

"Perhaps some hot soup?"

David Wise looked at her again with a smiling face, touching his beard. He said in a slow voice, "I really fancy something strong, like, like…"

Then he stopped.

"Tell us and we will provide it for you if it is in our means," said another reporter.

"Thank you," said David. "A bottle of Johnny Walker, Red or Black label, will do. That's all I need right now."

Everyone gathered around was surprised at his simple, albeit inappropriate for that time of day, request. He probably could have asked for a million of pounds and received it.

"This is your only request?" said Michael. "A bottle of whisky? Not even a whole box?"

"Yes, please," David Wise replied calmly. "I'll settle for just one bottle. I need to be able to remember all the details. But I'll only talk once I've gotten that drink."

The officers and reporters looked each other in dismay. Then they sent someone off for the bottle of whisky. As they waited, the reporters set up their many cameras, microphones and lights, all focused on David Wise's face. His eyes shone in the lights and he felt a bit embarrassed and shy at being in the centre of it all.

Then they brought him his bottle of whisky. He took it with a smile and looked at the people around him. Then he took a long drink straight from the bottle, gulping it down noisily like someone who has gone days in the desert without water. Then he stopped and wiped his mouth on his sleeve and burped loudly. The bottle of whisky was almost half gone. The reporters waited eagerly and impatiently.

Finally Michael said to him, "We have fulfilled your request. Now tell us what you know about the disappearance of Big Ben."

David Wise was the only man on that sad morning who had made worldwide reporters believe he could really reveal something about the mystery surrounding the disappearance of Big Ben. Not even the satellites in space or CCVT had been able to do that. He held up his right hand as a sign that he was about to talk. Cameras, lights and microphones all focused on him.

Michael told him, "Soon you will be live on television. People from around the world are waiting for answers."

"I am ready," said David. "I will tell the world what I know about this mystery. Although I know I won't be able to convince everyone. But at least I can bring some hope to all of us. Tell me when I can begin."

"We are going on live now," said Michael, "so be sure to be speak slowly and clearly."

"Thanks for the advice," said David, "I've never been on the telly before."

The reporter Julie offered to fix up his face and hair a bit. One reporter even lent him his tie. His interview was a short break of relief for Sergeant Bank and Inspector Bing after giving so many interviews since early morning. Now the focus turned on David Wise. When he saw his face in the cameras zoom lens, he began to feel a bit nervous but that was normal when he was about to be on live television for the first time in his life.

He cleared his throat. Then the interview began.

"My name is David Wise. Around ten after three this morning, I was walking along the river bank near Westminster Pier. That's when I saw these colourful lights shining in the sky. They were focused on Big Ben. I never saw anything like this before in my whole life. I kind of started to panic at that point. I went to hide behind the statue of Queen Boudicca. Then I heard the bells ringing haphazardly like if they were rung by someone pulling a rope really fast. Then it was quiet again and the lights disappeared with Big Ben. I don't remember anything else after that. Next thing I know I'm being woken up in the snow."

Everyone listening, both in Parliament Square and through the television, was silent. That was not what they had expected. No one was sure how to react to his claims, which sounded more like a fantasy story, impossible to believe. But in this situation who could contradict him without any other explanation?

The reporters began asking David Wise questions all at once.

"You said you saw strange lights taking Big Ben away just after three o'clock in the morning?"

Yes, that is correct," David replied.

Then Chief Milk interrupted.

"How could you know it was three in the morning without a watch?"

David Wise took the opportunity of the police chief's interruption to take another swig.

Then he said as though it were obvious, "I know it was three in the morning because Big Ben was still in its usual place and rang three times."

This made things even more interesting. While all the clocks and watches of London stopped mysteriously around half past two the previous night, Big Ben was still running at three. A few of the reporters looked less sceptical of what he was saying. But the police were not. The man seemed to be enjoying the attention he was receiving, and he did not seem to be taking the disappearance seriously. To them, David Wise was just a drunk taking advantage of the situation to get more free booze. If the CCTV surveillance cameras did not record anything, there was no way he could have seen what he claimed to have seen.

"Can you give us any more details?" asked the reporters.

David reiterated that he saw bright colourful lights coming from the clouds and taking Big Ben away. The chains that bound the bells to the great clock were loose underneath and bumping wildly into each other making a sound that could shatter an eardrum or woken a patient from coma at St Thomas Hospital nearby.

"I'm not exaggerating, if you could have seen it as I saw. I could hear as the bells ringing wildly in the clouds, almost like an alarm. After the sound disappeared from my ears, there was silence. I heard nothing more until I was found this morning."

Everybody was quiet, listening to David Wise's account. He had them all captivated. So he continued further.

"Ladies and gentlemen, and all of you watching across the United Kingdom and around the world, I will conclude my account as follows. My true and faithful account with sincerity, impartiality, objectivity and honesty seems to be the only solid evidence we have of what happened last night. It is clear CCTV and satellites have let us down. Personally, I hope many of you will agree with me too and be very disappointed and frustrated at how useless CCTV has proven to be. By some miracle I was able to witness this sad mysterious event so that I could tell it to the world. Without any doubt, if I didn't witness what had happened I am sure we would be completely lost, without any idea how to solve this mystery. I've been very fortunate and lucky to not go mad after seeing this happen before my eyes. No one should describe himself as brave, others should say it for him. But I can say that I was brave and maybe also a bit lucky, if these unknown people who took Big Ben away with them came in search of humans, I could have been taken too. Thank you."

"What kind of lights are so strong they could carry Big Ben away?" asked the reporters.

"They were not something I could describe easily, it was something beyond belief. They did it as easily as ripping a sheet of paper, effortlessly."

David drank more until the bottle was almost empty. He wiped his mouth on his sleeve again.

Michael asked him, "Could you point us in which direction these lights appeared from in the sky? And in which direction exactly they took Big Ben?"

"Yes, of course," David replied calmly looking into the cloudy sky as though he were searching for something. Then he got up with the empty bottle in his hand and shaded his eyes with the other. Everyone looked in the direction he was facing.

After a short moment that seemed like an eternity for the reporters, David finally pointed his finger.

"There. I saw the strange lights appear and take our Big Ben away from that way. I'm sure it was in that direction."

Everyone was looking into the sky. The reporters were becoming frustrated at his vaguely pointing into the sky.

"Could you be more precise? From which direction exactly did the lights appear in the sky?"

"Yes, I'm showing you," David replied, pointing again. "It was up there in the direction I am pointing now, just follow my finger."

"We don't see anything just the cloudy sky," they said frustrated. All the cameramen were focusing their cameras where he was pointing as if something would appear any second.

The crowd was also becoming fed up with this man. Some people began yelling and booing.

"He's a liar and a drunk! He's just filling us with false hope. Shame on you!"

"I'm sorry to disappoint so many people," said David. "This was my account. Everything happened so fast, it's hard to remember it all clearly now."

The Chief Milk said to the reporters, "Do not take him seriously, he has invented this story for a free drink."

"That's not true. I do not lie!" said David. But his argument was weak with the empty whisky bottle hanging from his hand and no concreted proof to support it. Still he insisted his story was true. But no one could entirely deny his account. The fact remained that Big Ben was no longer in its place. David began to get worried, realising his face had just been shown on people's televisions all over the world.

To defend himself against the accusations he said in a loud voice, "I'm not a liar, I have spoken the truth about what I saw happen. You'll all see one day."

The Chief Milk spoke privately with a reporter. A few moments later, that reporter came to ask David Wise a question to test his honesty.

"Do you want another bottle of whisky before any further questions? It seems like you have something more to tell us."

David Wise looked at the reporter and brushed his long thick hair from his face. Before he could answer, a large murmur went out among the reporters who were all looking at Twitter and Instagram on their mobiles. Then they turned their backs on David Wise and left him sitting alone below the statue of Gandhi in Parliament Square.

"Where are you going?" called David. "Where are you going? Something happened?"

Nobody looked back or answer him.

The reason the reporters and the police had left so suddenly was due to the incredible news that had just come from Iceland, from the small town called Húsavík. The local newspaper Skarpur had posted a photo on Twitter of the finding of a small grey piece of metal with the serial number GC-118-GB. At first, not much importance was given to this picture. As the news was coming from Iceland it seemed to have nothing to do with the disappearance of Big Ben in London. But all that changed when Michael approached the master clock keeper Mr Smith to show him that picture. He recognised it immediately. It belonged to Big Ben, he was sure if it. How could it get to Iceland overnight? The mystery of the disappearance of Big Ben had taken another turn.

The people at BBC Radio immediately took action, contacting the journalist in Húsavík to confirm that the story of how it was found and that it really was a part from Big Ben. It was not long before the priest, Johannes Jenssen, become another unbidden star of the world news. He had no idea that the unidentifiable object could belong to the missing Big Ben. Immediately, the British Government chartered a special plane to go fetch the priest and bring him to London along with the part. He accepted, honoured at the invitation and the opportunity to pray in front of the Elizabeth Tower.

After his live television interview, search parties were sent out across all the Scandinavian countries, accompanied by the RAF, looking for any trace of Big Ben.

Back in London, media attention had turned again to David Wise. He was surprised to see the reporters return suddenly back in front of him. He was still sitting in the same place at the statue. Many people from the crowd were looking at him. Between his story and the confusion about the news unfolding from Iceland, the public's opinion in the United Kingdom and around the world was more split than ever. Many people started to believe in the possibility that David Wise's account was true, while the other half did not believe him at all. Especially Chief Milk, who considered his account dubious at best. The media was divided as well. Some reporters believed in his account. Others did not. But after finding the small part of the mechanism of Big Ben near the edge of the Arctic Circle, David Wise's version of events could not be entirely fake.

To settle matters and avoid unnecessary arguments among the people, the BBC organised an interactive survey asking the public what they were really thought David Wise's account. The result were divided in half. The discovery of the small part in Iceland over one thousand kilometres away, rather than answering questions, only added more mystery and confusion.

The reporters told David that the public was divided on whether or not they agree with him.

"I am not surprised," he said. "I had predicted that the public opinion would be divided. It wasn't intended to convince everyone."

As they were talking, the news arrived from NASA and the Pentagon that their satellites in space had not recorded anything of what happened in London. In fact, when they checked the recordings they found nothing but white static for exactly thirty and a half minutes just after three in the morning. Their satellites had never failed before and definitely not all at the same time. This was another unexplained mystery. Even the astronauts at the International Space Station had been asleep during that time. They noticed that the station had even stopped for a few minutes in orbit. Instead of sixteen laps around Earth, the computer showed just ten. This last day of the year turned out to be the saddest. People were desperate and in fear of what might happen next. Everyone prayed that nothing more would happen.

Chapter Forty-Five
The Police Doubt David Wise's Story

Chief Milk said to David Wise, "Your face is recognised worldwide after this. But we do not accept your account of the disappearance at all. Worse, the report coming from the Pentagon and NASA is that their satellites didn't record anything of this last night. It seems very hard to believe that you were the only person happened to see it. The only thing that seems to match with your account and theirs is the time."

"Sir, you should be thanking me for all the information I gave you. The police on duty last night did not even see this. You are being unfair. What about the part found far away in Iceland. How did Big Ben get there? I stand by my story," said David Wise.

The Chief Milk was becoming annoyed with the foolish man and his stories that distracted from the real issue. Many people were beginning to believe his account of the event.

Chief Inspector Jason Long said to the reporters, "We do not believe Mr Wise's account due to lack of evidence. He has just gotten lucky that his story and NASA's coincidentally coincide."

"On what do you base these doubts?" the reporters asked the spokesman.

"On this: first Mr Wise said he heard the bells toll up above in the sky. A very loud sound that they would have woken anyone nearby, if not half the city. But after asking all staff and patients at St Thomas Hospital, we learned that no one heard anything. Even the priests and bishop of Westminster Abbey and all the residents in this area heard nothing. Everyone claimed to be fast asleep.

Second, how could Mr Wise have seen something CCTV and satellites did not? We know for sure that the CCTV cameras are constantly recording. How did they not record this? We consider this ignoble act a theft, not a disappearance, because a giant clock cannot just disappear. Someone stole it and ensured no one would find out who they are.

"Third, the CCTV cameras can never fail if the power does not fail. We have not received any report yet of any electrical failures last night in London or any part of the United Kingdom. Therefore we will continue to trust what the CCTV cameras tell us. Remember in 1999 when it caught those two figures many people believed to be ghosts? So after examining all the footage without seeing anything they could have recorded of this incident, you can understand why we have very strong doubts about the account of Mr Wise."

The reporters asked David if he had anything to say after all this.

"I have nothing to say. Only time will tell," David replied.

During all this time no one in London had noticed the black bird quietly perched in the bicorn Hat on top of the statue of Horatio Nelson Trafalgar Square. The bird was Ser, still camouflaged as a crow. Neither had anyone noticed the sadness reflected in the faces of the statues in the city, wondering who could be the next to disappear like Big Ben. More and more people were arriving around the Palace of Westminster. There was no place left to stand on the bridges across the River Thames. In the windows of St Thomas Hospital, doctors, staff and patients were staring at the empty clock tower. The mother of the baby Britannia Mary Johnson recalled why the reporter had questioned her earlier that morning. They watched as people on the bridges and surrounding areas knelt down to pray. It was a lovely gesture of solidarity to witness. Murmurs of thousands of different voices and languages was heard praying together among the many religions and beliefs practiced in London. Catholics, Protestants, those of Eastern Orthodoxy, Jewish people, Muslims, Hindus, Sikhs, Buddhists, Taoists, Shintoists, Jehovah's Witnesses, those of Baha'i Faith, Humanists, believers and non-believers alike could be seen praying together.

London had always been a melting pot, a multicultural metropolis now with over fifteen different religions and faiths and three hundred and fifty different ethnic groups of different languages that made up the mosaic of society of London. All prayed together over the disappearance of Big Ben. Many people were praying with their eyes closed and some with their heads down. Others were just moving theirs lips. Some just stood still, having lost the habit of praying long ago. Many hoped for a miracle. Unfortunately, nothing happened. The unbearable silence of Big Ben created an emptiness in the normally loud, hectic city.

Then to everyone's surprise, David Wise began speaking loudly.

"Oh, beloved Big Ben, you were a unique and unforgettable clock, the most famous in the world. You were a steadfast, reliable presence to all. You treated everyone equally. Oh, Big Ben we cry for your loss. As they say, you don't know what you've got 'til it's gone. Although just a clock, you were an honorary citizen of this city too. We hope that your example of dignity and integrity will inspire us all and bring us together as one to honour your legacy."

After his stirring words, Michael the reporter asked him, "Do you fancy another bottle?"

"Not at all," David Wise replied and added, "I do not want to spend another night unconscious under the snow. Whoever stole Big Ben could have taken me too. I won't be so lucky a second time."

Then more strange news arrived from a short distance away in Piccadilly Circus. A young couple was arguing. A girl wanted to go home after hearing about all the strange things that had happened in the London. Her boyfriend wanted to go see the tower without Big Ben. Witnesses claimed to have seen the Eros statue coming alive and shooting an arrow of love at them with his bow causing them to start kissing, ending their argument. Then the statue returned to just that, a statue, as if nothing had happened. Those who saw it could hardly believe their eyes. Only the fact that others had seen the same thing, confirmed that they had not imagined it. Another surprise came when everyone discovered that somehow none of their devices had recorded it.

The famous and popular Eros statue at Piccadilly Circus became another mysterious attraction in the city as well. Crowds gathered there waiting to see if the Eros statue would move again. But it did not.

Chapter Forty-Six
More Strange Occurrences with the Monuments

Moments later, similar news was reported from New York, where people claimed to have seen the Statue of Liberty moving her hand holding the torch and a stream of tears flowing from her eyes before returning to normal. The tourists fled in panic from the island. Also people gathered and skating around the world most famous Rockefeller Center claimed to have seen the Christmas Tree there rose up from the ground to the high of the skyline and back down to the ground, people fled in panic. The incredible news shocked the world.

While everyone was commenting on social media, another similar incident occurred in Paris where the iron structure of the Eiffel Tower stretched its long neck like a living giraffe, seeming to peer into the windows of nearby apartments and hotels. People ran screaming in shock at the sight in their windows and people below and around the Eiffel Tower at that time ran away. But then the Eiffel Tower returned and stood in its usual place as if it had not moved at all. When they reported that mysterious incident to the police, no one believed them.

Similar news was reported in other countries around the world. In Berlin people saw the Golden Angel of Peace flying towards Brandenburg Gate and return as before on the Column of Victory. Berliners and tourists were in shock. Many were surprised to find that their devices did not record any of it. In the city of Rio de Janeiro in Brazil atop Corcovado Mountain, the world's largest Art Deco statue, Christ the Redeemer, moved his large hands. People were in fear and panic at first and then took it as a miracle. When that news spread around, the area was full of thousands of pilgrims, coming to him move again. No one could explain why this strange phenomenon happened or what it meant. In Rome, the horses inside the Trevi fountain come alive and neighed enthusiastically. Another mystery occurred in Amsterdam where people saw The Night Watch sculptures in Rembrandt square come alive, playing with their muskets while the girl and boy smiled and waved at people. At the sound of the drums all of them took off their hats and helmets on their heads and bowed. Even the small dog barked. And then they were back to being statues like before. Also people standing outside the historic Tower of the Winds in Athens Greece, saw the frieze turning above showing the eight winds god alive looking at them blowing the airs into the wind, and second later they were back to being like before, people ran away in fear after seen such unthinkable thing happen.

Even as far away as the Easter Islands in the Pacific, people reported having seen all fifteen monolithic figure heads moving from left to right as if dancing. Then they leaned on one another and turning around, before becoming as still as they had been for centuries. The tourists who saw ran away in fright. Those who stayed to record found that their video cameras and mobile phones had captured nothing. The inhabitants of Easter Island had never seen anything like it before in their lives or heard any legends of something like this from their ancestors. In Egypt, people saw the Great Sphinx of Giza's body transform into a giant living lion while the head of King Chephen moved from left to right. In Spain in Cibeles Square, the most famous iconic statue and symbol of Madrid of the goddess sitting in a chariot pulled by two lions came alive. The chariot wheels raced while the lions raised their legs and roared in and then returned to normal just as suddenly. In Denmark, they reported that in Copenhagen the Little Mermaid statue had jumped into the water and then returned to her seat of stone. The sculptor Edvard Eriksen would never have believed such thing. All of this strange phenomenon was impossible to explain.

Chapter Forty-Seven
A Mysterious Bird in Trafalgar Square

While people were still trying to digest all of incredible news, another mysterious thing happened in Trafalgar Square in London. A group of thirteen crows was flying aggressively around trying to attack another crow perched on the bicorn hat on the statue of the legendary Admiral Horatio Nelson.

Why were so many birds acting against one single bird? Perhaps it was an issue of territory. All the aggressive birds formed a circle flapping around the single bird to make it fall to the ground or fly away. To prevent something worse from happening, some people called the RSPCA and the fire department to come to rescue the lonely bird.

As the people watched, they had no idea what the group of crows was saying to the single bird.

"You're a fake crow camouflaged to hide your true identity. We have already discovered your game, and who you really are. A fake crow, an alien on our land. We know that you are from another planet. You're one of those who came to cut our clock tower to steal our beloved Big Ben. You can barely talk like us or smell like us. You are lucky that we cannot communicate with the humans, otherwise we could tell them what you've done. Because of you, people will fear us and mistrust us. We and the humans have been living together side by side for thousands of years without any problems. Your shameful act could break our friendship and trust with them."

Just as the flock of birds was becoming more aggressive, group of fire fighters arrived at Trafalgar Square with a team from the RSPCA. Without wasting time, they raised a crane up to the height of the Column. But strangely the aggressive crows were not frightened by the humans' presence. To drive away the aggressive crows, the fire fighters lit firecrackers, and they flew off in fright. Just as one of the fire men reached with a small net to rescue the bird, he opened his eyes and dodged it. He tried to fly away and then fell to the ground. No one dared pick it up. The strange bird walked to the middle of the plaque erected by Parliament in memory of Admirals Earl Jellicoe and Earl Beatty. A member of the RSPCA got off from the crane and came closer to try to pick up the crow with his net.

But the birds screamed, making an awful sound not familiar from a crow species. The people from the RSPCA thought maybe they had found a new species. That encouraged them even more to rescue him, to check him over thoroughly. Perhaps that was why the crows were attacking this strange bird.

But the strange bird was still dodging them. After more unsuccessful attempts to catch it, the bird gave one last loud scream like an out-of-tune trumpet combined with a bellowing elephant. The RSPCA rescue team stepped backwards cautiously. Then they tried to grab it again with the net. The strange bird dodged them again and suddenly a kind of strobe light seemed to come from the bird and began flashing on and off. The strange bird transformed from a crow into an eagle with feathers like a parrot, seeming to move in slow motion from the effects of the strobe lights all the while trumpeting loudly. People in the vicinity were quite alarmed at the sight and attempted to run away while shielding their eyes. Then the mysterious bird transformed into ashes, leaving everyone standing there blinking from the brightness of the flashing lights. Only the small ring it wore on its leg was left on the ground.

When a man from the RSPCA tried to pick up that small ring, it rose up in the air and became a white ring of smoke with sparks flying from it. It floated over a metre high and then flew into the sky and disappeared inside the clouds. When the firemen tried to collect the ashes left on the ground by the bird for New Scotland Yard, they disappeared too. Trafalgar Square went up in total panic. Some people went to hide under the Christmas Tree from Norway. Were these birds hidden only in London or were they elsewhere in the world? And where had they come from? Was this related to Big Ben's disappearance? People became suspicious of every bird they saw fly by.

When this latest news about the crow reached Inspector Bing, Sergeant Bank and Mr Smith, they were certain it was one of the crows from yesterday. The reporters asked them if the birds they saw made a sound like an elephant or became eagles with feathers like a parrot.

"No, nothing like that," they admitted. "The birds we saw yesterday sounded like normal crows."

This latest news was reported around the world again, adding to the growing list of mysterious events that day. This was certainly not turning out to be just another ordinary day in London.

Chapter Forty-Eight
The Latest Update on the Mysterious Event

Around four o'clock, news reporter Peter Piers Putney of BBC-24 gave the latest update on the incredible events that had occurred that day in London and around the world.

"Today we woke up in London to the shocking discovery that Big Ben had disappeared. No one saw or heard anything of what happened. Not even the guards who were on duty last night at the Palace of Westminster. The only thing that seems certain about last night is that almost everyone slept an unusually deep sleep, like they had never experienced before. The vibrant, dynamic London was completely silent for probably the first time in its history.

More mysterious events followed this one. The discovery of people asleep standing like white statues covering in snow from Regent Street to Piccadilly Circus below the Eros statue fountain, at 10 Downing Street, the Queen's Guard at Buckingham Palace and on Tower Bridge. A big breakthrough came when a man named Alex Mel was discovered standing asleep near Derby Gate in Whitehall and then another man, David Wise, was discovered asleep under a thick layer of snow, next to the statue of Queen Boudicca. He claims to have seen powerful multi-coloured lights taking Big Ben away into the sky around three in the morning. What is more strange, is that all the people who were found asleep under the snow were perfectly fine and completely dry. David Wise's account now has the public opinion of the disappearance totally split in half.

The discovery of a fishing net that appeared to be electric at Westminster Bridge came next. After the strange net was dropped into the River Thames, part of the river froze like a white island between the Waterloo and Lambeth bridges. These ropes turned out to be stolen from a nearby tourist boat, whose owner had reported them missing not long before. This layer of ice quickly melted and, the surprise of the many bystanders, roses appeared on the River Thames and then, somehow, dolphins jumped out of the water over it as the flowers formed the six letters of Big Ben's name and then its initials BB. They then rearranged to form the Union Jack flag before disappearing underwater.

"Speaking of this, the missing winter flag on Victoria Tower at the Palace of Westminster is another unsolved mystery of the day, possibly linked to the disappearance of the clock. Also possibly linked is the thirty-three missing items from the House of Parliament gift shop, in which the thief left behind an apology note with a rare blue diamond as compensation for what they had stolen. The discovery of the small part from Big Ben's clockwork in Húsavík, a small town in northeast Iceland, is thought to be the first clue in relation to this mystery, and is a small ray of hope and consolation for British citizens.

Adding to the peculiarity of this event is the fact that not a single one of the 500,000 CCTV cameras in London managed to record a single thing. The Pentagon and NASA reported that their satellites did not record anything either. Every satellite in space seemed to have stopped working for thirty and a half minutes exactly last night. All the recordings are blank. Even at the ISS, astronauts reported having all fell asleep at this time and losing six laps around the Earth. These strange occurrences are still left unexplained.

Finally, the famous Eros statue fountain in Piccadilly Circus made headlines after it came alive and shot its arrow at a young couple. Related incidents were reported around the world. From the statue of Liberty in New York, and the Rockefeller Center Christmas Tree, the Christ the Redeemer in Rio de Janeiro, the Eiffel Tower in Paris, the angel on the Victory Column in Berlin, the Trevi fountain in Rome, the Tower of the Winds in Athens, in Egypt, the Great Sphinx of Giza's of King Chephen, the heads on Easter Island, the Cibeles statue in Madrid, the Little Mermaid in Copenhagen, to The Night's Watch statue in Amsterdam. And now we have reports of the most recent incident in which a crow in Trafalgar Square was screaming and then turned into ashes before people's eyes. People are beginning to refer to these events as supernatural. Some believe these are signs of the end of the world. Others believe we have just had our first encounter with the third kind.

Now we have the latest report from the central power plant of London. Their computers show a lowered intensity in power occurred from three until half past three in the morning. Nothing like this has ever happened before. This would explain why CCTV was not recording. The charity English Heritage has just reported that the remaining 1,500 gas lamps in London all went off mysteriously last night. The five remaining lamplighters say that this should not be possible. They left the lights well-lit last night as they always do.

Similar unexplained and strange phenomena have just occurred to other clock towers worldwide. They are reported to have been autonomously making strange movements with their hands and their figurines turning back and forth as though malfunctioning. Their hour hands were apparently turning anticlockwise before returning themselves to the correct time as before. Among the famous clocks towers were the Zytglogge tower in Bern, the Astronomical and Olomouc Clocks in the Czech Republic, the Old Joe Memorial Clock at the University of Birmingham, the clock tower in Edinburgh, the Venice and Brescia clocks in Italy, the clocks of the Lyon and Beauvais Cathedrals of France, the astronomical clock of Lund Cathedral in Sweden, the Aker Brygge clock in Oslo, the Verdensur in Copenhagen, the Helsinki Central Railway Station clock tower in Finland, the Hallgrimskirkja clock tower in Reykjavik, Iceland, the clock of the Zimmer tower in Belgium, the Munich Town Hall clock in Germany, the Gdansk Town Hall clock in Poland, the Philadelphia City Hall clock in America, the Peace Tower in Ottawa, the Iquique clock tower in Chile, Cape Town's City Hall clock in South Africa, the Jaffa Clock

Tower in Israel, the Rajabai Clock Tower in Mumbai, Deira Clocktower in Dubai, the old Clock Tower in Qatar, the Custom House clock tower in Shanghai, the old Victorian clock tower in Sydney, the Victoria Clock Tower in New Zealand, the clock on the Spasskaya Tower in Moscow and the Vatican City great clock in St Peter's Basilica in Rome, Italy. The Japanese newspaper, *Yomiuri Shimbun* reported that the Osaka Station City Water Clock inexplicably stopped working for two minutes and displayed Big Ben's name in the water and showed the hour as half past three. Then the water clock went back to functioning normally as if nothing had happened. Something like this has never happened before."

Moments later, the Mayor of London appeared on live television to assure people that the authorities were taking all the necessary measures to protected people' safety. Even his words could not take ease the sadness and fear felt across the city. But they were not alone; the entire world was with them in solidarity, thoughts and prayers.

"The celebration of the New Year will take place tonight with or without Big Ben. But there will be less fireworks and music than usual. There will be one single firework set off in Big Ben's honour. Instead, I would ask that everyone light a candle to hold up at midnight. We will applaud the name of Big Ben, along with many other cities and towns around the globe. These gestures of solidarity will show whoever stole Big Ben that we will never allow them to frighten us or take away our spirit. London is still standing strong."

Those listening to this speech burst into applause. It was the first time since waking up that people felt safe and secure.

At seven in the evening, the Icelandic priest from Húsavík landed at London Gatwick airport with the small part from Big Ben secured in a small glass box. The Mayor of London greeted him and took him to Central London. After arriving at the Palace of Westminster he was received by the Archbishop of Canterbury with other members of all creeds and religions practiced in London. Finally, the priest Johannes Jensen was introduced to Peter Bank and Mark Bing. Also present was Chief Milk and David Wise. Mr Smith had the sad honour of taking the small glass from the hands of the priest. As the only memory left of the great clock, it was to be kept in a secret place. It was already dark in London, but the temperature remained mild. While they were waiting for midnight to arrive and close the chapter of this sad day, the Archbishop of Canterbury and the Icelandic priest with other religion members of the United Kingdom began to pray together, some kneeling, others standing.

As all of this was happening, the ring of white smoke left behind by the strange bird was still intact and making its way through the galaxy at high speed back to the mysterious village of Black Cloud on planet Oxon.

Chapter Forty-Nine
Ser returns to Planet Oxon

When Ms Moxum saw the image of the ring of white smoke arriving through the Potsat she was relieved and hurried outside to catch it. All the birds surrounded her shouting, "Ser has arrived!" Moxum opened a magic ring on her index finger that shone with an azure blue light to guide the smoke ring through the invisible net. Then she took her magic wand and first turned it into the black ring the bird wore before, then a crow and then a normal sized golden eagle.

Then she said, "At last I see you, and I have you here."

The bird Ser tried to smile to her. Moxum looked at him with a serious face and said, "You have behaved very badly on this secret mission by staying behind. Because of you, the humans witnessed your transformations when the real crows attacked you, exposing the secret of your true identity. I expected that the disappearance of Big Ben would remain an eternal mystery for humankind. Now they may be able to figure it out. Your irresponsible act betrayed us. Therefore the only punishment you deserve is to be returned to the dry mosquito you were before. Never again will you become a bird or go on any secret missions anywhere."

The bird Ser was startled by the harsh words of anger from Ms Moxum

He cried saying, "Please forgive me master! I beg your pardon, it was my first mission. I will never doing anything like that again, you have my word. I have learned my lesson."

"I have made my decision and cannot change it. Your offence was very serious."

Ser cried again in despair, "Please forgive me, I accept full responsibility for my actions. The dose of your magic formula I took wasn't enough for me. I was tired after the long trip and had no strength left. That's why I couldn't participate in the work of the secret mission. I was lost in London without knowing that my colleagues had already returned home. Still, I managed to return here on my own without a human catching me."

"You seem to doubt the effectiveness of my magic power," said Ms Moxum angrily, "although the other birds obeyed all my instructions without failure. Only you have failed me. Now you disappoint me with your excuse making. I have been very kind to you, offering you an opportunity to go discover another planet, even though you weren't as fit. I trusted you in spite of this to go on this secret mission. But you did not do anything at all. And the most serious and unforgivable of all your mistakes was revealing to humans the secret of you identity. Your actions left clues to the mystery that I wanted to remain intact so that the humans would never discover anything about the theft of Big Ben. But now they already know something, because you helped them.

For all of these very serious offences, I cannot forgive you. You have failed in your duties. Look around, I have awarded your colleagues by allowing them to stay normal birds forever. I return you as you were before, a lifeless speck, like a little mosquito locked in the small glass bottle. This is the punishment you have earned."

The bird Ser cried again, still asking for forgiveness and flapping his wings in desperation, but Ms Moxum ignored him. Without another word, she grabbed the bird Ser and put him inside the water of the Potsat. Within seconds, the bird had become a tiny black speck again. She took it out with a skimmer and put it alone into the small green glass bottle and sealed it well. Then she shook the small bottle near her ear and said, "Never again you will get out of here."

Then she began laughing loudly.

Her sister Eris watched all of this happen and found it very hard to accept that the bird Ser she saw alive just a moment ago was now inside the small bottle as if he never was a golden eagle.

Chapter Fifty
Uncertainty in London

Meanwhile in London, people were still afraid of any bird flying near them. It was not easy for them to distinguish which were crows and which might not be. People were most afraid of what might happen to them if a bird touched them. The mysterious incident at Trafalgar Square caused an unfortunate mistrust in crows especially, after millennia of peaceful coexistence between the two species. In fact, people had become cautious not only of birds but towards anything unusual. The birds on their part continued flying around. They did not want to leave the city or lose their centuries-old friendship with the humans.

In despair they squawked at the humans, "Do not reject us please, we are the real crows you have always known. We know you cannot understand us, but we too are victims of this mystery. Those damn impostor crows camouflaged themselves as us. The single crow we were attacking was one of them. Let us remain friends as we always have been!"

During that time the police formed a human fence in Central London to protect people who were gathered from Trafalgar Square to Whitehall and the Palace of Westminster where a symbolic ceremony of New Year's Eve was to take place. At the New Green Yard below the Elizabeth Tower, many government members were present, including the royal princes and princesses, the clergy and members of other religions, ambassadors, Chief Milk and the two officers, Inspector Bing and Sergeant Bank, the master clock keeper and of course David Wise, the only man who claimed to have witnessed the mysterious disappearance of Big Ben.

Chapter Fifty-One
The Sad Celebration of the New Year

At eleven o'clock in London, the countdown to the new year began with much less enthusiasm than usual. The main part of the celebration was dedicated to showing solidarity with the United Kingdom and remembrance of Big Ben. Masses were held everywhere, even in Vatican City by the Pope. People worldwide were waiting for midnight London time to light their candles and hold a moment of silence.

The Mayor of London was ready and waiting to push a button that would launch a surprise that his technicians had installed in secret beforehand. And so it was he who did the countdown to midnight. The familiar sounds of the bells of Big Ben surprised all who gathered there and those listening in. They had not expected recordings of the bells from four large speakers installed on the roofs near the Elizabeth Tower as well as others on the Victoria Tower. People lit their candles in silence. Then they watched the single firework lit in the sky in the image of Big Ben. It stayed lit for fifty seconds. The crowds there and worldwide applauded and chanted, "Big Ben, Big Ben. We love you. We miss you. Big Ben" The astronauts in the ISS reported being able to see the lights of the candles from outer space. Then there was a silence, as if all those gathered there had agreed to stop speaking at the same time.

There was a realisation that this was the first time in centuries that New Year's Eve was celebrate in London without hearing the bells of Big Ben. Even when the great clock was stopped for repairs, the striking and tolling of the bells was maintained for important events such as New Year's Eve and Remembrance Sunday. But there would never be chimes from Big Ben again. People began to leave in silence. And then one last strange thing occurred. Every gas lamp on Westminster Bridge flickered on and off, the rays of light connecting to form triangles over people's heads. People began to run away in fear of what might happen next, others crouched down to protect themselves, and a few even tried to jump into the freezing water of the Thames. The police attempted to calm everyone down to avoid a stampede and another tragedy occurring.

"Please everyone, do not run. Remain calm, no pushing or shoving!"

Miraculously the crowd settled down.

Then someone said loudly, "Listen, listen to me please! I teach history at the University College London and I can tell you that the gas lamps did light mysteriously before our eyes. But I would like to remind you that it was a day like today, the last day of the year in 1813 when this Westminster Bridge was lit for the very first time with the gas lamps. And back then no one could explain why they did what they did. With all these unexplained mysteries today, I would like to advise you all to carry on like normal. We have seen enough strange things today. Hopefully this was the last. We must be strong, things will return to normal."

People listening to the man speaking, dressed in the fashion of the Victorian era, cheered and whistled at him for his warm words of encouragement Then they began to leave Westminster Bridges quietly, their minds still full of unanswered questions. Now that the solemn celebrations had ended, the special guests gathered inside the New Palace Gate said goodbye to each other until tomorrow, when they would attend Parliament the next day to discuss these mysterious matters more thoroughly.

Sergeant Bank and Inspector Bing said to Chief Milk, "We would like to speak with you about something important, sir."

"Go ahead," said Chief Milk.

"Sir, myself and my colleague Sergeant Bank have decided that we ought to be punished for our responsibility in the loss of Big Ben. We really feel as if we did not fulfil our duties fully as we should have done."

After hearing this Chief Milk looked at them and said, "Are you mad? You shouldn't condemn yourselves. You are innocent until proven otherwise. Everything that has happened today is still a mysteries to all of us. You cannot go to prison of your own will, as you know very well."

But Sergeant Bank and Inspector Bing continued to insist.

"Your request is beyond my comprehension," said Chief Milk. "I have never seen or heard anything like this in my entire career. If you insist on going to prison voluntarily without any sentence, you'll bear the expense of your voluntary stay in jail. Do not expect to be fed with the taxpayer's money. If Her Majesty's prison guards allow you to enter in the first place. But if this is your wish, let me see what I can do. I'm going to consult with the attorney general about your unusual request."

Inspector Bing and Sergeant Bank looked at each other uncertainly. They went and locked themselves inside the Elizabeth Tower where no one would think to look for them. They sat down and ate a large cheese pizza that Sergeant Bank's fiancée, Marcela, had brought for them and then fell asleep. When the Chief Superintendent came back looking for the two officers, he could not find them in the crowd and so he left. That same night the story of their request was sold to the tabloids. People woke up to that headline in the papers. This caused more commotion as the pity people felt for the unfortunate policemen. They were not guilty of anything.

Early that morning thousands of people gathered in Parliament Square with banners saying, 'Free the Guards!', 'Innocent until proven guilty', 'The law must act now' and 'No justice, No democracy, No life'. The crowd was chanting these words in loud voices. Others whistled and beat drums to be sure they were heard inside the House of Parliament. The message of the protesters was clear. Not a single MP could enter into the House of Parliament without seeing them or ignoring their demands for the release of the two officers who were missing.

Chapter Fifty-Two
The Emergency Call of Parliament

On the morning of 1 January, all the MPs of the House of Commons and the nine members of the Intelligence and Security Committee of Parliament arrived at the Palace of Westminster at ten o'clock with the usual punctuality of the British. All the Lords, wearing their full ceremonial dress, came to assist in this special session of the Parliament concerning the mysterious incident of the disappearance of Big Ben and other strange phenomena. In the public gallery of the Parliament, there were many people, among them Chief Milk, the master clock keeper Mr Smith and Mr David Wise, well shaven, wearing a new suit with a small bottle of water in his hand.

The Speaker, the Right Honourable Mr Maxim Moran, appeared through the library corridor of the Parliament dressed in state robes of black satin damask trimmed with gold lace and frogs and a full bottomed wig. He was escorted to the chamber by a doorkeeper and a Sergeant-at-Arms in traditional court dress with black buckled shoes, a small sword and the ceremonial mace on her right shoulder. They were followed by the trainbearer, Chaplain and Secretary. As they passed the police shouted at everyone to remove their hats. The Speaker solemnly entered the House of Commons. Many MPs were surprised to see him dressed in full state robes while others were not surprised at all due to the seriousness of the session. The Speaker stood up from his canopied green chair and called for a two-minute silence in honour of Big Ben's memory.

Then he said, "Lords of the Intelligence and Security Committee who came to assist in this session and all the honourable MPs of this House of Commons, it is with great regret that I officially announce to you the sad news of which you all know by now, and that is that our great beloved clock Big Ben has disappeared. It will be the first time that we gather here in this illustrious without the Ayrton Light since Queen Victoria established that tradition in 1885, a custom that we continue to respect as part of our democratic history and tradition until now. I am grateful for your presence here today, for coming to this extraordinary, unexpected session call of the Parliament.

I urge all honourable members to remain silent. Please do not interrupt the Prime Minister in his presentation of the present situation of the search for Big Ben and for other interventions that will follow. Please remain calm. The debate should be constructive; we are not here to blame anyone. No one knows how all this happened. Our duty is to reach a conclusion to ensure the peace of the population. Do not forget that this special session will be broadcast live on television around the world. In a few days' time, Her Majesty the Queen will address the nation. Thank you all for your understanding. The Prime Minister has the floor."

"Thank you, Mr Speaker," said the Prime Minister, "my first words are addressed towards our brave citizens for the strength in character they have shown in these confusing and difficult times. I would like to assure everyone that the country is safe and, as such, they must continue with their daily lives, Of course I will not ask them to forget what has happened. Bear in mind that this vibrant city of London and this great country has passed many difficult tests throughout history and overcame them all. We will carry on. I would like to take this opportunity as well to thank our partners and allies who have been helping us since the news broke out. Unfortunately, the RAF and other aircrafts have not found anything yet. You'll receive an update if any important information comes to light.

Mr Speaker and everyone here today, let me read to you the session agenda. We shall discuss the theft of Big Ben and the role of the satellites and CCTV surveillances cameras in this. We will also discuss if we should build another Big Ben in its place. It is known to everyone here that Big Ben was the honorary ambassador of our city and the most visited landmark attraction by thousands of people each day. And above all, I would like to suggest working on another, better security system to protect London to avoid losing any others important monuments in the future. Thank you for your attention, honourable members."

The MPs and the nine Lords listened quietly to the Prime Minister. But when he mentioned the last point, a new security system to protect their cities, murmurs went around the room.

"Order, order," the Speaker shouted to calm down the MPs. "Silence, please. You will have time for questions! The Prime Minister has the floor."

"Thank you, Mr Speaker," said the Prime Minister, "Lords and Honourable MPs, I beg you not to misinterpret my words. I am a pragmatic man. Yes, I may use the word 'theft' in referring to what happened to Big Ben. This does not change the reality and uncertainty surrounding this mystery. Please accept my words in all their sincerity."

The leader of the Opposition Rt. Hon. Mr Paul Johnson Wright now spoke.

"I agree with the solemn words spoken by the Prime Minister. Today is not a day of political confrontation. Today is a day to be united and not divided, because we are dealing with an unknown enemy, one that seems to have great power and abilities."

Then said the Speaker of the House, "I would now like to invite one of the members of the Security Committee of the United Kingdom who has joined us today in this special session. The Honourable Lord Benjamin has the floor."

"Thank you, Mr Speaker," said Lord Benjamin, "I will keep this short. First, Mr Prime Minister, you have my support in dealing with this mysterious affair and I would like to agree with you about the words you used concerning the event. My only issue was your assurance that we are all safe right now in

London. When we look at what has happened, not only to Big Ben, I believe that it is not wise to say we were safe here at this time."

"Thank you, Lord Benjamin," said the Prime Minister. "I appreciate what you have said, but at this particular time my duty is to ensure the people that they are safe, and avoid causing a panic, as the leaders of the United Kingdom have always done."

During all this time the nine lords were listening without saying anything. They were familiar with the more lively debates that took place in the House of Commons, compared with the calm discussions the House of Lords had.

More murmuring began.

"Order, order," shouted the Speaker of the House.

Then another MP spoke up and said, "My concerns are in line with Lord Benjamin's. I believe that we are not safe here at this time. Since Big Ben is still missing without any logical explanation for its disappearance, I think it is rather premature to assure people that they were safe. We cannot ignore that these strange events extend outside of London to the rest of the world. Nobody really knows the meaning of these moving statues, monuments, and clocks, but I think it is safe to say they are all connected. Personally I believe that we are no longer safe here on planet Earth."

"The floor now goes to the Secretary of State Mr Samuel J. Smirte to explain to this house his department's role in the Preventive Defence of Planet Earth in case of an attack of aliens or the interception of asteroids."

When the Secretary walked to the table, there were more murmurs.

"Order, order, order!" the speaker said, "Please let the secretary of security affairs speak without interruption."

"Thank you, Mr Speaker!" said Mr Smirte, "My Lords and honourable MPs, my presence here today is to explain something that we were all victims of. The mysterious disappearance of Big Ben is a fact we cannot deny or change. So is the mysterious movement of the statues and monuments around the world. All of these strange events have never happened before in the history of mankind. I knew beforehand that the I am about to give explanation will not convince any of you. It is not my intention to. But I am fulfilling my duty as the one in charge of the Department of Space Security that many of you here do not see as important. Some even suggested disposing of this department for better use of taxpayers' money. Many argued that danger would never come from the space and instead all the danger is here on planet Earth. How wrong you all were. Today we do know that Space Security is vital for our existence.

I say all of this only to tell you that there is nothing new to inform you at this stage. Scotland Yard is working with Interpol to try to solve these mysteries as soon as possible. The search for the great clock continues. It is still very early to draw conclusions about this mystery. There is still a chance that Big Ben could be found. We must continue the search. But if a whole month goes by without finding Big Ben, the Parliament should be called again to decide what to do with the empty space left by the clock above the Elizabeth Tower. Thank you very much for listening."

Eventually the Parliament voted in favour of meeting again within a month to assess the situation of the search for Big Ben.

Before closing the session, the Speaker of the House said, "I would like to report to all members that I have received a request from the Chief Superintendent John Milk to discuss the disappearance of the two police officers. Although he is not a parliamentarian, we have made an exception owing to the circumstances."

Chief Milk stood in the public gallery and said, "Thank you, Mr Speaker and all members of both chambers of the House. As you may know, the two officers on duty that night went missing yesterday after midnight. Many of you may have heard the two asked to be placed voluntarily in Her Majesty's prison without any charges against them or a sentence. I told them this was illegal, however, they felt this guilty for failing to protect Big Ben. But the good news is that Inspector Bing and Sergeant Bank are safe and well. Today they sent me a text message with another request to leave their hideout. They would like to resign from their duties at Westminster and to be part of the Yeomen Warders of Her Majesty's Ceremony of the Keys at the Tower of London. They would like to keep their ranks of inspector and sergeant after serving more than twenty-five years in the police force. They will be very proud to be new members of the Sovereign's Body Guard. If you consider this request to be reasonable, they would come out of hiding now. As you can hear the crowd shouting now, they do not believe the officers went into hide. They believe they were locked in a cell somewhere by the authorities. Nor do they believe they wanted to go to jail voluntarily. So grant their request. Thank you."

Mr Speaker waved his hand to the Prime Minister without saying anything.

The Prime Minister said, "For me, this request made by the officers was legitimate and understandable after what they went through. I will submit their request now for the MPs to vote on it."

All members raised their hands in approval of the request. All the people who were sitting in the public gallery applauded, including the master clock keeper and David Wise. When the news appeared on social media, there was a loud applause from the crowd outside in Parliament Square, which could be from heard inside the House of Commons. Inspector Bing and Sergeant Bank saw the news through their mobiles. They embraced and came out of their hiding place in the Elizabeth Tower and walked towards the Carriage Gate. When the crowd saw them coming, they came to carry them on their shoulders, taking them towards the Tower of London, their new service post. They thanked the crowd for their support.

"We would also like to thank the Lords and MPs for having accepted our request. Nobody locked us in a cell. We have had been hiding in the Elizabeth Tower after our ordeal."

"You hush!" said one woman in the crowd. "Amnesty International made a worldwide campaign in twenty-four hours to free you. We have received more than 700 million signatures worldwide online for your liberation. You do not need to thank anyone else. Just enjoy your freedom at your new post in the Tower of London as you had requested."

Finally the Parliament closed the session in the Palace of Westminster on this special day in the lives of all the members of the Commons and the Lords of the Security Committee. It was a unique experience in their political careers. Then trumpets sounded in the room. Everyone came out, walking with discipline and dignity that has characterised the British for centuries.

Days went by, and more and more tourists came to visit London to see with their own eyes the empty space left on the Elizabeth Tower. Although many had already seen it on television, seeing it in person was something quite different, and it caused tremendous impact on people. At first, many looked courageously at the empty tower, but after a few minutes their eyes stared at the empty space with disbelief. It very difficult for many to come to terms with it. Many cried in shock. Some even fainted. Others just stood asking the two unanswered questions, "Why? Who did this?"

A group of guides was quickly formed to create an almost pilgrimage-like route to take tourists to visit the landmarks where the mysterious events had occurred. From the Elizabeth Tower at the Palace of Westminster and the part of the River Thames that froze, toward Trafalgar Square where the crow lit up and disappeared to Piccadilly Circus and the Eros statue. People gathered there day and night hoping to see another impossible miracle, and perhaps to get shot by his magic arrow of love.

Chapter Fifty-Three
The Second Meeting of Parliament

After a month without any updates about the search for Big Ben, Parliament met again in the Commons to discuss what to do next and above all to accept the reality of the loss of Big Ben.

The Right Honourable Mr Maxim Moran said, "To all honourable members, please be silent. Do not interrupt the presentation of the Secretary in State. There will be a time for questions, and your questions will be answered. The debate should remain constructive and reach a consensus on this matter. This session will be broadcast live on television. Mr Samuel J. Smirte, you have the floor."

"Thank you, Mr Speaker. Before beginning this session I would like to ask all honourable members of the chamber to observe a minute of silence in tribute to Big Ben."

Everybody stood up in silence. One minute later, they took their seats and the session began.

"Mr Speaker and honourable members of the house, after a month of intensive search for the great clock in the Northern Hemisphere and on every continent by land, sea, and air, nothing was found. Not a single clue with which to make a reasonable hypothesis. I ask you to be understanding and open-minded towards the proposal, which I will present to you shortly. I hope for the discussion to be constructive. First, we must design a new security system for London and for our air space. Second, we must to build a new clock identical to Big Ben. We cannot leave the Elizabeth Tower empty, disfiguring the magnificent, historic Palace of Westminster. We should keep it in its original splendour as symbol of the greatness of our Democratic Institution. Finally, I would like to let you know that I have received public consensus on the building of a new clock tower. Thank you for listening. I am open to questions."

There was loud murmuring throughout the room after the Secretary's proposal. Almost all the MPs stood up from their seats after hearing the proposal to build a new Big Ben. His proposal was received by many as provocative and outrageous, and caused anger and fury among the opposition members, and the party members of the secretary, alike. They accused the Secretary for avoiding his responsibilities related to his department with his nonsense and pointless proposal when they had barely cleared up the mystery of the clock's disappearance. The peaceful atmosphere maintained during the Secretary's speech changed completely.

"Resign, resign, resign!" some voices were shouting.

"Order, order, order!" the Speaker shouted. "Silence, please! Everyone take your seats. Now is the question time to ask the Secretary any question you may have."

Mr Samuel J. Smirte could understand why his proposals caused such fury and outrage for so many MPs, even within his own Conservative Party. Barely half out of the hundred supported him.

Then the Speaker said, "The Honourable MP Mr Will Winston has the floor."

"Thank you, Mr Speaker. I would like to ask Mr Secretary, what was the real meaning of his proposal. I am as confused as the rest of the members, as you can see. You have proposed to build another great clock, If we accept, do you not think the same unknown thieves, or extra-terrestrials as you would have us believe, might come to steal it again? Could you explain to this house who stole the previous clock? It seems to me that you and your satellites are useless if they fall asleep as soon as we need a reliable. I hope the members of this house will agree with me that we will not vote for such if we cannot ensure our safety in the first place."

"That's right, that's right!" many voices shouted, while the group of young MPs still shouted, "Resign, resign, resign!"

"Order, order, order!" said the Speaker, "The Secretary has the floor."

"Thank you! Mr Speaker, I am very surprised by the almost hostile attitude some of our MPs have exhibited towards my proposal. An easy question I have for all of you is that perhaps there is a better solution to boosting the moral of the people? Or another landmark that can draw the most tourist revenue year after year? I cannot see any other better solution to provide to our city another historical landmark which would accomplish this. This is a reasonable proposal from someone who loves his city. Is there any other better solution?"

Nobody said anything; there was silence in the chamber. So he continued presenting his case to convince the majority of the MPs to accept his proposal.

"As the head of the Security Department, my second proposal is to build another security system not for London only but to protect and cover all the United Kingdom air space. I sincerely believe that the two proposals I have submitted to you are the best solutions to move forward from this incident."

More loud murmuring was heard and the young MPs continued chanting, "Resign, resign, resign!"

The Speaker intervened to calm them, "Silence, please! Let the honourable MP of the Liberal Democrats speak."

"Thank you, Mr Speaker. Mr Secretary, after listening to your proposal very carefully I did not see any clear idea on you propose to support such notions. First, long or a short term we do not have any guarantees that another event like the one might not happen again just because of a new system of security. We cannot be sure that a new security system would be effective at protecting the entire country. Second, both of your proposals, frankly, are going to be expensive. In the United Kingdom today we no longer have the people with the skills and knowledge to recreate an identical clock or to cast a bell of thirteen tonnes. I am sorry but my group cannot support your proposals. Thank you."

Another, more straightforward, MP took the floor.

"Mr Secretary, your proposals are scandalous and outrageous. I cannot accept your vague proposals without any guarantees that another event won't occur. I really believe strongly that it is better for the Elizabeth Tower to remain as it is now. Perhaps that could function to dissuade the unknown thieves from coming back again to steal something else. Because if something like this happens again in this city, no one knows the consequences it could have on the population. No one feels safe on Earth since the mysterious disappearance of Big Ben. We are exposed now to a constant danger as never before. For these reasons, I cannot vote in favour of your proposals. Thank you."

Then the group of moderate MPs demanded from the Secretary further explanation of the actual benefits of the costly satellites in orbit and the role of the CCTV cameras if they could not protect London and the United Kingdom in general.

"Why we do need them if they cannot protect us as we thought? We should classify them as useless and ineffective because they could not even record a single thing on the night they were needed most. The loss of Big Ben shows that these modern technologies we have are not as sophisticated as we thought. In fact, they were completely ineffective. So from now on, we shall not rely on this technology to protect us. We need a different, safer form of security."

Mr Secretary took the floor, first thanking the Speaker for his support after the previous intervener.

"I understand fully your concerns, they are mine as well. If you would allow me to say this: first, I will not sugar coat my answers for the sake of fear and insecurity, which every one of us feels. It is normal to feel fear, but then we must continue with our lives.

Second, we shouldn't dismiss or underestimate the useful role the satellites in our daily lives because of one thirty-minute malfunction. If it were only the United Kingdom's satellites that did not record anything, that would make sense. But every single satellite in space suffered the same mysterious failure at the same exact time. All this means that something very strange and unexplained happened."

"What do you mean exactly, Mr Secretary?" another PM asked him.

"We should not disregard the usefulness of our satellites both for civilian and military use. They have been serving our interests for a long time. Money is not an issue should we choose to build another security system in space. I would also like to remind all members of this House that the Palace of Westminster was listed a UNESCO site in 1987. If the majority of you do not want to approve the budget to build another Big Ben, I am sure that the many good citizens and philanthropists of the United Kingdom would be very proud to finance it with donations. Many people from around the world, in fact, would be very pleased to join the efforts."

A young, radical MP took the floor and said, "Mr Secretary, it seems to me that you are challenging us for not accepting your unreasonable proposal to build another Big Ben. Would it not be better for you to resign?"

"No, not at all. I won't resign," replied the Secretary, "I have done nothing wrong, unless of course you could show me or prove to me that I have. I cannot run away from my responsibilities because of false accusations made against me. It is unfair to condemn one without proof."

Then the Speaker of the House said, "Is there anyone else here, who would like to say something?"

"Yes," said an MP called Pranav Rahul." I would like to give my support to the Secretary, he should not be blamed for what has happened."

Another MP, Abdullah Alan, stood up and said, "I second the words spoken by Pranav Rahul. Mr Secretary you have my full support."

An MP called Arpita Patel said, "Mr Secretary, you have my full support as well."

Then the murmuring began again around the room.

"Order, order, order!" said the Speaker.

"I would like to speak," said MP Olivia Grace. "Personally I don't think anything any decisions can be made here today, as all the mysteries surrounding the loss of Big Ben still haunt our minds. But before finishing, I would like to ask Mr Secretary one last question: do you think Big Ben could ever reappear someday?"

"Ma'am, I do not have a clear answer to your question," Mr Secretary replied, "but my great wish is to see that clock appear before our eyes on its tower again. I can assure everyone in this house that my team will continue working tirelessly to do everything they can to find Big Ben. The investigations continue day and night without ceasing in coordination with other space agencies, analysing the images recorded by the spy satellites to try to find even a clue. I would like to inform the house as well that if the clock does not appear as mysteriously as it disappeared, my department would offer a reward of one hundred million pounds to anyone who could give true, valid and reliable information leading to its whereabouts. Maybe all these efforts could lead us to a place where the search of Big Ben has not yet been carries out."

His last words angered many of the MPs.

"Where on this Earth do you think the search of Big Ben has not yet reached?" some asked indignantly. "Do you really think that someone is hiding it in their homes? All evidence points to it not being on Earth at all."

"Resign, resign, resign!" others shouted.

"Order, order, order!" the Speaker said. "There will be order."

One young MP by the name of Bruce Buxton Bell asked Mr Secretary, "Who do you want to give the one hundred million pounds to in exchange for a promise of information? Do you want to just throw the money of the British taxpayers in the air? You'll be misusing and spending the taxpayers' money for nothing. Let me say this to you: perhaps you are an accomplice of whoever is responsible for this. I suggest this because of the carelessness of your proposal that reflects your attitude toward the grave situation we are in, for which we have yet to receive a rational explanation."

The Secretary did not answer the nonsensical, provocative questions about being an accomplice to the theft. He remained calm and quiet as he always did in these situations.

An older MP, David J. James, took the floor in support of the Secretary.

"A few days ago a man called David Wise told the world that he saw lights taking Big Ben across the sky and disappearing into the clouds. No one could deny that his story was a strange one. In this regard, I do not claim with certainty what I am about to say. I am only suggesting the idea that, as Mr Secretary said before, perhaps Big Ben could still be somewhere we have not searched yet. Not to belittle the diabolical cunning of those who stole it and hide it. On the other hand, the master clock keeper, Mr Smith, said he saw strange crows around the Elizabeth Tower, which later turned out not to be a crows at all, as was revealed at Trafalgar Square. We cannot ignore the relationship between these two incidences. We must be open-minded to any hypothesis."

Those words spoken by David J. James did not sit well at all with many of the MPs. One young radical MP took the floor.

"The honourable David J. James, we know full well that you hail from a more antiquated time. I understand your words of support for the Mr Secretary. But I am astonished that you trust the words of this David Wise, someone who was sleeping in the street? These are not my words, the police's. According to Scotland Yard, his testimony was far from credible. His only desire was to get a bottle of free drink. This does not mean I underestimate your honest suggestions and your wisdom after many years as parliamentarian. My only shock was at hearing you mentioning Mr David Wise, frankly."

"Mr David Wise has a fixed address, he lives in Pimlico. He is currently our only witness here in London."

This was the voice of an angry young woman in the public gallery.

Then more angry voices followed, "Stop criticising David Wise!"

"You're treating him like a liar and a fake."

"What have you contributed since the disappearance of Big Ben? Nothing and nothing, you just sit blaming others!"

"Order, order, order!" Mr Speaker said.

At that moment, the MP David J. James stood up by making a thankful gesture to the people in the public gallery for their support and then looked at the MP who had just spoken.

"You see? You are wrong."

The young MP did not take that gesture well. He sat down, embarrassed.

Another MP, John M Vincent, said, "Nothing we have agreed on here today can bring our beloved Big Ben back. It's contribution to this city was immeasurable."

Another MP, Alfred Samys, said, "As we will close this session soon, I would like to clearly say what I think about all this. Ii is not my intention to offend anyone, therefore I will not answer any questions. But I would like to say what I honestly believe from the bottom of my heart. The issue that brings us here today was not expected or able to be predicted by anyone. It caught us all by surprise. So I will quote the words of an English politician, who once said, 'Whoever wants to conquer the world, must come to conquer London first.' I have no doubt that the strangers who stole our beloved Big Ben have conquered London now. They have made a mockery of our security measures. Our technology that we thought was accurate and sophisticated, was no match for whatever the mysterious intruder used. Not only did they steal Big Ben and other small objects, they made the entire city sleep and thus easily took control of London and our lives without us knowing it. There are no words for the kind of fear and humiliation this causes. Thank you."

There was a brief moment of silence in the chamber. To liven up the session again, a middle-aged MP named Charles Iain said, "Honourable David J. James, do not be so pessimistic. You shouldn't give too much credit to those unknown intruders. I do not really believe that they conquered us or won any battle against us. They arrived in hiding to commit their theft. We must call a spade a spade. Yes, indeed, certainly they have stolen Big Ben, but I strongly believe that we have conquered them too."

There were murmurs in the chamber after hearing those words.

"Let me explain why I said that," he continued. "First, if they had come here to steal Big Ben, that means that they admired and envied us for having something that they could not. That means we may have knowledge they do not possess, in which case we are almost equal in knowledge and power. Secondly, they took other small objects including the winter flag and a small English dictionary with them. I strongly believe this is an indication that they are foreigners who do not speak English and have an interest in our culture. Perhaps they would like to become our friends or allies in the future? This of course is not ruling out that they might do something else in the future. After their daring audacity to take Big Ben away without anyone seeing them, who knows?"

"Don't be such a dreamer!" other MPs shouted at Charles Iain.

Then another MP said, "Mr Speaker, what my honourable friend Charles Iain has just said was pure speculation and complacency towards whoever took Big Ben away. How and why would it be possible that these faceless strangers could become our allies in the future? If what you are saying would actually happen at all. I can never trust these unknown intruders who had the audacity to remove our priceless object without our permission the way they did. I say 'remove', but it was better to say they stole, because they took what was not theirs. We should never expect to be friends or allies of any kind to anyone who would do this. You really are a dreamer, or just naïve to believe in such things."

Many MPs shouted, "You are right honourable friend, we cannot trust a bunch of thieves!"

"Order, order, order!" said the Speaker of the House.

Then another MP took the floor and said, "In politics, never say never. As my Honourable Friends have just said, we must be prepared to commit ourselves to some kind of contact. We are a modern, civilised nation. For this reason I would like to support the suggestion of my Honourable Friend Charles Iain. I would only like to see that they return our clock safely and ask for forgiveness for their actions. By repairing the moral damages caused to the United Kingdom and the world, and sharing with us the secrets of their technology, we can build trust between us and lay the foundation for becoming allies. In this way we can prevent this from happening again in the future."

"Another dreamer!" many MPs shouted.

"Order, order, order!" Mr Speaker shouted. "We are talking about a very serious matter here indeed. The public is watching us on television. Let us comport ourselves as the members of the Parliament that we are!"

There were more murmurs again in the chamber.

"Order, order, order, please!"

Chapter Fifty-Four
The Temporary Compromise

The Speaker said, "Lady Jane Jay Jones of the Green Party has the floor."

"Thank you, Mr Speaker. After listening to this debate go on without reaching any agreement, I would like to propose to all members of the house a compromise. Even I know already that this compromise won't satisfy everyone. But we all know that to build another clock would be very expensive. I propose that we build a less expensive clock in the form of a glass pyramid that could function on solar energy to tell the time, the date and the level of pollution in the air. We could even incorporate a mechanism to make speakers play the sound of the original bells of Big Ben. I may say it will be a clock fitting of the twenty first century and the Technology Era.

Furthermore, if the thieves who stole Big Ben before come to stealing this new glass clock (even though it seems unlikely they would try such an audacious thing), the impact of its loss, will not be as great as the loss of Big Ben. On top of that, it would not be very expensive to build another one in case something happened again. The only cost of its loss would be the effect it would have on people's sense of security. I would like to suggest this too: if Big Ben ever appeared as mysteriously as it disappeared, the solar-powered clock could be placed in the middle of Parliament Square or next to the statue of George Canning in the Little George green area as reminder of the mysterious tragic incident that occurred. As for the question of what the new clock should called, I will leave that decision up to the House. But if there should be a deadlock, the House will allow the public to decide since the clock will belong to the public like Big Ben did before.

My second proposal is this: I think a choir of children in red and white tunics should sing in the Parliament Square once a year in honour of Big Ben, followed by a trumpet playing "Last Post". This would be a great tribute to the most famous clock in the world. Thank you."

Then the Speaker said, "All honourable members of the House, as you know by tradition my position as the Speaker of the House is to be impartial. But today is a very special session. This House had never dealt with this kind of mysterious affair since its formation in 1215. Allow me to ask the Honourable Lady Jane Jay a question to clarify. What song do you propose the choir sing for the tribute to the great clock?"

"Simple," she replied. "The prayer that was inscribed on the plaque in the Big Ben clock room:

All through this hour Lord, be my guide
And by Thy power
No foot shall slide. Oh! Lord our God
Thy children call
Grant us Thy peace
And bless us all, Amen!"

There was a round of applause.

The Speaker spoke with her assistant quietly.

"I think this will have a positive effect, let us use it. All honourable members of the House of Commons, let us move to the vote on the proposal made by the Honourable Lady Jane Jay. I would like to emphasise that the nine Lords will not vote in this session, they have just come to attend as observers. Let us start the voting now."

The vote began. The results were presented to the Speaker to announce them.

"These are the results of the free vote of the MPs of the House of Commons without Party discipline: 524 for and 126 against. The motion of the proposal to have a solar-powered glass clock had been passed. There was no applause among the members of the Commons. There was nothing to celebrate.

The Secretary of Security and Space Defence has the floor for the last time in this extraordinary session of the Parliament," said the Speaker.

"Thank you, Right Honourable Speaker and members of Parliament," said the Secretary. "I have listened to your arguments very carefully. I am sorry to say that the disappointment at refusing to vote on my proposals was not only mine, but the people's too, who had hoped that we could have another Big Ben here in the London someday. I still insist that the best solution is to build another clock. Having said that, I am very grateful for the compromise put forward by the Honourable member of the Green Party, Lady Jane Jay. I sincerely thanked her for her contribution to this debate. Without her we would have left this House without reaching an agreement after three long hours of discussion.

What more could I have said more to convince you? Do not forget, people from around the world cried, fasted and mourned over the loss of Big Ben. I do not have any doubt in my mind that they would like to see a new Big Ben in London ringing its bells here like before. But let us be grateful to have the new solar-powered glass clock here in London. Thank you."

This session of the Parliament is now closed," said the Speaker.

The news was on the front pages of all newspapers that evening. Even the neon light in Piccadilly Circus announced the news of the agreement of the new glass clock, also the BT Tower in London display the rotating coloured lights of that news too. Many greeted this news with enthusiasm, others with disappointment. As always the public opinion was divided. But it is impossible to please everyone.

That same night giant television screens were installed across London awaiting the Queen's message to the nation the next day. From Parliament

Square, Trafalgar Square, Hyde Park to Wembley stadium, where there would be a concert in tribute to Big Ben to put a close to the tragic event that had struck London and allow its inhabitants to accept what had happened and move on with life.

Chapter Fifty-Five
The People Await the Queen's Speech

The next day the energetic Mayor of London made a dazzling speech to a crowd in Hyde Park on live television.

"Dear Londoners, are you ready to forget the past and move on with your lives?"

"Yes, yes, we are ready," the crowd replied.

"I am pleased to hear your positive response," said the Mayor. "I too, I am ready to move forward with my life and my duties. We are very proud to be Londoners. If it could, I feel London would be very proud of us too. In these modern times, London has been a leader in social evolution, development in sciences, arts, fashions, sports, business, technological innovation and a dynamic multicultural society. Any great person has been to London at least once in their lives. If you've never been to this great city, something is missing in your life. When you arrive you will feel at home, welcomed by the soul of a city that will wrap you in its embrace and make you feel safe and warm during your stay. Thank you."

Everyone cheered.

"Ladies and gentlemen, the time we have all been waiting for has arrived. Let us give a great round of applause to Her Majesty the Queen, whose speech will begin shortly on live television."

Cheers were heard around the city and as far away as Brighton over seventy-five kilometres away. Then the national anthem began to play.

Her Majesty the Queen began her address to the nation with a soft but firm voice.

"A few days ago something dreadful and unexpected happened in our city. A mysterious event that still has no rational explanation. I thank the display of calmness and rationality shown by Londoners and all British people after the shocking discovery of the disappearance of Big Ben in the uncertainty that followed. I thank the professionals involved for their unending effort, courage and energy put towards finding our great clock. I can assure you that we will continue looking for our irreplaceable and priceless Big Ben with our last breath. We will not rest until we find it. I would like to take this opportunity as well to thank all of our allies around the world, who helped us search from the very start. And I cannot forget the solidarity shown by millions of people around the world, who shared with us their sorrow in this tragic, unexplained event.

Many of you will agree with me that London has been orphaned by the loss of Big Ben. We have the right to know what had really happened. Big Ben had an irresistible magnetism, attraction and ability to captivate anyone who visited it with its unique beauty and charm. It was a symbol of the history and culture of our nation. With all these amazing qualities there is no doubt that this great clock was a very special part of British heritage. Whoever took it must have envied us for years.

Dear citizens, I have hope, as do many of you, that one day when we least expect it Big Ben will appear as mysteriously as it disappeared. In the meantime we will not let ourselves be overcome by this tragedy. As British citizens we will use the two qualities that have always characterised us throughout history: patience and resilience, our nation spirit and common endeavour will never be broken, better days will return, united and resolute, we will overcome this chapter in our history as we have done every other before. We will never forget Big Ben, our dear friend with whom we will always share a connection. We will not mourn the mysterious disappearance of the great clock, but we will never tire of waiting for its return. Big Ben has given us too much joy and offered its service for years without fail, and it is better to remember it this way. Whatever uncertainty surrounding this tragedy, London must and will continue to exist as it always has throughout the centuries.

I close my speech with words of hope from the great British poet, Dr Samuel Johnson. 'When a man is tired of London, he is tired of life… for there is in London all that life can afford.' We will never be tired of living in our great beloved city of London. This magnificent and legendary city will never tire of us either. Thus life goes on. Keep Calm and Move On."

"God save the Queen!" Thousands of people shouted across the many parks and squares in the city. They began singing the national anthem. Their voices were heard far from London all the way to the seaside in the cities of Brighton and Dover.

The message that Her Majesty, The Queen, addressed to the nation raised its spirits and gave it hope. People began to move on with their lives and to accept the reality of what had happened.

To be continued…

Meanwhile, in the mysterious village of Black Cloud in the planet Oxon, Ms Moxum followed the Queen's speech live on the screen of her Potsat while her nephews Winn Blitzzer and Valger were living as though in a dream after their spectacular adventure. But Winn Blitzzer was still waiting for his aunt's approval to begin the negotiations of their deliver of Big Ben to the king.

A few weeks later, the two former police officers on guard on that fateful night, Sergeant Bank and Inspector Bing, continued with their new jobs at the Tower of London as members of the eight hundred-year-old tradition, the Ceremony of the Key, which they seemed to enjoy very much. But they were always a bit nervous whenever they saw any ravens around, not knowing if they were real or fake birds. The bad experience with the fake crows was still haunting them. Unfortunately for them, they had to get used for it. There were many ravens inside the wall of the Tower of London.

And as for David Wise, he changed his life completely after his strange experience. He left the street life and the drinking behind, and became a tourist guide and a kind of celebrity, tell people the story of how he saw strange lights taking Big Ben into the clouds and disappearing and then being found asleep under the snow the next morning.

Chief Milk took an early retirement to pursue his own investigations into the unknown case of the mysterious disappearance of Big Ben. This dramatic experience took a heavy toll on him and, having previously been a believer, he became agnostic.

Mr Alex Mel, the first person to be discovered sleeping under the snow went to work with British space programme to study the mysteries of outer space.

As for the journalist Michael James, he became a writer of science fiction. And the reporter Ms Julie Claire went on to teach investigative journalism at the University of London. Ms Alice Mary continued working for BBC radio paying great attention to any call of news she received.

The master clock keeper, Mr Smith, continued with his work at the Palace of Westminster, maintaining the two thousand clocks there.

Far away from London in the small town of Húsavík, Iceland, Father Johannes Jensen continued life in his Church. After mass he spent more time meditating on the mysteries of life. The town Húsavík itself, which was previously not even on the map, was now a popular tourist site.

After a few months, people began to get used to living without seeing Big Ben above them. Atop the Elizabeth Tower there was a new solar-powered glass clock in the form of a pyramid, covering the empty space that was left by the missing clock. It was a very good solar-powered clock that changed colours every hour of the day. Every three hours a flag of the four nations that formed the United Kingdom reflected within it. It also showed the weather forecast and the level of pollution in the city. But all these attributes of the new solar-powered clock could not make Londoners forget Big Ben easily after being the icon and the symbol of London for so many years. People still hoped that one day when they least expected it, Big Ben might appear. Without Big Ben, something was missing not only in their beloved city but in their hearts as well.

The next book of this series will be:
The Mysterious Robbery of Big Ben: The Delivery of the Great Clock to the King of Planet Oxon.